Twelve criminal cases to  Tim Silvain, ranging from fir guy who swears he's been abd pen writer, the mystery of a guy who apparently returns from the dead and murder most foul.

But Tim Silvain has a private life which is often fraught with problems, as he finds it difficult to keep his sexual desires under control even knowing that the real love of his life is Paul Massingham.

Featuring a roll call of some of the best writers of gay erotica and mysteries today!

Derek Adams	M. Jules Aedin	Z. Allora
Maura Anderson	Victor J. Banis	Jeanne Barrack
Laura Baumbach	Alex Beecroft	Ally Blue
J.P. Bowie	Barry Brennessel	Michael Breyette
Nowell Briscoe	P.A. Brown	Brenda Bryce
Jade Buchanan	James Buchanan	Charlie Cochrane
Karenna Colcroft	Jamie Craig	Kirby Crow
Dick D.	Ethan Day	Diana DeRicc
Jason Edding	Theo Fenraven	Angela Fiddler
Dakota Flint	S.J. Frost	Kimberly Gardner
Michael Gouda	Roland Graeme	Storm Grant
Amber Green	LB Gregg	Drewey Wayne Gunn
Kaje Harper	Jan Irving	David Juhren
Samantha Kane	Kiernan Kelly	M. King
Matthew Lang	J.L. Langley	Josh Lanyon
Anna Lee	Elizabeth Lister	Clare London
William Maltese	Z.A. Maxfield	Timothy McGivney
Lloyd A. Meeker	Patric Michael	AKM Miles
Reiko Morgan	Jet Mykles	William Neale
Willa Okati	L. Picaro	Neil S. Plakcy
Jordan Castillo Price	Luisa Prieto	Rick R. Reed
A.M. Riley	George Seaton	Jardonn Smith
Caro Soles	JoAnne Soper-Cook	Richard Stevenson
Liz Strange	Marshall Thornton	Lex Valentine
Maggie Veness	Haley Walsh	Missy Welsh
Stevie Woods	Lance Zarimba	

Check out titles, both available and forthcoming, at
www.mlrpress.com

CRIMES OF PASSION

MICHAEL GOUDA

mlrpress
www.mlrpress.com

Published by
MLR Press, LLC
3052 Gaines Waterport Rd.
Albion, NY 14411

Visit ManLoveRomance Press, LLC on the Internet:
www.mlrpress.com

Cover Art by Deana Jamroz
Editing by Amanda Faris

Print format ISBN# 978-1-60820-397-0
ebook formatISBN# 978-1-60820-398-7

Issued 2011

CHAPTER ONE

Please Check on My Partner

"Mr. Sinclair?" asked the man, pausing irresolutely at the open door. I didn't know who else he expected to find when my name had been clearly painted on the frosted glass door outside, and I was the only person in the office.

I nodded, though, pleasantly enough.

"The private investigator?"

"That's right." That information had also been on the door, but some people are never really satisfied without confirmation.

"You look very young."

In other circumstances I might have taken that as a compliment, but it wasn't the impression I really wanted to give to prospective clients. I frowned and tried to look older or at least more mature. I was after all pushing twenty-six.

"Please come in and sit down," I indicated the only spare chair. If he was unable to identify me from the name on the door, perhaps he was also unable to recognize a chair.

He sat down, perching uneasily on the edge of the seat as if afraid that if he surrendered himself to its comfort, he might in some way become imprisoned by it. He was a small man, though. When sitting down he appeared of normal height, so he must have short legs, I reasoned. He was perhaps forty-five or in his well-preserved fifties. His hair, though greyish, was thick and well-groomed. He was wearing a dark, single-breasted suit that fitted him well, though I doubted whether it was bespoke. His tie was outrageously flamboyant, a dazzling arrangement of purple and orange, not good for a hangover. I wondered whether he had chosen it himself.

"What can I do for you, Mr...?" I asked, flipping open a

notepad on the desk. They like that. Even if I only write down a meaningless scribble, they think it shows I'm taking them seriously.

"You will of course keep this to yourself," he said, not replying to my implied request for his name.

"Rest assured. Everything you say is completely confidential. It remains within these four walls. Only you and I will ever know what goes on between us."

He nodded but still hesitated.

I tried to put on as trustworthy an expression as possible, eyes open candidly, mouth serious but not tight-lipped. I waited. He waited. This could go on for some time. I tried to resist glancing at my watch.

At last he appeared to make up his mind. "I think my partner is being unfaithful," he said.

With that tie, I wasn't surprised.

I sighed inwardly. Of course if I had expected something more exciting, a murder for instance, I should have joined the police force, but then I'd have had sergeants and inspectors and chief inspectors and all sorts of blue brass breathing down my neck. Now I was my own boss, but I did have to cater for the mundane: wives playing fast and loose on Wednesday afternoons with the window cleaner, guys screwing their bosses by pinching and selling the stock, employees pretending to be sick to work on the side. Discreet surveillance and investigation, not the heavy Constable Plod intervention, that's my scene. Later perhaps there might be a case for the police, but that was after I'd got all the details, found out all the dirt and, more importantly, got it all on video. You've been framed, chum.

"Let's take this from the beginning," I said. "Can I get some details? First, can I have your name?"

Almost operating under automatic pilot, I took down the usual details, wrote down his name: Alan Harrison, undistinguished (not that mine is likely to appear in Burkes' Peerage); the address, somewhere in Finsbury Park, the unpretentious part, the bit you tried to pretend wasn't Stamford Hill, just east of the reservoirs; home phone number, only to be used at a time of great emergency. He had a job in publishing, some sort of technical journal, didn't sound all that interesting but probably more exciting (and indeed remunerative) than mine.

Then came, for the clients at least, what is usually the most difficult part. It meant admitting that in some way they'd failed; failed to be sexually attractive enough, failed to be observant enough, failed to set in place the right safeguards, failed in some way, embarrassingly.

"Now what exactly do you want me to do, Mr. Harrison, find out what your partner is doing? What makes you think there's something wrong?"

"He's a good bit younger than I am. A person knows. A cooling of the affections I suppose. Excuses that sound more like lies."

I hadn't been expecting that, but I didn't think I allowed my surprise to register. Not that I have anything against gays, apart from the fact that most of them are fickle, unstable, devious, egoistic. Hell, I'm gay myself so I should know. It was just that he looked so "un-gay," so depressingly straight. Gaydar, huh! I mean he'd never given me any sort of appraising look (apart from remarking that I looked young), and I'm not exactly Quasimodo.

"And your partner's name is?" I asked.

"Philip Trelawny."

Now that was a name to conjure with. Yes, if I'd been inventing names, I'd have chosen one like that. "Cornish?" I asked. "As the saying goes 'By Pol, Tre and Pen, you shall know the Cornishmen.'"

"No, I don't think so. I met him in Shepherds Bush."

I didn't ask the circumstances. I had also met young men in Shepherds Bush, and the conditions and environment hadn't been all that salubrious.

"And you have lived together for…?"

"Three years. Three years next month."

Well, that wasn't bad. Certainly a longer period than I and anyone else I related to had lasted.

"You said Mr. Trelawny was younger than you. May I ask how old he is? It may not be important, but I'd like to know as many of the details as possible."

"He's twenty-one."

Poor Alan Harrison. A twink half his age. I could see the whole set up. Harrison earning the money, trying desperately to keep his little bloodsucker in the manner to which he wanted to become accustomed. After a while Philip getting fed up with an older person and looking elsewhere. I was surprised it had lasted so long.

"Does he have a job?" I asked, knowing the answer would be something along the lines of "Not at the moment."

"Oh yes," said Harrison. Another surprise. Probably just for pin money, something to keep him occupied. "He's got his own cyber company, on the web you know. Doing very well, in fact. Be a millionaire by the time he's twenty-five, he always says." This last was expressed in a rather rueful tone. I revised my impressions, quickly. So the money was mostly Philip's. That changed things considerably. And what had kept the two of them together for three years?

Now I am a bit of a cynic. Well, you couldn't be anything else in my job. Too many petty villains, too much deceit, deception and duplicity; the three Ds, which all mean the same thing—doing the other person down. I'm afraid I haven't much belief in the finer qualities of human behaviour, though I am occasionally forced to accept that they do exist.

So was it, could it be "true love," that had held this pair together for three years?

"A cyber company?" I asked, pretending an interest I didn't feel. Computers are okay, useful as a tool. I have one myself of course, but my database is hardly ever kept up to date, and I find notes scribbled on my pad are much more useful and accessible than buried somewhere deep in my hard disc. As you can see, I'm not really into technology. Some things are essential, mobile phones, etc., but I couldn't get emotionally involved with them.

"We keep our business lives apart," said Harrison. "I'm not really too sure what he does, but it certainly makes money."

"And is there anything specific that makes you think Philip is...er...being unfaithful?" Having it off with another guy, I nearly said.

"There's nothing concrete. It's just that he's more often out when I call him on the phone. Says it's business but won't go into details. His...er," Harrison paused, and I could swear a faint blush tinged his neck and throat. "His sex drive isn't as strong as it was."

I nodded sympathetically and made a note on my pad. Didn't mean anything, but by the time I looked up again, he was back to normal, if that wasn't too misleading a term.

"So, Mr. Harrison, you'd like me to check up on him, follow him if he goes out, find out who he meets."

Harrison nodded miserably.

"Get some pictures perhaps?"

He looked almost horrified. "Oh I don't think that's necessary."

"You want proof," I said brutally, to be kind, of course.

He nodded.

I passed over one of my data sheets. "Here's my charges. As you can see everything's itemized, time spent, etc., any subsidiary expenses will of course be extra."

Harrison looked a little alarmed. "Subsidiary?" he said.

"Sometimes I have to 'sweeten' people to give information. Rest assured, it's never usually more than five quid. Tenner, tops."

He agreed, a little reluctantly. Either he was mean or money was a bit of a problem for him.

"Okay," I said. "Now, what are Mr. Trelawny's plans for today? Is he indoors as far as you know?"

"Yes, he should be. He said he was working on a new website. It would take him all day."

"Leave it with me, then," I said. "How can I get in touch with you, perhaps other than at home?"

He gave me his work number and left, hopping off the seat as if it were red hot and almost scurrying out through the door.

I switched on the answer-phone, made sure my mobile was active and prepared to go to Finsbury Park. On the way out, I caught sight of myself in the mirror. Damn it, I did look young! Semi-smart in a white shirt, a little crumpled, and a dark tie with white dots, a concession to frivolity. I wondered whether I should grow a moustache.

Out into the mighty roar of London's traffic and the stink of exhaust and air that had been breathed in and out God knows how many times. Don't misunderstand me. I love London. I wouldn't give up its life and vibrancy for the cool clear nothingness of the countryside for a million quid, but it does have its effect on the lungs and the ear drums.

No, I don't leap into a black Mercedes and go zooming off into the night, or afternoon as it was in this case. Mainly because there's no place to park near the office in costly Jermyn Street, and anyway driving through London is not much faster than a brisk walk, so it's the tube for me. I do have a car, but it's an old cheapo, though not of course cheap in repair bills. I'd need it if I had to follow Trelawny in his car, of course, so I had to take the tube home, pick up the car and drive to Finsbury Park.

It took me only a half an hour to get there and another half to find the house. Randolph Street was a terrace of almost identical, red-brick Victorian houses, only made individual by the curtains in the front windows and the states of their miniscule front gardens. I parked a little down the street and walked past number 51, which had neat net curtains and a flourish of tasteful salmon-pink zonal pelargoniums in terra-cotta pots. Very neat, very tidy. Someone obviously had spent some time on the display.

Could it be Alan Harrison with the dreadful taste in ties?

I went back to the car and phoned the Harrison house. It rang five times, and I'd just decided that Philip Trelawny was out when the receiver was lifted. A voice, youngish, pleasantly modulated, said "Hello."

"Can I speak to Gladys?" I said.

"I think you must have the wrong number."

"Sorry." I rang off. Objective achieved. At least I knew he was in.

Now surveillance isn't what you'd call exciting. Generally speaking it consists of sitting in a car, staring at a shut door for hours on end, eating sarnies and drinking Coke, and then, when you really, really want a piss, the quarry comes out and you have to tie a knot in it and "pursue."

So from half past eleven to one o'clock, I sat in the car. Sometimes people passing give you odd looks, but if you're looking at an A to Z for instance, they think you're planning a route. Of course if they come back in two hours time and you're still looking for the way from Hackney to Putney, they begin to wonder.

At one o'clock I was beginning to think about the piss, and of course that was when the door of number 51 opened and a man came out. He must have been Trelawny. Certainly he looked in his early twenties. He was tall and blond, with that blondness that looks natural even though it might not be. His nose was straight and his eyes, I think—he was a bit far away to tell precisely— were blue. He walked with a sort of athletic grace, his hips, slim and masculine, tight trousers showing off a really provocative bulge. I dragged my attention away and buried my head in the A to Z while he passed. Then I got out my trusty camcorder and watched and indeed recorded his perfect arse as it sashayed along the street, proof, if needed, that young Philip had gone walkabout. Not that I couldn't think of a dozen perfectly innocent reasons why he shouldn't have popped out of the house. He obviously wasn't going far; he would have presumably taken the car if he had been. Probably he had run out of coffee, and he was off for a jar of instant from the local supermarket in the High Street.

He reached the corner and disappeared round it.

Instantly I was out of the car and in pursuit.

When you follow a guy, unless the street is full of other people, it can be a bit obvious, so it's necessary to keep a good distance between you and your quarry. Then when he's almost out of sight or round a corner, you race like merry hell until you can see him again. And so it proceeds. I ran to the corner, peered cautiously round and was greeted by an old lady with a pair of plastic shopping bags who gave a startled cry and obviously thought I was a mugger. I quickly converted my stoop to a crouch and bent down as if to tie a shoelace, forgetting, until I got there, that I was wearing loafers. The woman gave me another frightened look, obviously considering that, if I were not a dangerous criminal, I must at least a dangerous lunatic. I gave my ankle a rub as if it was paining, and she hurried on her way, obviously not convinced.

I stood up. Philip was halfway along the block, his blond hair distinctly visible. Now there were more pedestrians, so I was able to follow in a less suspicious fashion, keeping one or two passersby between us.

Another corner and we were in the High Street. I lost him amongst some of the shoppers and then caught him again about twenty yards ahead. Suddenly he disappeared behind a fat man and then, when my view was again clear, had disappeared completely. I caught up with the place I'd last seen him. Surely he could only have gone into a butcher's or a news-agent's, but he wasn't in either. Then I noticed the door between the two shops, one of those that would give access to the flats or offices on the first and second floors. There was a rather grubby plate fixed to the side, black letters on an off-white board. It said, "TwilightArt. com."

This is the situation I always dread. It's "make your mind up time." I have no car to shelter in, and anyway it's obviously a double yellow line, no parking zone. I can either hang around pretending to look at the cards in a news-agent's window (using the glass as a reflection of the opposite side of the street) and realize, after a while, I've been staring at a collection of telephone numbers advertising what used to be euphemistically called "ladies of the night," or get into the premises and allow my own face to be seen by my prey, which might be a disadvantage in the future.

I chickened out and phoned Alan Harrison.

"I think he's gone into a place called 'TwilightArt.com'," I told him. "Do you recognize the name?"

"No," he said.

"Have you any idea what it means?"

"No."

"Do you want me to go in and see what's happening?"

There was a long pause from the other end; I could hear him agonizing. I didn't help him in any way. Eventually there came a soft, subdued, "Okay."

"I'll get back to you," I said and cut the connection.

I avoided a double-decker bus intent on my destruction and went to the door, pushing it open and finding in front of me, as I expected, a flight of stairs that would take me to the first floor. They were uncarpeted, and I went up slowly, treading lightly to avoid making noise. At the top was a wooden swing door painted white with a small glass panel. It had the words "Office - Please Enter" painted on it. I peered through, but the small room with a desk, chair and a computer seemed otherwise unoccupied, so I obeyed the instructions and went in.

A window let in a certain amount of light from the front of the building, and I could hear sounds of traffic from the street outside. To the left was another of those swing doors with a glass insert. From behind this one though, a bright light shone, and I became aware of a strange, regular sound, a bit like heavy breathing, though exaggerated, amplified, almost artificial.

I crossed the room and peered through.

Now I'm not a prudish person. There have been occasions when I've exhibited my private parts to the vulgar gaze, but the scene that met my eyes was unexpected.

On a single bed covered with a burgundy-coloured bedspread was a tangle of limbs. A young man lay on his back, dark-haired, head thrown up, mouth open in a grimace of pain or ecstasy. His legs were raised while, pounding into him and emitting those moaning, groaning, gasping sounds, was another young man, blond hair and, surely, the arse I had been following down the street for the last twenty minutes, pushing and withdrawing with the speed and regularity of a jack-rabbit.

I stood for a second, lost in admiration until, remembering my job, I took out my camcorder and, through the glass, began to record. Poor Alan, I remembered thinking before I felt a certain excited feeling in the region of my own groin. Not really thinking, I explored the area, found a distinct hard-on, took it out and with my free hand began to do what any red-blooded gay would have done. Luckily I'm ambidextrous, and I don't think there was even a waver in my shooting arm, either of them!

"What the fuck?"

I spun round. Standing in front of me, fully clothed, was the blond-haired Philip Trelawny.

"What do you think you're doing?" he asked, though I think it must have been pretty obvious.

"Er…er…" I said.

Okay so let's get the embarrassment over. I explained. Well I explained about the camcorder bit, the Alan Harrison bit, the fear that Philip Trelawny was cheating on him bit and, after a while, Philip cooled down.

TwilightArt.com was his company. It shot gay porn. Then Philip advertised and sold the products over the web. No, he hadn't told Harrison, didn't think Harrison would have approved, but wasn't cheating on him. As far as he was concerned the relationship was as fine as it always had been. The sex bit, he explained by saying that when you see sex all day every day, it got a bit boring. Well that's what he said anyway, though I did notice that, before I actually put my own todger away, young Philip gave it a long, long look, then gave me one too and, very slowly, very suggestively, his long pink tongue licked around his lips.

But I don't cheat on a client…well not often anyway, and I never tell.

CHAPTER TWO

"I Think He Was Murdered"

"It's Timothy Sinclair, isn't it?"

"Tim," I said automatically and turned to face a mop of bright red hair, a sprinkling of freckles over a straight nose and a pair of wide brown eyes. The face was vaguely familiar, and I should of course have recognized him immediately, recalled the name and greeted him warmly. Whoever it was obviously remembered me; the generous lips were smiling. He looked genuinely pleased to see me.

Shit! Where the hell had we met? I hoped it wasn't from some scruffy interlude in a public convenience somewhere, but if it had been surely I wouldn't have given him my name. I scrabbled amongst my few remaining brain cells to come up with the memory, meanwhile stalling for time.

"Hi," I said enthusiastically. "How are you? Long time eh?"

"Fine," he said. "What about you? Still in the same line of business?"

Oh God. Getting deeper and deeper into the mire. What was I when I had met him? A journalist, the brief and rather sordid time I spent as a porn film dealer, a car salesman, a job I thought even less honest than peddling skin flicks? Was when we had met so recent that I had already started out on my private investigator career? Tim Sinclair P.I., struggling to keep head above water.

"'Fraid so," I said. "You?"

He gave me a look. "As a stripper?" he asked, a bit of a smile turning up the corners of his lips.

"Yes," I said. I guess the relief must have shown. A stripper? Yes of course. I must have seen him at some club or other, strutting his stuff, removing his clothes, showing his all or perhaps just nearly all. That was why the face was familiar though the name completely forgotten, if ever known. Then I started to think. Wait a moment! If that was the case how would he have known my name? "Er…"

"You've no idea who I am have you?"

"I'm really sorry," I said, feeling really mean. "Your face is familiar, but I can't remember your name or where we met." I gave him a smile that I hoped would indicate genuine regret.

The party swirled around us. Gay young things of indeterminate age chatted, drank and pulled each other's reputations to pieces in bright, artificial tones. I didn't even know whose party it was. I'd been invited by a sort of friend who always said he hated arriving at a party on his own but who always, once arrived, made a point of deserting his companion and looking for, and usually finding, someone more sexually stimulating. I didn't mind. There was free booze.

There was always the possibility that I, also, might find someone of similar attraction—hope springs eternal—and anyway I didn't have anything else to do. Trade was bad. I hadn't had a case to investigate for a fortnight. I'd have to get something, or I'd be back on the assistance, or have to find myself a 'real' job (as my mother used to say).

"Paul Massingham."

I determined to remember the name should we ever meet again, though I still couldn't recall where we'd met before.

"Of course," I said. "Sorry."

"We met at Joseph Carter's," he said, reading my mind.

Immediately it all became clear. Joseph Carter. Joe. Brilliant, both in looks and personality. Dark. Hair so black and glossy that it reflected the world around. Eyes dark and brooding, hot caverns of lust. In his company other people melted into the background, became "just scenery." No wonder I hadn't noticed, or at least remembered, Paul Massingham. Yet his was a nice face, a genuine face, one that you could really be attracted to. Just that, compared to the resplendence of Joe, it faded into vagueness, as no doubt did mine. I was surprised that Paul had in fact remembered my name.

"Ah yes, of course," I said, this time truthfully. "Didn't he…?"

"Kill himself." The words were out, blunt, brutal words. "That was the verdict of the coroner at the inquest."

I remembered the case. It had been in the tabloids a couple of months ago. A young man had thrown himself off a balcony of a high-rise flat and crashed to his death fifty feet below. I had thought at the time that it was such a dreadful waste. I wondered why he had chosen such a terrible method, the pause at the top, looking down, the unending seconds of the fall itself when there was no possibility of return. I felt a sort of internal shudder as I pictured the incident.

"What do you mean?" I asked. "Was there any doubt about the suicide?"

"I can't talk here," said Paul, glancing around to where a couple of "long-eared" gossip-mongers were already hanging around listening out for any trace of scandal. "Can I see you alone some time?"

I could have suggested the office the following morning, but I wasn't sure if this was a "case" or just a plea for some friendly advice, so I compromised with, "Well, if you're not too struck on the party, we could slip off now. I've about had my fill of it anyway. Come back to my place and we can chat. It's just round the corner anyway."

My "not quite a friend" who had brought me to the party saw us edging off together and raised his eyebrows in a complicated query, half questioning, half knowing. I shook my head indicating there was nothing like that, but I knew he'd be on the phone tomorrow morning, and I'd be in for a grilling.

The sky was clear, and there were even a few stars visible, bravely trying to twinkle through the light pollution of the street lamps. The air smelled almost fresh after the warm fug of clashing aftershaves and body-splashes from the party. I heard Paul give a great intake of breath as we stepped onto the pavement and knew he welcomed it too.

My flat was indeed just round the corner so it didn't take too long to get there. We didn't say much on the way, though I was aware of his body beside mine as we walked together, more or less in step. He had a graceful, almost athletic walk; his profile was attractive too, and I liked the way his hair curled at the nape of his neck. For the first time I suddenly thought of him as a pick-up rather than as a possible client.

"I was in love with Joe," he said suddenly, almost as if reading my thoughts and wanted to make things clear right from the start.

"Weren't we all," I said, dismissing any thoughts of a quickie from my mind.

Once inside the flat, I opened a bottle of Chateau Plonk and poured some into glasses. I suddenly realized I was hungry, and Paul said he was too, so I phoned for a pizza. There's a shop just round the corner. Everywhere is convenient where I live—except for custom and available cock—and they said the food would be round in ten minutes.

We sat and sipped, he in an armchair and me on the sofa. The wine was quite good for cheap stuff from the local supermarket. "Okay," I said, "tell me about Joe."

Paul looked at me, serious brown eyes. "I'm sure he didn't commit suicide," he said.

"If I remember rightly, there was an earlier attempt. The coroner, well, according to the reports in the paper, made a great point of that."

"Yes," agreed Paul. "Joe did. He was very depressed. It was just after we first met. He couldn't see the way his life was going, or at least, he saw only too well which way it was going. He thought it would be an endless array of one-night-stands until eventually he became old and not so attractive, and that would be it. He had also just lost his job. It was a silly attempt, and afterwards he regretted it. Might indeed not have been serious, but he swallowed some pills, enough to kill him if he hadn't been discovered and left a note."

"Was it you that found him?" I asked.

"Oh God, no. Some neighbour who lived in the same block of flats. I think she noticed the door to Joe's flat was unlocked and wondered if there'd been a break-in. She found Joe and called an ambulance."

"He'd left the door open?"

Paul shrugged. "That first attempt wasn't important," he said. "It was just the coroner who thought it was. Afterwards, Joe was completely different. We started a relationship. He was happy. We were planning on buying a house together. He got another job which he enjoyed. There was no reason for him to kill himself."

"Did you say all this at the inquest?"

"I wasn't asked. I told the police, but you know what happens when one half of a gay partnership dies. If you haven't got it all legally tied up, the authorities just ignore the survivor. His parents didn't want to know about us, or even see me at the time. Joe had tried to commit suicide once and failed. The second time he had succeeded."

I knew only too well. "Apart from what you know about his state of mind," I said, "is there anything else?"

"Yes. He wouldn't have done it that way. Not jumping off the balcony. He was terrified of heights. If he had wanted to, he'd have taken pills. He'd never, never have been able to jump."

I nodded, understanding quite well how impossible it would have been for me to jump off a tall building. I shuddered again at the thought as I had at the party. "So what did you do?"

"I told the police again, but then, of course, with the inquest result, they were even less interested. I kept on at them for a while until they told me to, well not to put too fine a point on it, they told me to piss off." He looked almost distraught, his eyes wide, the skin stretched taut over his cheekbones.

"What would you like me to do?"

He looked at me. "You'll help me?" His brown eyes for a

moment looked weepy, and I hoped against hope that he wasn't going to cry. I can't stand weeping guys, or women for that matter. They embarrass the shit out of me. Instead he got up from the chair and came and sat next to me on the sofa, close.

"Jesus," he said, "you don't know how grateful I am. No one listened to me. It's been like beating my head against a brick wall." He put his hand on my leg.

"Feels much better when you stop," I quipped. It was a nice feeling, the warmth of his palm through my trousering, but I didn't think I wanted to be the recipient of a sort of backlash gratitude, on the rebound. I like sex to be because they like me, not just out of thanks, but he seemed determined to make this physical. His hand moved gently upwards, and I could feel myself responding.

The doorbell rang. Pizza boy!

I don't know how it is that all pizza delivery boys are supposed to be young, attractive and available. The ones they always send round to me are either middle-aged or so unfortunately pimple-afflicted that I'd prefer to pay them for the junk food they're bringing rather than reward them with my sex. This one was genial but unattractive. I paid him and brought the box inside.

Paul was still sitting on the sofa, but I could see the moment had passed.

"Food time," I said. "Let's eat, and we'll talk more."

We finished the bottle with the pizza. I asked him what he thought could have happened if it hadn't been suicide. Accident?

"Impossible," he said. "There was quite a high balustrade to the balcony. He'd have had to climb over. I think he was murdered."

I looked at him in much the same as the police probably had done. Who would want to kill him?

"There's one thing more I haven't told you," he said. "The so-called suicide note."

"The second one?"

"Both," he said. "They were the same."

"You mean he wrote the same words in both?"

"No. It was the same note." He explained, "The first time it wasn't a police matter so the note just stayed there. I came across it later after Joe was back from the hospital. I wanted to destroy it, but Joe said, "No. It would remind him of a stupid episode and be a warning if he ever felt like that again." He paused and took a drink. "Then, when he was killed, the police took things away and must have eventually returned all the stuff to his parents. Personal things, you know. They didn't want them, so they asked me if I did. I suppose after they'd got over the shock, they felt a bit guilty. Amongst the things I found the letter. It was in a police bag, marked up with the date and everything. It was the same letter, used again."

That certainly sounded odd, but then people when contemplating suicide do behave oddly. "Have you any suspicions about who might have done it?" I asked. "Surely he was universally liked."

"Too much," said Paul. "There were some who were absolutely besotted with him. And until he met me, he was very much a one-nighter."

I nodded, thinking to myself that Joe and I were in some ways quite similar.

Paul looked at me. "You're a bit like him," he said, "to look at anyway."

That really freaked me out. What was it with this guy, reading my mind all the time. "Look," I said, "it's late. Why don't you come to the office tomorrow and we'll talk about it again? I need a clear head to think with."

Paul got up. Was it my imagination that he seemed a little reluctant? I think he'd have stayed, but I called a minicab anyway.

I went to bed and fell asleep almost immediately. A couple of hours later I was awake again, thoughts buzzing round my head. Joe Carter had left the door open after his first attempt at suicide. Was that carelessness, or did he hope that someone would find him before it was too late? But he had risen from the depths of depression after the affair with Paul had started, or so Paul had said. No more casual sex, or had there been? Talking about people being besotted with Joe, had that included Paul himself? What if Paul was the jealous type? But if Paul had pushed Joe off the balcony, why was he aggravating to get the case re-opened when it was all safely sealed?

It all sounded kosher, except for the method of suicide. If Joe really had a fear of heights, like I did, I knew that nothing on earth would make him choose that way to go. It was just impossible. Even the thought of standing on the balcony, climbing the rail, looking down at the space below, made the palms of my hands start to sweat. I lay awake for a long time, thoughts tumbling around, before eventually I dozed off.

The following morning I had begun to regret making the arrangement to meet Paul as early as nine-thirty. I felt like shit and looked like it too. Bloodshot eyes stared back at me from the mirror. There are some people who look pale and interesting after a sleepless night and half a bottle of vino. I decided I wasn't one of them, but I did the best I could.

Paul, on the other hand, who turned up dead on the stroke of nine-thirty, looked marvellous. His eyes were sparkling, his lips smiled, his skin glowed with health. He wore a green, open-necked shirt and white chinos. I hated him. Well I would have done if he hadn't been so fucking attractive.

I determined to put this on a business footing, hell I needed to. I couldn't afford to give out freebies to all the pretty young men in London, so, after explaining my terms, I asked him to tell me everything that had happened on the night that Joe Carter had died. I switched on the tape recorder.

"Okay," he said. "There isn't much to tell. I got home from work about six o'clock…"

"Home?" I asked. "Were you living at his flat?"

"Well, more or less. It wasn't really big enough for two, and

I did have my own bed-sitter which I'd kept on, but mostly I stayed at his flat. I told you we were planning on getting a house together."

I nodded. "He was there when you got in?"

"Well, first I thought he hadn't got home himself. The lights were out, and it's not a big enough place to lose someone in. But then I saw his coat was hanging in the hallway. I assumed he'd just gone out to get something from the corner shop." He paused and I could see he didn't like thinking about the next part. "Then, well, I started to get some food together in the kitchen. Nothing special, something on toast, I think. He still hadn't come back by the time it was ready, so I took mine into the living room to eat while watching the telly."

"Just let me have a picture. What did the flat consist of?"

"Okay. It was on the tenth floor of a high rise. There's a tiny hall, more of a little box as you come in the front door. The kitchen is off to the right, another little box. The living room is on the left and through that is the bedroom and a bathroom and toilet."

Again he paused. "I sat down and started to eat. The news was on. More unrest in Israel. Suddenly I felt a draught from behind me. There are some glass doors, well windows that open like a door, you know, French windows, onto the balcony outside. The doors were open. I couldn't understand why. It was winter, and Joe wouldn't have opened them or gone out at that time of year. Anyway I went out, just to see and glanced over the balustrade."

This time the pause was a dead stop. His face was pale, eyes strained, his skin taut over his cheekbones. I didn't like forcing him, but the details were important. I waited just a bit then said, "Go on."

"I…I…" He swallowed, "I looked over the rail into the open square below. It was still light enough to see - to see - his body sprawled below, so far below, he didn't stand a chance." Paul's face was agitated and I knew he was crying inside. Soon the tears started to run down his cheeks. I looked away.

In fact I went over to where I've got a small kettle and made two mugs of coffee. I suppose I could have gone to him and hugged him, but I'm not too good with emotions. When the coffee was made, there was no milk, since I had forgotten to bring any in; I took him a cup anyway. By then he had recovered a bit. He sipped at it. "Sorry," he said.

Now that's when I could have hugged him but I thought it might complicate things so instead I asked, "Did you go down first or phone the ambulance?"

"Ambulance. I knew it was useless, but I thought there just might be a chance, and I wanted to get help as quickly as possible."

"Who got the police?"

"The paramedics called them, as soon as they knew there was nothing they could do for Joe."

"And the letter?"

"Letter?"

"Yes, you said the suicide note was the same as the previous one."

"It wasn't the same as, it was the previous one. I didn't notice that at the time. I was in a dreadful state. All the police asked was if that was Joe's writing, and I said yes."

"Where did they find the note?"

For a moment, Paul looked confused. Then he answered, "It was on the balcony, in a corner."

I let him finish his coffee. If it was the same as mine, it tasted pretty foul, but he didn't complain. "Now you said last night that there were some people who hated Joe. Who were they?"

Paul pushed his fingers through his red hair. If anything, in its dishevelled state it made him look even more attractive. "There was one in particular, a guy named Ivor, Ivor Mitchell. He and Joe had had sex, I think only once or possibly a couple of times, and for Joe that was usually enough. But Ivor was obsessed with him. He used to phone him at home, and if I ever answered, he used to scream obscenities at me, saying I'd taken Joe from him.

Making all sorts of threats. I'd never keep him. He'd get him in the end. You know the sort of thing."

Well, I didn't, but I could imagine. "But, what makes you think he'd kill Joe? If anyone, surely it would be you that he'd want out of the way."

"At the start, yes, but as time went on, it was Joe that he began to hate. The phone calls changed. He'd scream at him, and if I answered he'd just say things like, 'You won't have him for long, you know. What will you do when you lose him?' I thought he meant that Joe would get tired of me, but…"

Paul left the sentence unfinished, so I ended it for him. "But he could have meant he'd get rid of Joe himself, by killing him."

Paul looked at me gratefully. "Yes."

"He'd be mad to make threats like that and then carry them out."

"But he is mad," said Paul. "I'm sure he's round the bend."

"Could he have known about the suicide letter?"

That brought him up short. He hesitated. "He had been to the flat," he said. "When Joe first picked him up, I think, and then a couple of times afterwards, before he became so insanely jealous. He was quite good company before."

"Did you tell the police about Mitchell?"

Paul nodded. "But they didn't take much notice, and of course, at that time I didn't know about the suicide note. I was in such a state I couldn't really think clearly about anything."

"Okay, Paul," I said. "I'll see what I can do, make some enquiries, perhaps even see Mitchell. I don't want to raise any false hopes, but I'll do what I can. Give me your telephone number so I can get in touch."

Just before he left he came over to me and kissed me on the lips, not a fully-fledged kiss but not just a peck either. He smelled nice. I was so surprised that I didn't really return it, in fact almost recoiled so that he looked a little hurt, as if I'd rebuffed him. I wanted to put my arms round him and really kiss him, but by that time the moment had passed. How easily do we let these times slip by.

After he'd gone, the office seemed a miserable place. I made some notes on my pad. Later I'd transfer them into the computer, if I had time. The telephone rang. It was my "sort of" friend from last night, demanding to know everything that had happened.

"Nothing at all," I said, sometimes I do tell the truth. "He's just a client."

"A very pretty one," said my friend. "Are you sure you didn't take him into your bed? Isn't he Joe Carter's ex-partner?"

"Yes, that's right." My friend knows everyone and everything, or at least thinks he does. "What do you know about him?"

"Just that he was the one that took Joe off the available list, much to everyone's regret. The meat market was all the leaner once that one got his claws into him."

That was unfair, I thought, but "fairness" isn't included in my friend's vocabulary. Sometimes he's useful so I don't fall out with him over it. "Do you know a guy called Ivor Mitchell?"

"Mad Miss Mitchell? Another of Joe's cast-offs," he said. I wondered whether my friend had been one of the few people who hadn't slept with Joe Carter and was a bit bitter about it. "You don't want to get involved with her. Talk about 'Fatal Attraction'. She'd boil your rabbit as soon as look at you. Last I heard of her, though, she was on the game."

"Do you think she…he would really do something desperate?"

"Shouldn't be surprised," he said. "Wait a moment, there's the most dishiest hunk just strolled by outside. I'm sure he's just panting for it. Talk to you later, love. And let me know when you get into the luscious redhead's knickers."

"Do you know—?" But he had rung off.

Many private investigators are ex-police. Those that are have the advantage of being aware of the way villains work; most indeed have spent many years in the company of villains. They also probably have contacts still within the police force and can often ask a mate to have a quick shufti at the PNC database to check on the whereabouts of a particular person they are interested in. Against the law of course, but it goes on.

Never having been a copper, I miss out on all these perks. Ah well, perhaps some time I'll be able to form a bonding relationship with a policeman. Until then I'll just have to work on my own. Paul didn't know Ivor Mitchell's address, though he thought he lived Balham way. I didn't have time to ask my friend, now no doubt in hot pursuit of the lovely who had walked past his window. I fell back on the telephone directory. Yes, there was a "Mitchell I." living in SW12, Lochinvar Street, highly appropriate! I could have rung him up, but I wanted a more casual approach. Everything I had heard about the sort of person Ivor was, suggested that he'd be someone who cruised around quite a bit. Weekends, probably up west, today being a Tuesday, he might be local. I checked up in my little black book of useful places, gathered over many years and quite a few adventures, and made a shortlist of some gay pubs and clubs in the area.

It might be a long night, so I shut up shop, went home and caught up with the sleep I had missed the previous night. I slept like a babe, just before dropping off, remembering the soft touch of Paul's lips on mine. No! I was not becoming in any way infatuated with the guy. Honestly!

I felt and looked much better when I woke up at six o'clock. I had some food and set off in my trusty old Vauxhall for Balham, Gateway to the South. The first two clubs drew a blank, though I knew my hunch was paying off because Ivor Mitchell was known in both. At the third, a rather tatty rent bar called "The Jam Factory," the clientele were making, or at least trying to make, a living. I could almost smell the acquisitiveness in the air. It came from the anxious searching in the older men's eyes and the weary availability in those of the younger ones. It was summed up by the dollar sign embroidered neatly on the arse cheek of one young man's jeans.

Or perhaps not so young. Though his hair was fashionably

cut and his smile engaging, his skin seemed to be almost too perfect for any but extreme youth. However underneath the almost professionally-applied make-up, there were tiny signs of Time's cruel fingers, mini-wrinkles that I myself noticed while looking at my own face in the shaving mirror, but which I hadn't yet felt the need to try to conceal.

I knew none of the three bar-staff here, all of whom looked just as financially available as the others though probably not until later in the evening, but I went up to the one who was at present rinsing some glasses.

"I wonder if you can help me," I said carefully.

The guy looked up. In his late twenties, he had dark eyebrows and a not unattractive smile which he immediately put on like a polite uniform, as soon as he saw a potential customer.

"I hope so," he said. "You'd make a welcome change from these other wrinklies."

I thought sadly of the desperate men searching for pleasure that had been condemned by this unfeeling man, who himself would be joining the same band before long.

"I'm looking for Ivor Mitchell," I said.

The smile left the barman's face. "That's him over there." He nodded towards the corner where a slim young man in his early twenties was standing in a temptingly alluring pose against the wall opposite. I bought two drinks and went over to him. He looked me up and down. He obviously thought he was the sort who could pick and choose his customers, and indeed he was an attractive guy, tall, slim, nicely developed under the form-fitting T-shirt and moulded jeans, which showed off what looked like a fair-sized priapic package.

Again I was surprised. I had expected a much older man, though I don't know why, possibly because the fuss he had apparently made sounded like someone who was desperate. This one looked much too street-wise and confident to behave in the unhinged way I'd had described to me.

"Ivor Mitchell?" I asked.

The guy raised an eyebrow, not giving much away, though could be asking how I knew. "You come recommended," I said.

"I come frequently," he said.

I acknowledged the quick-wittedness of his reply and handed him the drink I had bought.

"Do I know you?" he asked. "You look familiar." Oh God I thought, not another one who thinks I look like Joe Carter. "Never mind," he went on. "Let's sit." He led me to a small alcove with a table and a cushioned bench behind it. He sat down and patted the space beside him.

I joined him, and he moved closer so that our thighs touched. He certainly didn't waste any time. His hand went straight for my crotch, grabbed my cock through the material and gently massaged it. It had no option but to grow. Then he let it go and moved away.

"That's for the drink," he said. "Anything more is extra."

I decided he wasn't a very nice person. Not that I felt particularly frustrated; well, perhaps I would have liked him to continue for a little longer. "I really want to ask you a few questions," I said.

His expression of bland superiority altered slightly. "Are you the police?"

I shook my head but he still seemed worried. "Are you sure we haven't met before?"

"My name's Tim," I said. "Timothy Carter." I didn't see why I shouldn't make use of the resemblance if that's what it was.

Ivor jumped as if I'd stabbed him. "Carter!" he said. "A relative of Joe Carter's?"

"My brother," I lied modestly.

"Jesus," he said. "I didn't know he had one." He seemed genuinely upset, all his former cynical street cred evaporating, leaving him, I thought, looking a little, what was it? Frightened? "What do you want?" he asked.

"I'm worried about how he died," I said, which was true.

"Has that little Greek trollop been talking to you?"

"Greek trollop?" I said, genuinely mystified.

"Paul Massingham."

"I didn't know he was Greek."

"Oh he isn't, just obsessed with all things Greek, since he went on that trip with Joe. They both came back in love with Greek islands. Had the idea of forming some sort of gay couples' holiday agency."

I hadn't heard any of this before and determined to find out from Paul what it was about, but first I needed to get Ivor's slant on Joe. Not sure how to phrase it, I tried the tentative approach. "You were very fond of Joe yourself?"

"I was out of my mind," he admitted, I thought honestly. "I made a fucking idiot of myself for a time."

"But you got over it?"

"I had to, didn't I? He was dead."

"How did that affect you?" I asked.

"I was shocked, of course."

"Shocked?"

"Okay, I behaved like a jerk. I was jealous, and when he died, I went over the top." He sounded sincere.

He moved closer so that his thigh touched mine again. "You do look very like him," he said. His hand returned to my groin. This time it remained there, holding me. "I'm sorry I was like that before." His hand found my zip and drew it slowly down, then went inside, fiddled through my underpants until he found and grasped my cock.

"Do you want to come back to my place?" he asked.

I was sorely tempted. I didn't like him as a person, but physically he was attractive. I could feel myself weakening as my cock grew stronger so I shook my head.

"You sure? I didn't mean that about charging."

"Gotta go," I said before my hormones took over and stood up, forgetting for a moment how exposed I was. I sat down again and obeyed the injunctions which used to be displayed at the exit of every public toilet. 'Kindly adjust your dress before leaving'.

This time I made it to the door.

Outside I felt frustrated and wondered why I'd refused the offer. A clock from some nearby church or public building chimed. Eight o'clock. It wasn't all that late. I rang Paul on my mobile, not really expecting him to be in, but he was. He sounded almost pleased to hear from me.

"I've just seen Ivor," I said. "I don't think he had anything to do with Joe's death. He told me about the Greek thing, though, you never mentioned that."

"I didn't think it was important," said Paul. "It's complicated to explain over the phone though."

"We could meet," I said, leaving it vague.

"Do you want to come round? Where are you?"

"Balham," I said, "but I've got the car."

He explained where he lived, and half an hour later I was outside the house, another of the red-brick Victorian terrace houses that are so common in London. He'd obviously been looking out for me because by the time I'd parked and opened the gate to a small patch of garden, he had the front door open and was waiting for me, smiling, which was nice to see.

When I got in I found that the original, three-story house had been divided into three flats. Paul's was the downstairs one. He took me into the living room. It had a sofa and an easy chair, a pine table under the window, a CD player and a TV set with video. Bookshelves held paperbacks and some cassettes. A cabinet with drawers against the wall had some bottles and glasses standing on top. An open door in one corner led off to a tiny kitchen, another one was shut, presumably to the bedroom.

There were rugs on the floor and some pictures, framed views of sea coasts, on the walls. It was pleasant and comfortable. Rather more middle-class than I'd have expected from Paul, but much nicer than the tip that was mine. The lights were low, though whether this was for my benefit or because he normally had them like that, I didn't know.

I sat on the sofa, hoping.

"Do you want anything to drink?" asked Paul.

"I wouldn't mind a coffee."

"Only instant," he said and went out into the kitchen. I heard the rush of water into a kettle. I got up and went to the doorway, looking at the back of his head, admiring the M-shape that his red hair made at the nape of his neck. I fantasized about going in and planting a kiss on it. I took a step forward.

He turned around. "Milk and sugar?"

He brought the mugs into the room, and I sat down again on the sofa, leaving plenty of room next to me. He took the chair opposite.

"What's all this about the Greek islands?" I asked.

"It all started after Joe and I went to Greece. It was right at the beginning of our relationship, before things really got serious. Joe was down after the suicide attempt. He wanted a holiday; I wanted a holiday. We went together, not really as a couple, just as friends. We came back as…"

His face took on an expression which, had I not found him so attractive, I would have tossed off as a Mills and Boon one. I felt a twinge of jealousy, no, not jealousy so much as envy. No one, I knew, had ever looked like that over me. Perhaps no one ever would.

"So what happened when you came back?" Notice I didn't allow him to finish his sentence!

"Well I had this idea. It was only a suggestion at first, but Joe took it seriously. We'd had such a marvellous time in such a beautiful setting. I thought, why couldn't other gay couples, yes I thought of us as a couple by then, book up for their, you know, honeymoons through us."

It all sounded a bit corny but I suppose it could have caught on. "Gay Honeymoons?"

"It was corny, but it caught on."

There he was, doing it again, pinching stuff from my brain.

"We started making a bit of money. Then we got into difficulty. Cash flow problems, you know."

Did I. Had them all the time.

"Trouble was we had to pay for the bookings at the hotels before we got the money from the clients. After a while that caused an awful lot of…"

I nodded, understanding, not really listening. God, he was cute; serious brown eyes looking straight into mine, a mass of flaming red hair, a column of throat coming out of a black T-shirt. I wanted to kiss it, in the hollow where the shoulder blade was just visible. Hold him against me. I could almost feel his body against mine. Twice that evening I'd been aroused. I was frustrated. Let's face it, I wanted sex and particularly sex with Paul. I felt my cock twitch. It was uncomfortable and needed re-arranging, but I couldn't do it without Paul noticing.

He smiled. God, was he reading my mind again? He had stopped speaking.

"So," I said, wildly reaching for something to say. "So, how did it all work out?"

"That's when Nick turned up."

"Nick?"

He didn't say anything, just looked at me, a look that became more intense as the moments ticked by. I knew something was going to happen. I held out my hand and he got up from his chair, crossed that short space between us and sat on the sofa beside me.

I moved closer so that our thighs were touching and then

leaned over and kissed him on the mouth, lips closed, for a moment the sort of kiss an aunt might give. Then, when Paul responded, I let my lips open and my tongue pressed against his lips so that he opened up to the peaceful invasion.

Gently I pulled up his T-shirt and ran my hands over his chest, then down to his stomach. Paul lay back, happy to be caressed. My hands felt under the waist band of his jeans and the elastic of his underpants, delving into the pubic hair. Paul pushed upwards, wanting me to go further, to touch him, hold him. I opened the stud and the zipper slid down, revealing his white underpants swelling with the ridge of his erection. I lowered my face to the bulge, taking it sideways and nibbling it with my teeth, then licking it through the material. I could smell his maleness through the soft cotton.

Paul spread his legs wide, throwing his head back. I pulled down the waistband so that the cock was revealed, the skin soft and sensitive covering the rigid core. I cupped the ballsack in my palm and took the shaft into my mouth, sliding down over the head, the foreskin peeling back.

There was a sound from outside. In the hall? No it was a key turning in the front door. The door opening. "Christ!" said Paul. "My parents."

It was a word which in a situation like this still had the power to bring out the old instincts of terror and shame, as when I had been caught, once masturbating in the bath, the door carelessly left unlocked, and again with a friend from school who, on the pretext of helping with homework, had initiated me into rather more esoteric practices. Mother had entered my bedroom bringing coffee and biscuits for sustenance.

Luckily Paul and I hadn't gone far enough for concealment to be impossible. I was still fully clothed, he with T-shirt disarranged and flies unzipped, managed to make a recovery before the door opened and Mr. and Mrs. Massingham entered.

"Ah," said Paul. "I didn't think you'd be back so early. This is Tim Sinclair. Tim, my parents."

I stood to shake hands, well aware that I still had an erection making a sizable bulge in my trousers, but they either didn't notice or were too well-bred to acknowledge, even with a glance.

They were very pleasant and friendly, though at the moment I could have wished them in the bottommost circle of Dante's Inferno. "I see you've had coffee," said Mrs. Massingham. "Would you like some more?"

"No, thanks," I said. "Actually I was just about to leave."

Mr. Massingham smiled affably in the background. I could see where Paul had got his red hair from, though his father's was a little grizzled, salt amongst the pepper.

"I'll see you out," said Paul. We went into the hall together. I snatched a brief kiss before he opened the front door. "Why didn't you tell me you lived with your parents?"

"I moved in when Joe died," said Paul. "I wasn't expecting them back until after midnight."

"We have some unfinished business, I think," I said.

"I'll come round to the office tomorrow."

Driving home, I decided that today had been an unmitigated disaster, sex-wise at any rate. I wasn't even sure it had been much better in terms of the enquiry into Joe's death. I tended to believe that Ivor hadn't had anything to do with it. Perhaps it was all in Paul's imagination.

Next morning I learned a bit more about "Gay Honeymoons." It had all started in a fairly amateurish way, from Paul's initial idea. Joe had planned out the details and put the whole thing on a website. From there it had begun to take in some money but not nearly enough. Too soon the cash flow problems increased until it seemed that they would have to give up the idea. Then Nick Warren had arrived. Paul wasn't quite sure where Joe had found him. "Probably," said Paul, with a hint of sadness, "from one of his many pickups."

But Nick had proved a godsend, injecting much-needed

capital into the business so that it began to make more money than either Joe or Paul had ever expected or indeed hoped for. In fact he'd taken over quite a bit of the business, certainly the computer side, but then, as neither Joe not Paul were particularly interested in this, they didn't object.

"So everything was coming up roses?" I said.

He nodded, seemed about to say something but stopped.

"So what went wrong, then?"

"Well nothing really. I guess it was just a business difference. Something to do with the appearance of the website. Joe wondered why Nick had added something but I didn't really pay much attention. It seemed all right to me."

"Is the business still going strong?" I asked.

"Sure," said Paul. "As far as I know. I gave up my side of it when Joe died. Nick bought my share and I suppose Joe's share from his parents."

"You didn't inherit anything from Joe?"

"We'd never thought that far ahead," said Paul. "I guess we never thought anything could happen to us."

"Let's have a look at the site."

I switched on the computer, and Paul came and sat next to me. I could feel the warmth of his body and smell the clean, fresh scent of him. I let him type in the URL and waited while the screen filled with a picture of lush Greek landscape, a headland with the ruins of a temple on it, white in the sunlight, the sea in the background blue and sparkling. Bouzouki music tinkled in the background. The words "Gay Honeymoons" in convoluted lettering and rainbow colors headed the page. It was all fairly stomach-churning.

"Find your ideal Honeymoon island," enjoined the instructions. A list of hotels and islands followed, all praised and described in the most Mills and Boon language. A further page got down to the sordid details of price and availability. I suppose, to couples who were in love and wanting to spend a memorable fortnight, it was attractive enough.

"Was it all this," I gestured to the Technicolor flatulence on the screen, "that Joe objected to?"

"Oh no. That was our idea."

I took a look at his face. It was suffused with the sort of nostalgic expression that betokened love. Again I experienced a twinge of that envy I had felt before.

"So what was it?"

He pointed to a small white rectangle at the bottom of the page. It was so inconspicuous I hadn't really noticed it. "What is it?" I asked.

"A place to enter a password," said Paul. "It just gets you into a private area. Something to do with the accounts or something. I think he told me once but I've never tried it."

"Do you remember the password?"

"It was one of the Dodecanese islands, I think."

"They being?"

"Oh…" He reeled off a string of names, scarcely any of which I'd heard. "Adelphae, Agathonisi, Arki, Astypalea. Halki, Kalymnos, Karpathos, Kassos, Kos, Leros, Nisyros, Patmos, Rhodes, Ro, Saria, Symi, Tilos…and that's just some of them."

"Okay," I said. "You try them."

He began typing in the names. At the third one, the screen gave way to one filled with columns of figures. "There you are," he said. "Told you it wasn't very interesting."

He was right. There's nothing so boring as financial accounting. Nevertheless I took a printout of the pages. I've got a friend who's that way inclined, and I thought of showing them to him to see if he could find anything dodgy. While the printer was whirring and clacking away, I turned my attention to something infinitely less tedious. Paul's ear, or rather the space just beneath it, where the rich red hair curled under. It was the part I had desired, well, one of the many, when I looked at him the previous evening as he was making the coffee. I favoured it with an experimental kiss.

He responded with the alacrity of a puppy that has just been offered a stick to play with. Indeed he reacted with ardour, turning and gripping me with such fervour that I was forced to call a halt to the proceedings unless we were to have full-scale sex on the office floor.

"Let's wait until this evening," I said, in short, sharp gasps, my mouth releasing his only long enough to get out the phrases. "You can stay the night at my place. We won't be interrupted there."

After he'd gone, but before I'd quite cooled down, my "not quite a friend" rang. "How's Little Miss Red Riding Hood?" he asked. "Got into her knickers yet?"

The very thought triggered the usual response. Strictly speaking I had of course, but not in the sense he meant. "Not yet," I said.

"Ah ha! There's a chance then?"

"Possibly." I changed the subject. "What happened with your dishy hunk yesterday?"

"Oh that one!" My friend's tone was dismissive. "Doesn't know what she wants. Pretended to be straight, but when I lost interest, she started getting really uppity."

"So, no luck there, then?" I almost laughed. Well we both had been disappointed last night, but I obviously had got further than him, and knew I had the better chance of going the whole way.

I was about to ring off when a thought struck me. "Know anything about a guy called Nick Warren?" I asked.

"You know some funny types, Tim. My God, what hasn't Naughty Nicky done? Used to be a barman, I believe, somewhere down in the West Country. Branched out into all sorts of things after that, if the rumours are to be believed. Pimping, a bit of blackmail here and there. Was involved with a young rent-boy who got killed. Made some money on shady deals and ended up in London. Don't know what he's doing now, though."

I did, but I didn't say. Client confidentiality and all that.

I wondered whether I ought to see this Nick Warren. Of course making the meeting casual might be difficult. I didn't know anything about his movements as I had with Ivor, and my friend obviously didn't either. Even if I could find him, I doubted whether the "I'm Joe's brother" stratagem would work as Nick, being his business partner, had presumably known Joe much better than Ivor Mitchell had.

The telephone rang again. I picked up the receiver. A dark brown voice with more than a hint of attractive menace said, "Sinclair? My name is Warren, Nick Warren. I understand you are investigating Joe Carter's death. I think we should have a chat."

I didn't let my surprise show in my voice, or at least I don't think I did. It must have been Paul who had told him, I reasoned, though I wished he would let me know these things beforehand so that I could get myself prepared for them.

"Do you want to come over, Mr. Warren?" I asked.

Nick Warren, when he arrived, turned out to be dark-haired, mid-thirties, with an air of confidence, of always getting what he wanted. His slightly irregular eyebrows and the world-weary twist to his sensual lips gave him an attractively sardonic look. The suit he was wearing looked expensive, the grey tie discreet against his white shirt. He didn't waste any time on preliminaries.

"Joe was always neurotic," he said. "Paul thought he knew him better than anyone else, but it was his emotions talking most of the time."

"You mean there never was any doubt about the suicide?"

Nick shook his head.

"But…throwing himself off the balcony. How could anyone with a fear of heights do that?"

Nick made a gesture with his hand as if to dismiss my objection as completely groundless. "He was in a dreadful state," he said. "He felt things were going wrong like before. He'd started drinking again." He lit a cigarette and inhaled the smoke deeply.

I stared at him. "Paul didn't tell me any of this. He said completely the opposite. They were in love and happy. The business was flourishing, after you stepped in."

"Well certainly the business was in a good state," agreed Nick. "But Paul was wrong about everything else. Probably he didn't want to believe it, but Joe was looking elsewhere, and not only looking. He was fucking with everything in trousers or out of them. I know, I was one of them."

Nick's dark, saturnine face smiled twistedly at me through the tobacco haze. His dark eyebrows, his black hair springing from his forehead, the smile, or was it a sneer. I didn't want to believe him, but he sounded just too convincing.

I sighed, then tried to hide it. "Thanks for telling me this, Mr. Warren. It certainly makes a difference to what I was led to believe."

He nodded, crushed out his cigarette, and went out. Even from the back, he looked lithe, confident, even arrogant. Poor Paul! What was I going to tell him this evening?

But before that I faxed the figures to my accountant contact with a request to see if there was anything obviously wrong. I didn't think there would be and wasn't too surprised when I got a note faxed back saying that there didn't appear to be anything fishy and I owed him a large drink.

I bought some food on the way home and a bottle of the better sort of wine. If the evening was going to turn out as I expected and hoped it was, Chateau Plonk was not good enough.

When Paul arrived, though, it didn't immediately happen. There was no spontaneous hurling into my arms, no covering of my poor defenceless body with passionate kisses, no grappling for my, weakly protected, erogenous zones. Instead, after a brief kiss, he produced a small suitcase.

"I'd almost forgotten I had these," he said in explanation.

"This is what I got from Joe's parents after the funeral. I wondered if they might be something to do with all this." He took out some CDs and held them up with an air of triumph.

It was not exactly what I had planned. I had hoped that we could dispense with the Joe Carter affair, certainly after what Nick Warren had told me, and get down to my own pending one. But obviously Paul had other ideas. "What are they?" I asked.

"I think they're to do with 'Gay Honeymoons'," he said. "Have you got a computer?"

Of course I had a computer. Everyone had one of the bloody things these days. Not that I used it often, but it was up in my bedroom gathering dust so I was not all that averse to taking Paul up there. "Care for something to eat first? Or a glass of wine?"

He shook his head impatiently and we went upstairs, he first, I following with my eyes on that seductively moving butt, encased as it was in denim at the moment. I could scarcely keep my hands off it.

"First on the right," I said and ushered him into the sanctum sanctorum, now suitably cleaned and sweetly smelling with proprietary room freshener. The bed was even made, clean sheets and all. I switched on the computer and, while it did those things that computers do while they're booting up, Paul told me a bit more about the discs.

"Some of them are just copies of the site that we set up at the very beginning," he said. "Then they're some after Nick came in with us. There're a few which have some copies of personal letters from Joe."

"What do you expect to find out from them?" I asked, perhaps unfairly.

His brightness dropped. "I thought you might notice something," he said with that air of trust that I found very appealing but which I had no way of gratifying.

"Okay. Let's have a look."

They were indeed as he said, some early drafts for the website.

JPGs of Greek coastline and views which had been used, some copies of web creator files which showed what had been first proposed and rejected. I could see nothing significant in any of them. The ones after Nick had taken over also seemed quite as innocent. The letters from Joe were personal but most dated from way back, long before the suicide, so I didn't read them. "Isn't there anything from round the time when he died?" I asked.

"A couple," said Paul obviously growing dispirited. "Here's just a list of Greek Islands." On the screen was just such a list as Paul had reeled off this morning when we tried for the password to get into the accounts. There were however considerably more this time. "About 200," said Paul, "though there are even more than that, some of course just little more than bits of rock sticking up out of the sea." He scrolled down to the bottom where there was a gap, then a single word, and "see Nick."

"Parakeet!" I said. "Is that the name of a Greek island?"

"No, of course not."

"What does it mean? Did Nick keep birds?"

Paul shook his head looking genuinely puzzled. "I don't know what it means. Do you think it's important?"

"Probably not," I said, "but…" It sounded silly, so I hesitated.

"But what?"

"Well, if the names of islands were used as passwords, couldn't this also be one?"

"What for?" asked Paul. "We've found out about the accounts. What else would you need a password for?"

"I thought it was a stupid suggestion."

He typed in the "Gay Honeymoons" URL and then, in the blank space at the bottom put "parakeet." The screen cleared, to be replaced by a single request: "Please enter your name." Paul looked at me. I said, "Try 'Nick Warren.'"

The screen changed.

"Holy Shit!" I stared, horrified. Then turned to look at Paul.

"Is this stuff yours?" I asked.

From the look on his face I realized he was equally shocked. "Of course not."

"Do you think it was Joe's?"

"Christ, no!"

"It must be Nick's," I said.

"Jesus! And Joe found out about it. Accused Nick, and he killed him to stop him talking. What do we do? Go to the police?"

"There's no actual proof it was Nick. I'll have to go and see him, tomorrow."

"Jesus!" repeated Paul, appalled. He shivered and I held him until he stopped. Then I kissed him. After a while he responded. I took him by the hand and led him over to the bed. He lay on his back and I lay next to him, feeling the warmth of his body next to mine. Then I held him closer, and he moved to face me so that we lay mouth to mouth, chest to chest, groin to groin, and I could feel his hardness against mine.

I kissed him under his ear and on his neck. Paul's eyes were closed, but his hands fumbled at my shirt, then lower at my belt and zipper. The clothes were getting in the way. "Let's take them off," he said, trying to get up, but I pushed him back.

"Let me do it," I said.

I took off Paul's T-shirt, pulling it over his head, Paul lifting his arms, revealing the reddish hair in his armpits. Then, kneeling at his feet, I undid his trainers, taking them off and then his socks, my tongue cat-licking the soles and between the toes so that Paul twisted and turned with the sensation, which was both almost unbearable and yet at the same time too exciting to deny. At long last I stripped off his jeans and underpants. Paul lay there naked. His chest slimmed to a small waist just below which the honey of his pubic hair led to and surrounded his cock and balls.

I stood up and took off my own clothes. Paul lay back on the bed and I kissed his throat, his neck, everything, starting at the top and working downwards. My naked body was on top of him and the feel of skin against skin, cocks together, hard flesh against hard flesh was like an electric charge, driving out every other feeling. He pushed his body upwards, holding me and pulling me down on top of him. We held each other, our tongues and hands exploring each other's bodies. His mouth was moist, warm, wildly irresistible.

On top, I slowly inched down Paul's body, kissing and licking. I paused and sucked at the nipples, then went down and put my tongue in Paul's navel. Paul giggled and wriggled so I went even lower so that I could feel the fuzz of rust-coloured hair around that sprouting cock.

"Turn round," said Paul's voice, high with arousal, "so I can do the same to you." Soon both our faces were buried in each other's groins. I ran my tongue up and down his erect shaft and licked the firm young balls, taking each one into my mouth and gently mouthing them one at a time. Then I moved back and enclosed the prick as far as I could. I could feel my own erection being taken into Paul's warm mouth.

I put one arm over Paul's legs and gently explored his arse. I found the tender hole, stroked it and inserted my finger. I heard Paul gasp, then felt him doing the same to me. I pushed harder, at the same time sucking and stroking with my free hand.

Paul gasped, "I'm coming," and then clamped his mouth down again.

At the same time there was a warm, salty spurt into my mouth, but all I felt was my whole being centered in my own groin as a source of pleasure, exploding and pulsing again and again.

We lay together for a while, then got up and had some wine, discussing what to do. Later I took him back to bed again and we had another go, this time ending up in some other, equally pleasurable places.

The following morning I phoned Nick. I told him I'd seen Paul and that there were a couple of points I thought he might be able to clear up. Could we meet? He seemed a little reluctant.

Couldn't we do it over the phone? But I told him there was something I wanted to show him, which was true, and he agreed. Yes, he'd come into the office about eleven.

Paul was nervous. He wanted to come with me, but I said it would be better if he stayed away. If anything went wrong, I didn't specify, at least he'd be there to go to the police. This, of course, made him even more nervous, and the idea didn't actually have a calming effect on me either. We made some plans, had a little private business—God, that lad is insatiable, once he gets started—cleaned up, and I set out.

Nick was waiting outside the office when I arrived. I must have dallied rather longer with Paul than I'd intended. I apologized for being late, and Nick muttered something to the effect that if he treated his work as casually as I did mine, there would be little profit made.

"Okay," I said, unlocking the door and ushering him inside. "Let's get right down to the matter in hand." I switched on the computer.

Nick looked at me, a smile on his arrogant lips. "Well, what's young Paul been saying?" The emphasis he gave to the adjective implied that whatever it was, it had no value at all. Just jejune fantasy.

I turned and faced him. "Parakeet," I said.

Instantly his eyes narrowed and the smile disappeared. We both knew that the other understood exactly what the word denoted. "How did you find out?" he asked.

"Doesn't matter," I said. "What does is that Joe also found out. What did he do? Came and told you that he knew you were using his perfectly innocent site as an advertisement for your pedophile ring? Kids available for sex? So you pushed him over the balcony?"

Nick shrugged. "Well the first part's about right. Yes he did tell me, but I didn't push him. That was an accident. He went almost mad, flinging himself about, and I was just trying to calm him down. He tried to get away. The door to the balcony was open. He ran out, tripped and fell over the rail. There was nothing I could do, but obviously I didn't want the whole thing to come out. I'd no proof of my story. I knew about the old suicide letter. Joe had showed it to me, saying what a fool he had been, so I got it out of the drawer and left it on the balcony."

"All that story you told me yesterday about Joe going back to his old ways. That was a lie?"

"Yes," said Nick. "I didn't want anyone poking around. I thought I was covered, but you never know. And obviously I wasn't."

"The kids' stuff?"

"Oh come on," said Nick, "you're a man of the world. It's profitable. I'll give you a cut of the profits. There's plenty enough to go round."

I thought of the pictures I had seen. The innocent - well had been at one time - kids, laid out like meat on a butcher's slab, girls and boys, their slender limbs posed in spurious erotic positions, too young indeed even for pubic hair to have grown. I felt sick. "You're going to prison, Warren," I said. "Maybe they won't get you for the murder of Joe Carter, but they will for this."

Nick gave a short laugh. "And when the police look, they'll find the whole site wiped clean," he said. "It won't take me more than a couple of minutes."

"We've recorded everything that was there," I said, knowing I was on shaky ground now. "Paul's showing them everything and they're probably looking at the site at this very moment."

"There's nothing to link me with it."

"Only what you've just admitted, all of which is on my tape recorder."

Immediately when I said this I knew I'd made a dreadful mistake. Nick Warren wasn't one of those guys you can cower into submission, who'll give up without a fight.

"I think," he said, slowly and with menace, "that I'll take that from you now." On the last word he produced an object from his pocket, pressed something, there was a snapping sound and a long blade suddenly appeared, the light from the window glinting on it. From nowhere into my mind came the words "the vorpal blade went snicker-snack." I'd never really known what the line from Lewis Carol's poem, "Jabberwocky" meant before, but I did now.

I'm not a brave person. Something inside seemed to shrivel up as I saw that long, vicious blade and the man holding it. No compassion in his eyes, mouth twisted in a grimace, perhaps even of enjoyment, certainly of anticipation.

"Don't be a fool," I babbled. "Paul knows I'm seeing you here. If you kill me, they'll be after you straight away. Joe may not have been a murder but this will. They'll catch you. There'd be no way out. As it is, well, I don't know what you'll get for the kids' ring but it wouldn't be anything like what you'd get for murder."

I rabbited on, not really sure if I was making sense or not, but something must have got through. I saw the tenseness go out of his body, his eyes relaxed. He was thinking, which, as far as my safety was concerned, was probably better than him running purely on adrenaline.

"Okay," he said, with a return of his old sardonic arrogance. "Well, I'll be seeing you." He turned to go and, as I relaxed and thanked my lucky stars for my escape, he turned back and made a lunge at me with the knife. I was completely unprepared for the attack, and it was only instinct that made me dodge at the last moment. Too late though, to escape the wild rake of the knife completely. It caught my chin and then traveling down cut through my shirt and into my chest. I felt a hot shock, rather than pain, and the dribble of warmth down my skin.

As he raised the knife again, I saw, behind him, the door open. There were people there. Paul was one of them, his eyes wide with alarm. Others had on blue uniforms. They quickly had Nick in a hold and wrested the knife from him.

"Tim, are you all right?" asked Paul. A silly question as there was blood streaming down my shirt front, but I had to answer bravely.

"Just a scratch," I said, and then I must have fainted.

I woke to find myself flat on my back in an ambulance, with Paul holding my hand, under the somewhat disapproving gaze of a paramedic.

"We'll be in the hospital in a moment," said Paul.

"You'll be all right, son," said the paramedic. "I've stopped the bleeding and there's nothing vital been touched."

After I'd got patched up and sent home, Paul put me to bed, well on it anyway. He looked down at me. I lay there on the candlewick counterpane, completely naked, and at my fork my cock rested on my thigh, soft and, I hoped, inviting. Some of the rest of me was bandaged and I had a strip of plaster on my chin. Paul knelt down beside the bed.

"How are you feeling?" he asked. My face was puffy and sore, as were my chest and stomach. "I just need treating gently," I said and tried for a smile. It was not a great success.

"At least Nick's behind bars."

I didn't want to talk about him for the present. I'd always wanted to investigate a murder. This one had proved to be altogether too uncomfortable. "Kiss me," I said, "but not anywhere painful."

"I don't know where to kiss first," Paul said.

Our lovemaking was tender and gentle. I wasn't able to do as much as I wanted, so it wasn't quite what I had planned, but it would do, for the present.

There would be lots of time.

CHAPTER THREE

Back From the Dead

I was taking a pre-lunch break from my office in Jermyn Street. It was a hot, sunny summer day, the sort in England we get two of during June before the whole weather system collapses into thunder, lightning and torrential rain, and the office had been stifling hot and claustrophobic. So I'd slipped out through the back streets to St. James' Park and gone for a stroll round the lake, almost wishing I'd got some bread to throw for the ducks.

The fact that there was always a chance of meeting some unattached and equally randy young man didn't have anything at all to do with it. Of course not!

So there I was, with half an eye on a large pelican standing morosely on the bank, and the other one and a half on the slim figure of a guy dressed in a tight, white T-shirt and even tighter white shorts which, from the back at least, clasped two of the most perfect hemispheres I'd seen for many a long day. I rather wanted to get ahead so I could see what the front looked like, but as I was doing the old overtaking manoeuvre I bumped into someone coming in the opposite direction.

It was my oldest, dearest friend, whose name is Barnabas. I know, it's a terrible name. Can't imagine what his parents must have been thinking when they called him that. Of course "Barney" doesn't sound too bad, but really! We'd actually been at school together, then to University, though reading different subjects, discovered we were both gay, spent one, hilariously disastrous, night in bed together, and then settled for an amicable relationship that in some respects was almost closer than perhaps anything except marriage.

We trusted each other. We told each other everything even though we might not see each other for months on end. Well, I did say "in some respects."

"How's Paul?" he asked, smiling brightly.

Barney isn't strictly speaking drop-dead handsome. He has a rather long, horsy sort of face, brown eyes which he occasionally narrows almost menacingly when he's thinking hard or getting annoyed. He wears his hair rather longer than cropped and allows it to fall into a ragged fringe across his forehead. He looks like a student. In fact he works in the Stock Market, very successfully. He has an exceedingly smart flat in the trendy part of Islington and a gorgeous boyfriend whom I once, unsuccessfully, had tried to bed—before he took up with Barney, I hasten to add.

I didn't want to discuss the late-lamented Paul Massingham, not even with Barney. Paul and I had just gone through a particularly intense affair, and I still felt guilty about the way it had suddenly gone downhill and then finally fizzled out. Not of course that I would admit that the break-up was in any way my fault.

"It's over," I said.

Barney looked at me in surprise, tinged with concern. "I'm really sorry," he said, and sounded as if he meant it. "I thought you had a good thing going there."

I had thought so too.

Barney, though, knew me well enough not to probe but also knew that I'd probably tell him all the gruesome details in the fullness of time. He changed the subject.

"How's work?"

That was something else that I was pissed off with too, but didn't mind talking about. "Nonexistent," I said. "Haven't had a P.I. job for weeks. I think adultery's taken a back seat for the summer."

"I doubt it," he said, patting me on the shoulder in an understanding, affectionate, though completely un-patronising way. "Come and have a drink," he said. "Gin! And then you can sob all you want."

I took one last look at the guy in the white T-shirt and shorts, now disappearing over the horizon in the general direction of Buck House—the Queen was in residence, I noted, Royal Standard flying bravely, and accepted.

Three gin and tonics later, and I was ready to tell all. We were sitting on the patio of "The Lark in the Park" under a red and white Cinzano umbrella. We overlooked the greenery some twenty yards away, and it was pleasant. There were four guys, stripped to the minimum, lying on the grass and soaking up the rays. I suspected that they would soon turn bright pink, but at the moment, they were good to look at.

Barney wouldn't allow me to buy a round, and I was feeling quite happy. Hadn't got to the maudlin stage. That would be at least another two gins later. "I suppose we…" I started and then stopped.

Barney wasn't attending to me. Instead he was staring at one of the guys I'd noticed sunning themselves in the Park. There was an expression on Barney's face that I'd never seen before. I hoped it wasn't acute lust. Though personally I am not someone who believes in monogamy, I rather like to feel that it has an existence somewhere and that Barney, for one, is a particular example of the condition. His eyes were wide, his mouth hung open. He looked completely gob-smacked.

"What's the matter?" I asked.

"That guy over there," he said. "He's supposed to be dead."

I looked again towards where he was pointing. The particular young man was lying on the grass. For a moment I thought it was the one I had been pursuing earlier in the morning, but then realized that he had been dark while this one was fair, very blond indeed, with the whitest of white skins. Even through my gin-sodden eyes he looked anything but dead. As I watched he sat up and started to put on a cream-colored pullover. Very wise, I thought, without some Sunscreen Factor 8, he'd soon have been most unattractively frizzled.

I turned my attention back to Barney, waiting for an

explanation.

"Come on," he said. "I'll tell you on the way."

There was no way out straight from the patio into the Park, and we had to go back into the pub, through the bar, out the front door, turn right down an alleyway before we could get into the Park. When we actually arrived, the young man had disappeared.

"I'm sure that was Benjamin Cameron," Barney said. "He was supposed to have been killed in a car crash!"

The other three lads were still there, sun-worshipping. Barney went to speak to them. I contented myself with giving them a more basic scrutiny. One was really dishy, the other two WSN.

"That guy who was here with you," said Barney. "Where did he go?"

One of the "wouldn't say no's" spoke. "Dunno," he said. "Just said he'd gotta split."

"Did you know him?"

The three looked at each other. They shook their heads. "'E was just chattin'," said the dishy one. "'Bout 'ow 'ot it was." He shifted his hips to make himself more comfortable, and I stared at the really provocative bulge in his groin.

The others nodded in agreement. One of them said, "Never seen 'im before."

"Did he say what his name was?" asked Barney. "Could it have been Benjamin? Ben?"

"'E didn't say."

Barney sighed. "You can't tell me anything at all?"

"Sorry mate," said the dishy one. "Wus 'e a friend?" He put his hand in his pocket, I didn't think there could be room for it, and fiddled around, moving the contents of his shorts around a bit.

"Just someone I wanted to speak to." Barney gave me a surreptitious dig in the ribs. I was probably standing there with my eyes on stalks. Reluctantly I turned to go.

"'Cept of course he was an Aussie."

Barney turned back. "He said so?"

"Nah! You could tell from 'is accent, cobber," in a bad parody of Strine. Athletically he jumped to his feet without touching the ground with his hands. I watched enviously. I couldn't do that. Then he spoiled it by losing his balance and lurching towards me. He put out his hands and clutched me around the waist. I wasn't complaining. For a split second his body was against mine and I could feel his flesh, warmed by the sun. Then he drew away, smiling. "Sorry, mate," he said.

I smiled back to show that I wasn't the least bit upset.

Barney and I went back to the pub, where I had the other two gins while Barney told me the story. Apparently this guy, Benjamin Cameron, had been in a relationship with a friend of Barney's, an older guy called Jack something. Jack had been besotted, but Ben had gone back to Queensland for a visit or something and while over there had been involved in a car accident and killed. Tragedy! Jack was inconsolable, had wanted to go to Australia, bring back the body, bury it here, but of course the boy's relatives had objected.

Barney had apparently met this Benjamin a couple of times. He was sure that the guy in the Park had been him.

"Looked like him," I suggested. "He was a good bit away from us."

"And then he had an Australian accent," said Barney.

"So have quarter of the tourists in London in June."

"Could you find out?" he said. "I mean as a P.I. Professionally."

I looked at him. "Whaffor?" I asked a trifle indistinctly, five gins having had a bit of an effect.

"I'd like to find out, for Jack's sake. He's a good friend, and he was dreadfully upset. Still is, in fact."

I obviously still looked doubtful, perhaps even completely

canned, for he went on. "Look on it as a job. Nothing to do with our being friends. Your usual rates—I don't even want a discount. Just try to find out who that guy was. I could swear it was Benjamin."

I struggled to get myself into some sort of gear. "'T's goin' to be a bit difficult," I managed. "He's gone and those guys," I gestured over the green sward at the place where the three had been so attractively sprawled and now were also gone, "didn't know anything about him."

"There's another guy might know something," said Barney.

"Jack?" I asked, to prove that I had taken in something of what he had told me. "The boyfriend?"

"Oh God no! I don't want him to know anything about this. It would revive all the misery. No, this is someone who knew Benjamin in Australia. Guy called Josh. He lives in London now, Shepherd Market. I'll give you his phone number." He took out one of those mobile phones which contain everything so that, if you lose it, your life comes to a halt, and browsed through it for a while. Eventually he found what he was looking for. His eyes narrowed. "Haven't you got anything to write this down on?"

I felt around in my jacket pocket for an old envelope and found something like a small business card. I took it out and looked at it. Just as I'd thought, a rectangle of white cardboard. One side was blank. The other had a telephone number neatly written in black biro and the words, "Gi'us a ring sometime. Chris." I had no recollection of who Chris was or when he had given me it. That worried me for a moment so that I missed Barney's giving me the guy's name and telephone number, and he had to repeat it.

"Let me know how you get on," he said, and we parted, me back to the office to face a blank desk, and he no doubt to make a few hundred thou in a couple of hours before leaving early to go back to the gorgeous guy he lived with. Envious? Me? As if!

I was just turning into the bottom end of Jermyn Street when it struck me, struck me so forcibly that I stopped short in the middle of the pavement and three people bumped into me, cannoned off and passed by, grumbling. Of course Chris must have been the dishy guy in the park. He'd put the card into my pocket when he pretended to stumble and fall against me. Jeez, he was a brilliant dip! Suddenly worried, I felt for my wallet. If he was that good at slipping things into pockets, he would have had no trouble slipping a wallet out, but it was there, comfortingly slim.

I went into the office and took out the card again. On one side was Chris's number, on the other I had written that of the guy Barney had given me. Hormones versus professional duty! I phoned Chris. The number rang and rang. Of course, I thought, he'd hardly have had time to get home by now, even though the number I was ringing was an inner London one. I was just about to put the receiver down when it was answered. The voice at the other end sounded out of breath, as if he had been running up stairs to get to the phone.

"Chris," it said.

"Hi, Chris," I said. "I got your card."

There was a brief pause. Then "In the Park?"

"That's right," I said. "Congratulations. You'd make a good pickpocket."

He laughed. "Wanna come over? I'm in Lambeth." Lambeth is just over the river from the office. I was tempted. Only two stops on the Jubilee Line.

"I need a shower," I said.

"So do I," said Chris. "We can have one together. Gotta name?"

"Sure," I said. "It's Tim. Give us your address. I'll be over."

But before I left, I assuaged my sense of virtue by ringing the number Barney had given me, Josh of Shepherd Market. There was no answer, so I left with a clear conscience.

The address Chris had given me proved to be a block of

flats about a million miles high. Number 74 was on the seventh floor and the lift wasn't working—not that I'd have trusted it even if it had been—severely graffitied and the doors looked as if there'd been an attempt at being kicked in. I walked up seven flights of steps and arrived on the landing out of breath, much as Chris had sounded when he'd answered the phone. A depressing view looked over the balcony onto an inner yard of scrubby grass dotted with litter and no doubt dog shit, though I couldn't actually see it from this height. Some young kids were making the best of the area, racing round with the remains of an old pram and shrieking. The walls were rendered cement which hadn't stopped various comments from being spray-painted on them. I noticed one that announced "Chris is a poof." Well, I knew that already, though it was good to have confirmation.

His door was painted green which was the only way the separate flats were distinguished, apart from their number. I pressed the bell and waited. He opened the door with a smile and little else, just a towel wrapped insecurely round his waist and a couple of silver chains round his neck. And a small earring in his left ear. Obviously he hadn't been able to wait for the shower. There were still droplets of water on his shoulders and his hair, dirty gold, was wet. But he was even dishier than I remembered.

"Come in," he said. "Glad you've arrived. It was a bit lonely in there all by myself."

I followed him inside and down a passage, his butt beckoning me onwards through the skimpy covering. They turned right into a shower room. The towel disappeared revealing them in their glory. "You'd better get yer kit off," said Chris, "unless you wanna get it all wet."

Now that's the sort of invitation I don't need to hear twice. Jacket, tie, shirt, shoes, socks, trousers, jockeys, all stripped off double quick. Chris laughed, turned to face me. The water cascaded, and I joined him, pressed close, feeling his body against mine, and a growing erection to match.

I was almost unaware of the hot spray of the water, the steam filling the bathroom. Hands, made smooth and slippery-soft with soap, ranged over my body, under the armpits, between my legs, cleaning out the sweat and dirt of the day. The water rinsed, and Chris sank to his knees. I tried to go down with him but heard a whisper telling me to stay there. He turned me round.

A tongue licked between my buttocks, teased my arsehole and went between my legs to cat-lick under my balls.

His hands grasped my hips, bending me forward so that my buttocks separated, then went round over my stomach and down to grasp my cock, holding on to it while his tongue pushed deep into my hole.

Someone was groaning aloud, and I realized it was me. My cock hadn't had sex for some three weeks, and it knew it wanted it now and wasn't prepared to hang about waiting. My hands braced against the shower wall, keeping myself from falling over. I could feel the stuff inside me building up. "Whoa," I said, but it was too late. Out it all pumped against the shower wall.

"Bit of a waste," said Chris. "I could think of several places I could have used that."

For the moment I was exhausted, drained, helpless. "Sorry," I said. "I couldn't help myself." I touched his cock, which, erect and demanding, was pointing at me accusingly. "If we can lie down, you can put that wherever you think it'll feel most at home."

His arms held me, supporting me as I stood, my knees trembling just a bit. We didn't speak as we dried each other off, and Chris led me into the bedroom. I lay on the bed face down, let my legs be spread and then sighed as fingers and tongue found that special place again, which the Spanish call the *caverna oscura*, the dark cave.

After a short while sensations took charge of my body. I could scarcely believe I wanted to orgasm again, but those probing entities, tongue, fingers, eventually his cock, suitably Durex-coated, worked their magic. We both erupted into something fantastic, he into the condom, me into the bedding.

"Wow," I said, afterwards, lying there sticky and replete with sex. "That was really something."

Chris purred something I assumed was agreement.

"Why," I asked when I was thinking with my mind again, "why did you put the card in MY pocket?"

Chris giggled in my arms. "You were the one showing all the interest."

"True," I said, "though Barney was asking all the questions."

"Not the right ones, though."

"You really didn't know that guy? The one he was talking about."

"No."

"And hadn't seen him before?"

"He never asked me that. Yeah, I've seen 'im before. He goes to the Grenadier, down Hyde Park Corner, most nights."

When I left Chris's place I felt a bit depressed. I know some Roman bloke said, *post coitum omne animal triste*, after sex every animal feels sad, but I thought it was more than that. The sex had been great, and I wouldn't exactly have been averse to going back for a repeat performance some time, but that's all it was, fucking good sex, and I'd been used to something a bit more with Paul. Sex plus, sex double plus in fact, and lying together afterwards, being tender, and all that sloppy stuff had been great. Not that I'm one of those who say their cocks are joined to their hearts. Mine certainly isn't. Mine's a free-thinker and a free-doer. Too right. But all the same, I did sort of miss Paul.

Anyway, I'm pretty sure that wasn't the reason I felt a bit off. Probably still had the remains of a hangover after all those gins in the morning. I should have been feeling on top of the world. Great sex and a lead in the case! Already I'd earned enough to pay the rent on my flat for a week, though unfortunately not enough for the rent of the poky office room in Jermyn Street for a day. I wondered, as I often did, whether I ought to think about moving a bit down-market as far as premises were concerned.

A cloud obscured the sun. I looked up. Yes, it was clouding over. Already the sky had that distinctive yellowy look to it which confirmed that the mini heat-wave was over and that we'd soon be dodging thunder-bolts and forked lightning, in other words a typical third day of high summer in England.

I joined the waiting millions queuing at the station on their ways home.

I rather fancied a night in to rest and recuperate but knew that, come eight o'clock, I'd be off to the Grenadier.

By the time I was ready, it was dark, dark enough for ten p.m. and drops of rain were making marks the size of fifty pence pieces on the pavement. In a minute it would be a torrential downpour, and I knew I'd be soaked even getting to the tube. I was looking pretty snazzy if I say it myself, wearing a pair of Teddy Smith grey trousers with cargo pockets and a blue Duck and Cover shirt, none of which I wanted to get soaked. If I'd been working for a real client, I'd have gone by minicab, but this was for Barney. It didn't take me long to come to a decision. Hell, he earned more in a week than I'd take in a year. I phoned for a cab and journeyed through the rain to Hyde Park in style.

The Grenadier was dead smart, even if it was in what at one time had been a cellar. I, well Barney's account, had to pay a considerable sum just to get inside. And even there drinks cost the earth. And this Benjamin guy used to come here on a regular basis. Jeez. He must be a millionaire. Clutching a drink that looked cheap and nasty and tasted likewise, I went on a tour looking for the guy from the Park. I remembered him as pale and blond, his hair cut short, straight nose, a sort of sideways glance with the eyes, almost shifty. Not, in my view, all that attractive, but beauty is in the eyes of the whatsit after all.

I did the rounds. There were some real sizzlers there. Of course peering at them, lights in gay clubs are always flattering rather than illuminating, didn't do my image much good. Made me look desperate rather than laid back and receptive, but that couldn't be helped. Have a feeling one of these days I'll have to get some contact lenses, at least for close work.

Then I saw him. Standing by himself in a corner looking round, almost predatory, though that was possibly a reflection of my own usual attitude in gay clubs, or anywhere to be honest. Close to, he looked thin and gaunt and not all that well. He had a spattering of spots around his mouth. "Hi, Ben," I said cordially. He jumped and gave me that sideways glance I had associated with him when I first saw him. "It is Ben Cameron, isn't it?" I persisted.

"Er, no," he said, "you've got the wrong guy." He was either confused or lying.

"That's odd," I said. "You're the spitting image of him. We met at Josh's." The lie came easily.

The guy, who wasn't Benjamin, gave me another look. This time I associated it with pure terror, but I wasn't going to be put off. A terrier I was, with my teeth into a postman's ankle. "Care for a drink?" I asked.

Conflicting emotions seemed to be going on inside his brain. Perhaps he was thinking. "Er... Okay," he said. "Thanks. A beer." The Australian accent was noticeable.

I turned towards the bar and then back to ask if lager was okay. But in that fraction of time he was gone. Jeez, Cinderella couldn't have left the prince's ball more quickly on the first stroke of twelve o'clock. This time, though, there was no glass slipper. I saw a minor confusion towards the exit and made towards it, on the way handing my revolting drink to a made-up young/old queen who looked as if she deserved it.

I emerged into a cloudburst. Torrential rain streamed down from a purple-black sky. A pink flash of sheet lightning lit up the almost empty street, and I saw Ben's slim figure hurrying up Piccadilly, trying to keep as much under the shelter of the building overhangs as possible. I did the same, but in a couple of minutes I was drenched, as no doubt he was.

Now, stalking a quarry is my forte. I'd have got medals for it, if there were any available. I'm a master at using every passerby, every natural object, like a pillar-box, parapet or pissoir, as cover, at the same time not appearing to be in pursuit at all. Tonight, though, was not one of those occasions. I didn't care who saw me. Anyone who did would obviously think that I was just some young queen desperately scurrying to get out of the storm. Whether Ben knew I was following, I had no idea, nor did I really care. His cover was blown in that he had been discovered at the Grenadier. Probably he wouldn't use it again if hiding his identity was so important to him, so all I had to do was pursue and make sure that I didn't lose him.

I saw the station entrance of Green Park ahead and wondered if he'd duck in there, but he went past and then turned left down a side street. Puffing, I decided I was really out of condition. I increased my pace and skidded round the corner. Foreign territory here, all mewses and narrow alleys. This was Old London, little changed from the last century or perhaps the previous three, except the houses had been tarted up and now cost the earth and a little bit more. I wasn't sure where I was, Curzon Street, Clarges Mews, somewhere like that. The weather was still playing *ad alta voce* above and chucking it down as if it had no use for it at all up there. I couldn't have got any wetter if I'd jumped into the Thames.

But Ben was still in sight, at least when the lightning flashed. Then he turned into the doorway of a house, and when I got there he was gone and the door closed. From the outside it looked a rather pleasant Georgian house with three floors which didn't seem to have been split up into separate flats, certainly there were no little name tags with separate bell pushes. I debated whether to ring and face up to Ben (or whoever he was), but I wasn't in a very fit state, drenched to the skin, my hair plastered to my scalp, hardly a formidable opponent. I could see the number eighteen on the door but didn't have an idea what the name of the road was, though I thought I'd be able to find my way back in daylight.

The rain didn't show any signs of abating, and I knew I wouldn't be very welcome in a taxi so I squelched my way back to the tube and made for home, uncomfortably aware that I looked like a survivor from the Titanic. I could just hear my mother saying, "If you don't get out of those wet clothes soon, Timothy, you'll catch your death of cold."

I always used to tell her that colds are caused by a virus and not by getting wet, but the fact that I woke up the next morning with a sore throat and the sniffles seemed to cast doubts on my beliefs.

Barney rang before I left for work. "Yes, I did manage to find the guy last night," I told him in a blocked-up nose, gravelly sort of voice. "No, he denied his name was Benjamin Cameron, but I think he might have been lying. Yes, I've found where he's living. Yes, I'm going round to see him now. Yes, I have got a bit of a cold, thank you."

After last night's storm, the sky was clear and the air smelled (or would have done if my nose had been clear) clean as if washed of its impurities. Later no doubt the traffic exhaust would clog it up again, but at the moment it was almost like being in the country. The puddles on the pavement were drying as I watched. I called in at Boots in the High Street and bought some throat lozenges and a Vick inhaler (I like these old-fashioned remedies; they must work or they wouldn't have been hanging around for centuries). Then I took the tube back to Green Park.

Finding the street again was no problem. I discovered it was Shepherd Market, and that struck some sort of chord with me, though all I could think at the time was that Shepherd Market had been a well-known haunt of street prostitutes in the eighteenth or nineteenth centuries. If there were any now, they obviously were a much better class of person. Very high class indeed!

Number 18 Shepherd Market was as I remembered it, though drier. Some steps led up to an elegant portico with a front door painted in a rich dark red. There were window boxes with blue and white flowers flourishing profusely. I wasn't sure what I was going to say but there was no point in hesitating. I rang the bell.

The door was opened by a young man, but it certainly wasn't the Benjamin of last night. This one was tall and dark and looked like an actor with his dramatic good looks, dark, smouldering eyes under a beetling ridge of black eyebrows, eyelashes of a length that would have been the envy of any film actress and hair so glossily black as to make the proverbial raven's breast look positively shoddy in comparison. He even had a cleft chin. Perfection!

"Ah!" I said, momentarily at a loss.

He waited politely, presumably thinking I was collecting for some charity for destitute orphans or perhaps a Jehovah's Witness.

In the end I couldn't think of any credible story and, unusually for me, had to fall back on the truth.

"My name is Tim Sinclair," I said. "I'm a private investigator..." and I told the whole story. Towards the middle of my account, the super guy decided that the front doorstep wasn't exactly the right place for such revelations and invited me inside. I finished my story in an armchair with a cup of real coffee in one hand and a brioche in the other. Yes, he actually had brioches! How the other half lives!

At the end he looked at me, seeming to weigh me up, probably wondering what to tell me.

"The guy I followed here last night was Benjamin Cameron, wasn't it?" I asked.

He gave a sad sort of sigh, which made me want to put my arms round him and give him a sympathetic hug. "I told him it would never work," he said.

I waited, then when he didn't seem to want to carry on, I prompted. "So why did he pretend to be killed? I assume that's what happened."

The guy nodded. I suddenly realized I didn't know who he was. "By the way, what's your name?"

"Josh Travis," he said.

Suddenly what had worried me earlier about the address fell into place. This must be in fact the "Josh of Shepherd Market" whose telephone number had been given to me by Barney and which was at this moment in my pocket. "You're Ben's friend," I said, which hardly made me out to be psychic, as they were obviously living together in the same house.

"I try to keep him out of trouble," he said ambiguously.

"By pretending he's dead?"

"You don't understand."

"Try me, then," I said.

He seemed to hesitate and then said, "This thing with Jack, it was with Jack wasn't it?"

"You mean there were others?"

He ignored that. "It was all getting too heavy. Ben wanted out but Jack wouldn't even listen to him trying to tell."

"So he pretended to have an accident. How did he work it?"

"It's quite easy. He mocked up a page from a newspaper, wrote some letters from grieving relatives and sent them."

I looked at him, a god from the silver screen, telling me these appalling things, quite calmly. "But that's so cruel. Didn't he even consider the effect on Jack?"

"Crueler than just dumping him? At least he left the memories."

"Jesus," I said. Well, I'd got the answer, could relate it to Barney, earned my money. I got up to go. "Why did you go along with it?" I asked. "How close a friend are you?"

Again there was the hesitation and then, "Actually he's my brother."

I stared. There were no similarities I could see between this dark, handsome young man and the pale, blond, too thin Benjamin. They didn't even have the same surname.

He gave me a sideways look. "Actually half-brothers, but we're close."

I looked at him more closely, not that I hadn't been inspecting his face, and other parts, ever since he'd opened the door. Then I saw it. Okay, ignore the skin color, the hair, the complexion. Perhaps there was a hint of a likeness in the bone structure. They both had the same sideways look; in Benjamin it looked shifty, in Josh it was seductive. I wondered for a moment how such an acquired behavioural characteristic could have affected both of them when their genetic inheritance seemed so dissimilar, but perhaps there were other similarities I hadn't noticed. I had never seen both of them together after all, nor was I going to, well, not that time anyway.

We went out into the hall, a cream-painted room large enough to contain a piece of furniture, a wooden settee, and of course a staircase leading upstairs. "Could I have a word with Ben?" I asked.

For a moment Josh's gaze flickered up the flight of stairs then he gave me that sideways look. "He's not well at the moment," he said and opened the front door for me.

I was tempted to say "nothing trivial, I hope. " The more I heard of Benjamin Cameron, the less I liked him, but I said nothing except goodbye.

"What a fucking shit," said Barney.

I had phoned him almost immediately after I got to the office, and told him everything that had happened. I could just see his eyes narrowing in anger at Ben's behaviour. "Hasn't he broken the law? Isn't there something we can do?" he asked.

I wasn't sure about the legal situation. "Intent to deceive isn't the same as intent to defraud," I said. "Anyway what would be the point? If any of this became public, Jack would find out, and you said that's the last thing you wanted for him."

Barney mumbled something, presumably in agreement, though obviously still reluctant. "Well, thanks," he said. "You did what I asked. I'll put a cheque into the post straight away, unless you'd like to come round for a meal this evening when I can give it to you personally."

"Can't this evening," I said. I did say I'd phoned Barney almost immediately. In fact, the first call had been to Chris, and we'd arranged a return match for that evening.

"Okay," said Barney. "Some other time then. Take care, honey. Tell me about it later." He always could read me like a book.

That should have been it, but there were some things about this case that still bothered me. Not too much, but just enough to stop me worrying about where the next dollar was coming from. There had been a couple of things that Josh had said that, looking back, didn't seem quite kosher. I tried to think of what he had actually said. I wished I had had my recorder on. Often I did, but this time I hadn't bothered.

I'm sure he had said, "I try to keep him out of trouble." Surely that was going over the top. Dumping a lover you've got tired of is often traumatic and dispiriting, but trouble in the sense of a cause of real concern it was not.

Then there was the query which I had found so odd at the time, "It was with Jack wasn't it?" The implication was that there had been others.

But taken on their own they meant nothing.

I dismissed the whole thing, opened my mail, mostly junk, and thought about Chris.

I'm afraid second time around wasn't as good as the first time. I guess it never is, unless there's real commitment. What am I talking about? I don't believe in commitment. Anyway the sex was enjoyable and we both achieved satisfactory climaxes…well I assume Chris did. He certainly made enough noise about it.

So there we were, collapsed on the bed, spent, he sort of lying across me, and I was searching for something to say. I'd discovered that we didn't have all that in common, apart from poking parts of our bodies into other parts of same, so I mentioned Ben.

"I met up with that guy you told me went to the Grenadier," I said.

"Who?" he asked, obviously with his mind elsewhere.

"Ben," I said, lazily. "You know, the guy in the Park. The one my friend, Barney, was so interested in."

"Oh yes," he said, "the smackhead."

It took a couple of seconds to sink in, but when it did, I sat up so suddenly, I almost tipped the poor guy off the bed. He looked startled. "Whatsamarrer?"

"You didn't tell me that," I said. "If you didn't know him, how did you know he took drugs?"

"He took his top off," said Chris. "His arms had marks where he'd obviously injected."

I remembered then that as I'd looked at Ben, he had put on his pullover.

"There's something very strange about that guy," I said.

"Always is, with smackheads. Can't trust 'em an inch."

"Or their friends, or brothers," I said.

I left soon afterwards. In a way it was a bit sad as I knew that was it. The sex had been good but that was all it was, and we had nothing in common to become friends. I think Chris knew, too. We kissed on the doorstep, well just inside as the doorstep itself was a bit public. He'd helped me quite a bit with the case, and I was grateful. In fact without him, I doubt whether I'd have made any headway at all.

The following morning I was back at 18 Shepherd Market.

I rang the doorbell and waited. I thought there was no one in but at last Josh opened the door. He looked, I thought, tired, dark circles under his eyes, but still pretty desirable. He certainly didn't look pleased to see me.

"What do you want?" he asked.

"I'm sorry, Mr. Travis," I said, "but there are some things you didn't tell me about yesterday."

Josh sighed and opened the door, though very reluctantly. "You'd better come in."

There was no coffee and brioches this time.

"I'd like to see Ben Cameron," I said.

"He's not well."

"You mean he's drugged out?"

Josh started, and I knew I'd struck the truth. He sighed again, as if he'd come to the end of the line, and it would almost be a comfort to tell all. I felt sorry for him, but it didn't stop my probing.

"Is that why he left Jack?" I asked.

"Well, sort of. He needed money to get the stuff. He took some things from Jack."

"Stole them you mean?"

Josh nodded. "When Jack found out, Ben was afraid he'd go to the police. He thought, well, don't ask me what he thought. What he did was fake his own death so that Jack would think that was it."

"But," I said, and looked around at the opulence of the room. The property itself must have run to millions, and the furnishings weren't exactly Ikea. "Why did he need to steal?"

"He wasn't living here then. Anyway all this isn't ours. I suppose it will be one day, but it really belongs to my father, Ben's stepfather. When he quarrelled with dad, he'd some idea of being independent. Didn't do him much good. Afterwards I persuaded him to live here."

"Can I see him?" I asked.

"Do you really want to? He's in a bad way."

I just wanted to settle everything, make sure this wasn't another string of lies, so I nodded, and he took me upstairs.

It was dark in the room, the curtains drawn, but there was enough light to see Ben lying on the bed, his body bent into a curve, the legs drawn up. There was a sour-sweet smell, a mixture of sweat, shit and vomit probably. From time to time his body was shaken by uncontrollable shivering. It wasn't a pleasant sight.

Josh went in and pulled up the covers which had been kicked off. Ben groaned and Josh put his hand on his forehead. It was a gentle gesture. I could see the care Josh felt for his brother. He'd probably sat up all night with him. It would take at least a week before the symptoms finally subsided. Cold turkey can be cruel.

I went back downstairs and out, shutting the front door quietly behind me.

I debated as to whether I'd tell Barney. Probably would, in the fullness of time, though whether it would be better him thinking of Ben as an uncaring deserter or a thieving drug addict, I wasn't sure. Whichever way it wasn't a happy ending.

I don't believe in happy endings. Most actual endings are pretty unhappy things, like leaving or dying or losing. We just have to be satisfied with small happinesses along the way. God, am I becoming a philosopher? I hope not.

CHAPTER FOUR

Summertime and the living is easy…

Well, it was summertime certainly, but I had my reservations about the living being easy. I was sprawled on a park bench. No, sprawled is the wrong word, sounds too casually elegant. I was slumped on the park bench taking up as much of it as I could, with my legs spread out awkwardly. I figured that anyone passing by would give a look and then leave hurriedly. I wasn't a pretty sight. My clothes were filthy. I hadn't had a bath for three days and in this heat, I guess I smelled pretty high. But then you gotta smell right, looking isn't good enough on its own. I had a bottle of meths and cider mix, and every so often I'd raise it to my lips, though I made pretty damn sure I didn't drink any of the poisonous stuff. I'd spilled some down my jacket, more of the smelling right.

It was much too hot to be wearing all those clothes, but people on the streets don't take their jackets and shirts off at the first sign of a summer heat wave. Probably too aware that someone else might make off with them, not that I could imagine anyone wanting the stuff I was wearing. Even clean it had been pretty dire; a pair of trousers that would have scarcely fitted a man twice my waist size, tied round the middle by a frayed piece of string. A shirt, one of those ones that needed a separate collar, the sort grandpa wore. Needless to say it had no collar. The jacket, nothing to do with the pattern of the trousers of course, was worn smooth practically everywhere so that it had an almost uniform shine that occasionally caught the sun in a greasy sort of way. My shoes were scuffed, and one had its sole barely attached. The socks were better left undescribed. All purchased specially from Oxfam and grubbied up specifically for the part.

"The part." Yes, that gives it away. I was acting a part.

It was the only way I could think of to find out information about Adrian.

His father had come to see me the previous week, a stout, red-faced man with a bristling moustache and bad teeth. He looked like someone who drank rather too much and smoked likewise. Certainly he smelled like an over-filled ashtray. He limped in to the office favouring his right leg and helped with a stout walking stick.

"You've been recommended," he said shortly. His voice was gruff, plummy, a touch of the Cockney almost hidden by Sloane Square.

I gave him an enquiring glance, waiting for more. He mentioned a name, but it didn't register. Nonetheless I pigeon-holed it for later investigation and nodded gravely.

"And what can I do for you, Mr...?"

"Ponting." He paused as if I should know the name.

Suddenly I did. "Ponting of Ponting's Paints?"

He nodded, and his lips opened into a self-satisfied smirk. Pity they displayed the nicotine-stained teeth. "The very same," he said.

I pretended to be impressed. Ponting's Paints of course had been made famous country-wide after a very expensive TV advertising campaign in which a large dog had been trained to use a paintbrush held between his teeth. Not very original, but the more times an advert is shown, the more it becomes known. The dog was actually fairly cute.

"And the problem, Mr. Ponting?"

A frown spread over his coarse face and immediately he looked more like a cantankerous stall-holder at the local market who had seen a small boy running off with an apple, than the owner of a paint consortium worth millions.

"It's my son, Adrian," he said.

I nodded understandingly. Boys, I implicitly agreed, can be a great problem.

"He's run away," he said.

"The police," I suggested.

"Wouldn't be interested," he said. "You see he's nineteen years old. Old enough to make up his own mind."

I nodded again. "I assume there was some reason, a quarrel perhaps. I need to know the background."

It was hard work, like searching for the meat in a winkle, but eventually I got the picture. Young Adrian had been at University, red brick rather than Oxbridge, doing fairly well, average, was expected to get an Honours 2 degree. Then things had started going wrong. "Got in with the wrong crowd,", whatever that meant, certainly people Papa Ponting disapproved of. There were hints of drugs. Well, as probably ninety percent of undergraduates had experimented with drugs of one sort or another, I wasn't surprised at that. There had been "upsets" in the family which consisted of mother, father, Adrian and his sister, rows, accusations, things said which were better left unsaid

"Eventually," said Mr. Ponting, "everything came to a head. We had a terrific row and Adrian swept out. We thought he'd gone back to University, but he hadn't. We haven't heard from him since, and that's six weeks ago."

"What happened in that final row?"

"Oh you know. We each said things we didn't mean."

"Exactly what was said?" I persisted.

Ponting cleared his throat. He seemed to be trying to make up his mind about something. "Adrian said he'd run his own life. I said he couldn't afford to, that he needed my money, his whole life I'd paid for. He had no job, no real talent, no head for business, no application. He of course blew up, said he could do without me, without the money. Then he went."

"Could he have got money?" I asked. "Credit card, borrowing from friends, relations, his mother?"

Ponting shook his head. "I put my foot down. He had nothing."

"Where do you think he might have gone? Is there anyone he might be staying with?"

"Do you think we haven't tried all those? His friends. No result. I think he's been living on the streets, a tramp, probably here in London."

"Okay, Mr. Ponting, I'll do what I can."

There were those final sordid little bits of business like telling him my terms, which he accepted readily enough, taking down details of how I could get in touch with him, asking for the names and addresses of his friends, etc. He gave me a photo of Adrian, and I saw a fresh-faced young man with candid grey eyes, a mass of straw-coloured hair and a smile that made him look attractively disingenuous.

Ponting got to his feet and was about to go out when I stopped him. "One last point," I said. "What was that final row actually about?"

He tried to dismiss it with a wave of his hand. "You know," he said, "family things."

"I don't know," I said, "but I'd like to. It might be important."

"I can't remember," he said, and even though I thought he was lying, I left it at that.

So here I was, on the streets myself, an undercover job if ever there was one, and finding the living anything but easy.

There's so much to learn, where to go, what to do and, more importantly, what not to do. Who to avoid, the safe areas, the "comfort zones" which basically means where to avoid danger. Some people are suspicious, others surprisingly friendly. I asked around, carefully, not wanting to give the impression that I was actually searching for an individual. I had a name, a description, a period of time and, though so far I hadn't actually used it, the photograph. But it wasn't easy. London's a big place. People congregate in different parts of it, and I didn't know where to start. But I did get some clues. Someone had seen a guy like I described in the Finsbury Park area - I'd explained that I owed him a favour and wanted to find him again. Ask the Bag Lady, he recommended. She's always there. So here I was, lounging in the sunshine and thinking dour thoughts about how surely there was an easier way of earning my living when -

"Christ! Tim! What's fucking happened to you?"

A voice from the past, though not the too distant past. The red-haired Paul Massingham, ex-lover; still, if I cared to admit it, in my erotic fantasies. Looking svelte, slim, and eminently seductive and here was I, like something that hadn't been emptied out of the dustbin for three months. Shit! Shit! Shit! In that order...

And also, wallowing up behind him, like a galleon in full sail, plastic bag top-gallants and all, was the Bag Lady, the one I had been expecting to meet, so I couldn't go into any long, complicated explanations to Paul.

"On a job," I snarled at him out of the corner of my mouth. "Bugger off," slightly louder for the Bag Lady's benefit.

"On a what?" asked Paul.

"On yer bike," I said loudly. "I've got as much right to sit here as anyone else..." With the eye on the side away from BL, I gave him an exaggerated wink. "I'll be in touch," I whispered.

Paul's bemused expression cleared. "Have a bath first," he said and walked on, not looking back. I would have liked to have given him an appraising look, but there was work to be done.

The Bag Lady, no one seemed to know her real name, squatted on the seat next to me, leaning against the back rest and feeling the sunshine on her face. Around her she disposed her plastic bags, black rubbish bags, striped ones from Tesco, orange, rather stronger carriers from Sainsbury's. They contained her possessions, and she guarded them jealously, exposing her blackened teeth in a snarl if anyone came too close. In those bags were all the things she owned, gleanings from the rubbish bins of the more fortunate, broken toys, books with covers missing, damaged plastic ornaments; if it had been discarded, it was hers.

She wore all the clothes she had, layer upon layer of grubby materials which had mostly lost their original colors and now seemed uniformly dark and smelled, not so much rank as old, with that old smell you get in churches, composed of dust and damp and decaying hymn books.

She had no worries except that someone might steal her belongings. She often knew the pangs of hunger, but the Sally Ann would be round sometime with soup and bread. The cold at night she could endure, and company she certainly had no wish for. The fact that I was sitting next to her evoked her almost ritual response, upper lip drawn back in a snarl, a hiss of displeasure, enough, she knew, to frighten off most unwelcome visitors.

Then she saw the bottle in my hand, and her look changed to one of almost winsome ingratiation.

"I'm awfu' thirsty," she said. Her voice was gruff and rusty as if she didn't use it often.

I passed over the rot-gut brew, and she took a man-sized swallow, then another. I wondered what the stuff was doing to her insides. She handed it back. I was tempted to say "Keep it," but of course that wouldn't have been in character. An occasional expression of generosity is okay, but John Paul Getty-type magnanimity is sure to arouse suspicion.

"Ta," she said grudgingly, and belched. She looked at me and for the first time seemed to focus on what she saw. "I ain't seen you 'ere before," she said, suspicions returned.

I hadn't seen her before either, well, except from a distance, but I knew a lot about her. Everyone knew the Bag Lady, and, according to most, she knew everybody, which why I had chosen this bench at this time of day as I knew it was her regular place.

"Name's Tim," I said.

"Didn't ask you yer name," she said, though I knew she'd store it away somewhere in the ragbag of her mind. "Where you kip?"

Much more important than a name, a place to sleep at night. "Station." I said.

She gave me a look and then said, "Arsenal's better'n Finsbury Park."

I realized that, for some reason, I'd clicked. She was offering me good advice. I nodded. To be too effusive in my thanks would have given rise to mistrust.

I left it for a while, just passed over the bottle, and she had another two swallows.

Then I said, "Seen Adrian lately?"

She wiped her lips, then as an afterthought had another swig. If it was questions I was asking, she could exact payment in booze. "Poofy sort o' name," she observed, though it seemed a statement rather than anything requiring comment. "Old Adrian or Young Adrian?"

"Young Adrian."

She gave the question some thought, or at least I assumed that was what she was doing, though she might have been allowing the meths fumes to dissipate. "Saw him last week," she said. "'E said he was off North."

Reykjavik, I wondered wildly, the North Pole, or perhaps further afield. The idea of being in proximity to an iceberg was not unattractive at the moment.

"Belsize Park."

"That's the Adrian with blond hair," I checked to be sure.

She nodded. "Poof," she said.

"Is he?"

That was interesting, I thought, as I shambled off sweating through the sunshine. I wondered if that was the bit of information Papa Ponting had failed to tell me in his account of the final quarrel. Not that it was too significant. Gay or straight, a guy on the streets needs other talents to stay healthy.

Belsize Park. A long steep hill outside the tube station, upwards to the posh heights of Hampstead Heath, down to the murky depths of Camden Town. A row of shops opposite: greengrocers, delicatessen, travel agent, baker. I went into this and bought a sausage roll. The woman behind the counter obviously didn't like me coming into her hygienic shop, I hardly blamed her, but she served me civilly enough with barely a grimace.

I went outside and sat down on a seat conveniently situated so that anyone there could get the full effect of the exhausts from all the passing vehicles. A man, a fellow free spirit I assumed, was sitting at the other end. He wore a long grey overcoat that came down to his ankles, and from underneath protruded a pair of sandals. Inside these his sockless feet were dirty with what looked like mud. His ankles were scratched. I ate my sausage roll then prepared the way for conversation by producing my bottle of cider and meths, waving it in his direction so that he could hardly fail to see it.

"That stuff will kill you, you know," he said in an educated accent. He looked at me from under a pair of grey eyebrows. He didn't look well. There was a pallor to the skin of his face and a faint sheen of sweat, but then it was a hot day and he was wearing a thick coat.

"You're quite right," I said. "You don't fancy a swig, I suppose."

"If I wanted to kill myself, I could go home and put my head in the gas oven."

I didn't point out that natural gas isn't the lethal stuff the old version was and that he'd have to wait until it filled the room to the exclusion of all the oxygen before it suffocated him. Clearly he wasn't a gentleman of the road in spite of appearances. He might, however, if he were an habitué of this seat which overlooked all, know of some of them, or at least have noticed them.

"Sorry, guv," I said. "D'you see many guys hanging around here?"

The man bridled. "What makes you think I go looking for guys."

I realized I'd made a mistake. "No, I didn't mean that. I'm looking for a particular person. Someone told me he'd been seen in Belsize Park. Name of Adrian."

"I wouldn't know his name. What does he look like?"

I felt in the inside pocket of my appalling jacket and produced the photo. The man took it a little hesitantly, but after glancing at it, he gave a start and peered at it more closely. "Why, yes," he said, "I did see this young man. I remember the hair. He wasn't looking so happy of course. In fact I thought he looked a bit scared. Kept glancing behind him, as if he thought someone was after him."

"When was this?" I asked.

"This morning. Couple of hours ago, I suppose. Probably about eleven o'clock."

"Where did he go?"

"Up Rosslyn Hill. Towards Hampstead." He gestured with his head to the left.

I was about to get up when a thought struck me. "And was there?" I asked.

"Was there what?"

"Someone following him?"

"Not as far as I could tell. Didn't notice anyone." He paused. "Only you, of course."

I smiled and stood up.

"Well, perhaps a little drop," he said.

His hand was shaking so I left him with the bottle.

The hill was steep, and I sweated a bit more as I climbed it. I passed the hospital on the right and the road that leads down to Keat's House. Just past Flask Walk there were two twenty-something lads leaning on the wall outside the Flask public house. They were holding pint glasses of beer, and I envied them. They looked harmless enough, but you never can tell.

"Hi," I said. "I'm looking for this guy." I showed them the photo.

They looked at me suspiciously and, not for the first time, I wished I'd gone home and changed out of my hobo gear into something more respectable. I could have had a shower too. The thought of clear, clean water and a bar of soap suddenly seemed paradise.

"What do you want him for?" asked one of them.

"Hey, isn't that the guy who asked what the time was," said the other, clearly less mistrustful. "And you told him, time 'e got hisself a watch,"

"Thank you, gentlemen," I said trying to keep all traces of sarcasm out of my voice and moved sharply on, followed by a shout of "Wanker." But it wasn't threatening, and they didn't pursue.

Over the road was the gay pub King William IV, but I ignored it. It's rather piss-elegant, and I was hardly dressed for it. I did however look in the little courtyard outside where drinkers were sitting at tables and tearing reputations to shreds. Adrian, as far as I could see, wasn't amongst them.

I turned right at Hampstead Tube Station, incidentally the deepest one in the whole London underground system, and struggled up Heath Street, the steepest bit, which led to the Round Pond, Jack Straw's Castle and the Heath proper.

As I arrived I heard the sirens. Some people standing around the pond watching an overgrown schoolboy sailing a model yacht looked up with interest. A police car and an ambulance raced along Spaniards Road and screamed dramatically to a halt, officers and paramedics leaped out and ran down a narrow path that led into the wooded area called the Heath extension. I suddenly had a chill of apprehension and followed them. Perhaps a hundred yards further on under the trees there was a guy standing with a mobile phone in his hand. As the police ran towards him, he pointed into the tangled undergrowth of brambles at the side of the path. I could see something lying there, a patch of blue, a crop of yellow hair.

One of the paramedics knelt down beside and started busying herself. A policeman turned and faced me and the other curious onlookers who had followed.

"There's nothing to see," he said, which wasn't quite true. "Please stand back."

I took a breath and committed myself. "I think I might know who he is," I said.

The policeman gave me a look which took in my clothing, the dishevelled state, the general unreliability of such a person, and therefore any statement he might make. "This isn't a joke, sir," he said. I could see the "sir" stuck in his craw.

I got out the photograph and showed it to him. "Is this the man?"

He took it and had a look. "Wait here," he said and then turned and went back to the others crowding round the prostrate form. There was conversation, and the other policeman, a sergeant, turned. The constable pointed. The paramedic stood up and shook her head. The constable returned and gestured with a head movement for me to go ahead, at the same time holding back the others who looked as if they wanted to approach as well.

The boy lay on his back with the sunlight dappled through the leaves lighting up his face. The eyes were open and staring, the mouth wide in a soundless last cry. His hair lay around his head like a golden aureole. The blue I had seen was his pullover. As I arrived, they were lifting him onto a stretcher and I saw the back of his head where the blond hair was stained and congealed into a dark brown mass. Someone had bashed the back of his head in.

"Okay, son," said the sergeant "you'd better tell us what you know."

After I'd shown my credentials, explained my appearance, the commission from Adrian Ponting's father, how I'd tracked the boy from Finsbury Park following the information from various individuals along the way who, no doubt, could be traced and corroborate my evidence, I was allowed to go home.

As far as I was concerned the job was done. I had found Adrian and by now Mr. Ponting would have heard the news. I knew that later I would have to get in touch with him, if he didn't contact me first. Briefly I thought about the bill for my services but dismissed that for the time being as a little insensitive. I got out of the horrible clothes and stepped under the shower, where I remained for half an hour soaping myself until all evidence of the past few days was gone. The sight of Adrian's body, though, I could not wash away however much I scrubbed.

I didn't feel hungry. I didn't want to be alone. There were various people I could have phoned, but I knew that whoever I got in touch with, I'd start talking about Adrian, and for some reason I didn't want to. For most of them it would just be a subject of salacious tittle-tattle, and I was too close to it. Then I remembered Paul. I owed him an explanation, after this morning's meeting. Did I want to renew my acquaintance with him, though? The break-up had been pretty tough last time. Before I talked myself out of it I rang his number. If he was out, I told myself, I'd forget about the whole thing.

He answered at the third ring, and the sound of his voice made my knees tremble. Hopefully this wouldn't show in my voice.

"Sorry about this morning," I said. "You must have thought I was really down on my luck."

"God, Tim," he said. "I didn't know what to think. If you hadn't given me that wink, I'd have been back with a tenner to drop into your grubby little hand."

"Aren't I worth a bit more than that?" I asked, joking.

His voice was serious though. "Yes, you are," he said, and my knees trembled again. "What was it all about?"

"It's a long story," I said.

"You want to tell me? Let's have a drink, if you're free, but only if you've had a bath!"

I was free. I'd had a good shower. I smelled, I thought, ravishing. We met at the Cutlass and Pistol just round the corner from his place. I had a car, and he hadn't.

As we sat opposite each other in the snug, I looked at Paul, trying to see him as if for the first time: Red hair, spiked with gel; a deep red, not an anaemic shade of light brown or carroty; dark eyebrows. I studied his face, fresh complexioned, youthful. I could remember his whole body with that soft, smooth skin. Brown candid eyes and a smile that curled up a pair of invitingly generous lips.

He had changed from his shop clothes and now wore a white pullover, sort of cricket. Made him look clean and healthy. I thought about peeling it off as a prelude to even more delicious things and found myself getting quite excited. But I'd fucked up the relationship, and I doubted whether there was a chance of it ever getting off the ground again.

"It's good to see you again, Tim," he said. "I've missed you."

"Oh come on, it's only been since this morning."

He smiled, wrinkling up his nose in that way I remembered so well. "Always the same. You're never serious."

"Perhaps I don't want to get hurt again."

He looked me straight in the eyes for so long, I felt embarrassed, but I didn't know what to say or do next. Eventually I broke the contact. "I bet you want to know what was happening in the park this morning."

Paul gave a little sigh. "I didn't know what to think."

I told him the outline of the story, about how a father had engaged me to find his son who, he thought, was roughing it on the streets, about the Bag Lady sending me to Hampstead and the old guy in the grey overcoat up to the Heath. Then I told him about finding the body of Adrian Ponting.

"Who?" said Paul.

"Adrian Ponting," I said.

"Ponting's Paints?

I nodded.

"But I know, knew him."

I am continually surprised at the way the gay fraternity is one mass of interlocking relationships. Of course there are those who are so closeted that they hardly even come out even to themselves, but give me a gay name and the odds are that at least one of my friends will know him, probably have slept with him.

"Did you sleep with him?" I asked before I could stop myself. "Sorry, just curious."

"Once," he said. "He was really neurotic. Dead scared his parents might find out about him being gay and that."

"They did," I said. "I'm sure that's what caused the row."

"And now he's dead. What do the police think?"

"That it was some gay-bashing that went too far."

"But, in the middle of the day. Doesn't sound all that likely."

I agreed. "He was in a gay pick-up place, though hardly likely to be active at lunchtime. Still that's what they seem to think."

"So nothing will be done."

"They'll go through the motions I guess, but he'd probably been dead for about two hours when they found him. Whoever did it would have had plenty of time to get away. And if there's nothing to link the attacker with Adrian, the odds of their finding him are pretty remote."

"He shouldn't get away with it whoever the killer is," said Paul. "What are you going to do about it?"

"Me?" I looked at him almost at a loss for words. Then I found them. "Oh come on, what can I do? As far as I'm concerned the case is over. I've found Adrian. Mission accomplished."

Paul looked at me again and I could see he was disappointed. I tried to find excuses. "If the police can't find him, how on earth can I?"

He still looked at me. I gave in. "Okay. I'll ask around. See if I can find anyone who was in the woods at the time. They might talk to me when they wouldn't to the police." Suddenly I remembered something. "An old guy I met outside Belsize Park station did say Adrian was looking scared. Said he kept glancing back as if he thought he was being followed."

Paul smiled. I felt a warm hand on my knee under the table. "I knew you would." I covered it with my own. We were both leaning forward so that our faces were very close. I wanted to kiss him.

"I knew you would," he repeated. "In spite of all that laid-back talk, you're quite a nice guy."

I wondered if I would have agreed if it had been anyone but Paul who had asked me. "Aw shucks," I said.

His hand on my knee moved slightly upwards, towards my groin. "Do you want to come back to my place?" he asked.

I did! I did! I did!

My cock did as well. But…

"Last time we took it all too quickly," I said.

His expression didn't alter, but I felt his hand squeeze my leg. I think that meant that he understood. I kissed him in a shop doorway where no one could see us, and he pressed his body close to mine. I nearly changed my mind about going home, but he drew away and went off saying, "See you soon." I hope he meant it.

Next morning early I got a visit. And I mean early.

Four o'clock. Before even the sparrows had started to chatter outside my bedroom window, there was a loud banging on the front door. I didn't have much more time to open my eyes, notice that the LED display on my radio alarm showed 4.01 am when there was a shout from outside, "Police," a massive thud followed by a splintering sound and heavy size twelves pounding up the stairs.

Two massive six-footers burst into my bedroom—wouldn't usually complain about this, but this time it was quite scary—dragged me out of bed, naked as I was and quoted the old arrest spiel. "I'm arresting you on suspicion of the murder of Adrian Ponting. You do not have to say anything, but it may harm your defence if you do not mention, when questioned, something which you later rely on in court. Anything you do say may be given in evidence. Do you understand?"

"No," I said, but they didn't take any notice just told me to put my clothes on and come down to the station.

I could see it was no use arguing so I did what they told me. They allowed me to have a pee with one guy standing at the door watching me closely, and then I was off in a police car after briefly trying to put the bits of my front door together so that it wouldn't be obvious to every casual passerby looter that my house was open and available.

"There'll be some officers back to search the place," said one of the policemen, a statement which didn't give me much comfort. I had some fairly explicit pictures on my hard disc. I didn't think they were really against the law, but who knows?

At the nick, they searched me, thoroughly, even though they'd watched me get dressed and knew that I didn't have anything on me at all, and put me in a cell. "I want to call a lawyer," I said.

"Later," said the duty sergeant. "He'll hardly be in his office at this time." Which of course was true, though it didn't cheer me up any. I tried to think what could have happened. There was no way I could have been anywhere near the Heath at the time that Adrian had been killed. The old guy in the grey overcoat would tell them I was at Belsize Park, and then there were the tossers outside the pub.

Anyway if I had killed him, why would I have come back to the scene of the crime and identified him, and myself? It made no sense. All of a sudden I wondered if I was in one of those helpless Kafkaesque situations and felt a bit frightened.

A constable brought me a cup of tea a bit later which was

sweet and milky. I drank it even though I hate it like that. "The CID officers will be in at eight," he told me.

"Couldn't you have just asked me to come down to the station at half past?" I asked, but for some reason he didn't think much to that and went out.

I sat on the hard bench and waited.

A couple of centuries later I was taken for an interview; small room, no windows, vomit green paint on the walls, slight smell of disinfectant. A table, three chairs. Two plainclothes sat me down on one of them and sat down themselves on the other two. They introduced themselves as Inspector Rees and Detective Constable Parry. Rees was tall and thin and looked as if he permanently suffered from indigestion. Parry was young, good looking in a beefy, Rugby-playing way.

I know I should have stayed silent, but I couldn't stop myself. "What's all this about?"

"Surely you've been cautioned," said Rees. He turned to his partner. "Constable, hasn't Mr. Sinclair been cautioned?" His tone was dry, acerbic, obviously taking the piss.

"I don't understand," I said. "I was here yesterday. You seemed quite satisfied with what I told you."

Rees opened a folder which had been lying on the table in front of him. He looked at it as if he'd never seen it before. "Ah yes. You said you had been commissioned by Mr. Bernard Ponting to look for his son, Adrian."

"That's right," I said.

"We informed Mr. Ponting of the unfortunate demise of his son. He claims to have no knowledge of you, denies he ever asked you to look for him."

I was gob-smacked. It didn't make sense. I began to have dark forebodings, well, even darker ones than I'd already had since I'd been so rudely roused from my slumbers in the small hours. I couldn't cope with this on my own.

"I want to see a solicitor," I said.

"Do you have one in mind?" asked Rees smoothly.

I, of course, didn't. I'd never had occasion to use a lawyer, didn't even know the name of one. I shook my head.

"You are of course entitled to legal advice," said Rees. "We can supply you with one. Unfortunately he won't be available until 9:30, which is when he starts work."

"I'm not saying anything until he arrives, then," I said.

Rees sighed, as if I was being totally unreasonable. "Mr. Sinclair," he said, "probably a little chat and we can sort the whole matter out long before the duty solicitor can get here."

An arrest on suspicion of murder carried out in the small hours involving breaking and entering. It didn't sound like the sort of thing easily "sorted."

"You are, of course, perfectly within your rights, but look at it from our perspective. You have this strange story of following the victim, dressed as a tramp, and the reason you gave is denied by the very person you said told you to do it."

"But I was nowhere near the Heath when he was killed."

"Ah yes, this man in the grey overcoat and the two lads outside the pub. I'm afraid we haven't been able to locate any of them. But even if it was as you said, it would have been possible to kill Adrian then return to Belsize Park and come back to the Heath again."

"Why would I do that?"

"Yes, that's the question isn't it? What motive could you have for killing Adrian Ponting, a lad you say you didn't even know, had not even met before." He sat back in the chair and looked at me. This sounded like the only thing so far which was in my favour. I felt a slight lightening of my spirits.

Then Parry spoke for the first time.

"Are you a homosexual?" he asked.

Are you or have you even been a practicing homosexual? Only until I'm perfect at it. The old joke ran unbidden through my head. I didn't like that. No doubt they'd found the incriminating pictures on my hard disc. Not that there was anything particularly kinky on there, not in gay terms anyway. No underage stuff or anything like that. But it was pretty conclusive. I could scarcely deny it. Not sure that I wanted to. It wasn't any of their business. All of a sudden I felt very defensive.

"Yes, I am," I said. "It's not against the law, you know."

Parry had laid the groundwork, now Rees stepped in with the coup de grace. "And if you had tried to pick up Adrian Ponting as he was strolling through the woods, and he had spurned you, looking, and smelling, as you did, and you got cross and gave him a tap…"

"A 'tap,'" I said, remembering the blood-soaked mop of hair I'd seen. "Christ, that was more than a tap."

"Yes, that was unfortunate," said Rees. "It seems that Adrian Ponting had an abnormally thin skull. He might have never known it himself, but any knock could have killed him." He looked at me. "Is that how it happened?"

"Of course it fucking wasn't."

"So how did it happen?"

"Just as I told you yesterday." There was a silence. I tried to calm down. Then I said, "Aren't you supposed to be recording this?"

"It's just a little chat," said Rees easily. "No need to be too formal."

There was a discreet knock on the door. Rees looked annoyed. A constable in uniform came in and whispered in his ear. Rees looked even more annoyed. He got up and went towards the door. As he passed me he said, "It seems you've got a solicitor after all. Obviously one who keeps early hours."

The door closed, and I was left alone with Detective Constable Parry. He looked at me, and I looked at him. He had rather nice brown eyes. In fact if you like the well-built type, he was rather dishy. I smiled, and he looked away. He knew I was gay, and I suspected he was too, but of course he was not likely to come out, not to a suspected murderer, in an interview room, in his local Nick. For a moment I allowed my imagination to take control, being shafted by a prop-forward over the table. In spite of all the circumstances I felt the beginnings of a stirring in the loins.

Then the door opened again, and Rees came back, this time with a young/old man, who looked young until you peered carefully and saw the little lines around his eyes, the slight sag under his chin, the grey hair around his temples. So this was my solicitor. I'd never seen him before in my life.

"I'd like a word in private with my client," he said.

Rees grunted and motioned with his head to Parry. They left. The man held out his hand and we shook. His palm was dry, the grip firm. I hope mine was too.

"My name is Grant, Mr. Sinclair, Alisdair Grant." He had a Scottish accent, not pronounced but there, pleasantly. "Your friend, Paul Massingham, phoned me, early, to tell me you might need my assistance."

"Paul?"

"Apparently he rang you, again very early, and was answered by a strange voice who admitted to being a police officer. Paul was worried. The police wouldn't say what had happened to you. Paul came round, heard from the neighbours about your arrest and got in touch with me. We've been friends for a long time. I promised I'd help as much as I could."

Dear, dear Paul…I loved him like a brother. No I didn't, not like a brother anyway. I must have been out of my mind to let him slip away like I did. If I could get out of this mess, I'd do everything this side of Armageddon to get him back. But Grant was waiting.

"If you can get me out of this," I said and explained my side of the issue.

"Inspector Rees has told me what happened as far as he is concerned. I think the real problem is that there's been pressure on solving homophobic attacks from above. Things had to be seen to be done so Rees and his men were a bit 'over enthusiastic'."

"Kicking down my front door," I said bitterly.

"We'll get that sorted," said Grant. "In fact I think temporary repairs have already been effected. Now, as regards this other matter."

The "other matter" of course being my arrest for murder.

"I don't think he's got much of a case," said Grant. "Not even circumstantial. There's nothing to put you at the scene at the time of the crime. Probably we can find some CCTV cameras which will locate you getting off a tube at Belsize Park when you said you did, one coming from the other direction from Hampstead so that will clear you. I've no doubt with a little more effort they'll be able to locate the men you met yesterday. Now the only thing is Ponting's denial that he ever commissioned you."

"Jesus!" I said, slapping my head at my stupid forgetfulness. "I've got his signature. I had him sign his agreement to my terms. It's in my office."

And that was it. Well, nearly. A couple of hours later, someone had to go to the office and get the paper. For one dreadful moment I thought that perhaps I had dreamed it all, but the paper came back, duly signed. Not that anyone could really tell that it was Bernard Ponting's. Could have been anyone really, Brian Peasbody, Barry Piss-elegant, Harry Snogsworthy. Anyway, Grant got me out on police bail (473'd), which I suppose was the best I could expect in the circumstances. I was given the customary warning that I must return a week today, otherwise I would be arrested and not be liable for police bail again. DC Parry saw me out, and I gave him a cheerful wave, not returned, though perhaps secretly he wanted to.

Who was I kidding?

The air smelled good as I stepped out of the police station with Alisdair, even loaded as it was with exhaust fumes and the smell of curry from the Balti shop just down the road. We'd got so chummy now, I didn't think of him as Mr. Grant, the solicitor. He gave me a lift home. The front door had been cobbled together and, though it obviously wouldn't stand a determined onslaught, it would probably deter daytime opportunists. The first thing I did after Alisdair had left was to ring Paul. He sounded so relieved to hear my voice and that I wasn't incarcerated in the Tower that my heart went out to him.

"Why did you phone?" I asked.

"I don't know. I couldn't sleep last night, thinking about us. I wanted to sort things out, I guess, so I rang to catch you before you went off for work."

"You've saved my life," I said, exaggerating. "What can I do for you in return?" I have to keep everything on a jokey level otherwise I tend to get over-emotional.

"See me this evening," he said, "and this time I won't take no for an answer."

"Your place or mine?" I said, having no intention of saying "no."

"Whichever has most food for the weekend," he said, and I realized it wasn't just an evening's date.

That sorted out, I planned my itinerary for the rest of the day. Must contact Ponting, or even better I wanted to confront him. I also thought I'd stand a better chance of finding the old guy in the overcoat, and perhaps even the two drinkers from the Flask. Clearly the police hadn't been overly scrupulous in their search. I rang Ponting at home but got an answering machine. I didn't leave a message, thinking I'd try again later.

I shaved and changed and went out. It was still glorious June sunshine, Wimbledon tennis weather, though not quite as hot as it had been the last few days. I took my car and went via Camden Town to Belsize Park. There was no one sitting on the seat opposite the station so I went on up the hill.

As I passed the Flask, I saw the two guys leaning casually against the wall, holding their pints, exactly as they had been the day before. I parked the car in a side road and walked back. They did not recognize me until I got really close. "Jeez," said the less bright one, "You've come up in the world since yesterday."

"I hear your boyfriend got snuffed," said the more unpleasant.

I decided on a bit of bluff. "I'm a police officer," I said. "You obviously know more about this than we do."

They were taken aback, not scared but just knew that their previous attitude would hardly be appropriate. "I don't know nothing," said one.

"But you saw him yesterday?"

They nodded.

"I suppose you didn't see anyone following him?"

"Well, there were quite a few people around at the time."

"No one you noticed in particular?"

"Didn't see anyone follow him into the queer pub."

I looked at the one who was doing most of the talking. I guess he wasn't a bad guy, just wanted to seem to be normal and straight and all that that implied in their world.

"He went into the William IV?"

"Yeah. Me and Jed here had a bet that he was queer. I said he was, and Jed wasn't sure. Then he went to the pub so I won. Cost Jed a pint."

"And you didn't see anyone follow him in?" I persisted.

"No."

"There was that fat guy," said Jed.

"He's always in the William IV."

"And the one with the red face."

"Oh yes. Never seen him before."

I butted in. "Red face? Anything else you can tell me about him?"

"Old," said Jed's mate. "Grey hair. Posh sorta suit."

"And he followed the blond-haired guy into the pub?"

"Oh no! He just went up the street." Jed laughed. It had been a wind-up.

Slightly annoyed with myself, I crossed the road to the pub standing, squarely brick-built next door to a car showroom. It had two doors: one leading to the public, the other to the saloon, but as both areas met up around the central bar there wasn't any clear division once inside. A further door led into the garden, which was just a paved area with a couple of wooden tables and some uncomfortable looking benches. There was a mixture of young and not so young, looking summery in light clothes.

I bought a pint and just hung around on the fringes trying to overhear gossip. Not unnaturally most of the talk was about the "gay-bashing on the Heath." There was general outrage that such a thing could happen, a hint of fear from some. "I'm not going trolling up there again!" and a couple of mentions of a Geoffrey who would be upset.

One group to my right trilled away about Geoffrey.

"Have you seen him since?"

"How's he taking it?"

"He's out in the garden now," said one, and there was a general craning of necks towards the open door though not, I was pleased to see, any exodus to gawp.

I went out casually.

There was a bright group sitting round one of the tables obviously enjoying themselves, not one of whom looked the slightest bit upset. At another a solitary black guy was staring with a flat, expressionless gaze into a glass of what could have been gin, vodka or water. He had black cropped hair, not shaved, but very short, rather hooded eyelids, the most flawless, dark chocolate skin. It wasn't a hard conclusion to come to so I went up to him and said, "Geoffrey?"

He looked up, and was obviously trying to put a name to a face which was completely unfamiliar to him. I wondered whether to do the old "surely you remember me, didn't we meet at that party" ploy, but in the end I decided on the truth.

"My name's Tim," I said, "Tim Sinclair. I'm a private detective, looking into the killing of Adrian Ponting."

Well, he'd looked pretty miserable before, but my introduction doubled it. He had large brown eyes, and they filled with tears, running down over his cheeks.

I sat down on the bench beside him and instinctively put my hand over his, which was lying on the table. "It's going to be difficult," I said, "but you want to get the bastard that did it, don't you?"

"If only I'd been here, it wouldn't have happened," he said.

"What do you mean?"

"We'd arranged to meet," he said. "Here. But I was late. Adrian must have got here, seen that I wasn't around and left."

"Couldn't he have waited?"

"He probably didn't have any money to buy a drink. Didn't want to hang around."

"Why would he have gone up to the Heath?" I asked.

Geoffrey shrugged. "It was where we met about a month ago," he said. "Perhaps he thought I was up there. He was very insecure."

"You mean his father?"

Geoffrey nodded. "He hated the idea that Adrian was gay, and if he had known that I was black, I don't know what he'd have done. He hated blacks even more than gays."

Perhaps he had found out. The more I learned about Papa Ponting, the less I liked him. I suddenly thought of the description of the old guy in the expensive suit that Jed's friend had talked about. Though meagre, it matched more or less how I remembered Ponting from his visit to me. Only thing I hadn't asked was if the man had limped.

There wasn't much I could say to Geoffrey apart from recommending him to "hang in there, mate." If he wanted companionship there was probably some, of a sort, inside the pub. I guess though that for the time being he wanted to be alone.

I didn't realize how wrong I was. I was still holding his hand on the table, in a way which I felt was comforting, companionable, platonic certainly. Suddenly he turned his hand round so that we were palm to palm. His skin felt warm and slightly moist. Then, equally surprisingly, he took hold of my hand and transferred it into his lap. Wow! Talk about a banana. I could feel the whole diameter of it through the thin cloth of his trousers, but I'd have to explore to find the length.

In a strange way I felt let down. Here was this guy, one minute grieving over the loss of his lover and the next getting horny with the first stranger he met. Not that it wasn't affecting me. I didn't want him to think I was rejecting him so I did a bit of exploration, just to satisfy myself of the dimensions. Wow! Wow! And wow!

"Unfortunately," I said, "I've got an appointment to see someone. Otherwise well, you know, I'd love to…"

I looked at him, those tender brown eyes, the responsive mouth. I wondered what I was doing. Why shouldn't I take the rest of the day off, and the evening, and the night? Except of course for Paul. I disengaged.

"You've been kind," he said.

"I'll do my best to catch the guy," I assured him and left, arranging myself as best I could so that I wasn't obvious to everyone in the pub.

Jed and his mate had disappeared so I got back to the car and sat inside. I tried Ponting again on the mobile and this time a woman answered. She had a pleasant, soft-spoken voice with a catch in it. I think she might have been crying. "This is Tim Sinclair," I said. "I'd like to speak to Mr. Ponting."

"I'm afraid my husband is at work," she said. Work? The day after his son was killed?

"I really need to speak to him," I said.

"He should be back later, probably about six."

I rang off. I had two hours to fill. For a moment I thought of going back to Geoffrey. I argued with myself. Should I take advantage of someone's loneliness and grief? On the other hand might he not need some love and affection? Okay I admit it, I'm a slut. I didn't use either of those excuses. My cock was talking or at least his was! In the end though I didn't go back to the William IV. I drove down the hill to see if I could find my man in the grey overcoat, figuring that his evidence (if I could prompt it) might be more convincing than that of the two louts from the Flask.

As I drove past the seat I could see that he wasn't there, but I parked the car round the corner and got out, walking back. An old woman, a local if ever there was one, was hovering on the curb with a small dog of indeterminate breed and uncertain temper. It growled as I got near.

"Don't grumble at the nice man, Dolly," she said as I approached.

"Doesn't she like strangers?" I asked pleasantly.

"Doesn't even like me," said the woman. "Don't know why I bother to keep her."

"Company, I expect."

"Huh," she said. The dog yapped twice and looked at my ankles.

"I suppose you don't know a man who sometimes sits on that bench," I asked. "He wears sandals and a long grey overcoat."

"Fred Warburton," she said. "Oh, everyone knows Fred Warburton."

"Has he been around today?"

"Haven't seen him," she said. "Come away, Dolly." She tugged at the lead, and Dolly, who had been getting near to my trousers, was almost yanked off her feet. "Has a go at people's ankles," she explained. "Gives them a fair old nip if she can." She smiled with an air of satisfaction, exposing a set of unnaturally white false teeth.

"No idea where I could find him?"

"Who? Old Fred Warburton? Everyone knows where Fred Warburton lives."

Everyone but me, of course. "Where is that?"

"Why there," she cackled, as if it was a great joke. She pointed to a house over the road and next door to the entrance to the Underground station. It was a tall, three story house of elegant proportions though looking a bit run-down, the paint peeling from the windows. "In a flat?" I asked. "Bed sit?"

She thought this was really funny, gasping as if to catch her breath, and Dolly took advantage of her inattention to edge near enough to me to take a nip at my ankles. Luckily I was able to hop out of the way. The woman thought this was even funnier. I was glad I had made her day.

"In a flat," she repeated through wheezing breaths. "No, love, it's his house. Rich as Croesus, he is, though won't spend a penny unless he has to. Got some funny ways, has Fred Warburton." She went off, dragging her foul dog with her, and I heard her laughing until she went round the corner.

I sat on the bench and looked over the road at the house. Even from where I was sitting, I could see that the windows were dirty, and the curtains behind them looked unkempt. So he was a sort of miser, was he? Worth millions but not prepared to spend anything unnecessary. Presumably very little to keep him occupied, which was why he sat on the bench and observed the world—but not young men, as he had so peremptorily informed me—go by. I wondered where he was today. Perhaps I was completely wrong and he had some all-consuming passion, literary possibly, that he carried on behind that closed door and those grubby windows, only emerging when he needed a break for some fresh air.

I got up and crossed the street, walked up the flight of stone steps and rang the bell. It sounded hollowly through the house. I waited before ringing again, but I felt there would be no answer. Some other time, perhaps.

I felt a bit depressed. I wasn't really getting anywhere. So far all I was following was a hunch started off by a pair of piss-taking yobs. I had hoped that old grey-coat would have supported some of it, confirmed that a red-faced, grey-haired man with a limp had also come out of the station after Adrian and followed him up the hill. To kill him? Because he was gay and had a black boyfriend? Could I believe that?

I must see Ponting. I looked at my watch. Four-thirty. Still an hour and a half. It would be an imposition, perhaps even cruel, but if I went to Ponting's house, I might be able to have a word with Mrs. Ponting. They lived in Maida Vale; sounded a rather smart address. It would take me half an hour to drive there.

The house was smart and expensive, the Regency facade painted white and some black decorative iron railings to keep the hoi poloi out. I peered through them, feeling like a Bisto kid; a garage that must have put another £30,000 onto the asking price, masses of geraniums in tubs and a small car on the gravel. No BMW or Mercedes so I assumed his Lordship wasn't yet home. The gates provided yet more material for the metal-worker's art. They were oiled and opened without a squeak. The front door was painted an elegant forest green.

A girl, possibly Filipino, opened the door. "My name is Tim Sinclair," I said. "I should like to speak to Mrs. Ponting."

"Are you expecting?" she asked which had me for a moment. I was saved from answering by the appearance of a woman, tall, very beautiful in an elegant, anorexic sort of way. The words of the song flashed into my mind:

Oh, your daddy's rich.

And your mama's good lookin'.

But poor Adrian had had every cause to cry, and now he was dead.

"That's all right, Angelina," she said to the girl, who shimmied off into some, no doubt, lowly area of the house. "What did you want to see my husband about?"

"I really am sorry to trouble you at a sad time like this," I said, putting on my "caring" face, which wasn't too difficult. I suspected that the news of her son's death must have affected her much more deeply than her husband.

She brushed aside my condolences with a slight wave of her hand. "It's just that Mr. Ponting was employing me to find your son - "

"And you wanted your payment now that he's been 'found'?" Her eyes flashed with a sudden anger.

"No, it's not like that at all. Considering what happened, I'm quite prepared to waive the bill. It's just that he's got me into a bit of trouble with the police, by denying he ever gave me the job. I just wanted to sort it out before I got arrested again."

"It's affected him really badly," she said. "He and Adrian were very close."

Were they, I thought cynically. That's not the impression I, and others, got. "Yet he's gone off to work today, you say?" I made no attempt to leave out a touch of criticism from my tone.

"Unfortunately a problem arose, and he was needed. He was of course devastated when we heard yesterday. I know what he said about you to the police. I think it was a spur of the moment thing. He didn't want Adrian's being gay to come out, though I suppose it was inevitable, so he just said the first thing that came into his head. It was silly, and I'm sure he'll put it right with the police. In fact, I'll make sure he does."

"You knew Adrian was gay?" I said.

"Oh yes," she said "I've known for years. I think his father did too, though he tried not to believe it. I knew about the boyfriend, too. Adrian told me. He was so happy." Her eyes filled with tears. I wondered what she would have thought if she'd seen me and Geoffrey "fondling" in the William IV earlier.

She pulled herself together. She was a fighter all right. "And yesterday was going so well. I'd nearly talked Harry into accepting Adrian's 'problem' as he called it. We'd gone to Colchester to see some relatives, and on the way back in the car, we talked about it, so calmly, and then, when we got home, to find the police here, with the news."

I was stunned. That was my little hypothesis completely blown away. And no doubt his alibi could be checked with the relatives, etc. I didn't know what to say. "Life's a bitch" was probably the most apposite though hardly the most sensitive.

"I'm so sorry to have bothered you," I said and made my exit. She watched me from the front door until I'd reached the pavement. Then she shut it. Sooner or later her husband would get back from work, and they would share their grief together.

But I had other plans. Mostly they centered on getting myself fully ready, willing and able for a weekend of, I hoped, debauchery with Paul, so home for preparation and then round to his house. He had cooked a meal and we ate it together.

Afterwards I followed him to the kitchen where he took the dirty plates and stacked them in a corner. My heartbeat quickened. Was this it? The start to a wonderful weekend together? I'm not that over-effusive normally, but I had promised myself to do everything for him if he helped me to get out of prison. He had, and it wasn't just thankfulness I felt. He turned, the soft brown eyes commanding more than inviting when he stepped closer to embrace me, and all the old feelings I thought I had lost were there again.

His kiss was soft first, then urgent and demanding. He whispered some words near my ear I didn't understand, instead I concentrated on undressing him while he did the same to me. He didn't rush, and that was a thing I quite liked, nice and slow, as if it were the first time.

I remembered the previous times, the impatient guy who couldn't wait that long. This time was different though. It took him a long while until he had unbuttoned my shirt, opened it and bent down to flick his tongue around my nipples. I sensed his teeth biting me softly, and in no time my whole body was covered with goose bumps.

He still uttered some incomprehensible words while he opened the belt of my trousers and drew down the zipper, staring into my eyes with an unfocused gaze. I knew that look all too well, reached out and touched his crotch, where I was greeted with a pleasant hardness, long and hard. I don't have to mention mine was in the same condition, aching and straining against the waistband of my pants. I was sure it had already soaked the fabric by the time he finally managed to drop my trousers, went to his knees and soaked it even more with his saliva, outlining the shape of my cock. My head flung back, suddenly seeing where we were, in the kitchen, amid the used plates and dirty table from the effort he took to cook the meal. As much as I hated to stop him I did need a bed, a soft surface to lay him down and to do the things I had been dreaming of ever since I entered his flat.

I took him by the arms and pulled him towards the bedroom, our clothes scattered on the floor. Paul was all over me, the lovely red hair glued to his forehead; he lay beside me and I felt more than good. I struggled with his trousers and the shirt until he was naked except for his briefs, like me. If I ever had thought to find this in other men I was certainly wrong. There had been many naked bums and cocks, but there was just one Paul Massingham.

I rolled myself over his body, pressing our covered dicks together, heard him groaning in pleasure, his hands and tongue left me a squirming bundle between the dishevelled sheets, and once more I promised to give him everything. His hands cupped my buttocks, freeing them from the underpants, squeezing them hard and sliding into my crack, his lips kissing me until I couldn't breathe anymore. I panted for air, rolled down his body and started to wash him with my saliva; he smelled nice, fresh and like the soap I was familiar with.

When I reached his bellybutton he giggled, ruffled my hair and pushed me lower. I turned until my face was level with his lovely, hard cock and started to lick away the drops that had appeared, flooding down the shaft and wetting his reddish pubic hair. I was infatuated again. I heard his approving moans, his hands groping for my own penis, dangling in front of his mouth and then felt it vanish into the velvet warmth that was his mouth, gently grazing it with his teeth, alternating with soft sucks. I mumbled likewise incomprehensible words while breathing through my nostrils, spreading his legs apart to give me access to the sweetness down below his balls. He squirmed, tossed his head upon the sheets when I entered him with my fingers, then I looked up, my eyes searching for a yes. In answer he passed over the tube of jelly and pushed my hands aside. He gently rolled the condom over my cock and lay down again, pulling me with him.

I didn't need any other encouragement. Just to feel the tip of my penis at his opening was more than I could bear that moment. "Don't let me wait," he said, his face flushed with excitement. "I need you." I needed him too. This felt right...a little push and I broke the barrier. His face did not show any signs of discomfort, so I pushed forward, little by little; my arm supported my weight, the other hand I used to rub his member, smearing the drops all over. I was as deep in him as I could go and rewarded with the most blissful feeling I'd had in a long time.

I gave him time to cool me down a bit, until his eyes opened and started to glisten. His hands cupped my buttocks again and pulled me in even deeper, if that was possible, wriggling his ass and clamping the muscles in there. I smiled, and he responded. I bent down to kiss his luscious red lips, his tongue slipping into my mouth; he moaned while I increased the speed, still rubbing his cock until my neck muscles started to hurt. I sat upright, giving him one last sounding kiss and then started to fuck him seriously.

His eyes were closed, a faint smile around the edge of his mouth, and I stared into his face, withdrawing to the tip and pushing forward again in a steady speed until he hissed "more, more," and "faster." I followed his desires. We were in perfect rhythm, him pushing back against my body whenever I shoved in, his ass muscles squeezing my penis, faster and faster until the semen in my balls seemed to boil, and we were covered in sweat completely. I can't remember the next seconds; they are razed out in my memory. Just the blissful feeling stayed, the hot gushes as I emptied myself into him; a few moments later he came too without touching himself. His penis squirmed and squirted high in the air, hitting my chest and his belly, his abdomen and his hair.

"Jesus Christ," he muttered. "I didn't expect you to be that good..." I took it as a compliment. "Don't go," he said, looking up at me, and I bent down, kissing him feverishly, exhausted and happy.

I was surprised that I wasn't getting soft; he really must have turned me on. It was just so… We kept staring at each other and smiling, the muscles in his arse clenching and pulsating, I had no choice. Paul giggled boyishly and pulled me even closer, his legs spread so wide that I thought he would get a cramp. I was sliding along into the wet and slippery tunnel, rising to full erection once more. What was the guy doing to me?

"Oh yes," I heard him saying, "oh yes, oh yes!" I don't know how long we stayed glued together. I was madly pushing in and out of his body, overwhelmed, tired, drenched, drained and all too horny. My back ached, but I didn't mind. I sucked him while I loved him and the cries yelled in my ear, my yells and his. I hoped the walls were thick enough. And then again complete bliss, dark memory and hands, pulling at my neck to suck my tongue and bite my lips, his legs lowering, embracing me while I was lying heavy upon his body. Content and happy.

The following day we drove together to Belsize Park. It was nice and companionable. I could tell Paul thought the same even though he didn't say anything. I wondered what it would be like to have a partner, at work I mean. There were times when it would have been useful to have someone to stay on watch while I had to follow a suspect. To be realistic though, the job didn't pay enough for two, sometimes it barely paid enough for one, and, I reminded myself, I'd told Mrs. Ponting that I'd waive the bill this time. That had been foolish, more than that, incredibly, ineffably, unspeakably stupid.

I metaphorically kicked myself, and, as if he knew what was going on in my mind, Paul put his hand on my arm and squeezed it. I liked it, knowing that he was sitting next to me.

We went through Camden Town, Chalk Farm and up Haverstock Hill. People were out doing their Saturday morning shopping. As we turned the corner and Belsize Park station came into view, it was obvious something was wrong. I had that déja vu feeling. There were two police cars and an ambulance parked outside Warburton's house.

"Not again," I said.

"Shall we leave it?" asked Paul. "Just drive by and go home."

But I couldn't. I guess that's why I'm a P.I., just have to poke my nose into things. I found a place to park and we walked back. A small crowd had formed on the pavement outside the front door, and a policeman in uniform was standing there. He was a different one from the one on the Heath, but it felt the same. As we arrived a man came out. It was DC Ted Parry. We looked at each other and the recognition was mutual.

"What the hell are you doing here?" he asked.

"I came to have a word with Fred Warburton."

He sighed. "How did you know? Oh well, you'd better come in."

He turned, and Paul and I followed him back into the house. The crowd watched curiously. I saw the old lady with the snappy dog and gave her a little wave. Instantly she became the centre of interest.

Inside the hall—dark, high-ceilinged and with old-fashioned wallpaper—Parry turned and saw Paul. "Who's this?" he asked.

"Paul Massingham," I said. "My partner."

I could see from the expression in his eyes that he was wondering in what sense I had used the word. I suspected that Paul was a bit confused as well.

"Okay," said Parry, "now tell us what you wanted to see Warburton about."

"He was the man I told you about yesterday. The one in the overcoat who told me about seeing Adrian on his way to the Heath. The one you couldn't find."

"You didn't know his name when you talked to us yesterday morning," said Parry suspiciously.

"But I did by yesterday afternoon," I said. "I asked around

and the woman outside with the little dog told me. Ask her, if you don't believe me, but watch out for your ankles."

Parry grunted. "What's happened to Warburton?" I asked.

"Next door neighbour was worried that she hadn't seen him for a couple of days. Told the police, and when we broke in, we found him hanging, probably suicide. There's a note, but it doesn't make much sense."

"He was an odd man by all accounts," I said. "I thought he was a tramp, but apparently he had millions. What did the note say?"

"I can't tell you that," said Parry scandalized.

"Just thought I might be able to help."

Parry gave me one of those long, searching looks. "Okay," he said and handed me a sheet of paper enclosed in a plastic folder.

"I didn't mean to do it. It was an accident. He thought I was after him and grabbed hold of me. All I did was give him a push and he tripped and fell. When he didn't get up, I turned him over and saw the…"

"It doesn't really say why he hanged himself. It isn't even finished."

I felt a sinking feeling in my stomach. I thought I could see the explanation. I remembered the startled jump Warburton had given when I showed him Adrian's photograph. I could see the mud on his ankles, the scratches from the brambles. The denial that he was after young men. Had he been protesting too much? It had been a tragic accident after all, but Warburton had felt responsible and hadn't been able to live with the guilt.

"Oh God," I said, and started to explain.

CHAPTER FIVE

Me and Paul

"That's where the body was found," said Detective Constable Parry. He pointed to a patch of road which looked no different from any other. I almost expected the outline of a human form to be chalked on the surface, but there was nothing visible.

It was a quite unremarkable road lined with quite unremarkable Victorian red-brick houses, except for the spaces where some of them had been knocked down. Hiding one of the spaces was a large hoarding which stated "Lennox and Winters. Property Developers." It also announced that they intended to build several luxury houses and apartments and that enquiries should be made to the firm. I could hear the noise of a drill coming from behind.

"Just outside his own house," I said. "Unlucky for some."

"You knew him?"

I nodded. "What do the police think?"

D.C. Parry gave me a shrewd look.

When Parry and I had first met some months ago as a consequence of my being arrested in connection with the killing of a man on Hampstead Heath, I had suspected he was gay. He had shown too much interest in my own frank admittance that I was. He had, perhaps, kept eye contact rather longer than was absolutely necessary on our parting, when I had absolved myself from the crime and, in fact, had found the real killer.

Parry had not, of course, come out in any way, and I would probably have remained in doubt if I had not, purely by chance, come across him in a West End gay bar one evening when he was letting down his hair, as it were. I'd scarcely recognized him out of his conservative office uniform. The rather stocky, serious, young detective constable was wearing a beige crew-neck Versace number with matching jeans. I knew it was Versace because it had the name all down the left arm. Jeez! To think a copper can afford to splash out £100 on a pullover.

Anyway, he was bouncing his stuff almost in time to the music, and he did, I noticed, have quite a lot of stuff to bounce. It was, of course, too good a chance to miss so, in a gap when the DJ had obviously lost his way with his discs, I went over to the policeman and greeted him. Was he fazed? Actually he was not. The very opposite. "Tim Sinclair," he said, "I wondered if we'd ever meet on neutral ground." Then he moved close and groped me well and truly.

Now, I'm more or less involved with a guy called Paul Massingham. We've been up and down, emotionally, I mean, but, at that time, we were really getting it together, and I was having serious thoughts of settling down with him. But, you know, a guy is a guy is a guy, and when another guy, who isn't exactly Quasimodo, starts fondling your excitable parts, well you tend to react. I do anyway. So before long, we were dancing and getting along really nicely. Together we danced, Ted and I, that was his name, Ted Parry; our caresses, in that all-enveloping, drug-enhanced throng, becoming more and more intimate.

Actually we didn't, you know, go the whole way. There was a problem with where to go. He lived at that time in the Police Section House, and I, well I'm ashamed to admit it, Paul was already waiting for me in my house, so the evening remained unconsummated, as far as Ted and I were concerned. But, and this was the point, it meant that I now had a contact inside the police force, something I'd wanted, and needed, for a long time.

So while I dallied with this fine example of male pulchritude it was really just for professional rather than libidinous reasons.

Huh! Who am I kidding?

But we had remained friends, and he was now someone I could call on if I needed information. Useful. Like today with the body in the road, that was no longer there.

"So what do the police think?" I asked.

Ted said, "A hit and run driver. Probably an accident and whoever did it was too scared or drunk to stop and report it. What's your interest anyway?"

I told him.

It had been the night before. Paul had rung me at the office, where I was sitting waiting for a phone to ring or a client call, and asked if I'd meet him at a friend's house, Peter Squires. There was a problem, might even be a job, and Paul knew how much I needed work. You might think that Private Investigation is a glamorous job, but it's not so fine if there isn't any business coming in. And I was looking at work through the wrong end of a telescope. Small and much too far away.

Squires lived in a Victorian red-brick house, one of a terrace, built, according to a carved stone set above the door, in 1861. It had been a good, well-built house and cared for, but all the same it was showing its age. It had been through several wars, including two World ones, and had sustained some damage in the second of these. There were several cracks in the brickwork, not terminal, but enough to show that it needed a bit of restoration if it were ever to find its former glory. The others that were still in the row were similar. Some had already succumbed to the developers' ball and chain. The sun was still up and Granby Street, gap-toothed though she might be from the depredations, looked calm and sun-washed. The red brick houses had a rosy glow. I suddenly had a feeling of affection for the old street. Bruised and battered, she had stood up to time and wore her scars with dignity.

Peter Squires opened the door. He was a tall, thin guy, serious-looking with glasses. Looked older than he probably was. His voice and enthusiasm were that of a young man. Paul was already there, appearing in the hall behind Squires, and, as always, the sight of my lover's red hair, the particular cast of his features, the planes of his cheeks, the smile which lit up his whole face, made my stomach give that old familiar lurch.

"So this is Tim," said Squires. "I've been hearing a lot about you."

"Nothing good, I hope," I said with my usual lack of originality.

"Come in and have a beer."

I went in and on the way gave Paul a squeeze, not quite sure who or what Squires was and how a more demonstrative greeting might have gone down. We sat in the handkerchief-sized garden at the back, in the evening sunshine.

"It's nice here," I said.

"Until they pull the rest of the houses down and build some modern monstrosity for fat cat businessmen to lodge their mistresses in," said Squires. His tone was bitter.

"That's what they want to do?" I asked.

Squires nodded.

"Do you have to sell?" I asked.

Squires sighed. "They're making it difficult not to," he said. "First the golden handshake, generous purchase price, but…" he paused. "If you still don't want to sell, things happen."

"Things?"

Paul butted in. "Oh, come on, Pete, don't pussy-foot around. Nasty things happen, Tim. You get 'stepped on' by heavies if you come home late at night. Rubbish tipped onto your front garden. A burning cloth pushed through your letter box. Someone'll get seriously hurt soon."

"And then of course there's the constant noise," said Squires. He stopped talking, and I could hear the pneumatic drill from down the road. It vied with the sweet sound of a blackbird singing from a buddleia bush, and the drill won, hands down. "I tried to form a sort of Association. Figured it would be easier for us if we were together, but they're dropping out, and the fewer there are of us left, the more difficult it becomes."

"The police?" I asked, falling back, as I always did, on the line of least resistance.

Squires shrugged. "They just say it's local vandals, kids, you know. I don't think they're interested."

I didn't think I was either. Sounded as if anyone who investigated too closely might find himself seriously trampled. "You think it's the developers behind all the aggro?"

"I'm sure it's Arthur Lennox."

"I guess I could make some enquiries," I said tentatively. Paul gave me a sharp look. He could tell when I wasn't enthusiastic.

A woman suddenly came out into the garden through the back door of the house. Squires stood up and kissed her. Not a passionate one, more the sort of kiss a husband would give his wife on his return from work. All the same I was surprised. For some reason I had assumed that Peter Squires was gay.

"This is Laura." He pointed at me. "Tim Sinclair and you know P…"

"The Dixons are leaving," she said, interrupting in the dramatic sort of tone that would announce the start of World War 3 or the introduction of sex rationing.

"Oh fuck," said Squires. "I knew they were wavering, but I hoped they'd stick it out." He turned to me. "They live at number 64," he said. "Someone broke all their windows the other day. What's happened now?" he asked Laura.

"Their kid was threatened on the way to school this morning," she said. "Not hurt, but it terrified the shit out of him apparently. They decided it was the last straw, so they've accepted Lennox's offer. Reduced from last time, the bastard. Something's got to be done."

"I'm hoping Tim here will be able to help us."

Laura looked at me. I could tell from the expression on her face that she didn't think it likely. I made soothing noises, said I'd call on the Dixons, would get back to Squires the following day, and Paul and I left.

I knew he was mad at me. "What's the matter with you?" he asked. "Don't you want to help them?"

"It's not as easy as that, Paul," I said. "What makes you think

I can find something that the police can't?"

"They haven't even tried. You could at least see the Dixon family Peter was talking about."

Number 64 was just along the road. It was easy to identify. All the windows on the ground floor had been boarded up. The Dixons turned out to be an attractive young couple, though very suspicious. There was considerable reluctance to let us in, and even after we had persuaded them that we weren't criminal, they were guarded in what they told us. Yes, they admitted, their son, Shaun, had had an unpleasant experience on the way to school that morning. They wouldn't go into details; Shaun hadn't said too much himself, merely that it was "kids from around" who had told him the family "had better get out if they knew what's good for them".

"Kids?" I asked. That was what the police had said, of course.

"Put up to it," said Mrs. Dixon, a worried frown putting years onto her young face. "It certainly wasn't kids who threw the rocks through the windows."

"Did you see them?" asked Paul.

"Only as shapes," she said. "They weren't kids."

"What did you think?" I asked her husband.

"I wasn't there," he said shortly. "That's why it was so frightening for the family."

"Well?" asked Paul as we went out into the gathering dusk. The streetlights were popping on one by one. It was getting cooler, and I wanted to get home, wanted to get Paul home, all to myself. All of a sudden the street felt vaguely threatening, the gaps between the houses pools of darkness which could hide anything.

I sniffed the air; take-away hot dogs, onions and chicken tikka masala, petrol and exhaust fumes from the cars and taxis temporarily halted at the red traffic lights where Granby Street turned into the main road, air that had been breathed in and out, used air, tired air. But it was London air. For late August there was a chill. It felt as if summer was already over.

A guy, in his mid twenties, perhaps a bit older, appeared at the other end of the street, walking our way. I looked at him, taking in the thin, dark face, forehead furrowed in a worried frown, the brown eyes which looked as if he had problems. He glanced back, seeing my intense stare and smiled assuming perhaps that he knew me, that I was an acquaintance whom he must acknowledge. He passed.

I turned and watched the young man's figure as he walked away in and out of the shadowy pools between the lamplight, his body slim and elegant, his buttocks moving under the cloth of his jeans, athletically, his shoulders broad, his waist slim. He went up the path into a house along the way.

"You'll know him again," said Paul. His tone was light; I don't think he was jealous.

"Did you see where he went?" I asked. "A visitor for Peter Squires."

We went home, me to change, Paul to do some work for his job the following day. So, I'd made the decision, and now I was living with Paul. Of course it wasn't just my decision. We'd both had a hand in it, talked long into the night. In fact talked long into many nights, after we'd made love. His red head on the pillow next to mine. And me knowing that that was how I wanted it to be in the morning, every morning.

I know I said I'd never do it, never give way to that sentimental urge that afflicts the human male from time to time, setting up home with a significant other. But, well, there were so many things that had made me change my mind, some silly and sentimental like the way he looked at me solemn and serious as if he couldn't believe his luck, others because we got on so well together. Now I felt there was integrity and respect on both sides.

As I went out I looked fondly through the doorway of the living room at the figure of my lover crouched studiously at the table over his work. He was tapping away at the computer keyboard and the words streamed across the monitor screen. I admired the M-shape that his dark red hair made at the nape of his neck. For a moment I paused to view the picture, framed as it was through the doorway. I saw the watercolour on the wall that Paul and I had chosen together, the light from the table lamp which shone on the silky-soft red hair, the angle of his cheekbone. It was a sight that induced an almost physical spasm of emotion in the pit of my stomach and a desire to plant a kiss on that special place.

"You sure you don't want to come with me?" I asked.

"Gotta finish this for tomorrow," he said. "Important presentation." Paul worked for an advertising company, conning the public as I often remarked, not always in jest. "Don't be late, and don't pick up any strange men." He turned and smiled.

I promised. As if I would!

"If I'm asleep when you get back, wake me."

I went back to Granby Street and called in at the Granby Arms, the "spit and sawdust" pub at the end of the road. It certainly wasn't one of those trendy, theme pubs which are taking over all the old-style ones. It also wasn't doing much business.

A heavyset man with a stubbly chin was serving behind the bar. I suspected he was the landlord. He seemed disposed to chat, which was ideal.

"How will all this development affect your trade?" I asked.

"Couldn't happen too soon," he said, gloomily. "Look at it tonight. If they build some smart flats, then the brewery can tart this place up and really work up a clientele."

"So, you're not in favour of Peter Squires' campaign?"

He regarded me sharply. "I can see his point. He doesn't want to lose his house, but you have to move with the times."

"What do you think of the harassment of the remaining house-owners?"

Again I got that sharp look. "Exaggerated," he said shortly.

"I suppose Squires comes in here. I'd like to have a word with him."

"What are you? A reporter. We don't want scandal mags round here."

I assured him I wasn't a reporter. "Thinking of buying a house round here. Just want to get the local picture."

He nodded, apparently accepting my lie. "You missed him," he said. "He was in earlier." He paused as if debating with himself whether to tell, but eventually the urge to confide won. He was obviously a born gossip. "He had a bit of a punch up."

I looked suitably impressed. "Didn't strike me as that type."

He looked as if he almost regretted going so far. "Well, it wasn't a real fight. Just a big argument."

"About the development scheme?" I asked.

"Must have been," he said. "It was with Neil Winters."

When I didn't immediately react, he added, "One of the partners."

Then I remembered the hoardings, "Lennox and Winters."

"How did it end?" I asked.

"Squires rushed out, and Winters followed him."

Paul had already been in bed when I got home, lying, as he always did when we didn't get to bed together, down the extreme centre so that I would have to wake him when I got in. His red hair was tousled and his face seemed slightly flushed so that he looked indeed like the very kid that I always thought him. Remembering the instructions Paul had given me before I went out, I made no real attempt to creep in silently, but Paul didn't wake and only mumbled something incoherent as I wrapped myself around him.

The light from the street lamp outside lit the room, and I wished I had drawn the curtains but I didn't want to get out of bed again.

As always the feel of Paul's body aroused me, but I restrained myself and tried to sleep. My body, though, was not in the mood for sleep.

I tried another position and pulled Paul's limp body close to my chest. The smooth skin under my stroking palms felt warm as I followed his sleek body contours and finally sensed a stirring.

"Is it morning already?" I heard Paul's sleepy voice.

"No, honey." I sniffed the clean smell of his hair. "You said you'd be disappointed if I didn't wake you."

Paul wriggled in my arms and turned to face me. I kissed his tilted nose and smiled, then searched for the half open lips. "Or are you too tired?"

Paul still was a bit dizzy from sleep but smiled that ravishing smile of his. He reached up to my ear. "I'm never too tired for you. Take me." I reached down and gently squeezed his balls, which provoked a little gasp from my lover. I heard him giggle and pushed him gently onto his back, sniffing again the sweet scent of youth, allowing my hands to roam over his slim hips, down the long legs and up again, now caressing the insides of his thighs, approaching with every stroke the centre of Paul's body.

My gaze was locked on my lover's face, the half closed eyes, the smile around his lips, watching intently as my fingers cupped his ballsack and Paul let out a little sigh. I smiled, slid down while I covered that smooth body with little kisses until I faced Paul's hard cock and pressed my lips just at the junction where the shaft met the balls.

Paul stroked my short hair and thrust his hips in demand, but I rose to my knees and lifted Paul's legs before I began to trace my mouth along his calves, his feet and sucking his big toe into my mouth.

Paul gasped and opened his eyes. A hot wire seemed to lead from his toe directly to his cock. I went further, along his smooth legs, caressed with my tongue the inside of his thigh, tracing a path until without warning my tongue met the centre of Paul's body, pressing my mouth at his anal opening, inhaling deeply my lover's scent, feeling him lifting his legs even more, hearing him gasping in delight.

My tongue wandered, lavishing the smooth round orbs of his ballsack, up higher, sucking at the crown of his cock, circling round, licking the droplets, and finally taking Paul's twitching cock deep down my throat.

I heard more than saw Paul's mouth open in delight, making strange little noises, thrusting his hips until he hissed indistinctly. "Come into me. Please."

I hated to let loose of Paul's dick; slowly I pushed a wetted finger into his opening, breaking the little resistance while with my other hand I opened the drawer and pulled out an almost empty tube of K-Y.

It was then that the phone had rung.

At that time of night it had to be either a wrong number or something urgent. For a moment I tried to ignore it, but the insistent stridency of the sound distracted me from the job in hand.

"Fuck," I said. "Darling, don't go away."

Paul's eyes were still firmly closed, and his face was flushed, one lock of his unruly hair lay damply on his forehead.

I got out of bed, cock still erect, and took the three strides across the room. "Yes," I almost shouted into the receiver.

A woman's voice, no one familiar, said, "Is that Paul? Paul Massingham?"

"Who is it?" I asked. "Do you know what the time is?"

"It's Laura, Laura, Peter Squires' sister. He's dead." The voice was flat, expressionless. Immediately I regretted my anger, product of unrequited lust. My cock drooped.

"Sorry, Laura," I said. "Tim Sinclair here. Tell me what happened. Do you want us to come over?"

And the following day here I was, with my favourite Detective Constable, looking at the unmarked place where he had died.

"So," said Ted Parry, "you decided after all to try to help him."

"Too late, unfortunately," I said.

"How did you find out?"

"About his death? Laura Squires phoned late last night."

I didn't tell him the exact circumstances.

"Laura, that's his sister," said Parry, more a statement than a question.

I nodded. I didn't want to admit that when I had first met her I had thought Laura was married to Peter. What sort of a P.I. would that make me? "Do you think there's anything suspicious about his death?"

"More suspicious than a hit and run, you mean?"

"Well, there was the row he had last night with Neil Winters," I said.

"I can imagine he was always having arguments with the developers. They stood for everything he was against. Do you imagine it was desperate enough that they'd kill him?"

"Depends on how much they'd stand to lose if the scheme didn't go through," I said.

"You've got a nasty mind."

"Even though I'm not a policeman."

Parry laughed. "By the way, I've got myself a flat. Moved out of the police barracks."

I ignored the apparent non-sequitur, though later I realized its significance.

"I've got to go and see Laura," I said, serious again. "I said I'd come round when she phoned last night."

"She's pretty cut up about it?"

"Who wouldn't be?"

"Care for a drink afterwards?" he asked casually.

"No work today?"

"Day off."

"I'll see you in the Granby Arms."

I had arranged to see Laura at Peter Squires' house at eleven o'clock. As I went in through the gate and up the short path that led to the front door, I heard a clock striking. Even before I rang the bell, she opened the door.

She looked terrible. Obviously she had had no sleep and there were dark circles under her red-rimmed eyes. Her hair hadn't been brushed and stood out in a black tangled bush. She wasn't wearing make-up, and her skin looked dry and flaky. "They've done it at last," she said in a loud voice, before I could even say anything. "And the fucking police are doing nothing, as per usual."

I glanced back to where DC Parry was standing on the opposite pavement. He must have heard. He turned and went off down the street.

We went into the hall. "You've got to find some proof," she said. "They can't get away with it."

"Someone came to see Peter last night," I said. "Who was it?"

She looked startled. "I don't know. He said he was staying in. I left soon after you did, so I wasn't here."

I don't know why I pursued it. Obviously it couldn't have anything to do with the accident, if that's what it was; that had happened much later, after Peter had been to the pub, had a quarrel with Neil Winters and then, presumably, come home. All the same I wanted to get a general picture.

"Have you any idea who it might have been?" I asked. "Dark-haired, thin, mid- to late twenties. We saw him as we left the Dixons. He certainly came here."

She shrugged.

One more chance. "What sort of a guy was Peter?" I asked, perhaps a little insensitively. "Would he have kept an appointments diary?"

She gave a bitter sort of laugh and opened the door to the

living room, gesturing to a desk which had one of those flaps that lowered to provide a writing surface. It was open and contained an unruly litter of scattered papers. Peter was not, I surmised, the sort of person who would have kept a diary with all his appointments neatly entered.

I walked over to the desk. There were rough drafts of fliers announcing meetings of the anti-development group, copies of letters to and from the council, scrawled lists of ideas to scupper Lennox and Winters. On a more personal level, I found a couple of notes, unsigned but clearly of an intimate nature. "Longing to see you," said one, "perhaps Thursday." It was undated so didn't help much. A strong hand, I suspected male.

"Any idea who these are from?" I asked.

Laura shook her head. "He didn't tell me too much about his personal life," she said. "We only worked together against those bloody builders." She sniffed and dabbed at her nose with her handkerchief. I hoped she wasn't going to give way.

"I'll go and see them," I said.

I was about to leave when I noticed an official looking letter amongst the litter on the desk. The heading proclaimed "The British Museum." Intrigued, I looked at it. It didn't say much.

"Dear Mr. Squires,

Your discovery is very interesting. We should meet."

It was signed with an indecipherable scrawl, though printed underneath was the name "Professor Wallis B. Embury, Roman Antiquities." I would have ignored it except that scribbled on the side was the single word: "Eureka.."

"Is that Peter's writing?" I asked.

She nodded, though looked startled.

"What's it about?"

"Nothing important," she said and almost snatched the letter, screwing it up and throwing it in the waste paper basket.

"Get the bastards," she said as I went out of the front door.

But first I had promised to meet Ted.

He was sitting at the bar, looking quite at home and holding a pint glass. He turned round and smiled as I walked in and I realized, not for the first time, how attractive he was. A young man, perhaps a couple of years older than me, dark hair cut short, sticking up but not gelled, soft and silky, the sort you want to stroke or run your fingers through, straight-looking, pleasant, wearing casual clothes, light coloured loose trousers that showed little and a brown leather jacket over a plain green shirt. His smile revealed a couple of crooked front teeth which didn't detract. I asked for a low alcohol beer for me.

The heavyset man was behind the bar. "I'll have to get you a bottle."

"I've just got to make a call," I said. "Is there a phone I can use?"

He gestured to the passage between the public and saloon bar. The phone was a public one with a slot to insert ten pence coins. There were a few messages and numbers scrawled on the wall behind, and a card had been slipped into a gap between the coin box and the wall. I saw an advert for "Miss Diamond, Dominatrix," but of course it had no interest for me. I dialled the number for the British Museum, and when a polite receptionist answered, asked for Professor Wallis B. Embury.

I was a little surprised to hear a female American voice answer, but then remembered the woman who had married Edward VIII, Wallis Simpson.

"Good morning," I said and explained about the letter and Peter Squires' death.

She sounded genuinely regretful. "I was looking forward to meeting him. What he had found was really interesting."

"What exactly was it? Your letter didn't say."

She seemed very enthusiastic. "It'd probably look like a lump of old stone to you, but I think it's the end of a piece of statuary, a torch held by Cautes, which, if it is, means that it's probably the doorway of a Mithraeum."

I waited for more illumination.

"A temple to the god Mithras. It seems that Mr. Squires found this on a building site."

Instantly things started to click in my memory cells. "Could it be important?"

"If it's what I think it is, then yes, very important."

"And…?"

"Well the building would be stopped of course. At least until an archaeological dig had taken place."

"And that could take?"

"Well, depending on what the initial survey finds, anything up to a year. Perhaps longer."

Eureka, I thought, thanked her and rang off.

"So you see," I told Ted, "if it's true, then Lennox and Winters would have to give up the development scheme, at least for the foreseeable future."

Parry didn't look all that interested. He sat on his stool, positioned just far enough away so that, if you swung your knees round, you could touch your neighbour's—unintentional design feature.

"Perhaps they have sunk so much money into this, they couldn't afford to hold up operations for such a long time. So they killed him."

Parry's knees brushed my thigh, and, not expecting it, I instinctively flinched away, but then out of friendship I returned so that the fleshy part of my thigh was pressed against his knee.

"If millions of pounds are at stake it means they've got a very good motive for murder."

Parry's knee massaged my thigh gently, side to side. I wondered whether I was expected to put my hand on it. He settled the problem by putting his hand on mine. It rested lightly, not moving, just about halfway between knee and groin. I felt a twitch of excitement stir my cock. I allowed my legs to open a little, an invitation.

The barman came back with a handful of bottles held by the neck. "Sorry I was so long," he said. He opened one and then asked, "Do you want it in a glass?"

I shook my head. Parry hadn't removed his hand from my leg; in fact it was gradually traveling upwards towards the unmistakable bulge at the top. I picked up the bottle from the bar and took a gulp. Parry was gently massaging my groin, finding and straightening the length of my rigidly-outlined prick so that he could rub it. Thank God the barman had turned away, though I doubted whether he could see over the counter, and there were few enough other customers, none within viewing distance.

"Ted," I said, "pleasant though this is, don't you think you should be doing your job?"

"I'm off duty," he said with a smile which was almost a leer. "Is anyone at home this afternoon?"

"No," I said, without thinking.

"Otherwise there's always my flat. I'm sure you'd like to inspect it."

He looked at me, his hand on my cock, fingers gently caressing through the material, and I was sorely tempted. Yes, I know, all that talk earlier about Paul and me, about integrity and respect and love! Did I mention love? I can't actually remember but—

"I've got an appointment to see Neil Winters," I lied. "Even if you've got a day off from work, I haven't." It was an easy out, a coward's way out, because it left the opportunity open for sometime in the future. I should have said something like, "I'm sorry, Ted, but Paul and I are something special. Much as I like you, much as I fancy you, it can never be." Did I say that? Fuck!

Even so, we parted on friendly terms though he looked disappointed.

I tried to track down Neil Winters, first phoning the firm, to be told that Mr. Winters wasn't at work that day. Then I looked his address up in the phone book and went round to see if he was in.

His house was a marked contrast to Peter Squires', or in fact to mine. It was an elegant Regency house with a large, well-kept front garden. The front door was set under a Classical portico. There were five upstairs windows. I rang the bell and heard it sound hollowly through the house. I waited for some time, but there was no answer. Oh well, it had been a long shot anyway. I tried once more, just for luck, and then heard a sound from inside.

The door opened, and the young man whom we had seen last night calling on Squires opened the door. If Laura had looked bad, he looked twice as dreadful. Sharp lines creased his face on either side of his mouth, as if they had been etched with acid. He was unshaven and his shirt looked as if it had been slept in, or rather had been on while the wearer tossed and turned in a vain attempt to sleep. His eyes were deep-sunk into their sockets.

"Neil Winters?" I asked.

"Yes," he said curtly, without any expression in his voice at all. Although he was looking at me, or at least in my direction, I doubted whether he was actually seeing me at all. Certainly he didn't recognize me in the way that I had him. His eyes were unfocused. For a moment I wondered whether he was drunk.

"Are you all right?" I asked, which was stupid because he clearly wasn't, but it's the sort of thing we say.

He pulled himself together with what was obviously a physical effort. "I'm sorry," he said. "I've had some bad news. What do you want?"

"It's about Peter Squires," I said.

That really got him. He staggered and had to hold onto the door jamb for support. A sign of guilt, I wondered.

"He's dead," he said in a voice which sounded broken and lost. And something deep inside told me that I'd got it all wrong. "He's dead, and I'll never see him again."

"Look, I'm sorry, but I must talk to you. It is important."

Somehow my words seemed to get through to him for he stood back from the door and I went in.

He sat down, slumped in an armchair in the front room that overlooked the Square. It was pleasantly furnished with what my mother would have called "a woman's touch" but looked as if it needed a good clean. There was a layer of dust on the tops of furniture, a bottle of whisky stood three quarters empty on the table. It and the glass had made circles on the polished surface.

"Do you live here alone, Mr. Winters?" I asked.

For a moment he stared at me as if to say what the hell business was it of mine, and who was I anyway, then the fight went out of him. "My wife's gone," he said. "We had, differences."

"You went to see Peter Squires last night?"

"Last night," he repeated as if he couldn't believe it was such a short time ago.

"Then had a quarrel with him, in the pub."

He nodded. "Who are you?"

"My name's Tim Sinclair. I'm a private investigator. Laura Squires has asked me to find out what happened to Peter."

"Laura? She must be devastated. She never approved of Peter and me."

That surprised me. Laura had said she knew nothing about Peter's personal life. I wondered why she had lied.

I paused, then, "Did you kill him?" I asked abruptly.

"Kill him? Did I kill him? Of course I didn't. I loved him. I still love him. That was the reason my wife left. We, Peter and I, were going to live together…" He broke down.

I hate to see a grown man cry, and I felt sorry for him, but, for some reason, excessive potty training when young or something, I can never seem to be able to go to someone and touch them in sympathy, much less the full American hug, so I sat there until he got over it.

I'm sure he was as embarrassed as I was. "Sorry," he said.

"I understand," I said.

He poured himself a drink, offered me one. I shook my head, it was only ten-thirty in the morning, and swallowed. It seemed to settle him, for the moment.

"Do you feel up to talking about it?" I asked. "What was the quarrel about?"

"You know about the development? It was a dirty deal that Arthur Lennox proposed and a dirty-tricks campaign afterwards. I was sorry I agreed to it, but we were desperate to get the properties bought and building started. The money we'd put into it. Of course after I met Peter, and we, got together, it seemed worse than ever. He wanted me to split with Lennox, but it was difficult, and last night Peter got annoyed. We'd have made it up. In fact we did, after we left the pub."

"What about the Mithraeum?"

He looked puzzled.

"The Roman remains?"

"I don't know anything about that. Peter never said anything about Roman remains."

My proposed hypotheses must have been wrong. Certainly Neil's grief at the death of Peter argued against his killing him. And if they hadn't heard about the archaeology, then that was another motive up the spout. Perhaps it had been a hit-and-run as Parry had suggested and nothing to do with the development project at all.

I doubted whether there'd be anything for me at the office so I went home and phoned Paul.

"Hello, lover," I said. I was alone so it didn't matter.

"Hi, Tim," he said, which told me he wasn't. "What can I do for you?"

"What can I do for you?" I said. "Well for a start, you can unzip those trousers you're wearing and let me put my hand into the warm interior. Find something soft and responsive. Play around with it for a little until it…"

"I'm a bit busy at the moment. I think perhaps we'll have to put it off until later."

"Not even a little grope around?" I said.

"'Fraid not. It's a little inconvenient at the moment. What exactly did you want?"

I took pity on him, told him in a few, well-chosen words about Neil and Peter, and about the Roman discovery.

"And the developers didn't even know about it?"

"Apparently not."

"So, what are you going to do now?"

"I'll have to think about it. Are you going to be back early?"

"Busy, busy, busy," he said. "I may be late."

I groaned. "I want you," I said.

"Later," he said, and before I could blow him a kiss, rang off.

Almost as if it had been waiting for me, the phone rang again.

"Hello," I said.

"Is that you, Tim?"

A young male voice at the other end. For a moment I didn't recognize it.

"Who is this?"

"It's Ted. Ted Parry. Can I come round?"

"What do you want?" I sounded ungracious, but I wasn't sure that being alone with Ted was a good idea. Perhaps I could meet him in a pub somewhere.

"Just wanted to hear what happened when you saw Neil Winters."

"I thought you were off duty," I said.

"I thought you were at the office." Touché!

"Okay," I said. "When do you want to come round?"

Ted hesitated. "Actually, I'm just outside, phone box opposite."

I looked out of the window and saw him in the box. He was smiling broadly and carrying a plastic bag. He arrived with a large pizza and a six-pack of lager. "I don't know if you've eaten…" he said, and I suddenly found I was ravenously hungry. We ate from the box and drank from the cans, the beer feeling cool against my throat.

After we'd polished off the pizza, Ted perched on the arm of the settee, seeming a little restless. He got up and, sipping from his second can of beer, wandered round the room. I wondered whether he was debating a jump on top of me, and whether I would submit and spend the rest of the afternoon in a fantastic fuck orgy. Then have to face Paul this evening.

"Is that Paul?" Ted asked. Christ where? Got home early? But he was pointing to a photo on the sideboard. Smiling, eyes sparkling, Paul, wearing an open-necked green shirt and white jeans, looked at his happiest. I remembered vividly the occasion when I had taken the photo, one glorious green and gold day when Paul and I had escaped from the city and visited that anachronistic finger of countryside, Epping Forest that inserts itself into the northeast side of the metropolis. It had been a day of green and gold, gold buttercups and creeping masses of cinquefoil with their gold potentilla flowers, feathery bunches of bright yellow ladies bedstraw and overall the gold sun, shining through the leaves of the trees to make dappled shade on the grass. We had walked along a path probably created and used by deer, found a bank, sat and eaten our lunch and drank wine there, and afterwards made love. The expression on Paul's photographed face brought back every sensation, the fresh, clean smell of the turf, the warmth of the sun and of his body, the touch of flesh on flesh, the taste of the wine on his lips and tongue, the green and the gold, green shirt and red-gold hair, leaves, grass and the wild flowers of summer.

Suddenly brought back to the present by Ted's enquiring look, I realized that I hadn't answered the question. "Yes. Yes," I said, "you met him once, the Ponting case. You'd like him. Everyone does."

"He's important to you, isn't he?"

Up till then my life had always been full of the search for the next fuck, the constant looking, the contact, the acceptance, jolt of excitement, or the rejection. The play, the feel of unfamiliar skin against mine, the orgasm and the parting. And then on to the next. But Ted's question brought me up short. Yes, I realized, Paul was important, much too important to throw away on a casual liaison. Better to keep Ted as a friend, and infinitely more useful too.

"Yes, I guess he is," I said simply, and the moment passed.

I told Ted about my meeting with Neil Winters, about his relationship with Peter. He nodded and told me about the post mortem and forensics report. Not that there was much to tell. He had been knocked down by a car. There were a few shards of glass from a broken headlight and a scrape of green paint caught on a metal button from his jacket.

"Green paint?"

"Probably from a car, but not a common color and certainly one that's been discontinued. A Volvo they said, old model."

"Well," I said, "no doubt you'll keep your traffic boys alert." I felt depressed. It looked as if Peter Squires' death had been what the police had thought all along, a hit-and-run, a stupid, wasteful accident caused by some bastard who'd had too much to drink and had insisted on driving home.

"So, what are you going to do?"

"I guess I'd better tell Laura. She deserves that. If it's any consolation it looks as if the development will be held up to a good long time, what with the British Museum's interest. And if Neil Winters really does get out of the partnership, then the whole thing could fall through. A few houses have been knocked down, but no doubt someone'll put up some more in keeping with the rest of the road. At least some good could come out of the nasty business. I'd like to have seen Lennox in prison though."

Granby Street, as I turned the corner by the Granby Arms, was getting quite familiar to me, even though yesterday evening was the first time I'd actually ever seen it. The landlord of the pub, though, would be disappointed. No modern theme pub for him with a clientele of rich, upwardly mobile young executives and their girlfriends. I wondered, as I passed number 64, whether the Dixons would stay. Poor Peter, his street saved, but he wasn't here to appreciate it. Laura, though.

I slammed on the brakes as I realized what my subconscious had noticed as I passed the car park for the Granby Arms. The driver of the car behind blared his horn angrily and shook his fist as he zoomed out to overtake me. "Sorry," I said to his back.

I did a three point turn and went into the park. Yes, I was right. Parked there was a green car and, when I got out to look at it, I saw that it had a broken near-side front headlight.

"They're shut," said an elderly man, waiting by the closed door of the pub. "They say pubs can be open all day, but this one's shut."

I could understand it. The landlord had little incentive to stay open when trade was so scarce.

"I suppose you don't happen to know whose car this is?" I asked.

The old man gazed at the Volvo for some time as if it was the first time he'd ever seen it. Perhaps it was. Then he nodded. "It's young Peter Squires' car," he said. "Poor lad. He's dead you know."

It didn't make sense. Squires knocked down by his own car.

"But it wasn't here this morning," I said.

"No," he agreed. "His sister drives it. I expect she's at his house and left it here. Parking in the road's dangerous. You're liable to find you've got no wheels when you come back." He chuckled, morosely.

"Laura," I said, "you did know about Peter's relationship with Neil Winters."

We were sitting in the front room overlooking the road. Or

at least I was sitting, but Laura kept finding things to do. She'd perch for a moment on the edge of the chair and then spring up to pick up a book or something and put it in one of the large cardboard boxes arranged in a row along the side of the room. It seemed she couldn't keep still. If anything she looked more distraught than she had this morning.

"There was nothing going on between them," she said. "Peter wasn't like that, and if he had been, he wouldn't have taken up with Winters."

She wasn't making much sense, I thought, but I could see how she would feel about Neil and Peter, sleeping with the enemy, in a very literal sense.

"I saw him this morning," I said. "He wouldn't have done anything to Peter. He loved him. They were planning on living together."

She made a wide sweeping gesture with her hand as if she would erase the whole thing from her mind. "Then Lennox did it," she said. "He'd do anything to get the building started. He couldn't afford to have it held up for the archaeological dig."

"He didn't know anything about it," I said. "Nor did you this morning when I found that letter from Professor Embury."

"I was confused," she said, her voice rising slightly. "Of course he must have known. He wanted to stop Peter."

"But it was out of Peter's hands," I said. "The museum knew about it. Killing Peter wouldn't have stopped the investigation."

"They did it," she said, with the fanatical air of someone who knows for certain whatever the evidence to the contrary."

"Peter was hit with his own car," I said.

Her expression changed, crumpled. What I had previously thought was grief-ravaged, now I saw as guilt. She stared at me, her face a mask of despair.

"How do you know that?" she asked.

"The police found fragments of headlight glass, the scrape of green paint from a Volvo."

She gave a great groan, "Oh God."

"You'd better tell me," I said.

And so the story came out. Of that last evening when Neil had called and Peter had gone with him, and Laura, to the pub. The landlord hadn't mentioned Laura, and I, of course, having no reason hadn't asked. Then there was the quarrel over the usual thing, Peter's exit, and her more restrained following to find the two of them making up in the car park. She couldn't stand it and, after Neil had left, had borrowed the car to drive to her own home. Then there was the shouting match and Peter had stormed out from the passenger seat, crossing in front of the car to get to his gate. Furiously she had revved the accelerator, the clutch had slipped and she hit him before he had had time to get to the pavement.

She was, of course, aghast, but cold-bloodedly, now that the deed has been done and she realized Peter was dead, the thought struck her that she could turn the accident to her own advantage and blame the developers for murder. It was a stupid plan, born of desperation and bound to be discovered. All the same I felt sorry for her.

I didn't know what she'd be charged with, but it was obvious that the police had to be told so I rang Ted and explained.

"Hello, darling," I whispered, as I got in and found Paul sitting on the sofa. "How did the day go?"

"Good," he said, lying back in the cushions so that he was open and vulnerable to anything I wanted. "Now you can do all those things you suggested over the phone this morning."

But at the moment I didn't want to do anything, say anything. I just wanted to sit there and hold him quietly. Eventually I would tell him everything, and we would make love.

Me and Paul ~ Epilogue

A month or two later Paul and I paid a visit to British Museum. I hadn't been since I was a kid, and Paul said he'd never been. I thought there were some Roman artifacts from another Mithras discovery so we went to have a look. On the opposite side of Russell Square we passed some little shops selling archaeological curiosities, Roman coins, Egyptian ushabti figures, pieces of statuary. We did a bit of window shopping. Some were quite cheap.

"Let's buy a Roman coin," suggested Paul, "as a souvenir of today."

We went in. It was one of those shops that seemed to have remained locked in time since Victorian days. There was a smell of antiquity, like the interior of an old church, and, though there were some items displayed in glass-fronted cases, the valuable stuff presumably, many items just lay jumbled together in boxes for the idle seeker to pore over and discover rich treasure or rubbish.

I picked up a bit of stone which had been carved into a strange convoluted shape. I tried to puzzle out what it could be.

"It's part of a flaming torch," said a voice, and a bent old man wearing old-fashioned pince-nez appeared out of the shadows. "Came from a Roman dig in Ostia. We think it was held by Cautes or Cautopates who symbolized day and night and…"

"…guarded the entrance to temples of Mithras," I finished.

"That's right," said the man, smiling warmly and seeming disposed to chat. "I was saving it for someone who promised to return and buy it. He'd had one bit and said he'd come back for the other, but he never did."

A strange feeling tickled the back of my neck. "This man," I said. "He didn't give his name, I suppose."

"I always keep a record of who buys things. Wait a minute, I'll look it up." He searched through the spidery handwriting in a leather-bound ledger which looked as if it was nearly as old as some of his curiosities. Then he looked up.

"Here it is. Squires, it was, Peter Squires."

CHAPTER SIX

The envelope lay on the mat. A plain brown envelope. The sort that could contain anything, a bill, a circular, though nowadays these have rather more exciting covers to make up, I assume, for the depressing nature of their contents. A communication from that mail order company I belong to that offers books and videos of a certain nature and guarantees that the nature of the contents won't be obvious to anyone but the addressee, or at least to the person that opens the letter. Not that my postman, whom I suspect is gay anyway, would be at all shocked by a Gay Male Publishers catalogue.

The envelope, as I say, lay on the mat, seemingly innocent of anything but a desire to entertain or inform, surely not capable of disrupting a household, breaking up a relationship—but I jump ahead of myself.

We, that is my lover Paul Massingham and I, were having breakfast when the postman arrived that morning. Through the kitchen window, sitting on my stool at the compact little breakfast bar which had been built in by a previous owner of the two-up/two-down house, I could see him as he made his way up the five stone steps to the front door, hear him whistling cheerfully. Why do postmen and butchers always appear so cheerful? I heard the letterbox flap snap shut and saw the postman catch sight of me as I put a slice of whole-meal, multigrain toast into my mouth. He waved. I waved. Paul looked up inquiringly, red hair shining, brown eyes candid.

"Postman Pat," I said.

"His name's Harry," he said.

"Is it?" I said. "How do you know that?"

He smiled, in an attempt to appear mysterious. When I failed to rise to the bait, he said, "I went to school with him."

"I like you with your hair short," I said, changing the subject. It made him look clean-cut and younger than twenty-two. It also made his ears stand out, though I didn't tell him this.

And the envelope lay on the mat while we ate toast and drank tea and smiled at each other because we were in love, me for the first time in my life, he possibly, if what he had told me was the truth, and I had no reason to doubt him, for the second. Paul finished his mug of tea and went out into the tiny hall. He came back with a handful of letters, putting them down on the shelf beside me.

"Why don't I ever get any mail?" he asked, mock petulant.

"How many letters do you write?"

"I don't even get junk mail."

"You can have mine," I said, and offered him the bunch, including the brown manila one. "You have just won five million pounds, a villa in San Tropez and a Porsche."

He grinned and kissed me. "You have won a red-haired lover. Must dash. I'll see you this evening." He went out, the door slammed and I watched him, lithe and athletic, jump down the steps outside. A turn, a wave and he was gone. When I saw him next, everything would have changed.

I wondered whether to have another slice of toast, but decided I ought to get off to the office. I opened the mail. As I thought, nothing of any consequence, just junk, two bills, a bank statement showing an overdraft of £27.32 and a brown manila envelope with a handwritten name and address on the front, postmarked Central London. I slit the envelope with a buttery knife.

What I saw brought me up short with a shock to my guts almost like a physical blow. Scrawled on one side of the page were the words, "fucking faggot." I turned it over.

I had had some experience of homophobia; I guess every gay has, even when it isn't directed at him personally. My first boss, when I was a junior office boy in an Export Merchants, had been an intolerant bigot. I had even seen some of these letters before written by people with hate in their hearts and a desire to wound. They say that "sticks and stones may break my bones but words will never hurt me," but it ain't true.

And coming as it did so unexpectedly, I was entirely unprepared, and the shock was considerable. The sheer malice of the wording caught me unprepared. I felt a tightness in my chest as if I could not breathe. Even though I was sitting down my legs felt weak and shaky. I wondered for a moment if I was going to faint. Deep breaths, I told myself. Take deep breaths.

Slowly I regained control and thought what to do next.

Whoever had written it obviously knew who I was, knew quite a lot about me. It was handwritten, or rather printed, on a piece of ordinary paper looking as if it had been torn from a pad. The envelope was plain brown manila. It was a nasty letter. The writer hadn't minced his words, even managed to include an element of racism into the message.

"You are a sick piece of shit. How can you speak of feeling pride in being gay. Sticking a prick up another man's arse is not natural. Why do you think God made women? So that we could procreate. Men that go with other men are freaks. You are outcasts. You should be gassed. Gays are even less human than niggers. Die soon, you cunt. And that Paul of yours. You think the sun shines out of his arse, don't you…he's been having it off with all and sundry. How does that make you feel, fuckwit?"

And that was just the first paragraph.

The usual, sensible, advice when receiving letters like this is to throw them into the dustbin immediately and forget all about it, but, apart from the obvious dislike of me and gays in general, there was that other accusation about Paul. Of course I didn't believe it but…

I thought about my friend, Ted Parry, in the police. I wondered if I should show it to him, fingerprints and things like that. And people sometimes forget it's possible to get a DNA profile from spittle left on the envelope when it was licked. Of course you have to have the person's DNA profile on record to get a match, but still…

I thought of Paul's candid smiling face as he said goodbye, but could it hide a lie? I wondered who could have sent the letter. Ostensibly it would have to be a straight, though how that word could be applied to someone as bitter and twisted as the writer obviously was, I don't know. But it might just as easily be a gay, using the homophobic attitude to throw off suspicion.

I wasn't happy as I set off for the office in Jermyn Street.

There were three letters in the wire cage under the slot when I reached the office. One of them was a now familiar brown manila one. I ripped it open first.

As I feared it was another of the anonymous letters, if anything more malicious than the one I had opened at home. I actually felt my flesh crawl as I read the comments and realized that, whoever it was, this person knew a great deal about both Paul and me, knew intimate details about our relationship. Even knew a physical characteristic of Paul's body which no one, except his doctor or a lover, would surely have known.

I slumped down in the office chair behind my spindly old desk and stared at the rings made by innumerable mugs of coffee. On the way to work I had, almost, made up my mind to ignore the letter, tear it up, erase it from my mind, but this later one…

I reached for the phone and rang Detective Constable Ted Parry. He wasn't on duty, the desk sergeant told me, so I rang him at home. We'd got quite friendly since first meeting him when I'd been arrested on suspicion of the murder of Adrian Ponting, back in the summer. Almost too friendly on a couple of occasions when the opportunity of sharing his bed had arisen, but Paul had been too important. I'd almost lost him once, and I didn't want to risk that again.

The sleepy sound of Ted's voice told me that I'd roused him from his bed. He sounded husky and deep and, in spite of my concern about the letters, for a brief moment I visualized him, hair mussed, eyes half-closed. I wondered if he wore anything in bed. He said he'd only just got in after working a night shift. I apologized. He said it didn't matter. You know all the sort of things we say in those circumstances. Then he asked what I wanted, and I explained about the letters. He sounded concerned.

"Give me a few hours," he said. "I'm no use at the moment. While you're waiting can you make a list of people whom you might have offended in some way, however slight. These things sometimes rankle in the mind and come out, perhaps months later, in a burst of vitriolic spite."

"Okay," I said.

"Don't worry, Tim," he said. "We'll sort it out."

His obvious sympathy made me feel better. A bit.

I made a cup of instant and got out a sheet of paper. Then I decided to put it on the computer. I switched it on, found I had e-mail and checked. It was another of those damned anonymous letters "from no one at nowhere." For some reason, although it was only electronic pulses, it seemed even more intrusive than the physical paper and ink. I deleted it before reading. Christ! Who was it? He seemed to know everything about me. For a moment I had a creepy feeling that someone was looking at me from behind my back, and I whirled round, to see the same wall, blank and featureless, painted with the same bland magnolia paint. The windows to my right looked out to the windows from the buildings on the opposite side of the street. Could there be someone behind those featureless rectangles with binoculars trained on me? I took a mouthful of coffee which tasted as foul as it always did. At least that was one thing that hadn't changed.

I struggled to think. What had Ted said? Anyone whom I might have upset, however slightly. If you think about it, for most people, that could be dozens and, as a P.I. whose work often resulted in people being sent to prison, or at least messed up in some way, it was likely to be even more than most.

I thought back to my first case. Alan Harrison, who had suspected his partner, Philip Trelawney, of being unfaithful. Well,

I had solved that quite easily, so neither of those would have had any reason to feel offended. Not unless Alan had somehow discovered that Philip and I… That was before I met Paul of course, but why would Philip have ever told him about the casual one-nighter (or more accurately, one-afternooner)? I put Alan Harrison's name down as a possible.

The next one was Nick Warren. He, of course, would be a prime suspect, ending up as he had been convicted of manslaughter. But Nick Warren was safely locked away in prison, wasn't he? It would be relatively easy to check if he had escaped, of course, but it seemed unlikely. Wouldn't I have been told? I put down his name, even though I didn't really think of him as a likely suspect in the circumstances.

Who was next, I wondered.

The third case of course had been the one where the guy had passed himself off as dead in order to escape the clutches of some older bloke, and also to avoid being prosecuted for theft. Well, both him and his brother, I supposed, could have had it in for me, but nothing had happened as a result of my investigations. They hadn't been prosecuted, and to start something which might lead to the case being reconsidered would surely be the worst kind of folly. I just couldn't see them being so stupid. I nearly went on when I suddenly thought of the guy who had put me onto the real solution of the case, Chris, that guy in Lambeth. Funnily enough I thought I'd seen him in Jermyn Street only the other day. Just a brief glimpse and then he'd vanished in the crowd of Christmas shoppers and office workers out for lunch.

I felt in a way that I'd treated him badly, but surely he wasn't the sort of guy who expected long-term relationships. He'd picked me up in the Park, we'd had a good fuck, twice, if I remember rightly, and that was it. I didn't even know his surname. I couldn't imagine his bearing a grudge. All the same I put down "Chris" and then a question mark.

Who was next? The Ponting case. Sad one that! Adrian Ponting killed on Hampstead Heath, his killer, a complete accident, had been so overburdened with guilt that he'd committed suicide.

End of story. No one left, except of course Adrian's parents.

But they couldn't bear a grudge, surely, except that, as a result of my investigations, Adrian's gayness had been made public. There always seemed to be these exceptions. I noted them down.

The latest case had been the business with the guy killed by his sister. Anonymous letters are always supposed to be women's work, but I couldn't see Laura Squires writing the sort of letters I'd received. Of course the real people who had suffered, apart from Peter who had died, had been the developers, Arthur Lennox and his partner. As far as I knew, they still hadn't been able to start work on the building as the archaeological survey was still in progress, and, though they hadn't actually found anything, and I knew for certain they wouldn't, the money they had tied up in the undertaking must have been considerable. I put down Arthur Lennox's name.

That made five possible suspects all together: Alan Harrison, Nick Warren, Chris, George Ponting, and Arthur Lennox.

"You're not off out again," said Alan Harrison.

"Who's going to bring in the money," asked his partner, Philip Trelawney, "if I don't do some work?"

It was true, but it didn't make anything easier in Harrison's mind. "We never seem to have any time together these days," he complained.

At first he had been only too pleased when Philip's cyber enterprise had taken off, but then, as Philip himself said, porn will always sell. Sex is one thing that isn't affected by the price of oil or the latest Middle East crisis.

Conventional Alan had been slightly uneasy about the pornographic nature of TwilightArt.com, but the increased income had overcome any reservations he initially had experienced. Money spring-cleans a good deal of dirty linen, he openly admitted to himself, but Philip's business, in taking off, had also taken up more and more of his time.

Alan remembered how, months back, when he had not even known about the filming but suspected that Philip was being unfaithful, he had hired a private detective, a Mr. Sinclair, young chap, dark hair and attractive light grey eyes, who had followed Philip and discovered the truth.

At first Philip had been understandably upset at this obvious lack of trust on Alan's part but later had treated it as a joke. "I always thought P.I.s were seedy, middle-aged men in raincoats," he had said to Alan, "but you had to pick a real hottie to send after me."

Was it his imagination, wondered Alan over the intervening months, but Philip had seemed to mention this Tim Sinclair, that was his name, more times than absolutely necessary. Why had it been necessary at all? Like, when passing a good-looking guy in the street, he had asked, "Doesn't that one remind you of the P.I. you hired to check up on me?" Or there was that night when in the extremes of coital orgasm, now sadly so rare, Philip had cried out a single syllable. It certainly could have been "Tim," and at the time Alan was too astounded to probe. So doubt had festered into suspicion and then into certainty.

"So where are you going?" asked Alan. "To see Tim Sinclair?"

Philip looked startled, or was it guilt? "Tim!" he said. "You must be insane! I never see him."

But Alan did not believe him. All the same his hatred, if anything, was directed more against Tim Sinclair, rather than towards Philip.

In his Lambeth flat, Chris thought about Tim Sinclair, thought about his dark hair, springy to the touch, his sexy, light-grey eyes, the way his body felt underneath when he had ploughed him so vigorously and Tim had bellowed his lust into the mattress. Twice only and then the brush-off.

Dumped! Chris could scarcely believe it. It was always he who did the dumping, not the other way round. His first reaction had been anger. How dare Tim do such a thing? Then, he tried to think rationally, to say it didn't really matter all that much, what was one amongst so many? But somehow he couldn't seem to get Tim out of his mind, and the thought festered so that it seemed to color all his subsequent pick-ups. Instead of the casual, confident approach, he suddenly began to have doubts. Might he not be successful? Would he be refused? Was he, the worst yet, getting old, becoming less attractive? He started to peer anxiously into the mirror, noticing for the first time the tiny, as yet, wrinkles round his eyes. What did they call them, crows' feet?

It was irrational, but he felt he had to see Tim Sinclair again. He had his phone number, of course, but he sensed that ringing the guy up would be no use. If Tim hadn't wanted to see him after those two sexual escapades, he'd hardly have changed his mind since.

Chris looked him up in the phone book and found that his office was in Jermyn Street. Perhaps he would wander along there one afternoon, see where Tim worked, find out more about him.

Suddenly the urge to know more about Tim was irresistible. He'd discover where he lived, whom he lived with, if there was someone. Information is power, they say. Perhaps he'd find out something to give him a hold over the guy. Perhaps he'd think of some way to use the information against Tim. Almost without realizing it, he knew that he'd formed a half-plan to hurt him in some way.

Mrs. Ponting looked at her husband. He was sitting, slumped in his chair, looking, she thought, ten years older than he had before Adrian had died.

"Will you be going to the office this morning?" she asked, but he didn't respond, perhaps hadn't even heard. She sighed.

"George," she said more loudly. "You'll have to snap out of it. This is not doing either of us any good."

There was still no answer. His eyes were open but seemed to be staring blankly into the distance. She put her hand on his shoulder, and he jumped with a sudden spasm so violent that it must have been painful.

"Why?" he gasped.

"Why what?" asked his wife. "Why did Adrian have to die?"

"Why did he have to be queer?"

"I don't think he had much choice. They don't usually."

"But now everyone knows. I was his father and only able to produce a nancyboy for a son."

"So it's you you're feeling sorry for." Mrs. Ponting suddenly realized that the dislike she had felt for her husband for some years had turned to hatred.

"I suppose I was the father," he said, his eyes suddenly focusing on his wife.

She would leave him soon, she resolved.

"That damned private eye," he said.

"Whom you hired," she reminded him, "to find out about Adrian."

"That damned, fucking private eye. I'll get him. I'll make him wish he'd never been born."

Mrs. Ponting didn't answer.

Arthur Lennox crashed down the telephone receiver onto the rest with such force that it was surprising it did not shatter. He had just been talking to his bank manager, who had informed him that there was no more money to be advanced. The hold-up on the development caused by the archaeological survey was costing him millions. He could see bankruptcy staring him in the face.

Neil Winters, his business partner, had withdrawn from the partnership after the death of Peter Squires, and Lennox felt completely alone and powerless.

If it hadn't been for that interfering P.I. everything would have gone smoothly; the remaining owners and tenants scared into selling their properties cheaply or moving away, the construction of luxury flats and penthouses for the upwardly mobile. A great fat profit for Arthur Lennox. But now! He ground his teeth in fury and thought what he could do to get, in some small way, his revenge.

Ted didn't call back that morning, and by lunchtime I'd had enough of the office. There was no work to be done on any outstanding cases—to be honest, there were no outstanding cases, business was tight—so I switched on the answer phone and went out into the city. The West End was its usual pre-Christmas rush, people thronging the streets and going from department store to department store to find last-minute presents for relatives and friends they would not see for another year.

Each shop window vied with its neighbour to present a Christmas scene, whether celebrating God or Mammon, the Christmas crib or Santa's mob of little helpers. Overhead, above the streets and stretched between buildings, were strings of lights which by this evening would be gay and festive, but in the cold light of day looked merely grey and electrical against a leaden sky.

It was probably the letters, but I kept looking around to see whether I was being followed. Once I thought I saw Mr. Ponting, but, if it was he, then he'd changed considerably, looking much less well-fed, if not gaunt and haggard. Soon, I decided there was no point in aimless wandering, and I caught the underground home. My answering machine at work would give any potential client who phoned my home number, and, if it was important enough, they'd try that.

It was half past two when I unlocked the front door. Immediately I was certain someone had been there since I'd left that morning. I'm not exactly house-proud, but I knew that I hadn't left a worn shirt in the middle of the stairs. I recognized it as Paul's. There was no reason why he would have returned, unless he'd been taken ill, and I called out.

No answer.

The house was absolutely silent and I felt the hairs at the back of my neck raise. Apart from that shirt, there was nothing else I could see that was unusual, but all the same I felt a strange atmosphere in the house. Was someone up there, waiting for me, knowing now that I'd returned early? There was little I could do. Phoning the police on the evidence of a discarded shirt would be deemed stupid, and I knew that I'd have to go upstairs and find out. I didn't relish the idea. I quickly went into the kitchen and took a carving knife from the cutlery drawer, then, feeling foolish, but more than a little scared, I slowly made my way upstairs.

The fifth stair creaked, and I cursed myself, knowing I should have stepped over it. The landing was dim, the doors to the various rooms, toilet, bathroom, the two bedrooms, were shut. Again I knew that at least some of them would have been left open this morning in our rush to get out.

I opened the bathroom door. It was, as always, untidy, some towels draped over the side of the bath. In the wash basin though there was a rim of blue color as if someone had washed their hands of perhaps paint but failed to rinse the bowl.

I tried the spare bedroom but here there was nothing unusual; a cold, rather sterile room, comfortable enough but without any imprint of character from either of us.

Taking a deep breath I tried the last door, our bedroom, opened it and stood horrified. The bed was unmade, the covers thrown off onto the floor. The bottom sheet was crumpled, as if someone, or several people had had a very energetic night. What was worse, though, was that the centre had been smoothed flat and, in blue letters, paint or ink, was scrawled the sentence "I fucked Paul HERE." Amongst the letters was obvious evidence of semen, still wet.

I felt sick. Scarcely thinking what I was doing, but knowing that, at all costs, I must get rid of this violation, I pulled off the soiled sheet, ran with it downstairs and put it into the washing machine, on hottest, filling the detergent container as full as I could.

The machine chugged into life, and I sat down on one of the

breakfast stools, gasping for breath. Then I shot up again as the front doorbell shrilled. "Jesus fucking Christ!"

For a moment I imagined it to be the desecrator returned and my heart gave a great lurch, but of course that was unlikely, to say the least. Who thinks rationally in circumstances like these? I opened the door, and my relief must have been obvious. It was Ted Parry.

He took one look at my face and said, "What's happened, Tim?"

I was pretty incoherent I guess. There was so much, the intruder, the letters, the e-mail. Okay some of it he already knew, but he led me into the kitchen, heated some coffee in the microwave and held me while I blabbered on and on. As I did so I became calmer and realized that I'd acted like a fool, first in trashing the e-mail. Whoever had written it would obviously have used a fake address, but there's always a trail, and one which an experienced computer buff could track. Then the evidence for the bed was even now swirling away in the washer and though Ted immediately switched it off, his look told me that in all probability the detergent and hot water had done its work. All we had were the two written letters, and the rim of blue dye around the hand basin upstairs.

"Call myself a P.I." I said bitterly. I felt like crying.

But Ted didn't recriminate. Instead he was sympathetic, taking me in his arms and giving me a hug, a hug that went on for so long that I suddenly realized I was enjoying it, and he was too, and I drew away. For a moment I thought he wasn't going to let go, his arms held me fiercely, but then he relaxed. He took a step back.

"Try to ignore this stuff about Paul," he said. "I'm sure it's just a product of this guy's sick mind."

I nodded.

"Have you thought about anyone who might be doing it?" he asked.

I took out the piece of paper with the five names. "Alan

Harrison, Nick Warren—he's in prison though, Chris, I don't even know his second name, Adrian Ponting's father and Arthur Lennox. Could be more, and some of these are pretty unlikely." I explained the circumstances, however embarrassing it was.

"I'll look into them," said Ted. "You probably don't want to make this official, not even the break-in."

"Thanks," I said gratefully.

"That's where he got in," he said, pointing at a pane of glass in the back door that had been broken. "Unlocked the key through that. You should always use a bolt as well." It was the nearest he got to a reproof.

"Do you want me to stay?" he asked.

He looked as if he wouldn't mind, but staying might lead to more "sympathy," and I didn't feel strong enough to resist, wasn't even sure that I wanted to. If Paul was having it off with someone else… I banished the thought before it appeared, well, almost.

"Paul will be back soon," I said. "I don't want him to know anything about all this."

"You don't think you should ask him?"

Ask him what? Of course I didn't want to ask him. What if there was a reluctance to answer, a hint, perhaps, that he wasn't telling the truth.

I shook my head and Ted left, saying he'd be in touch the following day, or earlier if he found anything relevant. I watched him walk down the street, broad shoulders, stocky, straight-looking. Good old dependable Ted Parry. At the corner he turned and gave me the thumbs up and I waved back.

I cleaned up the bathroom, made the bed with clean sheets, picked up the shirt from the stairs and, after examining it, put it in the laundry basket. Doing something practical took my mind off things, a bit, but soon I was worrying again, thinking thoughts I didn't want to. I kept looking at the clock, my watch, the radio alarm to see when it would be time to expect Paul back.

Eventually I knew I had to do something so I rang him at work. He'd just left, I was told, so that meant another half an hour of waiting.

I stood at the window, looking down the road, cursing myself for my disappointment every time a figure came into view which wasn't his, even though I knew I hadn't left enough time.

At last, at long last, after eons of time had passed, I saw him, turning the corner at the end of the road, his red hair aflame, catching the last rays of the dying winter sun, walking quickly, not quickly enough, with a spring in his step.

I met him at the front door and he looked surprised, though pleased.

We kissed in the hall, a long kiss.

At last he drew away.

"Do you want some supper?" he asked.

"There's only one thing I want from you at the moment," I said and pressed my body up against his as we stood together in the hall.

"Insatiable," said Paul, but he responded. Our bodies moulded into each other with a relaxed, unreserved familiarity. We knew every aspect of each other's bodies, but there was still an excitement, enhanced today on my part at least by the new situation, by my relief at his return.

"Shall we go upstairs?" he asked, but I didn't want to go into our bedroom, that room.

"No. In here," I said, almost dragging him into the living room.

All at once I felt an almost frenzied elation. I wrenched at my pullover, pulling it over my head. I wanted the touch of skin on skin. I tore at my shirt, and the buttons shot across the floor. Paul laughed at my eagerness but then was caught up in the intensity of the passion.

I took the initiative, kicking off my trainers, unzipping my jeans and pulling both them and my underpants off, flinging them aside. Then, deciding that Paul's undressing was too slow, I did the same for him, pulling down his trousers, revealing his firm, flat belly with the tattoo above the curly spring of pubic hair, into which I buried my face, smelling the clean smell of soap and underneath the subtler, more arousing smell of man.

Paul's erection probed my chin, insistent, demanding attention, and I grasped its hardness, gently ran my tongue tip from helmet to base before enclosing the head of his long prick in the warm, wet closeness of my mouth. I cupped his ballsack in my hands and delicately fingered the passage between his fork. Paul gave a low moan of pleasure and arched with his hips so that his prick filled my mouth.

"Turn round," said Paul indistinctly, but I understood. We lay on the carpet and I swivelled my body so that it was above Paul's, my own cock imprisoned in Paul's mouth. My hands grasped Paul's boyish buttocks, a long middle finger probing into the secret fastness of his anus.

I lowered and raised myself so that the pricks were fucked in our mouths. I was in charge, dictating the rhythm, speeding the pulse. Then, as the excitement built up, the structure collapsed onto the carpet, and we rolled on our sides, two bodies coiled on the floor, naked as God intended, hands, tongues touching, caressing, stroking to a living flame the two elements of our separate beings, then the coming together in the orgasm.

Paul came with a great cry, and I, more quietly, a second or two later.

Half lying on the sofa afterwards, naked, though Paul still had on one sock, I held him tightly and looked at him as if I was seeing him for the first time. The glory of his red hair, on his head and down there, where the tattooed dragon swirled. I thought of that second letter which had talked about the tattoo. How had the writer seen it, unless...

Suddenly I shivered. It was cold in the room without the fire. We started to put our clothes on and Paul chatted. "Where are the summer days gone?" he asked. "Will there be a white Christmas?"

"One snowflake on the roof of the meteorological office in London constitutes a white Christmas," I said.

"I don't like winter," said Paul.

"Cuddling up with someone in front of a fire?"

"Yes, that's good," he said, and we went into the kitchen and started to get some food ready.

"But lying in the sunshine with the warmth on your body, that's really sexy," said Paul. "Do you remember that time on Hampstead Heath?"

I did indeed, could picture the green and gold of the afternoon, the sunlight glimmering through the delicate tracery of the leaves, making patterns on the ground, Paul and I lying naked on the grass, no, not naked. We had our shorts on, I remembered, though Paul had rolled his down to the level where the red-gold of his pubic hair showed and the dragon had frolicked in the sunlight. That dragon, which Paul had had tattooed after he and his previous lover, Joe, the one killed by Nick Warren, had returned from their holiday in Greece. No need to get mealy-mouthed, it was their honeymoon, but that was another time, and besides the wench was dead.

Afterwards we'd drunk wine and made love. The memory brought back every sensation; the fresh, clean smell of the turf, the warmth of the sun and of his body, the touch of flesh on flesh, the taste of the wine on his lips and tongue, the green and the gold, green shirt and red-gold hair, leaves, grass and the wild parsley that grew everywhere.

"We sunbathed there," I said. "Why didn't we strip off completely? We did afterwards if I remember rightly."

"Oh you know," he said with a smile. "You were doing your prudish dame bit. Didn't want me to strip off completely in front of Ted."

It came back to me. Of course we'd gone with Ted, but he'd had to go back on his own, on duty or something, leaving us alone, but he'd been there, when Paul had shown off the tattoo.

Something hit me. Realization, though for a moment I found it hard to believe. Ted? Friendly, sympathetic Ted? I knew he had a thing for me but… Things started falling into place. If I'd split with Paul, did he think I'd turn to him? Were his feelings for me so strong that he'd go to these lengths? Certainly he knew enough about us to write the letters. He could have got to the house before me, done the dirty and then come back again, to be sympathetic, to take away the evidence and, of course, to find nothing, while my suspicions about Paul grew and gnawed into our relationship.

Suddenly I felt sick, but I had to know.

"I've gotta go out," I said.

Paul gave me a startled look. "But supper's ready."

"It'll have to keep."

I ran out of the house and jumped into the car. I think I broke all the speed limits, but luckily there were few other vehicles around, and I arrived outside Ted's house without accident or being pulled over by the police. Ironic that!

Looking a bit apprehensive he opened the door after I'd angrily pounded on it and rung the bell a few times but his frown cleared when he saw who it was.

"You bastard," I said, wiping the smile from his face. "It was you. It was you all the time."

He didn't say a word, confirming I was right.

"Why the deceit? Why this vile way of attacking through Paul?"

His eyes filled with tears. Remorse? More from feeling sorry for himself.

"Why did you do it?" I asked.

"You don't know how I feel," he said eventually. "You were so happy with him, and yet you led me on. Remember the time at the gay club? You would have slept with me if we had had anywhere to go."

It was true, and I regretted it. To give up Paul and all that that stood for, for the sake of a one night mindless fuck. Yet it had been honest lust, not some devious, convoluted plot to blacken Paul in my mind.

"What were you trying to do? Split me up from Paul?"

The reply was delayed and hesitant. Perhaps he hadn't even worked out exactly what he hoped the outcome would be. Then as if dragged from him, "Yes."

I wanted to flail into him, punch him but good sense prevailed. He was stronger than me, stockier, with Rugby player muscles.

"Well, you've failed. You disgust me," I said ignoring the tears, ignoring the stricken look on his face.

"What are you going to do?"

I hadn't thought about it. By rights I should report him to the police, but of course he had all the evidence in his possession, anyway they were probably all his mates, and the police always stick together.

"I won't be seeing you again," I said and turned away. It was weak, but it was the best I could do. I blinked the tears from my eyes, not sure if they were rage, frustration or just sadness.

I went back to Paul and explanations and a dried up supper though I wasn't all that hungry.

CHAPTER SEVEN

Burn-Up

It was late as we turned into the street that led to our block of flats. We were suddenly aware that, at the other end, there was a red glow, a brightness that filled the exit leading out onto the High Street. Drawn by curiosity we went to investigate and joined a small crowd of bystanders who had either been passing or had been attracted by the sound of the fire engines to the scene. Over the road the Internet café, which we had christened "Gay Gladys" after its camp owner, was burning furiously, flames fanning out from the broken front window then flattened by the stone arch to make a canopy of fire. We could feel the heat on our faces.

Groups of firemen were directing streams of water into the fire which hissed and crackled as if resentful at being disturbed.

"Wow!" said Paul. "No more sexy pictures from there then."

"Serves then right," said a stocky onlooker with a red face and cropped hair to his two mates standing with him. "It was a place for queers."

One of them, presumably a little more politically correct, said, "You mean for gays."

The other laughed.

We watched as gradually the fire was brought under control, the flames dying down to be replaced by rolling clouds of acrid smoke and at last just damp spirals rising from the grey waterlogged ashes. Several policemen and other official-looking men in plain clothes were peering at the scene and making notes. A sergeant whom I recognized came over and asked the crowd to move on. There would be no more excitement that evening.

Well, of course it all depended on what he meant by excitement. I firmly intended that Paul and I should have a considerable amount of excitement before the night was out. I reached for and held his hand.

The red-faced man noticed. "Fuckin' poufs," he said.

I was about to respond in kind, but Paul squeezed my hand so I bit my lip.

"Hello, Tim, Paul," said the police sergeant, smiling. I knew Charlie Shepherd from way back. It's useful to have friends in the force for obvious reasons, especially now I had lost Ted Parry.

The red-faced man snorted with indignation. "Shit," he said, "even the police know them."

"How did it happen, Charlie?" I asked, being on first name terms with him.

He shrugged and gestured to the two guys in suits. "The accident investigation blokes are looking, but it'll be difficult to find anything until the whole thing goes cool."

"I feel sorry for Gladys," said Paul. "He's tried so hard to get things going, make it a success."

That's Paul, always thinking of others, considerate. Me? I was thinking of other, well, other things. "Come on," I said, "I want you, in bed."

"Okay," said Paul. That's another thing I like about Paul. He doesn't argue with me when I'm obviously as horny as a rutting mustang.

We turned away.

But it was not to be, or at least not immediately.

There was the sound of a car horn hooting desperately, and I could see a white Cavalier stopped by the police ribbon across the road. Apparently deciding that he was not going to be allowed through, the driver flung the door open, got out and strode towards what cindery remains there were of his shop. It was Gladys, carrying a case over his shoulder, hair dishevelled and blowing in the breeze, a pair of jeans and a leather jacket over a shirt of a rather virulent yellow. Looked as though he'd just got out of bed, which was where I wanted to be, mine and

Paul's, not his, of course.

John Gladwyn, Gladys to his friends.

"Oh God. Oh God." I heard him muttering as he got closer. "What a mess."

"Here's another one," said the red-faced man who seemed to be the main spokesman of the trio.

One of his companions sniggered. "Look at his handbag," he said.

"That's a shoulder bag," said the other one.

"It's a pouf-bag," said the red-faced one. They all thought this was very funny.

Gladys has a face a little like a camel, long, with a thick bottom lip, large rather complacent brown eyes with particularly long lashes. Tonight he looked distraught. Charlie stopped him or he would have been into the ashes and probably have incinerated his feet through his Gucci slip-on shoes.

"But I must see if there's anything I can salvage," protested Gladys.

"I'm sorry, sir," said Charlie, "but you'll have to wait until we're sure it's safe."

Gladys looked completely crazy, wringing his hands. "I don't believe it," he said.

"Why don't you go home and then come back in the morning," said Charlie.

"Drive all the way home?" He looked as if the concept was an impossibility.

Paul gave me a glance, raising his eyebrows in an unspoken question. I wasn't exactly sure what he had in mind but knew it would be considerate and probably thoughtful. I knew that it would probably also result in my not getting away as soon as I had hoped. I nodded though and felt his hand cup my right buttock, the fingers just inserting themselves into my cleft where they probed intimately.

"Come back and stay at our place, Gladys," he said, his voice normal, as if he weren't groping my rear end. "You'll be right next door in the morning."

Gladys was clearly torn. "I don't want to put you out," he said.

I felt I had to back up Paul's invitation, whatever it was doing to my sex life. "Sure," I said, "come over to our place."

Paul's middle finger showed his approval and I almost jumped.

We turned to go.

"Just a minute," said Charlie. "You can't leave your car there. We'll be opening the road later and it's blocking the way."

Gladys looked a bit as if he'd forgotten how to drive. "Give Tim the keys," said Paul. "He'll move it to our parking place."

Charlie gave us a cheerful wave and the red-faced guy gave a scowl.

Later we sat round the kitchen table and force-fed the shell-shocked Gladys with some microwaved chicken nuggets washed down by a particularly nasty white plonk, but, to some extent, it seemed to deaden his pain.

"I don't understand who could have done it," he said, clutching his head histrionically.

"Could have been an accident, an electrical fault," I suggested.

Gladys shook his head. "No, I'm sure someone did it out of spite."

"You are insured against fire?" asked Paul.

"Of course I am, darling, but it will take ages to build up the business again, premises, stock. By that time all the queens who came will have forgotten about it completely."

"Forgotten 'Gay Gladys'?" I said, hoping to cheer him up. "I doubt that's possible."

But he wouldn't be consoled.

Eventually I gave up the hopeless task and concentrated on casting lascivious glances at Paul.

He'd grown his hair longer now, and it hid those jutting ears that I found so beguiling. The light from a lamp over his left shoulder brought out natural gold highlights. He caught my eye and smiled, then looked seriously back at Gladys, nodding at something he'd said.

I wanted to run my fingers down the planes of his face, feeling the hollows of his eye sockets and the mounds of cheek, nose and chin. My phantom touch was arousing.

My Paul, my golden boy, the collar of his blue shirt open to reveal the column of his throat, which I love to kiss, and just the top of his white T-shirt. I see him as others would, tall and slim, curly golden-red hair, a serious expression on his face, the jaw line strong, straight nose, nostrils a little flared, brown eyes under arched eyebrows. I know him so well; know every expression from this quiet, contemplative one, through angry and happy, to the abandoned openness of unrestrained passion.

I imagine my hands straying down the sides of his neck, across his shoulders and chest, feeling the broad expanse of muscle and flesh through the thin material of his shirt. My fingers find the buttons and one by one undo them so that the shirt gapes open, my fingers entering and gently brushing the surface of the skin.

Lower and lower drift my caressing hands, undoing his belt and gently opening the zip of his jeans, allowing them to slide down to his ankles. My hands pass over the flat stomach, round the slim waist, around the back to cup the firm buttocks, then down the outside of the long slim legs. Then, teasing, the fingers stroke up the sensitive inside of his thighs to find and gently cup his ballsack, and finally to clasp his erection still in the restraining softness of his underwear.

"What do you think, Tim?" The question jerked me from the reverie. Paul was looking at me with a slight smile on his lips. For a moment I wondered whether he knew what I had been thinking, and I glanced at his groin to see if the erection I had imagined was in fact there.

"What do I think about what?" I asked. Obviously there was no way I could pretend I had been following the conversation.

"Will you take the case on?"

"The police will do it," I said. "The fire people will find out what caused it and then the police will do their best."

"Oh come on, Tim," said Paul. "I don't know how you'll ever hope to make a success of this P.I. business. You're always so reluctant to take on a case."

That was unfair. I needed the job. It was just that, as I said, the police would have it in hand, and anyway I wanted to get to bed. "Let's leave it until the morning," I said.

Paul turned to Gladys. "He'll do it," he said.

We parked Gladys on the sofa which pulls out into a sort of bed, not all that comfortable but it does at a pinch. Then we went to our room. I was surprised to find it was nearly two o'clock in the morning.

"I'm sure you'll help Gladys," said Paul. He sounded tired, and I knew I wasn't going to get my long-awaited sex that night. There was no way I would insist; Paul had to be up early for work in the morning.

"What makes him think it wasn't some kids?"

"Kids who are serial homophobes?"

I didn't know what he was talking about. "Serial?"

Paul yawned. "Weren't you listening at all? His wasn't the first gay place to get burned down. There was that pub, the Hussar, down Camden way."

"Coincidence?" I said vaguely. I remembered the incident now. It had happened about two weeks ago.

"And the club, 'Stinky Fingers'?"

I hadn't heard about that. It wasn't a club I'd ever been to. No one's ever accused me of being over particular, but the name didn't exactly inspire confidence. "All the more reason for the police to take it seriously if that's what's been going on."

"Oh you know them," said Paul. "If they think this is a gay thing, how much effort will they put into finding out who's responsible? Like gay-bashing."

I nodded. He was probably right.

Paul yawned again. "God, I'm whacked. Tell me about it tomorrow." I watched him as he stripped and almost fell into bed. He lay there, red hair dishevelled into curls on the pillow, looking at me. "What are you waiting for?" he asked. "Am I sleeping alone tonight?"

I joined him, and he cuddled into our old sleeping position, his back against my chest, his buttocks into my groin. I ran my hand down his stomach, into the hair at the base and felt for his cock.

"Mmmm," he said sleepily. "That's nice."

I could think of even nicer things, but it was pretty obvious that getting my jollies that night was out of the question. I even thought of Gladys next door, snoozing fitfully or perhaps lying awake with the worry. He wouldn't want to be disturbed by sounds of revelry. Personally I'm quiet in extremis but Paul has been known to utter wild shouts which I find quite exhilarating and indeed rewarding. Already Paul's breathing was low and regular, and I realized he was asleep so settled myself to do the same. Perhaps in the morning we could indulge in a bit of cosy one-on-one congress.

But it was not to be.

When I awoke Paul was already up and the place next to me was only slightly warm. Sounds from the kitchen and low conversation told me that he and Gladys were organizing breakfast. Or at least, when I wandered out in my shorts and a bleary smile, Paul was eating buttered toast and Gladys was looking gloomily out of the window from which he could just see the corner of his incinerated premises.

"I'm late," said Paul. "I'll leave you two to discuss." He gave me a buttery kiss and rushed out.

"Do you think it'll be okay to go and have a peek now?" asked Gladys. Clearly he didn't want a long, lingering breakfast.

"Hang on," I said. "I'll come with you. Just let me have a cup of coffee and put on some clothes."

Gladys sat down unwillingly and I poured him a cup, then drank mine while I dressed. "You'd best ring up the insurers," I said.

I heard him phoning and giving a not-very-coherent report to someone at the other end.

"Now tell me about these other burnings," I said through the open door when he'd finished.

Apparently both The Hussar and Stinky Fingers, top and bottom ends of the market, I guess, were owned by one Roderick Boyston. I didn't believe in the name either, but Gladys assured me the name was kosher.

"Did your and Boyston's establishments have anything in common?" I asked, "apart from the fact that they all catered for gays."

"What do you mean?"

"I don't know," I said. "Perhaps they all bought from the same supplier."

"I doubt it," said Gladys. "Rod would have bought alcohol mainly. I didn't have a license."

"Just clutching at straws," I said. "I think we'll find it was either an electrical fault, or kids." I emerged from the bedroom looking somewhat less than drop-dead gorgeous in a scrubby pair of jeans and a pullover. If we were going clambering over a cinder patch, I didn't see the need for dressing up.

Gladys was looking gloomy.

"Well, let's go and see," I said, giving up the idea of a more substantial breakfast.

The scene appeared even more depressing in the light of morning. A mist hung over the wreckage, looking as if there was still smoke coming from the derelict building, the blistered paint. Someone, the police I assumed, had hammered some boards across the door and now glassless window. Gladys gently picked at one of the planks as if he was wary of breaking his fingernails, but it was firmly nailed down. There was a smell of burnt wood and paint and plastic, and also something else.

"Can you smell it?" I asked. "Petrol."

Gladys nodded.

"You didn't keep petrol on the premises?"

"Of course not."

"Could have been used as an accelerant," I said.

It was a long, long morning, what with the insurers who turned up at 9.30, the police, who seemed upset that we'd crossed their line to investigate the damage, the fire investigators who confirmed that the fire had started at the door and spread inwards and upwards and was almost certainly started by petrol being poured through the letterbox. They'd actually found the remains of a burnt rag which presumably had been pushed in afterwards to set the whole thing off.

I held Gladys' hand, metaphorically, while he was interviewed by all of them and told the same story three times, that he was coming to the premises in the evening to do some clearing up when he had seen the fire, that, as far as he knew, he had no specific enemies who wished him, or his business, any harm, and that he was doing quite well, so that, unspoken comment, there wasn't much likelihood of his setting light to it himself to get the insurance money.

None of the interrogators seemed much interested in the other two fires, when I suggested there might be a common link. In fact one of the police muttered something which sounded like "coincidence," before he made a note of my comment in his diary. I knew that would never reach the light of day again.

Eventually I left Gladys pacing through the debris looking vainly for anything to salvage. I promised I'd be in touch as soon as I had anything to report.

The only person I could think of calling on was Roderick Boyston. I looked up his number, gave him a ring, explained who

I was and what I wanted and asked if I could call to see him. As owner of two gay clubs, I imagined him as fat, prosperous, middle-aged, and probably bald, and I couldn't have been more wrong.

He buzzed me up from the intercom, and I climbed the four flights of stairs to his door. He was tall and slim with a well-developed body under a dark blue open-necked shirt and some reasonably tight black trousers. His hair was black and designer tousled, looking as if he'd just run his fingers through it. Dark eyes, high cheekbones, olive, almost Mediterranean skin and, when he smiled, perfect teeth. Almost too good-looking to be true. He was probably a couple of years younger than me. Immediately I regretted not having gone home to change.

I shook his hand, introduced myself, apologized for looking like a tramp. His grip was firm, dry and warm. It lingered for just a little longer than was perhaps absolutely necessary. I told him that I was investigating last night's fire which had destroyed John Gladwyn's Internet cafe. He looked startled at the news, worried almost, but didn't comment.

His smart top floor flat made mine look like a hen-coop.

"Coffee?" he asked and without waiting for an answer poured me a cup of best Arabica from a flask on a warmer, none of your bog-standard instant for Mr. Boyston. He gestured to an armchair which seemed to enfold me in its depths as I sat down. He perched on the arm of one opposite.

"Poor old Gladys," he said. "He never did seem to have much luck."

"The police don't seem to want to connect it to your two fires," I said, "but it does seem a bit of a coincidence. Gay premises all three of them, and all in the same local area."

He looked noncommittal.

"Have you any ideas about who might have done it, Mr. Boyston?" I asked.

"Rod," he said, "call me Rod."

Subtly he had altered his stance, allowing his right leg to swing open, perhaps looking at me in a less than conventional way, a calculating, almost sexual manner. Suddenly I realized that Rod was coming on to me. His smile was no longer just polite, it was downright seductive. I could see the shape of his upper body under the midnight-blue shirt. His olive skin at the open neck was smooth and would, I was sure, feel velvety under my fingers. I felt my own cock stir and wondered, if Rod were to stand up, whether there would be an answering response inside those expensively-tailored black trousers.

I fumbled with the coffee cup, drank the last few drops and looked around for somewhere to put it.

He got up and took it from me. My question answered. There was a distinct bulge around the groin area. For a moment he stood in front of me, the projection at roughly eye level, or to be more accurate, mouth level, and I knew he was waiting for me to make a move, a grab, a grope. I was sorely tempted. I'd been frustrated since last night, and who, apart from me (and Rod), would know? I had no objection to mixing business with pleasure. I had done it before, but Paul was special, and though we had never sworn undying monogamy there was an unspoken undertaking that we'd more or less stay faithful.

So there were no excuses for what I did, and I knew I'd feel guilty afterwards, but that didn't stop my putting my hand onto the fork and feeling, through the material, the softness of scrotum and balls and then a hardening shape. Rod breathed deeply, and I grasped hold of his cock, using my other hand to find and draw down his zip, inside, the whiteness of underwear. His trousers slipped to his knees. I felt his hands on the back of my head drawing me towards him, and I could smell the exciting scent of man, see the outlined shape obviously impatient to be out of the confines.

I obliged and took it out, feeling the soft silkiness of the surface skin surrounding the hard stem. I kiss-licked the top, prepared to take the whole thing into my mouth when—

There was the sound of a key turning, a door opening, a call.

"Rod, you in?"

"Shit," he said and drew back hastily.

Frantic adjustment and doing up of zip fastener. Rod slipped back into his chair and I looked, I hope, composed.

"Come in, Dominic," said Rod. "We have a visitor."

Another tall, good-looking creature came into the room, though this one was more blond. Autocratic nose, the sort over which the owner looks down on the world. A mouth with a smile which bordered on a sneer. He was gorgeous. Unfortunately he knew it only too well. And he wasn't pleased to see me. He gave me what I can only describe as the sort of look usually reserved for the sight of a dog turd brought in on a shoe and now resting on a thick pile carpet.

"You brought back a bit of rough trade?" he said to Rod. The tone was unpleasant. I could see there were deep waters between these two.

I bridled. I know I wasn't wearing my best whistle and had been tramping over what could have been described as an incendiary bomb site all morning, but even so, I'd have thought my basic good breeding showed through. Obviously not! I tried to ignore the fact that, had he been ten minutes later, Rod and I might have been locked in some form of coital combination on the sitting room floor.

"This is Tim Sinclair," said Rod, ignoring the insinuation. "He's a private investigator. He's making enquiries about the fires. Apparently John Gladwyn's place was burned down last night. Tim, this is my partner, Dominic Bradley."

I was prepared to forgive Dominic his suspicions, especially as they were well-founded, so I held out my hand. It was ignored, as was I. "And what conclusions has he come to?" he asked, pointedly addressing his question to Rod.

"We haven't had much time, actually. I've only just arrived," I said.

"Looks like I was just in time then," said Dominic nastily.

"I was asking whether there was anyone Rod suspected," I said, after the briefest of pauses as I struggled to remember exactly what we had been talking about, before, before what nearly had happened, hadn't (if you see what I mean).

Rod cleared his throat. "There was a guy I had to sack about a week before the first fire," he said. "Found him with his hands where they shouldn't have been." He paused, perhaps thinking, as I did, that that was exactly what I had been doing a couple of moments earlier. "In the till," he added.

"He'd hardly have had a motive for the Gladys fire," I said.

"Unless he wanted to divert suspicion from the others," said Dominic.

"What's his name?" I asked.

"Sid," said Rod.

"Ah, easy to find," I said. "Sid what?"

"I don't know," said Rod. "He just drifted in, said his name was Sid and asked for a job at the Hussar. I needed someone so I took him on. He didn't stay long enough for us to get on intimate terms."

Dominic snorted. "Doesn't usually take you that long."

"What progress have the police made with the investigation into your fires?" I asked, jumping in before the fur started flying.

"Zilch," said Rod. "They don't really seem to be putting much effort into it."

I could see I wasn't going to get very far, not with Dominic here anyway, so after I asked a few questions about the M.O. (same as for Gladys, petrol through the door followed by a lighted rag) I left. Rod winked at me behind Dominic's back as I went out, but it was Dominic who saw me out. Perhaps he was afraid I'd hide in the stair cupboard and leap on Rod when he was alone.

"What do you think about these fires, Mr. Bradley?" I asked.

"Perhaps they deserved them," he said and shut the door

behind me.

The sun had burned off the morning mist and was now shining brightly. Even the London air, though with its perennial background of petrol fumes and exhaust gases, smelled reasonably fresh. A warm summer's day, temperature in the 20s. I decided that I needed sustenance. I'd missed breakfast and had only had a cup of coffee since. There was a café I knew at the end of the street so I made my way there avoiding the passersby, most of whom seemed to be coming my way.

Two youths barged through the crowd, almost running and obviously not giving a shit who they knocked into in their overtaking rush.

Coincidence, but I recognized one of them as he approached me. It was the red-faced guy who had been standing with his two mates, watching the fire last night and who had been so unpleasant about gays. For a moment I considered putting out my foot as he passed and tripping the guy up, but there were two of them, and I didn't feel in the mood for a fight, or, in fact, being beaten up.

They passed me and disappeared into the crowd as people filled in the space they left behind them. The café was on the corner, a couple of shops away, one of which was a sex shop, a gay sex shop. The windows were of course blanked out and the doorway hidden by one of those hanging curtains made from individual strands of silver chain. As always, whenever I pass one of these places I automatically try to glance in. Sometimes I even pay a visit, but this time my empty stomach took precedence so I walked by.

As I did so, a guy, youngish, attractive-ish pushed aside the curtain and burst out onto the pavement. In fact he came out with such momentum that he propelled himself right into my arms which I'd raised to protect myself. For a moment he remained there, and I clasped him, not unwillingly, I must admit.

"Nice," I said, "but we haven't been introduced."

He gasped for breath, temporarily winded, but wasn't in the

mood for pleasantries. "Fire," he said. "There's a fire in the back room." He looked around wildly as if he didn't know what to do. That sort of behaviour always brings out the masterful in me.

"Have you rung the Fire Brigade?" I asked.

The young man shook his head.

"Gotta phone?" I asked.

"In there," he said and nodded towards the shop.

Pretending to be brave, though feeling not-a-little foolish, I pulled aside the curtain and peered inside. All looked normal. "Where's the phone, and where's the fire?"

"Phone's on the counter, fire's in the back room. I told you." He joined me at the doorway, his body close to mine. I felt protective. He was very young.

The main room was like all the other sex shops I'd been into, lined with racks of magazines, empty video boxes and DVD cases. Behind the counter which ran down the right side of the shop were some sex toys. I could see an over-large penis marked with what looked like genital warts, not pretty. A door at the back of the shop was shut, presumably the back room. There were no customers.

"What did you see?" I asked.

"I opened the door and the whole room was ablaze. It's the store room," he said. "Lots of boxes, magazines and stuff. I slammed the door and ran out."

I knew it was unwise, but I had to have a look. It was hot inside the shop. I approached the back room door, reached for the handle but then decided against. I could feel the heat even through the wood. There was a smell of smoke, and as I looked a wisp appeared curling out between the top of the door and the jamb.

"Better ring 999," I said.

The guy dithered, so I stepped over and punched in the numbers. A female voice asked me which service I required. "Fire," I announced. "There's a fire at the Sex Shop in the High

Street. Think it's quite big. It's really hot in here."

"Can you get out?" she asked.

"Yes," I said.

"I should do so," she said.

I put the phone down. "Anything you want to save? If the fire gets through the door you will lose everything." I asked the guy. "The brigade's coming." I had a thought. "Is there anyone upstairs?"

The guy shook his head, then he opened the till and grabbed the money inside. A few ten pound notes and some change. Then he took the artificial penis and stuffed it inside his jacket. I sighed.

We went out and stood on the pavement. I introduced myself.

"I'm Sidney Lane," he said. "I'm the manager."

"Who owns the shop?" I asked.

"Rod," he said. "Rod Boyston."

Another coincidence? "I know him," I said.

"So do I." His tone was coy, and looking at his face I realized that he meant that in a special way. Suddenly something clicked in my mind. Sidney, Sid.

"Did you use to work at the Gay Hussar?" I asked.

He nodded. "Then Rod made me manager of this shop." He glanced fearfully inside to see if the fire had escaped from the back. There was more smoke but as yet no flames. I looked down the road to see if the engines were coming.

Rod had said that he'd had to sack a guy called Sid from the Hussar because he'd found him stealing. Surely he'd hardly have put the same guy in charge of another of his businesses. Unless…unless, it was all a lie to stop Dominic becoming too interested in Rod's relationship with Sid.

"So," I said, "you're quite friendly with Rod Boyston?"

"Oh yes. We get together quite regularly. He's a lovely person. Do you know he can actually…" But he was cut short from what would no doubt have been an intimate confession by the sound of a siren, and a fire engine turned the corner at the bottom of the High Street. I waved and it drew up next to us. Six lusty firemen jumped down, and we were immediately surrounded by butch masculinity.

"In there," I said, pointing out the obvious as the smoke was now flowing out in billowing waves.

One fireman went in with an axe while, with practiced familiarity, the hose was unrolled and two others took it inside. I heard a splintering crash as the door was smashed open and saw the flames leaping out as they were fuelled by the inrush of oxygen. I thanked my stars I hadn't opened that door.

A small crowd gathered, held back by another fire officer.

The hose belched water and after a short while managed to take control.

Another officer approached us. "Are you the one who called us?" he asked me.

I nodded. "But this is the manager," I said. "He found the fire."

Sid's moment of glory arrived. He rose to the occasion. "I went to the back room to get some new videos," he said. "It was a quiet time, no customers. I found the place alight so I shut the door and ran out, but Tim here said we should phone you." He smiled almost proudly, but unfortunately the huge plastic penis chose that moment to drop out from underneath his coat. It bounced twice and then lay on the pavement, pink and proud. The crowd guffawed. There was a brief pause while the fire officer looked down.

"Thank you, sir. I see you chose to rescue what you considered important."

Sid blushed. "I did take the contents of the till," he said defensively.

Poor Sid.

Leaving the firemen in charge, I took him to the cafe and

bought him a jam doughnut and a coffee, his choice. I had pie and chips as I'm on a diet.

He was a nice kid, if not very bright, and obviously besotted with Rod. While he chattered on about how lovely he was, I pondered about the fire, or as I thought of it, the latest fire. What worried me a bit was that whoever had started it had obviously used a different method. He, or she, I acknowledged, hadn't done it at night, nor had petrol been poured through a letter box followed by a lighted rag. In fact I had no idea how this fire had started. Sid swore that no one had gone into the storeroom that morning until he had. So how had it started?

The fire officer offered an explanation. The fire apparently hadn't started anywhere near the electrics. It seemed to have begun in the middle of the room where kindling of some sort had been piled so that it soon caught hold. "A smart arsonist," he told us, "can make a time-delayed incendiary device by mixing brake fluid and antifreeze in a Styrofoam coffee cup. He could plant the little bomb in some tinder at night and stroll away. Once the temperature reaches sixteen degrees Celsius the next morning, whoomph, you got fire."

So it could have been someone during the night.

"Was there any evidence of a break-in this morning?" I asked Sid after the firemen had gone and left soggy porn magazines all over the floor.

For a moment he looked uncomfortable, but then was obviously too ready to tell about his adventures to be embarrassed. "I stayed here overnight. Rod came and we slept, well, you know, in the room above. There's a bed and things there. Rod has it for occasional visitors."

I could imagine. I wondered what excuse he'd given Dominic for being away most of the night.

"But even so you must have locked the shop door."

"I think I may have forgotten, or perhaps Rod left it open when he left. At any rate I found it was unlocked when I came down to open the shop first thing."

"So anyone could have come in last night," I said.

Briefly the memory of a red-faced lout pushing past me just before the discovery of the fire jogged into my mind. Could he have been checking up on the state of his homemade bomb? The temperature was well into the 20s by then. If he had planted the device, he'd have been expecting sparks at least. But how would he have known the door was open? Or perhaps he had gone on the off-chance, expecting to have to break in, and the open door had been a bonus. I wondered why he, or indeed anyone, had changed their modus operandi. Perhaps to divert suspicion, make it seem an altogether unrelated crime.

I said goodbye to Sid, advising him to inform Rod of what had happened. Before I actually left he shyly thanked me for my help and handed me the artificial penis, giving me a diffident smile at the same time. I controlled an automatic cry of horror, not wishing to hurt his feelings, but it was hell trying to hide the ghastly object on the bus on the way home.

John Gladwyn was waiting outside his burned-out premises. He looked starved and miserable so I invited him back into the house for something to eat. I told him about my meeting with Rod. I don't think it was the information, but the very mention of Rod seemed to cheer him up.

"He's a nice guy," he said, smiling a bit.

I agreed, though I hadn't personally had much contact with him except for a brief—but I pushed that out of my mind guiltily. Paul would be home soon.

"And sexy too," said Gladys.

"Ah," I said, "so you've had experience."

He gave a sigh, a little reminiscent one as if of a happy memory. "I guess, just one of many. I'm surprised he didn't come on to you."

"Dominic was there," I said with a half-truth.

Gladys nodded, understanding.

Then I told him about the fire at the sex shop, in the middle of which Paul arrived, looking slim and scrumptious and sexy as always. Not that I could do anything about it with Gladys looking on.

I started again and told them about the fire and also my near miss with the red-faced guy. Gladys didn't know whom I was talking about but Paul did.

"I remember him," he said, "and his mates. One had jet black hair. He's got an odd sort of mouth, twisted, sort of smiling and sneering at the same time. Quite attractive." I gave him a look but said nothing. "The other one had brown greasy hair, longish, and a puffy, bland face which gave nothing away at all of what he was feeling or thinking."

It was an accurate description and certainly seemed to spark off some sort of memory for Gladys.

"I do know them. They used to hang around the café, creating trouble. A couple of times I had to get the police to give them a warning, get them off the premises."

"They were watching the fire last night," said Paul.

"Were they?" said Gladys. "I didn't see them."

I wasn't surprised. The state Gladys was in, he'd hardly have noticed if Joan of Arc herself had been standing by observing the conflagration with a hint of nostalgia.

"Do you know who they are? Their names?" I asked.

Gladys shook his head. "I suppose Lily Law would probably have a record," he said.

It was an idea. I gave my friend Sergeant Charlie Shepherd a ring. If he wasn't straight as a ruler I'd say that he fancied me, as he was always prepared to help me out with information, etc. I explained the situation. "There'd be some record, wouldn't there, Charlie, if they'd been interviewed by the police. Do you think you could have a search around and find out who they are?"

"No need, Tim," he said. "I talked to them myself. Nasty group of yobbos. You'd best keep clear of them." But he told me their names and an address, and I thanked him and rang off.

"Well, we know who they are and at least where one of them lives," I said.

"So, what do we do now?" asked Gladys.

"You go home," I said. "They know you, so you wouldn't be any use trailing them."

Gladys was a nice guy, but after more than thirty-six hours of abstinence, I wanted Paul all to myself for a while.

"Alone at last," said Paul, clasping his hands in a Victorian melodrama pastiche.

I entered into the spirit of the thing. "I'm at your mercy," I said. "Please treat me gently."

He twisted imaginary moustaches and advanced on me. I fell back onto the bed uttering a tiny shriek of alarm.

Paul changed roles. "Would sir like a massage?" he asked.

"Parts of me would," I said.

He put his hands on my chest. "Here?" he asked, standing by me and bending over.

"Stay there," I said. His groin was just on a level with my eyes. Gently I reached out and clasped the bulge, feeling the soft collection of balls and cock that I loved so much.

Already I could see the results of my ministrations as the bulge in Paul's groin grew, making a thick ridge that demanded attention. I unzipped his trousers to find a semi-erect cock needing to be rescued from his underwear.

"Beautiful," I said.

"I bet you say that to all the dicks you see," said Paul smiling.

"Come closer."

And attention it got, as I nuzzled his prick, gently nibbling it under its cotton covering, smelling the fresh, clean smell of his flesh and musky excitement. I tucked the elastic top under his balls so that his genitals hung over, topped by a golden-red bush of pubic hair.

From the top of his cock appeared a clear drop of liquid which I licked away, then the shaft which I traced with my tongue, and finally the ballsack with its sensitive burden of eggs, each of which received a tender and ardent sucking. Then I returned to the prick itself, taking it into my mouth while one hand massaged Paul's testicles and the other felt the crack between his buttocks, insinuating my middle finger into the hole.

Paul gave a soft moan of desire, opening up to my probing finger, pushing his hips so that my mouth took his prick right down to the roots where the curled hairs sprouted. He was impaled fore and aft, my tongue and finger which together enclosed his whole being, sucking out his essence while his orgasm built up in his loins. His head jerked back and from his throat emerged a cry of lust fulfilled. I gulped and swallowed as the juices spurted and felt the muscles in his arse contract at each spasm.

Paul gave a great shuddering sigh. We lay quietly for a while. At length I gave a moan of frustrated desire. Paul lay flat on his back looking up at me. He smiled and licked his lips with the tip of his tongue. I took this for an invitation. I grasped him with both hands, one on each side of his pelvis, gently turning him over. Limp, acquiescent, Paul allowed himself to be turned. I put a pillow underneath him so that the twin curves of his buttocks bulged upwards. They looked defenceless and white. Slowly, with great care I parted them to display his entrance, and entrancing it was.

It deserved a kiss and then more as my tongue licked, leaving moisture, lubricating. With a knee on either side, and the weight of me above him, I settled my hard warmness in the centre of his anus.

The sphincter muscles clenched automatically, but I lay on top, whispering my love. I pushed my hand underneath him, gripping his tool, rubbing it up and down, and, half-hard, he relaxed his arse. My prick slid in, in and then farther, was withdrawn and then pushed as far as it would go. Paul gave a sharp gasp, and then the excitement took over. He pressed his buttocks upwards into my pelvis, enclosing me with his warmth and tightness. My cock almost seemed to pierce him through. He and I were one, joined, linked together at the roots of our sexual being.

There were animal noises gradually rising to a crescendo of excited yelps as I pushed against him and felt Paul's tense body straining, the passion building up and then the orgasm pulse and pulse inside him. I shuddered and collapsed onto him, murmuring his name again and again.

We lay together, one on top of the other.

Afterwards we cleaned up and went out.

Unlike me, who only wants to cuddle up and go to sleep afterwards, Paul is a "get up and do something," guy, so, the relationship being what it was, we went out.

First to the address Charlie had given me, a seedy part of Kentish Town, the house a red brick Victorian with peeling paint and dingy windows, rather like our own. We stood on the opposite side of the road.

"So," said Paul, "what do we do now?"

"I guess, wait and see. I'm not going to knock on the door and ask if they can come out to play."

There were lights on in the downstairs windows and music, or what passed for music, blared out. I felt sorry for the neighbours. So, we stood outside for a quarter of an hour while the dusk deepened and the street lamps started to pop on one by one, orange brightening to sodium yellow. We felt conspicuous though there weren't many people about and the traffic was light.

That's one of the "perks" of being a P.I., hours and hours of just standing around waiting. Paul's been out with me before, and he always sets out with a sense of excitement, usually to be disillusioned when the boredom set in.

"There must be something we can do," he said, casually groping me.

"Insatiable." I sighed.

"Anyway. What makes you think these guys will do anything tonight?"

"I don't, but if what I think happened, they did two fires last night and got away with it. They're getting cocky, and cockiness means mistakes. So, I just want to follow them, see what they're up to, get to know their—"

I broke off. The music had suddenly stopped and the lights in the house disappeared. The front door opened and three guys came out, laughing and leaping around in a laddish sort of way.

"Get down," I whispered, and we crouched behind a car.

Not that we need have bothered as the trio took no notice of anyone around. They walked along the pavement, three abreast so that anyone who was coming along in the opposite direction had to step into the road. It was too easy following them, their noise made them obvious from way back.

What did I say about being cocky, making mistakes?

In the middle of the block, they turned right into a dimly lit alleyway which, presumably, led to the town and the main street. We followed carefully, but, not seeing them as we turned the corner, quickened our pace. Major mistake!

The street lamps were fewer in the alley, and the pools of light, giving a dramatic cast to the cobbles and piles of rubbish, were interspersed with zones of darkness which by contrast seemed impenetrably black.

It was from out of one of these that the figure of "red face" emerged. In the darkness a menacing figure, dressed in studded black leather jacket, baggy jeans and stout Doc Martens, kicking boots. We turned but behind us were the other two, "black hair" and "pudding face."

"You following us?" Red Face said. "Where are you off to at this time of night?"

"It's them two queers who were at the fire last night," said the one with no expression.

"Want to suck my dick?" asked the dark-haired one, a sneering invitation that was no invitation.

I assumed that the question was not serious and whatever answer I gave would be objected to. I said nothing, trying to edge past the lads who blocked our way.

"Not good enough for you?" The first sneered, the flat planes of his slab-like face distorted with an irrational anger and hatred. I managed to hit out and felt my fist sink into flesh before the lead attacker's foot shot out, catching the calf of Paul's leg and knocking him forward. He lost his balance and fell to the ground.

Two of them crowded round aiming vicious kicks at his groin and head while the leader hit out at me. I tried to get to Paul but a boot got me in the thigh. Shocks of pain spread through my body as I tried to protect myself with useless hands. We might have stood a chance, but we were outnumbered, and I knew we were for it. I hit out in all directions, but I doubted I was doing anything but prolonging the agony.

Suddenly there was a shout and I caught sight of another figure entering the alley from the way we had come. I despaired. Four of them now.

But the newcomer was swinging some sort of object on a rope, or so it looked like, and it wasn't aimed at us. He caught Pudding Face's head with a clunk that I could hear, even though I was occupied, and the guy dropped to the ground like a sack of soggy manure. Red Face was momentarily diverted, and I took the opportunity to kick him where it hurts most. He gave a strangled shriek and grabbed hold of himself. I turned to where Paul was lying, the last guy standing over him. Even as I did so, Paul grabbed the guy's foot as he aimed another kick and hoisted it up. He fell over backwards and hit his head on the cobbles. Paul got to his feet and came over to me. I looked at him anxiously.

"I'm okay," he said.

There was a pause, punctuated only by the groans of Red Face, holding his testicles. I turned to our rescuer. In the pale light of an obviously insufficient street lamp, I recognized the long camel face of Gladys, his features distorted in what must be an expression of triumph.

"What are you doing here?" I asked amazed.

"You think, just because I'm as camp as a row of tents, I can't do my bit in a fight? I followed you. Didn't want to miss out on the party."

I looked around. Two of the guys were limping off, but the one Gladys had hit was still flat out on the ground.

"What did you hit him with?"

Gladys looked rueful and held up his shoulder carrier. He shook it, and the contents rattled a bit. "Computer," he said. "Doubt if it'll be much use now."

"You can always claim for it by saying it was part of the stuff lost in the fire," I said.

His face cleared. "Good thing I download everything onto my hard disc at home," he said.

Paul went over to the shape on the ground. "I hope you haven't killed him," he said.

"What do you think he was trying to do to you?" I asked.

But the guy was coming round, moving and groaning. He put his hand to the side of his head.

"Jesus," he said. "What the fuck did you hit me with?"

"My handbag," said Gladys. "That'll teach you to mess with gays."

"Jesus," said the guy again, holding his head.

It seemed a good opportunity to probe. "Why are you setting fire to these gay places?" I asked.

For the first time the guy's pudding face showed some emotion. It was surprise, or rather bewilderment. "Setting fire?" he said. "We haven't set fire to anything."

For some reason I believed him. "Nor your mates?" I said.

"'Course not," he said. "Please can I go home? I gotta fucking headache."

I felt almost sorry for him. There was quite a lump on the side of his head. "Okay," I said, and he limped off into the night.

"So much for your theory," said Gladys.

"Let's go and have a drink," I said.

"There's a gay bar just down the road from the end of the alley," said Paul.

"How do you know?" I said irritably. I felt cross with myself; the fracas with the three had been my stupid fault after all, and here I was taking it out on Paul.

"It's no longer a bar," said Gladys. "It's been a club for ages, but I'm a member. We can get in."

So, however Paul had known about it, it had been a long time ago. I felt instantly contrite. I went to him and stroked his cheek. "How are your bruises, lover?" I asked.

"The same as yours, I guess," he said and kissed me there in the alleyway under the fitful street lights.

"Okay, lovebirds," said Gladys, "the first round's on me."

"We owe you for saving our butts," said Paul.

We went in on Gladys' membership card. The actual club was a single long rectangle of a room with a padded form running almost all the way round three sides of it for customers to sit on. A couple of doors made breaks in the seating. I assumed they were the conveniences and of course the entrance/exit. The fourth side was the bar. In the middle was a long narrow dancing space where two or three couples did a slow smooch to one of those records which have little melody but a slow, languorous beat. Decoration was minimal and relied on three of those revolving spheres covered with small squares of mirror glass on which coloured laser beams caught and reflected a myriad colors into all corners of the room. Anyone with a tendency to fits would have hated it.

The club wasn't all that crowded, a few young/old guys by themselves either looked around with a predatory air or, if in groups, chattered and laughed. Some seemed to know Gladys and called out a greeting. Gladys waved back regally and led the way to the bar. Behind it was a young man with thick dark eyebrows and nicely-filled jeans.

Or perhaps he wasn't so young! Though his hair was fashionably cut and his smile engaging, the lad's skin seemed to be almost too perfect for any but extreme youth, and underneath the almost professionally-applied make-up, there were tiny signs of crows' feet that I myself had noticed while looking at my own face in the shaving mirror, but which I hadn't felt the need to try to conceal.

"That's the owner," said Gladys. "His name's Don."

While we waited to be served I glanced around. The lights weren't too marvellous. Who wants glaring lights that reveal every imperfection in a gay bar? Someone came out of one of the doors. His figure for a moment looked familiar. "Isn't that…?" I started to ask, but the guy disappeared behind a pillar and when he came out was too much in the shadows to see clearly.

"Isn't what?" asked Paul.

"Never mind," I said. "He's gone now. I'll have a beer."

"Piña colada," said Paul, and then to Gladys' raised eyebrows, "Okay, a beer."

"Hi Gladys," said Don. "Sorry to hear about the fire."

"Seems to be getting a bit too frequent," said Gladys. "There was another one at the Sex Shop in the High Street today."

"No," said Don, his eyebrows joined in a frown. "That's Rod's place isn't it?"

"You know Rod Boyston?" I asked.

"Who doesn't?" said Don, removing the tops from three bottles and putting them on the counter in front of us.

"He's a nice guy," I said. "Met him for the first time today."

"Good sex too," said Don. The guy wasn't shy about his personal life. "Don't you think?"

I could feel Paul's body next to me suddenly grow rigid. I

pretended to ignore it.

"Don't know," I said casually. "The subject never came up."

"You'd know it if it did."

I veered the conversation onto safer ground. "Not many people in tonight." I said.

"You wait a bit," said Don. "It'll hot up later."

He was right. Hot up it did, and for some reason, though I couldn't exactly decide why, that worried me.

Even on a Tuesday the club reached its brightest and most eardrum-shattering best an hour later. Laser lights flashed and probed in time to the pounding rhythms, with the bass notes on drums and bass guitar, a tune on keyboard, romantic and haunting, contrapuntal to the throbbing pulse. The coloured beams of light reflected on skins shiny with sweat, lighting their masculinity and emphasizing sex, smells of aftershave, sweat and young, healthy manhood.

We drank, dropped the occasional E tab, courtesy of an obliging mate of Gladys, and had a marvellous time. I danced with Paul, and around us were all the others so that it seemed as if we were all dancing together, a dance that encompassed the whole gay community.

"I love you," I shouted to Paul. "You are the best thing that ever happened to me." I'm not even sure that he heard though a guy on my left gave me a look. Deciding that long-range communication was out of the question, I moved closer to Paul and whispered in his ear. "Must go to the loo," I said.

"You say the sweetest things," said Paul.

I weaved my way through the dancers to the door which I thought was the bog only to see a notice on it which said "Club Staff Only." It was the door out of which I had thought I'd seen the barely recognized guy come earlier. The one I thought was Dominic Bradley. Out of curiosity I put my hand on the door to see if it was open, only to take it back quickly. The wood was burning hot. A sudden memory jolted through me, something

Don had said about things heating up, and connecting with the fireman's information that a time-delayed device could burst into flame once the temperature reached the twenties.

A fire in this crowded room could be a tragedy. Turning, I ran round the edge of the room to the bar.

Don was still serving drinks.

I called him over.

"Be with you in a minute," he said.

"It's urgent," I said.

He came over.

"That room over there," I said, "the staff room. What is it?"

"Just a private room. I sleep there sometimes, the part-time bar staff have time off in there."

"I think there's a fire there," I said.

Don looked disbelieving.

"Ring the Fire Brigade," I suggested.

"It's been locked all evening," said Don, as if that would have made any difference to an accidental fire.

"Someone came out just after we arrived," I said.

"There's no key except that one," said Don, gesturing to a key hanging from a hook behind the bar.

"No one?" I said.

"Well, only Rod."

"That's it," I said. "It was Dominic who came out. I'm sure of it. You'd better ring 999."

"Dominic? Dominic Bradley?"

"Yes, don't you see. He's getting his own back on the people Rod has had it off with."

"But some of the places were Rod's own."

"Getting his own back on Rod," I said. "There isn't time to argue. Get the Fire Brigade."

But Don wasn't convinced. He took down the key and, ignoring the customers who were now clamouring for drinks, came out from behind the bar and approached the door of the staff rest room. He put the key into the lock.

"Don't open it quickly," I warned.

Too late. The door opened outwards and with it came a gout of flame, catching Don, who screamed and fell down, clutching his face.

Dancers froze in mid step, and there were confused shouts as people made their way towards the exit, some tripping over each other and making even more confusion and panic. I tried to shut the door but the flames were belching out, and it was too hot to get close. I compromised by dragging Don out by the heels.

"Somebody ring for the Fire Brigade and an ambulance," I shouted, hoping that at least some of them would have had the sense to bring mobiles, "and then get out." Not that they needed any encouragement to do this. "Can anyone help me with Don?"

There was a sudden sputtering of electrics and the lights went out, the music dying to an eerie wail, though the room was still lit by the leaping flames so that shadows danced on the walls.

I was vainly trying to lift him up when someone arrived to help, fighting his way through the mob trying to get out. It was Paul.

"Take his shoulders," I said, and picked up the lower half. "Has anyone phoned for help?"

"Gladys did," said Paul. Trust Gladys, the only guy who went out for an evening's entertainment armed with mobile phone, computer and God knows what other technological contraption, probably a satellite location device, in case he ever got lost.

The flames were licking at the walls now, the padded seats all round the room giving off thick, black smoke I knew was a killer. Bottles of alcohol from behind the bar burst and flared, sounding like gunshots. We had to get out. It was impossible to see to the end of the room where the exit was, but the shouts of people there gave us direction. "Get down on the ground and crawl," I said and together we crept across the floor dragging Don's body between us. It seemed to take an eternity. The flames crackled and all the time the air above us filled with smoke so that it became more and more difficult to breathe.

I started to choke. If we left Don here, we might get out safely. I was going to suggest this to Paul, but I couldn't breathe. The smoke was everywhere. There was no air. I was dying. Darkness and I knew I was dead.

Coming round was even more painful. My throat was so sore, I couldn't swallow. A great weight like someone sitting on my chest. A paramedic was asking me if I knew my name. "Where's Paul?" I croaked.

"Is your name Paul?" she asked.

"Tim," I said, or tried to say through my smoke-ravaged tonsils. "Where's Paul?"

"Just lie quietly, Paul," she said and tried to put an oxygen mask over my face.

I pushed it aside, suddenly panicking. "Where's Paul?" I struggled to sit up.

A hand clasped mine; a familiar voice sounded close to me.

"It's all right, Tim. I'm here."

"What about Don?" I asked.

"Lost his eyebrows."

I wanted to laugh, but it was too painful. "Dominic did it," I managed.

"Don't talk for the moment," said the paramedic.

"I know," said Paul, holding my hand. "We'll sort it all out later."

I lay back reassured. Everything would be all right. As soon as I got up and about again, I'd sort out the Dominic problem. He obviously couldn't be allowed to go on as a serial arsonist. I felt sure that Rod knew about it, or suspected at least. There was more to be done, but that could wait.

At the moment all I wanted was some rest, and Paul, and I was going to get both.

CHAPTER EIGHT

U.F.O.

Steps on an iron staircase, the echoing clang of metal doors, the smell of dirt and old sweat. Overall the pervasive sense of despair. All this summed up, for Nick Warren, the prison in which he was and would be incarcerated, unless some miracle happened, for the next five years. He sometimes wondered whether he would be able to cope with the sentence which seemed to stretch endlessly in front of him, minute by minute, hour by hour, day by day.

He couldn't stand the isolation which being so close to so many people seemed to accentuate, the bullying, the eruptions of violence from both fellow prisoners and prison officers alike. His cell mate, one Fred Green, a weedy chap with an angular face, yellow as a nicotine stain, breath to match, was perhaps the only person who showed any signs of understanding.

"You mustn't bottle it all up, mate," he said one evening, from the bottom bunk after the lights had flicked off and the echo of the clanging doors had died away down the corridor. "You've gotta do your time, get through it as well as you can."

"I shouldn't be here," said Nick.

"We all say that. All prisons are full of 'innocent' people."

"I don't mean I didn't do what I was found guilty of. It's just that I'd have got away with it, if it hadn't been for…" He paused.

"You got it in for some bent copper?"

"Some fucking private investigator sticking his fucking nose into my business. Found out more than he should have." He slammed his fist against the brick wall in frustration.

"And you think there's nothing you can do about it?"

Nick laughed, a hollow, mirthless laugh, "In here, in this

fucking soulless place?"

"There is a way," said Fred. "I have a friend outside who owes me and is prepared to carry out instructions. What's this guy's name?"

"Tim Sinclair," said Nick. "How far will your friend go?"

"All the way," said Fred. "Tomorrow I can get in touch."

"You'd do that for me?"

"I'd want something in exchange," said Fred.

"What?"

There was no answer, but Nick felt a hand come up from the bunk below, grasp his knee and then climb slowly towards his groin.

"All the way," said Fred in a lust-filled whisper. "In exchange."

Nick tensed and then relaxed. It was dark, and anyway he was fucking horny. Certainly he would have no intention of allowing this to happen again, not with Fred Green at any rate, but he could put up with it this once if it meant getting back at Tim Sinclair and that red-haired fancy boy of his.

He didn't look like an alien when he walked into my office. He was just an ordinary sort of young man, clean cut, nice eyebrows, shortish, cropped hair, though not a skinhead, wearing a grey, loose-fitting sweatshirt and nicely fitting trousers. The sort of guy who looked as if he ought to be holding a basketball; cute, next-door type. About twenty-six, I guessed, which is my age. Nothing like the loopy freak I immediately classed him as when he started out on his story.

"Mr. Sinclair," he said, coming through the door with its black painted name and the initials "P.I." to show my profession.

He had such a pleasant, candid smile; not just lips and teeth, but it seemed to include his eyes as well, that I immediately said, "Tim," even though I usually prefer clients to be on a not too familiar level, at any rate to start off with.

"Hi," he said. "Mike Lowell. Mike will do fine."

I gestured to the only other seat in front of my desk, and he sat down, arranging his legs comfortably, looking at ease, which was good. Too often my clients are jumpy, nervous, not knowing how to start their tales of woe. Anyway, he certainly cheered up my office with its scruffy old furniture and lack of anything pleasant to look at. I wondered whether I ought to get some pictures to brighten the bland, magnolia-painted walls.

"Coffee, Mike?" I asked, but he shook his head, which was a wise decision as I know how dreadful my instant coffee can be.

"How can I help, Mike?" I asked.

"This is going to sound a bit weird," he said. "You see, I've been kidnapped by aliens, and I think they turned me into one."

Problem. How to react? One: the, you must be making a joke, so, "It doesn't show, Mike. I mean you haven't gone green or got antennae coming out of your head." Two: the flatly disbelieving, "I'm sorry I don't have time to take screwballs seriously, so please stop wasting my time."

I compromised, nodded as if it was a perfectly reasonable statement and waited for the punch line.

"I suppose you want the details," he said.

I pondered. The guy was obviously nutty, though I didn't think dangerous. Perhaps a bit simple, but I had nothing better to do. There were no outstanding cases, and I had no appointments for the morning. In fact, as always, business was scarce, another word for non-existent. The deciding factor, I admit it, was that he was nice to look at. So I said, "Yes, please," and got out my notebook and biro.

"We were in the pub," he said, "and the talk got round to football."

I sighed inwardly, feeling depressed. Two things I can't stand are straight pubs and the game of football. I mean twenty-two butch sportsmen are fine to drool over, but the shorts the guys wear have become much too long, and baggy, and the sort of discussion which goes on in pubs about footballers isn't often about what tackle they've got under the shorts and whether they'd be willing to share it out amongst members of their own sex. It's usually about tactics and whether a four-two-four is better than a five-three-two formation. I mean - big yawn.

"But, I'm not all that into football," he went on, and I warmed to him. "So I changed the subject to aliens. That's more my interest."

I stared at him, trying to imagine the scene. Four guys (would it be?) holding their pints of lager, no bottles probably, chatting about the relative merits of Millwall or the Gunners, and suddenly Mike here says something like, "I bet aliens from outer space could get up a better team than either of those."

"How did that go down with your mates?" I asked.

He gave me a look of surprise, eyebrows raised, eyes widening, staring into mine, brown eyes, straightforward, beautiful.

"I guess they were okay," he said. "They know I like to talk about space and stuff."

"And do they believe in it, like you do?"

"They think it's funny, but they've stopped trying to talk me out of it."

"Good friends," I said.

"The best." He smiled, and his face lit up. For a moment I forgot the impossible story I was hearing and almost started believing him.

"The kidnapping," I reminded him.

"Oh yes. It was later the same night. I'd had quite a lot to drink."

"You didn't try to drive home, I hope," I said. It was a bit like talking to a child, in a man's body.

"No way. Joe was driving me home in his car."

"Joe being?"'

"My best friend. He always looks after me. Anyway, I'd dozed off in the front seat when suddenly he jammed on the brakes. Good thing I'd got the safety belt on, or I'd have been through the windscreen. Of course I woke up, and there was this bright light shining through the glass."

"From above?" I asked.

"No," said Mike. "It was in the road in front of us, but so bright I couldn't see what was behind it, but Joe was scared. He swore and jumped out of the car and took off."

"Some friend."

"He was going for help I guess."

"To rescue you from a light?" I tried to sound incredulous.

For a second Mike seemed bewildered. "No, no," he protested. "It was a ship, an alien ship."

"You saw it?"

Mike shook his head. "No, I only saw the light, but I was taken into it."

"Tell me."

"I was almost blinded by the light," he said. "For a moment I couldn't understand what was going on. Then these four people suddenly came up to the car, opened the door and pulled me out."

"People?"

"Aliens."

"You knew they were aliens?"

"They had sort of grey smooth skin and faces with big almond shaped eyes, no hair, no noses, just holes for mouths." He didn't sound frightened or angry, and he obviously believed in what he was saying.

"Clothes?"

"No clothes," he said, "unless the grey smooth skin was a sort of covering."

"Like Lycra?" I suggested.

Mike nodded. "Smooth and shiny and close-fitting."

I was pruriently curious. "And did they have, you know, breasts and genitals?"

Mike looked uncomfortable. "Not exactly," he said. "They all seemed to be male. Er - they had bulges."

I was quite interested, but felt I couldn't afford to probe too deeply into that aspect. "And they took you into this space ship?" I asked.

"Sure. Though they blindfolded me first, but when they took it off, it was obvious where I was."

"Sort of high-tech equipment? Flashing lights? Low background hum? Like the set of Star Trek?"

He looked at me almost suspiciously. "That's right. You haven't been kidnapped too, have you?"

"What did they do to you?" I asked.

"They put me on this sort of operating table, held me down and stripped me bollock naked. Then they fastened my wrists and ankles so that I was sort of spread-eagled and…"

My somewhat fertile imagination pictured the event. It was quite exciting. "You struggled, of course," I said.

"At first," he said, "but their investigation when it got, down there—" he glanced down at his groin "—was…er…" he hesitated, searching for the right word.

"Arousing," I suggested.

"Certainly not," he said, obviously not understanding, "but I got a hard-on. They were very interested in that, got quite excited. Chattered away in their sort of twittery language. Kept touching it and stroking it."

"They didn't speak English."

"'Course not. They were aliens I told you."

"And did you, did you have an orgasm?"

"I came, if that's what you mean, and they collected it in a bottle. Perhaps they wanted it for analysis. It was quite a lot," he said proudly.

This was getting a bit spooky. "How," I began, and found out that I was speaking in a high-pitched squeak, so I sank an octave, "how did they make you into an alien?"

He blushed. "They turned me over," he said, and paused.

"And?"

"And they porked me."

"Using a condom, I hope."

"Aliens don't need condoms."

I was cross. "You let four pricks fuck you and didn't use protection. That was seriously stupid, Mike. Don't you realize what diseases you could catch from that? Have you been tested?"

"They didn't use their cocks."

That took me back. "What did they use then?"

"I think it was a sort of syringe, shaped like a cock though."

"They fucked you with a dildo?"

"I suppose so."

"How did that make you feel?"

"Hurt a bit at first, but after it was good. Wished it could have been a real prick though."

"And afterwards?"

"Afterwards I was different. I had powers I didn't have before. I was an alien." He looked at me with that frank, open gaze. I knew he believed it implicitly, but the story seemed full of holes to me, or at least sounded like an elaborate practical joke. I could imagine his "best" mates sitting around planning it. "Let's play a joke on Mike. He believes in aliens so we'll kidnap him, make believe he's been caught by men from Mars and have a bit of fun with him."

"It wasn't like that," Mike said.

"Like what?"

"A practical joke. Joe wouldn't do that to me."

I stared at him. I hadn't said a word. Somehow it seemed that he'd read my mind, but that was impossible. Surely he must have just interpreted my doubtful look and had a lucky result.

"I can you know."

"Can what?"

"Read your mind."

Jesus, I thought. That was incredible. I looked at him. A final test. There he was sitting opposite me, broad chest covered by a grey T-shirt, strong thighs, I could see the muscles under the material of his trousers. An unmistakable bulge in the groin. I'd like to fuck you, I thought.

"Come on then," he said, smiling.

"And did you?" asked Paul.

"Certainly not," I said. "As if I would."

It was late evening, and my partner, Paul Massingham, and I were sitting at home in that quiet time after the evening meal, not sure whether it was worthwhile switching on the TV, still chatting about the day's events.

"There was a time when you'd have needed much less encouragement than that to fling yourself on and into any available guy," said Paul smiling.

It was true, but I'd long ago decided that Paul was much too precious to me to risk losing for a temporary fuck, however easily attainable, or at least I thought so. "I was just testing him," I said.

"You believe he could read your mind?"

"Not really. Lucky guess," I said and then added, "Probably."

"What did he want you to do?"

"Apart from fuck him? I don't really know. Find out the truth, I guess."

"It's an odd story. Is he as innocent as he sounds?"

"I think he believes everything he claims happened," I said.

Paul frowned. "So, what are you going to do?"

"I'll get in touch with this 'best friend' of his, Joe, tomorrow and see what he has to say."

Paul nodded though in an absentminded sort of way.

"Don't you think that's sensible?"

He seemed to pull himself together. "What? Yeah, sure."

"Is anything the matter?" I turned to look him full in the face. He looked tired, no, perhaps more worried. There were some vague shadow-circles under his eyes. To me, as always, he was infinitely desirable.

"You look worn-out," I said. "I'll make us some coffee." I stood up and switched on the side lamp. It lit up his red hair, his white T-shirt, a smile that was so attractive that it could persuade me into doing absolutely anything.

He said, "Kiss me before you go."

"Go?" I said, mystified. "I'm only going to the kitchen."

"Kiss me," said Paul and there was an urgency in his tone that made me look at him intently. I saw the smile, the eyebrows raised quizzically, the lock of red hair that always flopped uncontrollably over his forehead, the highlights dyed a coppery orange by the touch of the lamp.

I brushed the waiting lips with mine. "A proper kiss," Paul demanded and took me in his arms.

His lips, soft and inviting, pressed like a contract against mine and then opened to allow his agile tongue to enter my mouth, to find and embrace my tongue, to play up my hormones and arouse my prick so that our erections pressed hard against each other. I felt my emotions surge. This was my love, my life, my all. I had never felt like this about anyone else before, and was sure I never would again. The kiss seemed to go on forever. The world turned but here it stayed still.

"Are you sure there's nothing wrong?" I asked.

His hand strayed down and grasped my cock. "Doesn't seem anything wrong here," he said.

Which led to other things, the coffee forgotten, and I didn't pursue whatever might have been troubling my lover, to my later regret.

The following morning I gave Paul a lift to work. I don't usually take the car into Central London, but I knew I'd need it later to get to Joe's place of work. Paul seemed pleased to get the lift, and I put it down to not having to struggle with the crowds in the tube. Traffic, though, was heavy, and he was almost late by the time we reached Green Park station, the underground station he usually went to. Just goes to show that the tube is quicker than a car when we're talking about traffic in London.

Paul seemed to want me to take him further. He works in Shepherd's Market which is a bit further along the road towards Marble Arch, but by then the traffic had slowed to an almost dead stop, and I suggested he'd be quicker if he walked. He'd even be on time if he relied on his feet.

Reluctantly, it seemed, he got out of the car, looking round as he did so and then walking on. I watched my partner's back as he walked away, his body slim and elegant, his buttocks moving easily, athletically under the cloth of his jeans, his shoulders broad, his waist narrow. A couple of times he half turned to look back. At first I thought he was looking at me, caught in my jam, but he didn't answer my wave. I looked to see if there was perhaps someone from his office behind him, but couldn't see anyone I recognized.

Eventually he disappeared into the press of people.

Something happened ahead and the line of cars moved and for a moment I thought I'd be able to catch up again with Paul. I could see his red hair which made him stand out from the rest of the morning rush hour crowd, but we ground to a halt and again he disappeared.

Then I saw this guy, or at least I saw someone, behaving in a way I recognized, recognized because I'd done it myself so many times. The guy was following someone without wanting to be noticed. In crowds it's difficult because it's so easy to lose the prey. Hidden by others they can slip into a shop, and no one the wiser. This guy was careful. He kept behind others but his eyes were, I'm sure, on that distinctive red hair. As he drew level with me I got a good look at him.

His own hair was black and uncut and needed a good wash. Thick eyebrows arched above cold and unfeeling eyes. He had a bristle of stubble on his cheeks and chin. He didn't exactly look dirty, but he was hard and street-toughened. I knew the type. He'd probably started out as a petty thief in his early teens, and now he'd graduated to something much more dangerous. For a moment a feeling of fear caught at me, but there was nothing I could do. I couldn't leave the car here, but then, I reasoned, nor could he do anything to Paul in these crowded conditions.

I wondered if I'd made a mistake. Perhaps he wasn't after Paul at all. Again the car ahead moved forward, and I followed. Momentarily the crowd thinned and I saw Paul again. He was going up the steps to the building where he worked. He reached the top and went inside. I looked for the black-haired guy but couldn't see him. At least I was sure he hadn't followed Paul into the building, and I breathed a sigh of relief.

Imagination can do funny things.

"Joe" turned out to be a not-unlikeable lad who worked as a warehouse assistant in an electrical wholesale firm on the outskirts of Islington. He appeared to be in his early twenties. I caught him on his lunch break where he was having a kick-around in the yard with some other employees. He was tall and thin with straight, straw-coloured hair and a cheerful smile. The only really noticeable physical characteristic that made him stand out was a slight cast in one eye, so that it was sometimes difficult to know where he was actually looking. Like the others he was wearing a pair of blue overalls and a T-shirt.

He didn't seem to mind my taking him away from his scratch

game of footie and down the road to a hole in the wall pub with hard wooden benches for a swift half, which actually turned into quite a few pints; the lad could certainly take his ale. I didn't mind buying, though I kept my own intake down.

"Tell me about the evening when Mike says he was kidnapped by aliens," I said.

I wasn't sure whether his inability to look me straight in the eye was due to his astigmatism or a feeling of guilt.

"That Mike," he said, "he sometimes imagines things." He sounded uncomfortable though I may have fancied it.

"So, what really happened?" I asked. "I've got Mike's version, but you were in the car with him driving home. What did you see?"

"What did he say?" asked Joe.

"You first," I said.

"It was really strange," said Joe. "There was this bright light in the middle of the road suddenly shining straight at me. At first I thought it was it was the headlights of a car or lorry, but there was just the one light. I braked and skidded a bit but didn't hit anything. Mike was asleep but obviously woke up when I stopped. I got out to investigate."

Well, so far, that corroborated Mike's story.

"What did you find?"

His wandering eye failed to make contact with mine. "Nothing," he said. "I don't remember what happened. All I know was that when I got back to the car Mike was inside, but it was two hours later. Somehow we'd lost two hours."

Oh yes, I thought, the old lost-time scenario. And almost impossible to prove or disprove, especially if Mike stuck to his story.

"Where exactly did this happen?"

Joe was vague. "Out of town a bit," he said.

"A little more specific."

He hesitated, disguised it with a swallow from his glass, then said, "On the stretch of road between Potters Bar and Barnet."

I knew the area; my sister lives in Hatfield and to visit her I have to take that route. "Can you tell me where on the road you stopped?"

He seemed to make up his mind seeing that my persistence was not to be ignored. "I can show you, if you've got a car. We'll go now, if you like."

"What about your work?"

Joe shrugged. Obviously he took quite a cavalier approach to his job, but it was nothing to do with me, so I got up. As he stood, Joe staggered slightly, and I put out my hand to steady him. I could feel the hard muscle under his overall. In spite of the drinking, he looked, and felt, fit.

He slumped down comfortably into the passenger seat, hands resting in his lap as we drove north out of London. The traffic was light, and the sun came out as we passed East Finchley and took the Barnet road. We hadn't spoken for a while, and I took a sideways glance. His hands were rubbing himself and there was a sizable cock shape outlined under the blue material of his overalls. I figured he couldn't be wearing any underwear.

Shit, I thought, why was it that, now that I was in a stable relationship, people seemed to come on to me all the time whereas while I was single and available I could scarcely find cock for love or money. It wasn't fair.

I tried to concentrate on the road. Not easy!

We passed Barnet church and got into the real country. Town houses gave way to open fields on one side and a wooded area on the other.

"I need a piss," said Joe.

There was a lay-by just ahead so I pulled over. He could take his piss hidden from any passing cars behind some thick scrub by the edge of the road, but when I stopped it didn't seem to be all that urgent. His hands went for my groin and found a growing tumescence. Just to be sociable I reached over and felt his. A mutual companionable grope would be fine, I thought. Nothing heavy, nothing serious. Nothing to feel guilty about, but Joe was having none of this. Suddenly his head was in my lap, and my cock was out of my trousers and in his mouth, where lips and tongue gave it a really significant workout. I don't think I've ever experienced such mobility as I was taken in and in and in. His left hand fondled my ballsack and his middle finger probed underneath so insistently that I was forced to lift myself so that it could find access to my arse.

I was pleasurably entertained, and the people in the cars driving by us couldn't see below the level of the driving wheel where all the action was taking place, but anyone in the passenger seats of the much higher lorries had a pretty good overview. In fact one must have conveyed the news to the driver, for a long blast on the horn as he disappeared into the distance expressed either disapproval or regret. I only hoped that Joe's back would have been mistaken for that of a female.

Nevertheless, and in spite of the mounting excitement I was feeling, the imminent danger of another car swinging into the lay-by or a lorry grinding to a halt, made me protest.

"Joe," I said, "hold on. Pleasant as this is, we were looking for the place where you stopped when whatever it was shone the light at you."

He took a moment off from his sucking efforts "We're here," he said and raised a spare arm to point out of the window where some black skid marks on the other side of the road indicated a vehicle had braked suddenly. His probing finger found a place which sparked off something really stimulating. I could feel the juices stirring.

"Nggg," I said, or something like that. "We nearly are here, but this isn't a good place. There are guys passing all the time."

He stopped, and I tried to calm myself. I took a long breath, some of it disappointment and frustration.

"There's a hut over there," he said.

I didn't ask how he knew. Perhaps this was a regular haunt of his.

It was a wooden construction painted black on the outside with a single window that had been boarded up, perhaps a relic of some hole in the road repair job which had failed to be removed. The door was fastened with a chain and padlock which looked secure, but the board to which it was fastened was loose, and Joe had no trouble opening it. He slipped inside, and I, after a brief hesitation and with somewhat mixed feelings, followed him.

After the sunlight outside, inside was pitch black. Whatever its ramshackle appearance, the hut was apparently well-built and not a chink of light came through the boards. I could see nothing, but obviously I was silhouetted against the rectangular light of the doorway, and Joe could see me, or at least my outline.

I felt an arm grab hold of me, pull me in so suddenly that I lost my balance and fell on the floor. His body fell on top of me, fingers scrabbling at my clothes, wrenching at the fastenings, pulling them aside so that soon I was as good as naked, the bunched up clothes at ankle and wrist. He, on the other hand, was naked. He'd used the short interval while I hesitated outside to strip himself of overalls and T-shirt. I suspected that he'd had a lot of practice.

I could feel Joe's cock, hard and thrusting, against my stomach and knew that mine was erect as well. Joe could not keep still. Like a young animal he worried and played with me uttering little whimpers of enjoyment. First his head was under my arms and I felt a tongue licking the bushy hair, then in an instant his head lay on my stomach and his teeth were gently nibbling at my skin. Meanwhile one hand was on my chest, the fingers playing with my right nipple while the other hand crawled up the inside of my thigh until it reached just below my scrotum. I was entranced; it was as if I were having sex with at least three people. I tried to respond by grabbing hold of him, but Joe would not allow himself to be caught, first rolling aside and then almost immediately rolling back to mould to my body all the way down, lips kissing mine, chest and stomach joined, my legs under Joe's, my cock imprisoned, happy captive, in the moist fork between his legs.

Now Joe was quiet and still, his lips gently meeting mine, and then the point of his tongue emerged, insistently probing inside mine, past my teeth, into my mouth and meeting my answering tongue, tasting the saliva, joining our two tongues. It was as if this inspired a fresh urgency in our groins, each pushing against the other, his hands cupping my buttocks, the middle finger of his right hand now exploring the deepness of my cleft until it found and entered the crinkled hole. I gasped. I was aware of what Joe wanted and knew that this was what I wanted too. Joe was taking the initiative. I felt another finger inserted and both moved, enlarging the hole. I opened my legs and then raised my knees so that the access could be easier, and the fingers probed deeper.

Now Joe's cock had found the cleft, and I experienced a moment of caution. "Safe sex," I muttered. I heard him laugh, and I reached down to find his cock was already protected, the surface slick with lubrication. Talk about Speedy Gonzales! What a wizard. I raised myself up even further, Joe's body between my legs, his cock piercing the sphincter, sliding in and out, finding the special place.

Again there were little animal noises gradually rising to a crescendo of excited yelps, and I pushed against him and felt Joe's tense body straining, the passion building up and then the orgasm pulse and pulse inside me. He shuddered and collapsed on top of me.

I finished off with him still inside, rubbing myself against his belly.

All over, and the troublesome task of cleaning up and, in my case, dealing with the guilt, remained. I couldn't find my clothes and groped around for them before giving up.

"You'll have to open the door and let some light in, Joe," I said. "I've lost my shirt and jeans."

There was a hint of a chuckle from somewhere in the

darkness, and suddenly a light appeared from a bulb hanging in the ceiling. I hadn't realized there was electricity on. Joe was almost dressed. He was incredible with clothes. I picked up the scattered remnants of mine and struggled into them. Now I could see clearly, there wasn't much inside the hut of interest. A wooden table on trestles stood against one wall and a few traffic cones were piled up in a corner. Reasonably presentable, I made for the door when something caught my eye. Under the table were a tangle of wires and a glint of red. I inspected. It was a series of LED bulbs attached to a transformer. It seemed unlikely road repair equipment.

"What's this?" I said.

Joe looked. "Rubbish," he said dismissively.

But I wasn't to be put off. There was a power point in the wall under the trestle table and I plugged in. Immediately they came to life and started winking in a steady pattern.

"Joe," I said. "This was where you had your joke on Mike wasn't it? The 'operating table,'" I pointed to the trestle. "And here, part of the 'alien technology'?" The lights blinked accusingly.

Joe's roving eye steadied. He looked me full in the face and then nodded. "It was only a bit of sport," he said. "Mike didn't really mind. He enjoyed it. Well, the sex bit."

"The costumes?"

"The masks were from the local 'Hire a Costume' place. The body stuff was from the Cycle Club."

"He thinks he's an alien," I said.

Joe seemed to find that funny. I suppose it was in a way. Mike loved and believed in his aliens. Would showing him it had all been a trick, disappoint him?

"I'll have to tell him," I said. "He's employed me to find out."

Joe shrugged. "Tell him then," he said. "I'll make it up to him if he's upset." He winked suggestively, and I was sure he would.

"I'll take you back," I said.

That evening I told a suitably edited version of the afternoon's events to Paul. "Afterwards I dropped Joe off at his work place which he entered cockily and with a grin. I'd no idea what story he'd tell for taking the afternoon off, but I was sure he'd get away with it."

"So it was a joke all the time," Paul said. He glanced out of the window. "Have you told Mike?"

"I suggested we meet this evening in the William IV pub in Hampstead. You'll come along too, won't you?"

There was a brief hesitation and Paul again looked out of the window. This time I really noticed.

"What's the matter? What's out there?"

Paul shook his head. "Nothing."

"So what's with the 'out of the window' casual but frequent glancing?"

He couldn't help it. He looked out again. Suddenly things clicked in my head. Occasionally I am a P.I. "This morning," I said," when I took you to work, there was a guy following. I wasn't sure at the time."

"Black hair, sort of hard eyes?"

I nodded.

"He's been doing it for the past few days. I've managed to give him the slip most times, but today he was behind me when I got to the end of the road. What do you think he wants?"

"Let's ask him," I said. I went over to the window and looked up and down the road. There was no one in sight. Nor did the guy appear as we got ready to go out, and there was no sign of him as we went to the tube station, the Angel, Islington, and then seven stops on the Edgware branch of the Northern line to Hampstead. If the guy was following us, he was good. Neither of us saw anything, though at that time of the evening, the platforms and trains were crowded.

Hampstead is the deepest station on the Underground, and we emerged from the lifts into pleasant evening dusk. The sun was sinking behind a bank of clouds over Hampstead Heath towards the west. Mike was waiting at the pub, sitting in the garden, if you can dignify the small square paved courtyard dotted with a few potted shrubs by the name. He waved and we went through the pub where I bought three pints and joined him.

He smiled when I introduced Paul, obviously liking him. We sat down, and I started on my explanation.

"Mike," I said, "I had a chat with Joe this afternoon."

"Yes, I know," he said, which brought me up short. I hadn't expected that they would have been in touch so soon.

"He admitted that the meeting with the aliens was all a joke. It was just a bit of fun, knowing how keen you are on aliens and stuff. They mocked up an old shed on the Potters Bar Road and…"

I tapered off. Mike was smiling.

"Of course," he said. "That's what they made him believe. Aliens can do anything."

"No," I said. "You don't understand. I saw the place. Joe was there."

If anything Mike's smile grew broader. "He's good sex isn't he?"

That got me. In spite of myself, I flashed a glance at Paul, sitting opposite me, holding a glass of lager, his brown eyes fixed on me. He could see the momentary guilt in my face, and I saw his look change. It was as if I had suddenly kicked him.

"It was nothing," I lied. "Just a fumble in the car. It didn't amount to anything. Honestly, Paul."

But Paul was on his feet, had turned and walked away into the High Street, up the hill towards the Heath.

"Now you've done it," I said to Mike, though my anger was really directed at myself. I followed Paul though I didn't really know if I was doing the right thing. Mike tagged along.

I could see Paul's figure up the hill. The darkness was gathering and the street lights had come on, their yellow sodium glow lighting up his hair. There were quite a few other people around, late-shoppers, groups of youngsters congregating, drinkers outside the pubs, glasses in their hands, and Paul disappeared behind the figures of these others from time to time.

We kept him in sight though, my eyes as far as possible riveted on him, when suddenly someone shoved by us. I'd scarcely have noticed except that the man pushed right between us and jostled me out of the way. There was no word of apology, but he turned briefly as he passed, and I recognized him, dark, dirty hair, ice-cold eyes. It was the man whom I had seen that morning, the man who had been following Paul.

I nearly grabbed at him while he was within arm reach, but stopped myself, deciding to find out what was happening, what he would do. The pedestrians thinned out as we came to the top of the hill, where the Round Pond was, where kids and grown-ups sailed boats on Sunday lunchtimes. This was where the path started that led down onto the Heath, a noted trolling area for gays.

The sun was almost down, sinking beneath the bank of clouds. A few shadows of figures lurked amongst the trees. To the casual observer, they might have been the last of the daytime loiterers, catching the final few moments of light, but I knew better. These were an entirely different species, one to which I was both drawn and repelled. I knew that to wander amongst them would lead to tentative gropes in the anonymous darkness and then the unidentified, exciting, frightening sex.

What was Paul doing? What was the stalker doing? I hurried my pace, not wanting to lose them in the shadows. The path was a pale snake in front of me, Paul invisible, the follower hardly less so. I knew I had to catch up with him. Mike, from behind, whispered something.

"What?" I asked, barely pausing.

"He's got a knife. Tim, he's got a knife."

How could he know this? It was much too dark to see, but the words frightened me. I darted forward and nearly caught up with the guy. He must have heard my footsteps for he turned. In the last greyness of dusk I could make out his features, but he didn't seem to have anything in his hands.

A shout from far behind. "Tim, be careful. He's not after Paul. He wants you."

The guy spoke, rasping. "Are you Tim Sinclair?"

I didn't understand what was going on. I still thought he was after Paul, couldn't understand why he was asking my name, how in fact he knew it anyway.

He took a step towards me and I sort of rugby-tackled him. Not that I've ever played Rugby, or knew how to tackle, but I made a furious dive at him. He sidestepped, and I cannoned into him, both of us falling onto the ground.

I scrambled to my feet, but the man had got up before me and in a single stride was next to me, clasping me in a two-armed grip around my chest. I could smell his sweat, feel the heat from his body through both layers of clothing. His breath was harsh in my ear.

"So you're Tim Sinclair. I thought eventually Paul would lead me to you." One of his arms released and groped for something in his short jacket pocket. I wrenched myself out of the grip and turned to face him.

His body was low in a threatening crouch. In his left hand he held a knife; how had Mike known? It had been completely hidden up until then. The blade glinted with the reflected yellow lights from the street behind and above us. I tried to think back to a course I'd once taken in unarmed combat. Keep your distance. Hit the assailant's wrist with a stick. Talk to him. The first I could see the sense of. Unfortunately I had nothing to hit him with. I tried the third.

"What do you want? We haven't got much money. I haven't even got a mobile phone."

"This ain't a mugging. What you're going to get is from Nick

Warren. He sends you his best."

Nick Warren? In spite of the fear, I remembered the man, the sardonic half smile on his attractive face. Five years for manslaughter, the killing of Paul's ex-lover. Prison couldn't have agreed with Nick, the sort of guy whose life consisted of doing just what he wanted to do. I tried to reason. "If you kill me, you'll never get away with it. There's two witnesses. The police will pursue you forever." Even now, from the corner of my eye I could see Mike catching up.

The guy gave a sudden lunge, catching me by surprise. At the last moment I dodged and the knife scraped past my ribs, cutting through my jacket and shirt. I felt a sharp pain and a dribble of something warm run down my side.

"That's enough," said a voice from the shadows. The man whirled around, the knife threatening whoever it was. For a brief moment he had his back to me, and in that fragment of time I kicked out at the back of the guy's legs, losing my own balance as I did so. Shouting, the man fell spread-eagled, the knife bouncing away across the ground.

The shadow stepped forward and twisted the guy's left arm behind his back. After a short while he stopped struggling. From the ground I stared up into the face of Paul Massingham.

"You came back," I said, before I passed out.

Later, after the police and ambulance had been called, the whole story came out. That guy was a great talker once he started, and rather than face a charge of attempted murder all on his own, he implicated everyone else, the seedy nark in prison and behind him, Nick Warren.

Nick of course had known where Paul worked from when they had known each other. Following Paul was an easy way of finding me, after I had moved my office address from the prestigious-but-way-beyond-my-means Jermyn Street to the less salubrious but cheaper Roden Street.

"But what I don't understand," said Paul, "was how Mike

knew the guy had a knife and was trying to kill you?"

I was sitting up in bed, the bandages feeling tight around my ribs, but I was okay. The hospital had insisted I was going to live and had sent me home.

"He's an alien, with powers," I suggested.

Paul looked at me. "You know that can't be true."

"Thank you for coming back," I said.

"I decided I needed you." His stare was frank and open, more than I deserved. "Next time you won't get away with that so easily."

"I promise you," I said, "there won't be a next time."

But even as I said it I wondered whether I could keep my word.

I nuzzled his ear, one of his most favourite erogenous parts and prelude to so much more, though that night I had to take it very gently.

CHAPTER NINE

Ghosts

"I don't believe in ghosts," I said.

"That's what everyone says," said Paul, "until they actually see one. Until clammy hands reach out of the darkness and touch your cringing flesh."

"Sounds like you after a night out at the Clubs."

"I don't have clammy hands," objected Paul.

"No," I agreed. "You are in every way perfect."

"I know," said Paul complacently.

Paul Massingham is my lover. He has red hair, deep red with gold highlights. Sometimes he wears it long when it has a habit of curling softly. Then again he cuts it short and his ears stick out, which I love because they make him look like a gawky adolescent. His eyes are brown, and he smiles a lot. I'm very lucky. Sometimes, though, I take him for granted, and then I feel guilty afterwards.

"But there's no getting away from it, there's a ghost in the house," said Paul. "Everyone's seen it."

"Everyone?"

"Well, you know, lots of people."

"I don't investigate ghosts," I said. I'm a P.I. Most of the work I do is chasing after people whose partners are having it off with someone else extramaritally. It's boring work, but it brings in a crust or two. Just.

"You aren't investigating anything, Tim," said Paul. "When was the last time you had a commission?"

It was true. Employment had been scarce recently. Paul always accused me of being "picky," and he was right. While often wishing that the cases I was offered could prove to be more exciting, perhaps in the police tradition, I was frequently reluctant to accept those that seemed even a bit out of the ordinary. Laziness, perhaps, fear of failure. Knowledge of my own (lack of) capability.

"Give it a go," said Paul and stroked me encouragingly in the place he knew would make me agree to almost anything.

"That's unfair," I said, already weakening, in spirit at any rate. Another part of me was doing the exact opposite.

"Will you do it?" he said, taking hold of me/it firmly.

"Why is it so important to you?"

"They're my friends," he said. "I told them you'd do it."

I sighed. "Run it through me again." Paul smiled and attempted to remove his hand. "Leave that there," I said.

"Pleasure," said Paul.

The tale was simple, if not all that credible, especially for unbelievers in the supernatural like myself. Two friends of Paul's, Martin Kasmir and John Sweet, owned a house in Potters Bar, Hertfordshire, just north of London proper. It was a fairly modern, four bedroom house, said Paul, which they used commercially as a Bed and Breakfast place. They'd only been there for a few months when they started to notice thumps and bangs coming, they thought, from a bedroom. One guest had sworn that he'd seen a person standing by the bed. Some others had complained of the room feeling very cold, even at the height of summer.

"And that's it? No turreted castle?" I asked. "No guy in an Elizabethan ruff with his head tucked underneath his arm? Ouch!"

Paul had playfully pinched me in a particularly sensitive area. Even through the material of my trousers, it was a bit painful.

"Sorry, darling," said Paul, "but it's not a joke."

"Certainly isn't," I said, pretending distress. "My left testicle has undergone major trauma."

"Shall I kiss it better?"

That sounded a much better idea. "Okay," I said.

"And you'll take the case?" Lips prepared, mouth open, warm aperture approaching.

I could do no other. I'm a sucker for sexual invitation, often literally.

"Okay," I said.

The following day we both went round to the house. It was a pleasant, detached, two-story building, red-brick, with bow-fronted 1930s-style windows on either side of the central front door. Apart from minor differences like the color of the paint and the curtains in the windows, there was very little to distinguish it from the houses on either side. The bell was a two-tone. I had no experience, of course, but it didn't exactly look haunted. A sign on the gate read "Buddleia House." Hardly Gothic.

A tall, dark-haired man with thick eyebrows and a sensual mouth opened the door. He was wearing a white T-shirt and skin-tight, light-blue jeans. From the look of his equipment bulging provocatively out from his groin, he wasn't wearing any underwear. Paul greeted him with what I thought was an over-enthusiastic hug which went on for just a little bit too long.

I manufactured a cough.

"Martin, this is Tim," Paul said after a while.

Martin and I shook hands. We went in out of the sunshine and were led into a brightly lit kitchen which doubled as a sort of eating room. It was all pine and strove to give the impression of Scandinavian hygiene, an image which was slightly spoiled by the dirty plates and remains of what was obviously a hearty breakfast for clearly more than one on the draining board.

"Haven't got round to doing the washing up yet," said Martin, noticing the direction of my glance. "We've got guests this week. Care for a coffee?"

"Yes, please," said Paul before I could answer. "Where's

John?" He turned to me. "You'll like John. He's a dish."

Martin sighed. "Everyone fancies John. He'll be back soon. He's out getting the week's groceries at the moment."

For the first time, I warmed to Martin. He was obviously in the same position as I was with Paul. Everyone thought Paul was a dish. I was just the other one in the background. From time to time I had attempted to explain this to Paul, but he always refused to accept it.

Martin fiddled with a coffee maker which started to thump enthusiastically. I decided that a rush of caffeine was a good idea. We sat down round the pine table, on pine chairs.

"About this ghost," I said.

"There isn't a ghost," said Martin, looking into his coffee cup. Then he raised his head and looked at me. He had dark blue eyes and long eyelashes. They were the sort you could lose yourself in. "There can't be. No such things."

"So how did the whole thing start?" I asked, trying hard not to gaze into his eyes.

"I don't know. Some hysterical queen got cold in bed all by herself and imagined it, I suppose. The people in the house next door told her the story of this guy who was killed. This house was apparently unoccupied for some time, and it became a squat. The windows were boarded up, but they still managed to break in. This was long before we bought it of course. It seems one night some skinheads, drunk, got in after them, chased this guy upstairs and beat him up. He died later. That's the story they," he gestured with his thumb at the side wall, "told us."

"What happened then?" asked Paul.

"The queen left, but the story remained. Other people said they had seen something in that room at night, a guy lying on the floor in a pool of blood. Of course there's never anything there in the morning."

"Paul said there were thumps," I said.

"It's probably the central heating," said Martin, "the pipes, you know."

"So what can I do?" I asked.

"Prove that there's no ghost. We don't want to lose any more guests. It was hard enough starting the whole business arrangement. As if we didn't have enough problems and opposition, both John and I have sunk all our savings into it and mortgaged our bollocks to the bank."

I thought about it. There's no way anyone can prove the nonexistence of something. If there's enough evidence you can prove something is there, but how to prove it isn't there? Martin looked at me. Paul looked at me. Deep blue eyes, dark brown eyes. I weakened.

"Let's see the room," I said. I was always a sucker for beautiful eyes.

At the top of the central staircase which led to the first floor, a landing split into two, each coming back on itself, three doors either side. Martin pointed to the right.

"Those two are ours," he said, "John's and mine. The third door's the bathroom."

We turned to the left. "Guest rooms," he said, "ensuite bathrooms for the doubles and this," he put his hand on the third door, "is 'the' room, the one the ghost is supposed to have appeared in."

He opened the door. It was a single room, or at least had a single bed. There was a chest of drawers opposite and a mirror above, and some rather gloomy-looking prints on the wall. A corner had been divided off with a shower curtain. There was an easy chair in another corner. It didn't look too comfortable. A window overlooked the back garden. As I crossed to peer out, I noticed how cold the room was. The other parts of the house had been warm with a close, almost airless heat. Here there was a distinct chill. I noticed that Paul and Martin both felt it too.

"Something wrong with the central heating," said Martin. He went across to a radiator and gave it a kick. There was a liquid gurgle but nothing more. The temperature didn't increase.

Paul didn't say anything, but he gave me a look meant to convey something meaningful. I ignored it and looked out. A metal staircase led down from a platform.

"Fire escape," said Martin. "Regulations, must be two escape routes. We had to have it put in."

"And this is the room where the guy was killed?" I asked.

"So they say," said Martin.

"Don't you know?"

Martin shrugged. "That's what the people next door said."

There was a noise from downstairs and a shout. "Mart!"

Martin smiled. "It's John," he said. "Come and meet him."

Paul went out and I followed. As Martin and I went through the doorway, he brushed against me. I could feel the warmth of his body in that sudden touch. I gave him a sharp look, and he smiled. It was a friendly smile, and the contact might have been accidental, but I had a feeling it wasn't.

John Sweet was standing at the foot of the stairs. As Martin had said, he was a strikingly handsome man who looked more like an actor with his dramatic good looks, dark, smouldering eyes under a beetling ridge of black eyebrows, eyelashes of a length that would have been the envy of any film actress, and hair so glossily black as to make the proverbial raven's breast look positively shoddy in comparison. Perhaps it's envy or jealousy, but I never trust people who are so stunning.

"Here's Sherlock Holmes," said Martin touching my arm as we went downstairs, "and Dr. Watson you know." He pointed to Paul.

John laughed. "Take no notice of the comedian," he said. "You must be Tim Sinclair." We shook hands and went back into the kitchen where Martin again started on the coffee machine. "So, what do you think?"

"I think your central heating needs looking at," I said.

"He noticed how cold it is in that room," said Martin.

"We all did," said Paul.

"So are you going to stay overnight?"

I looked at Paul. "You're in there on your own," he said.

Martin smiled and winked at me. "Otherwise nothing appears."

I nodded.

Terms and conditions agreed, Paul and I left. The car was just down the road, and we had to pass a man who was standing at the gate of the house next door. He was a dried-up, shrivelled guy who I thought at first glance was old. Close to, though, he couldn't have been much out of his forties, but a perennial frown and downturn of his mouth had left deep creases etched into his face. Despite the weather being fairly mild, he was wearing brightly coloured woollen gloves and a scarf around his neck. He looked, as he sounded when he spoke, antagonistic.

"You two staying there?" He aimed a vicious jab with his forefinger at John and Martin's house.

"Well," started Paul, and I knew he was about to explain the whole situation so I jumped in hurriedly.

"We're thinking of it," I said. "Why?"

"It's haunted! There was a dreadful murder done there and something was left behind. Folks who have seen it are never the same again. It's an evil house. You'd best not stay there overnight."

"We don't believe in ghosts," I said.

"They killed him with their knives. You'd never believe the amount of blood there was in that room. They say you can still hear him thrashing about in his death agonies."

Disbeliever that I was, I still felt a chill run down my back. "Thanks for warning us," I said.

"Poor lad," said the man, "black, he was. Shouldn't have been there, of course. Squatters they were, lowering the tone of the neighbourhood."

"Well, they're long gone now," Paul said.

"To be replaced by what?" The man gave us a vitriolic glance. Was he referring to the ghost or to the fact that the house catered for a mostly gay clientele and was owned by a gay couple? I preferred not to ask.

As I got into the car, I looked back. A woman dressed in grey, her hair tightly shingled, had come out of the house and joined him at the gate. They were both staring after us.

"Perhaps the ghost would be preferable to people like that," said Paul and gave my leg an affectionate squeeze. "I suppose this means we won't be sleeping together tonight. I guess we'll have to make up for that this afternoon."

I broke a few speed regulations on the way home.

There were no other guests at Buddleia House that night.

"Perhaps the story of the ghost has got about," said John gloomily.

In spite of my disbelief, I wasn't exactly looking forward to the night. I'd got used to sleeping with my arms around Paul, feeling the warmth of his body against mine. A single bed and moreover a room which, in spite of all Martin's attention to the central heating, still felt cold—if not damp—was not inviting. Paul, I knew, would be in the next room, also alone, but in a double bed. Perhaps I might creep out later, as I was sure nothing would actually happen, and join him.

I looked out of the window onto the garden which was lit by a half moon. It was full of shadows, a couple of which, in my imagination, looked man-shaped. No doubt in the morning they would be bushes. I pulled the curtains and went to bed.

Well, of course there was no way I was going to be able to sleep. It was an unfamiliar bed, I had no one to cuddle up to and, in spite of a double ration of blankets, kindly provided by Martin who seemed anxious to make sure I was okay and had hung around for quite a while before leaving me alone, it still felt cold. My mind centered on the story.

A black guy, beaten to death in this room, thumps and screams as the skinheads killed him, lying in a pool of blood on the floor next to where I was myself trying to go to sleep. The whole thing was stupid, I thought. Why had I ever agreed to it? And now I was going to lie awake for the whole night and nothing was going to happen.

It was about that time that I fell asleep, or at least I don't remember anything apart from wondering why I'd been such an idiot.

I woke suddenly. The room was lighter than it had been, and I saw that the curtains, which I had drawn, were now open. The moon was shining in. It must have been the light that had wakened me. Then a shape moved in between me and the rectangle of light.

"Paul?" I said and then jumped as a burst of adrenaline, or at least fear, pumped through my body. There was a hand resting on the pillow beside me, a dark hand, a black hand.

I think I must have screamed or at least shouted. Certainly I've never got out of bed quicker in my whole life. I made for the door, wrenched at the handle, fearing for one dreadful moment that I'd find it wouldn't open, but it turned and I pulled it open and dashed out. Before I scuttled down the corridor I took a last look behind me, not sure whether the "thing" was after me. In that brief moment I saw the figure, standing on the other side of the bed. It hadn't moved. A male figure, I could see that, hands and face dark-skinned, wearing a white shirt, light trousers, on both of which were splattered, dark-spreading stains.

A door opened on the other landing, and a rectangle of light spilled out. Martin came out. I stood, shaking, dressed only in underpants. He came to me and wrapped himself around me. It was, I'm sure, meant as a gesture of comfort, but the fact that he was stark naked and that we were pressed front to front, chest, stomach and loins, would have been in other circumstances exciting, to say the least. But, at the moment, I was in no mood for sexual stimulation.

"It was there," I babbled, almost face to face, "the ghost.

Standing by the bed."

Other doors opened. John came out of his room and Paul from the one next to mine. Martin and I were, as it were, "discovered." There was a brief pause and Martin let go of me.

"Do you have to be so public in your indiscretions?" asked John, coldly.

"No, no," I blabbered, "it's nothing like that. It's in there." I pointed to my room.

"Perhaps you two should have stayed there."

I looked in despair at Paul and got a very frosty glare back. "Back to your old tricks," he said in a low voice but loud enough for everyone to hear. That was a bit unfair, though I must admit that, in the past, I had played around. But this time I was innocent.

"The ghost," I said, "it was standing by my bed. I ran out, and Martin came from his room. We weren't doing anything. I was in a state. It was terrifying."

Paul looked dubious. "You really saw something?"

"Yes, a black guy, covered in blood. Look, if you don't believe me." Feeling somewhat braver, now that I had some company, I thrust open the door and switched on the light, to reveal... nothing. There was no one there. The curtains were drawn closed. Only the bedclothes were thrown back and onto the floor to show the speed and force of my exit.

"Looks like a bed of passion," said John, sarcastically.

We stood at the doorway: one naked guy, Martin; one in Y-fronts, me; Paul in shorts and a T-shirt; John in a pair of black silk pajamas. The narrowness of the doorway meant we were standing close, and I found I was pressed against Martin. I stepped in away from him quickly, and then jumped as my foot stood in something cold, and wet.

"Oh God. It's blood!"

John looked down. "It's water," he said. "The radiator's sprung a leak."

"Where was the ghost?" asked Martin. He walked to the middle of the room and stood there, buttocks curved and clenched a bit against the cold. He didn't seem to mind that he was the centre of attention.

"Couldn't you put on some clothes?" asked John.

Martin looked down at himself. "Hmm, yes, you're right," he said. "This chilliness isn't doing the best for my equipment." He picked up a blanket from the floor and wrapped it round himself.

"It was standing between the bed and the window, and the curtains were open because I saw the moon. In fact he, yes it was a he, was silhouetted against the moonlight, but I saw his hand on the pillow. It was black."

Paul went round the bed. "There's nothing here" he said.

John went to the window and pulled open the curtains. "Nor here."

I joined him. The window catch was locked. I undid it and pulled open the sash window. It slid up without a sound. A cold breeze from outside raised goose bumps on my legs and arms. I shivered.

"You'll catch your death of cold," said Paul and brought over a pullover and my jeans which were on the chair beside the bed. I clambered into them.

"Are you sure you weren't dreaming, Tim?" asked John. "There's nowhere he could have gone."

"Unless it was a ghost, a real ghost," said Martin, wearing his blanket like a toga. "In which case he could have walked through the wall."

"Are you sure you saw something?" asked Paul after we'd gone to bed. I'd refused to sleep in the single room and was now in Paul's double, cuddling up to him, as I'd always intended to later in the night.

"Of course I am."

"But where could he have gone?"

It was indeed a problem. He couldn't have come out of the door as we were all there on the landing. There were no cupboards in the room, and the window had been locked. Suddenly something struck me. "I suppose John could have slid the latch to when he drew the curtains," I said.

"John?"

"Yes," I said. "There was a moment before I joined him. He could have done it. In which case the window would have been unlocked and whoever it was in the room could have got out, climbed down the fire escape and made his getaway while we were all chattering away on the landing."

"While you were clutching Martin's naked body," said Paul.

"I wasn't clutching him," I protested. "He was clutching me, but anyway it was only for humanitarian reasons. I was in a state."

"Huh! You'd have been in an aroused state if we hadn't arrived so soon."

"You know," I said, drawing him closer, "it's only you who make me really aroused." And I was too, my prick hard against Paul's stomach. I kissed him, long and deep and hard. There was an enthusiastic response and then suddenly a withdrawal.

Paul came up for air. "Why?" he asked.

"Why?" I repeated, not understanding. "Because I love you. Because I need you."

"No, I mean why would John have done that? What possible motive would he have had for hiding an escape route?"

Clearly Paul's mind had been on other things. But he was, of course, right. It made no sense for John to do anything that would perpetuate the idea that there was a ghost abroad in Buddleia House. It was clearly to his and John's disadvantage if potential clients were frightened away. I wasn't really in the mood for trying to work this out at the moment and attempted to continue making advances. My prick was anxious to find somewhere to bury itself and discharge, but Paul was insistent.

"Come on," he said, "you're the detective. What's the motive?"

I didn't know, and, at the moment, I didn't care. I said as much.

"Then, if John didn't lock the window, where did it - he - the ghost - go?"

"Do you want me to say that I imagined the whole thing? I assure you I didn't. I can still see that hand, on the pillow, inches away from my face…and the breathing -" I broke off. It was something I hadn't thought of before.

"Breathing?" said Paul. "Ghosts don't breathe."

"Nor do things conjured up be the imagination. I'd forgotten that. Yes, whoever it was, was breathing hard."

"Let's go back," said Paul. "Look a bit harder, without the other two."

"Do we have to?" I asked, pleading a little.

"Come on," said Paul and was out of bed and struggling into his trousers and pullover. I groaned but got up and did the same.

We tiptoed into the landing. There were no lights under either John nor Martin's doors, but I remembered how Martin had come bursting out before and assumed he must be a light sleeper. I opened the door to the single room. It was as we had left it; that is, the curtain was drawn back, the moonlight came through the window and lit the room with a pale light. The bedclothes were still on the floor except for the blanket which Martin had worn and discarded at the door when he had gone back to his own room.

I shut the door behind us and let my eyes become accustomed to the moonlight.

"Well, what now?" asked Paul.

"Get into bed," I said.

Paul groaned. "Can't you ever stop thinking about sex?" he said.

"No, I just want to see if I can place things." He lay on the bed, and I arranged him so that he was lying as I had been. "Now, whoever it was, was standing between me, that's you, and the window, so that I saw his silhouette. And his hand, his left hand was resting on the pillow."

I stood where I thought he must have been, and Paul moved me a bit to the right so that I blocked the light. I took a step forward so that I could put my hand on the pillow. "Okay. He was here, in this spot," I said, "Now switch on the light."

"Is this what Watson had to put up with?" asked Paul but did as he was told.

I got down on my hands and knees and peered at the spot on the neutral grey carpet.

"Footprints?" asked Paul, a tad, I suspected, sarcastically.

"Nothing." I looked up. The bed was in front of me, bedclothes hanging untidily down, but leaving, I suddenly realized, enough space underneath for someone to crawl under and hide. I got up. "Help me move the bed," I said.

Together we shifted the bed, and again I got down and peered. This time there were some dark marks on the carpet. I touched them, felt the wetness, looked at my fingertips. Blood-red!

"Oh Christ," I said, holding my hand out dramatically.

Paul looked at my fingers and then bent over and sniffed them.

"What are you doing?" I asked.

"I don't know what it is," he said. "Blood smells of old coins. This smells of, different, something familiar."

He licked the ends.

"Oh God," I said. "That's gross."

"Tomato ketchup," he said.

I sniffed. He was right. "So, unless someone's been eating their fish and chips under the bed, my visitor hid under there while we were in here, the ketchup on his shirt rubbing off onto the carpet, waited until we left and then went out of the window."

I walked over to check. The latch was undone. "There's your

proof. I locked that window when I shut it."

"I still don't understand the latch business," said Paul.

"Let's leave it until the morning," I said and reached for his groin, feeling the softness. "Now if we can get back to the matter in hand…"

We went back into his room. It was late. The others must have been asleep, but I was wide awake and feeling randy. Paul sat on the bed and looked at me. He was smiling, a smile I knew of old, and one that meant he felt as I did. His red-gold hair was ruffled, and his smile impish, that of an adolescent about to commit a forbidden but nevertheless enjoyable illegality.

I stood in the middle of the room and unzipped my jeans, letting them fall to my ankles. Paul inserted his fingers into the waistband of my Y-fronts and pulled them down. His face was inches away from my cock which was showing interest in the only way it could. He gave it some gentle kisses, holding the shaft in one hand while the other fondled my testicles. Almost overbalancing, I stepped out of my clothes.

I removed Paul's pullover and knelt down. I kissed the defined pectorals of his chest, the stomach, hard and divided. His skin was smooth and cool and smelled of soap. I licked his nipples tentatively. "Stop that! You know I can't stand that," he cried out, pushing me away.

So I turned my attention lower and pulled down his jeans. Under them my slim, twenty-year-old lover wore only blue briefs. There was an obvious swelling in the soft cotton material just crying out to be released from its confinement. He raised his buttocks from the bed, and I pulled his underwear down to his feet and off in one smooth, swift move.

His penis was released and sprang up straight away. I gazed almost in awe at the magnetic beauty of his uncircumcised cock, his low-hanging testicles, the nest of red pubic hair. Paul smiled as he acknowledged the look of lust and hunger on my face.

"I want that," I said.

"Come and get it," he said, lying back, offering himself to me, vulnerable and open.

I didn't need any further invitation. It was no time for a tentative move. I launched myself and spread-eagled across his body, my face nestling in the soft, man-smelling cushion of his groin. My own cock and balls swung above his face. I could smell his excitement, a combination of clean sweat, soap, sex. My fingers gently pulled back his foreskin to reveal the helmet-shaped head. Then I stroked the length of shaft down to where it sprouted from the wrinkled skin of his scrotum.

Suddenly from underneath me he lifted his head and took my dick into his mouth. A shot of adrenaline rocked my body; my loins felt as if they were on fire, the passion building up. If possible I became even more fully erect. My cock was deep in that moist, warm mouth, his tongue caressing as if it had a life of its own, his face plunged into my pubic hair.

I gasped.

His hands grasped my buttocks and pulled my hips into each thrust, and with each thrust, he played on me like an expert fisherman.

With the tip of my tongue, I licked his ballsack and trailed the length of his penis from the base to the top, caressing the tip with quick butterfly kisses. Paul shivered with pleasure as my hand took hold of his cock and gently began to stroke.

With my free hand, I cradled his balls, rolling them between my fingers and stroked the sensitive perineum under his ballsack. Paul gave a soft groan.

"Do you like that?" I said, as if I needed to ask.

"Ummmmm." he replied, his mouth full, a long drawn-out moan of pleasure all he was able to make.

"What about this?"

My fingers traced the way between his buttocks and found his hole, gently rubbing the area. I felt a brief instinctive tension and then a relaxation, a giving. My middle finger probed, gently found entrance.

"Aaaaaaaaaaaaahhhhhhhhhh," Paul moaned softly.

I took his cock into my mouth, feeling the hard core, the soft velvet of the outer skin, tasting the saltiness of his pre-cum from the tip.

His mouth opened in a great sigh as my mouth sucked his cock all the way down, his pubic hair tickling the end of my nose. The centre of his sexual being impaled between my middle finger and throat. And there we were joined cock to mouth, mouth to cock, a perfect circle.

Gently I fucked his mouth, but the steady build-up in my loins refused to be denied. I was getting near, and, though I didn't want it to end, the inevitable orgasm refused to be denied. My thrusts grew more urgent.

"I'm coming," I said.

"Wait a minute," said Paul. He stopped, and I moaned with unsatisfied desire.

I wanted the pressure of the other body on mine closer, closer, inside me. I raised my legs, opening myself to Paul's probing fingers, along the path which leads from the base of the ballsack to the hole. And all the time our tongues twining together, one finger in. I could feel it exploring the soft interior, finding something, some part of me that had never been touched before but which sent waves of pleasure through my whole body. I tried to cry out, but the mouth on top of me stopped the sound, and I did not want to lose it.

But I had to. "I want you in me," I said.

"Are you sure?" asked Paul.

Waves of pleasure.

"Yes. Yes."

I sighed as the finger withdrew, the warmth of the body removed.

"What are you doing?" I asked.

"Condom."

"Don't bother with one."

Paul didn't answer but reached behind to a drawer in the table for the little safety package.

I felt my legs lifted, the coldness of a lubricant inserted on a finger, another finger entered and both moved, enlarging the hole. I opened my legs and raised my knees so that access could be easier, and the fingers probed deeper then withdrew. Paul's cock, suitably protected, found the cleft, and I raised myself up even further, Paul's body between my legs, his cock piercing the sphincter, sliding slickly in.

I pushed against him and felt Paul's tense body straining, the passion building up and then the orgasm pulse inside me. I arched myself upwards, lungs bursting, body rigid, my cock spurting without being touched, at last gasping moans of satisfied desire. Paul shuddered and collapsed onto me murmuring my name again and again. I held him tightly as he finished, our bodies pressed together.

I gazed into his face and saw it change. The rictus of desire smoothed into a seraphic smile.

"I love you, Tim." he said. "I love you."

At the time I felt that I loved him too, but failed to say so.

The next morning Martin woke us with mugs of tea. "The famous detectives discovered in a compromising position," he announced, posing in the doorway and pretending to snap us, paparazzi-style. "If you're going to do your detecting on the fire escape, you'd better get up. We've got people arriving later this morning."

I would much have preferred staying in bed. Paul's naked body was next to mine; I could feel the warmth, the silky smoothness of his skin, but the job called, and anyway Martin looked as if he planned on getting us up as soon as possible.

"Breakfast is in ten minutes," he said. "If you're not down by then, I'll be back to join you." His quizzical expression suggested that he wouldn't have been averse to doing just that, and, thinking back to last night on the landing when his naked body, with that hanging dick, had clasped mine in an embrace that, at the time, I hadn't been able to fully appreciate, I wondered what a threesome would be like.

Paul, though, was getting up, disentangling himself from my embrace, poised, a naked faun by the side of the bed, before covering that seductive body in the clothes he had discarded so readily earlier.

I sighed and got dressed myself. We washed and did what was necessary as quickly as possible. From downstairs a gong sounded. So Martin wasn't intending to carry out his threat.

"What about that window catch?" asked Paul as we went downstairs. "Do you still think John locked it, and if so, why? What possible reason could he have?"

I didn't reply, firstly because we were about to enter the breakfast room and I could see John Sweet sitting at the table, and secondly because I had absolutely no idea of an answer.

Martin did the serving, and very prettily he did it, twitching his butt in a most provocative way as he passed us plates of egg and bacon and poured the coffee. John, who was obviously not a morning person, chewed on a slice of toast rather morosely and said nothing apart from grunting a "Morning" to us as we entered.

"So," said Martin, after he'd put the food on the table and joined us, "was there a ghost last night?"

"There was certainly someone there," I said. "He left his mark."

John looked up with a start. "What mark?" he asked.

"Tomato ketchup under the bed," said Paul.

Martin and John looked suitably puzzled so I explained.

"You think there was someone under the bed while we were all in there?" asked Martin.

"While you were showing everything," added John.

"He should be so lucky," said Martin.

"So, what's to be done now?" asked John.

"Paul and I will have another look around," I said. "We may have missed things last night, and I want to look at the fire escape."

"I'll help," said Martin, looking eager. "I've always wanted to do some sleuthing."

"I've got an appointment to see the bank manager," said John. "You've got work to do, Martin, before the new arrivals come at ten. No pratting around for you."

Martin looked disappointed, but obviously agreed that there were tasks to be done. "Cinderella, that's all I am," he said, as we finished breakfast and Paul and I went upstairs.

"Do you think everything's okay between those two?" I asked Paul as we went up to the "haunted" room. "Could it be that John wants the whole enterprise to fail?"

"Don't forget Martin said they'd both put all their money into it," said Paul.

"Martin seems a bit of a tart," I said.

"It's mostly put on. He really cares for John."

"Ummm," I said and put as much disbelief into my tone as I could.

There was nothing we could find in the room so we examined the fire escape. The window opened soundlessly. If someone had come in last night through it, I wouldn't have heard anything. We climbed down. The last flight, the final twelve steps, was fixed on a counter balance some eight feet from the ground. Obviously anyone climbing down could unhitch it, but could someone from below jump up, or be hoisted up in some way to grab it and pull it down? We tried. I couldn't get it on my own, nor could Paul, and lifting him didn't make it any easier, but standing on my shoulders, precariously, he was only inches away from the bottom step. He grabbed at it before I overbalanced, and he had to jump down.

"I'm not up to this circus balancing act," I complained. "You're putting on weight. No more bacon and eggs for breakfast." I rubbed my shoulders where his shoes had been.

"I saw something," Paul said, and he bent down to examine the bottom step. "Look, here it is." He held out something between his finger and thumb.

It was a small scrap of red wool. "A clue, Holmes!"

"I'll take it to forensics," I said.

"Oh come on, now," said Paul. "Sherlock never had that scientific stuff to fall back on. Just look at it, and tell me what you see."

"A piece of knitting wool," I said, "bright red. Could be from anything."

I looked round the garden. It was neat and tidy. Probably in summertime it would have been bright with flowers. At the moment it had a sad, grey November-ish look to it, the sky leaden, what plants there were, drooping.

"Oy," said someone.

It was the neighbour we had seen the day before. This time he was hanging over the fence which divided his property from Buddleia House. His scarf and gloves still suggested that he wasn't very good at withstanding the harsher elements, and I wondered why he spent so much time outside. Perhaps that wife of his preferred him out of her way.

"Good morning," I said.

"Did you see the ghost?" he asked.

"I saw something," I said, carefully.

"Told you so," he said. "Gave you a bit of a shock, I expect!"

I admitted it had. "Tell me some more about the ghost," I said.

He beckoned us over. "There was this group of squatters…" he started, peering over the fence, his spectacles gleaming.

"Could we go inside?" I asked. "It's not very pleasant here, and you look as if you'd be better off in the warm." His scarf was wound tightly around his neck.

He looked a little taken aback, but, apart from saying no, which would have made him sound rude, especially as I had phrased my request with his apparent welfare at heart, he couldn't do much else.

"Come in," he said. "This cold weather does make my rheumatics act up something cruel." We trailed round to the front gate and up his front path. He let us in, holding the door just wide enough for us to slip through and then shutting it firmly behind us. He showed us into the front room. It was furnished pleasantly enough with two easy chairs and a sofa around the TV set. There were some photos of what looked like family groups scattered around on small tables, the mantelpiece, and the like. The grate was filled with some red crêpe paper, perhaps supposed to imitate a fire.

Paul and I sat side by side on the sofa. The man, still standing and still wearing his scarf and gloves, launched into his story. It was the same as we'd heard before though with added details about how dreadful it had been with the noise the squatters had made at night, how there had been needles and worse scattered around in the garden, how the authorities hadn't seemed concerned however many complaints they, he and his wife, had made. How the whole neighbourhood had been going downhill until the night of the murder. Then at last the police had had to take action.

The door opened and his wife came in. Her hair still looked like tightly-coiled barbed wire. "I thought I heard voices," she said. "Who are your friends, dear?"

"Paul Massingham," I said, "and I'm Tim Sinclair."

"My husband, Mr. Preed," she said, as if she knew the man hadn't told us his name. She turned to him. "Do take your scarf and gloves off, dear," she said, "or you won't get the benefit when you go out again." Even her voice had a steely tinge to it. I suspected that, as soon as Mr. Preed had finished his story, he'd be dispatched outside again.

Obediently he unwound his scarf and removed his gloves. His fingers were slightly bent as if he suffered from arthritis. He looked around vaguely as if not sure where to put the clothes.

"Oh, give them here," said Mrs. Preed, snatching them from him and laying them on the table next to the sofa. Something about the color of the gloves caught my attention. They had been knitted from a rainbow of different shades as if from the odds and ends of other garments which had left remnants of wool behind. Amongst the colors was a particularly bright red which I was sure I recognized. I would have liked to have taken the snippet of wool which Paul had found on the fire escape and compare the two, but of course I couldn't at the time.

"Something wrong with the gloves?" asked Mrs. Preed sharply, and I was aware that I had been staring at them rather too fixedly.

"No," I said. "Certainly not. I was just, er, looking at the photograph. It's you and Mr. Preed isn't it?"

The framed photo stood next to the gloves. It showed five people frozen into an attitude of forced jocularity, the smiles etched on Mr. and Mrs. Preed were obvious, and a woman who looked younger than her but had the same bone structure stood next to a black man. In front of them a child, perhaps seven years old, looked as if he had just been reprimanded. He was dark-skinned but not as dark as the man.

"With my sister and her husband," said Mrs. Preed. "That's our nephew, Clark."

"A fine looking boy," I said, feeling that some complimentary comment was necessary.

"Oh that was ten years ago, wasn't it, Stan?" She turned for confirmation to her husband. "Clark's seventeen now."

Mr. Preed grunted. It seemed he didn't want to talk family matters. "So," he continued, "finally the house was cleaned out, and a right mess it was in, I can tell you. The damage those louts had caused. There were girls there that ought to have known better." Clearly Mr. Preed had ideas about the feminine gender which consisted largely of preparing food and clearing up afterwards. "And then, even when it was all tidied up, the noises started. At first we thought it was more squatters had got in, but it wasn't cos they'd boarded up the doors and windows. A right mess it looked, didn't it, Ethel? And we had to live next door to it."

Mrs. Preed nodded. "And then them two bought it," she said.

"You didn't approve?" asked Paul. It was the first time he had spoken, and the Preeds looked at him rather as if they hadn't realized he could talk.

"Well, you know, with children around." Mr. Preed waved his hands in the air. "You can't trust them sort."

I wasn't going to argue with his homophobia, but I had no scruples about getting out the scrap of wool we had found and comparing it with the red bits of the glove. As far as I could tell it was exact.

"What are you doing?" asked Mrs. Preed. She sounded worried, which was good, as far as I was concerned.

"This," I said, holding up the bit we had found, "is a scrap of wool which was caught on the bottom rung of next door's fire escape. As you can see it's exactly the same color of the wool on your husband's gloves. The only way it could have got up there was if he'd somehow reached up, perhaps on the shoulders of someone else and pulled it down."

No one said anything.

"Now why should you have wanted to do that, Mr. Preed? So that someone else could nip up the stairs, get into that bedroom and frighten the fucking shit out of whoever was asleep there."

There was a sharp intake of breath from Mrs. Preed. I hoped it was because I was onto the truth rather than because of the language.

"And who was that someone else?" Mr. Preed still had an ounce or two of defiance left. "Just tell me that!"

Well, I thought I knew, but of course I hadn't any proof, and then, right on cue, I couldn't have stage-managed it any better myself, the door opened and this black guy came in. He had black, cropped hair, not shaved, but very short, rather hooded eyelids, the most flawless, dark chocolate skin. He was wearing a white open-necked shirt and dark jacket. He was in a single word, hot, and I'd bet my last dollar that he was gay.

"Not now, Clark," said Mr. Preed, but it was too late.

I went out on a limb. There was no way I could have recognized whoever it was from last night, but I chanced my arm, anyway. "That's the guy," I said, pointing dramatically. "That's the guy who was in my bedroom last night, pretending to be a ghost."

"You've got no proof," said Mr. Preed.

But the lad knew that the game was up. "It were only a joke. Uncle Stan said it was only for fun."

"But your Uncle Stan hoped they'd go out of business, that the ghost would frighten potential customers away. No joke for two guys who have mortgaged themselves up to the hilt to keep their business going."

Clark had the decency to look ashamed. As for the Preeds, well, they realized the game was up, and, frightened that we would go to police, they promised to stop the impersonations. I said we would try to persuade Martin and John not to take further action.

And that was almost all to the story. John and Martin hadn't got a ghost after all. They didn't take the matter any further with their neighbours, and I assumed that would be that.

Some months later though I happened to be skimming through a copy of Gay Times, as one does, when I noticed an advertisement. It was recommending a bed and breakfast place in Potters Bar.

"Stay at the Haunted House, where the ghost of a murdered young man appears regularly in the haunted bedroom. Are you man enough to stay overnight alone? Other rooms available."

For a moment I couldn't believe it was the same place, but the address and telephone number were the same as were the proprietors: John Sweet and Martin Kasmir. And these two, fearing that the news of the haunting would frighten off potential guests, had paid me to prove that there wasn't a ghost, and now here they were advertising the existence of such a one.

I had nothing to do that afternoon so I paid them a visit.

Martin opened the door, his tight jeans, white this time, still showing all that he'd got.

"Tim," he said. "You're by yourself? How lovely. And I'm all alone too. Do come in."

Without waiting for an answer, he dragged me in.

"What's all this about?" I asked, showing him the advert, after he'd sat me down on the sofa and plumped himself down beside me so close that our thighs touched. "I thought the whole point was to prove there was no ghost."

Martin smiled. "But then we found that trade dropped off even more. It was the idea of having a ghost which was attracting people to us."

"But you haven't got one now."

"Oh yes, we have! That guy, Clark, is a very accommodating lad."

"He's working for you now," I said. "That must have upset the Preeds."

"Oh they've moved out, and Clark needed somewhere to stay near to his college. Our house was the perfect solution, and he fits in so well. As I said, he's very accommodating. All we have to make sure is that no one sees him around the house, except at haunting times. But we've had some alterations done upstairs to make that possible."

"But what happens if someone stands up to him when he appears as a ghost, rather than running out of the room like I did?"

"Very accommodating indeed," he said. "No one's complained so far."

I looked at Martin. He had his mischievous, I've-done-something-bad-and-I don't-give-a-toss look about him. "Come on upstairs and I'll show you."

He held out his hand in invitation.

I knew I shouldn't go up with him, but I did.

CHAPTER TEN

Murder Most Foul

The body was lying on the bed. It was still wearing the clothes it had worn when I saw it last. It? Not "it," him, him, him! Him, as I had seen him when we ran into each other in the coffee bar earlier that same afternoon. He, taking refreshment, innocently; me, cruising, I guess you could call it, guiltily.

Why 'guiltily'? Well, mainly because I'm married, or actually not married, though we've talked about it, me and my lover, Paul, who, as far as I know and believe, is monogamously faithful. Whereas I, well, I've got a recurrent problem, a sort of linguistic impediment—I can't say "No," certainly not to a guy like the one who'd come in to the Coffee Experience earlier that day and sat down on the stool next to me at the counter.

I thought at first he'd been out jogging. Mid-twenties, I guessed. A dark blue vest exposed his arms, tanned lightly from the early summer sunshine, light blue baggy pants, showing nothing until they stretched over two hemispheres of more than earthly delight. Brown hair bleached at the tips, expertly done so that it looked natural. Dark eyebrows, the left one raised slightly, quizzically so that I knew he saw everything—life, love, the stock market, the Danish pastry he had bought with his café latte— as a universal mischief and could be treated with equal lack of seriousness.

I won't go into the episode too fully as I'm not all that proud of what I did. Suffice it to say that I smiled as he took out a respectable bite from his pastry, and he smiled back. Smiles led to chat, and chat to a casual brush of leg against leg from our adjacent stools. Pressure and an answering pressure. He obviously wasn't quite so innocent as I'd first thought.

"I'm Tim," I said eventually, when I was sure the way things were going.

"Pete."

"Hi, Pete. Got any place to go?" Very forward on my part, but we'd discussed the weather already, and there didn't seem to be any point in hanging back.

"I'd like to, Tim, but…I'm seeing someone in a quarter of an hour. It's only business, and I have to go. I wasn't expecting to meet up with…"

He looked at me, and I filled in the gap, "a guy as attractive and sexy as you." Oh well, I thought, perhaps it was for the best. At least I wouldn't have to feel guilty afterwards.

Then he said, "But later. I'll be free later. Come round to my place, if you like, about four o'clock." He looked at me, the quizzical eyebrow raised. "It'll be fun."

And that was it. He gave me the address, a flat off the Balls Pond Road, and out he went, sashaying into the street, those perfect hemispheres doing a caramba samba which juggled me into an erotic fantasy which kept me as good as comatose until the guy behind the counter, not my type at all, asked me if I was okay, and I came to and left.

I never saw Pete alive again.

At about two minutes to four I climbed up the two flights of stairs leading to the flat he'd given me the address of, pressed the bell and waited. There was no answer, but then I saw that the door was open so I went in. Not, you might think, the most sensible thing to do. In films it's always that scenario, the open unlocked door, which leads to the heroine getting jumped on, ravished, killed, but I didn't think too much of it. I was expected. He'd left the door ajar. Sounded sensible to me.

I went in and shut the door behind me. Inside there was a narrow sort of hall/lobby/passageway, some coats hung on hooks fastened to the wall, more doors further down on each side of the corridor. The carpet was thick and felt expensive underfoot. Wallpaper, not magnolia emulsion.

"Pete," I called out. No answer.

The flat, I could see, was all on one floor so all the rooms presumably led off this central corridor. I tried the first on the left, a small kitchen, a couple of mugs upturned on the draining board, tidy. There was another door on the other side leading to a lounge/dining room. That sounds rather grand, but it was one of those rooms which did for both. A table on one side with four upright chairs around it, a comfortable-looking sofa on the other faced a TV/entertainment centre. Pete, or someone, wasn't short of a bob or two.

On the walls were some pictures, bright, Mediterranean colors, sort of abstract landscapes. Windows looked out onto the central courtyard with the windows of the flats opposite looking straight at me. There was no one around. Just a sweet-smelling aroma which I recognized as Homme Epouvantable, an expensive aftershave I loathed. It hadn't been on Pete when I'd been with him earlier. Was there someone else there?

A further door led me back into the passageway. I shouted his name again, feeling, for the first time, some twinges of doubt. He was expecting me so why the silence? Surely I wasn't in for a surprise party! I tried the door opposite, a bedroom, the curtains drawn so that everything was dim. I could just make out a figure on the bed, lying still, turned away from me.

"Pete," I said, though he must have been fast asleep indeed not to have heard my other calls. He didn't stir. Doubts now turned into an unpleasant feeling of apprehension. It's a cliché to say that my hackles rose, but I did feel the hairs on the back of my neck stir.

I touched him. He was warm, but he didn't move and, when I felt it, there was no pulse in his neck.

The obvious thing was to phone for an ambulance or the police, but I hesitated. Did I want to get involved with this? I didn't know the guy, and here I was in his flat, and he was dead. The best thing, even if it was the cowardly thing, was to get out, find a public call box some way away and phone from there. I'd be clear. There'd be no embarrassing questions. Even better Paul wouldn't find out. Okay, I was behaving like a selfish shit, but, there was nothing to be done for Pete now, apart from finding out why he had died, and that was a police job.

The only thing that troubled me was whether I had touched anything in the flat. Would my fingerprints be all over the place? I tried to think back. The door handles. I'd wipe them on the way out. I turned to go and jumped as the front door bell shrilled.

Jesus!

I froze. Perhaps whoever it was would go away if I stayed quiet.

But the bell went again, and I heard a shout from outside, "Police!"

Oh God! If I was found skulking here with a dead body, it would look worse than ever. I ran out into the hall just as something heavy crashed into the other side of the door. I wrenched it open before it was kicked off its hinges. Two policemen in uniform were outside.

It was stupid of me, but I wasn't thinking clearly. "Is there anything I can do for you?" I said.

I should have said something like. "Thank God you've come! There's a body in the bedroom."

"We've had a phone call, sir," said one of the cops, with a thin, ferrety face and a moustache. "Is everything all right."

"Phone call?" I said. "I don't understand. Why shouldn't everything be all right?" As I said it I knew I was digging the pit for myself even deeper.

"Are you Mr. Palmer?" asked the other policeman, whom I might have fancied in other circumstances.

So that was Pete's name. Peter Palmer. Not a particularly euphonious choice by his parents. "Er no," I said. "He's - er - not in at the moment."

"So you are?"

"A friend of his," I said, putting off the evil hour for a moment.

"And your name is?"

"Tim Sinclair," I said, finally capitulating.

"Could we come in for a moment, sir?" said the ferret, and it was less a question than a statement of intent.

I knew the game was up.

"There is a bit of a problem," I admitted.

The next hour was something of a blur. I showed them into the bedroom. They rang for a medical team, though I knew it was too late. They took me down to the station where an Inspector Skipton saw me. Coolly efficient, hair parted conventionally on the right-hand side, so young-looking, he was obviously fast-track. Up the police ladder so quickly that he had nothing of the usual 'I've been a sergeant for twenty years' cynicism. Too bright for his own good, I thought, but I tried not to show it. For some reason I took an inexplicable dislike to him, but then he was trying to fit me up for murder. I told all. My story sounded tacky, especially the bit about picking Pete Palmer up in the coffee bar. The inspector, who appeared fishy-eyed the whole time, looked even more sceptical when I mentioned his name.

"We've established that Mr. Palmer, who owns the flat, is in his forties," he said. "His first name is Harold. The person in the bed wasn't Mr. Palmer."

"So who is Pete?" I asked, genuinely bewildered. "And where is Palmer?"

"We hoped you'd tell us," he said. "Have you found any more bodies in your visits to other people's flats?"

I ignored that one, but he made me go through the whole story again.

"Did this Pete say whom he was seeing when he left the coffee house?"

"No," I said. "Just that it was business, and he'd be back home at four o'clock."

"'Home' being Mr. Palmer's flat."

"Apparently," I said. "That's the address he gave me."

Skipton didn't look as if he believed me, but after we'd gone exhaustively through my credentials, confirmed that I was a registered private investigator who had actually helped the police in the past, he cautioned me not to leave the area without informing him and finally let me go, I felt, a trifle unwillingly. I'd been a murder suspect once before, and it didn't feel any more pleasant this second time.

"We'll probably need to talk again," he said.

I had no doubt about that, but at least I was able to go home, and start explaining to Paul.

I love Paul with all my heart, it's my body that occasionally lets me down with other guys. I didn't want him to know about my most recent indiscretion, which in fact hadn't of course happened, through no fault of my own, so I invented a little white porkie.

In my story Pete became a client who had called me on the phone asking for help. He'd said he didn't want to come to the office so I'd agreed to go round to his place. The rest of course was the truth. If you're telling lies, keep them simple, and use as much of the truth as possible. It saves on the memory.

"How did he die?" asked Paul.

I shrugged. The police hadn't told me, perhaps they didn't know themselves at the time. There had been no obvious signs, no dagger sticking in his heart, no rope around his neck. "Suspicious death," I said.

"You don't think the police really suspect you," said Paul.

"I was the only one in the flat," I said. "I'm the obvious one."

"Well, you'll just have to find the real murderer," said Paul, with, as always, supreme, though sometimes unfounded, confidence in my abilities. "What about this Palmer guy?"

"Yes. I think that's the only reason they didn't actually arrest me. It seems he's missing so it does look a bit suspicious."

"Was Pete living with Palmer? Were they gay?"

"Pete certainly was. I don't know anything about the relationship," I said.

Paul was on me in a flash, though the tone wasn't accusing, just interested. "How do you know Pete was gay? You only saw him after he was dead."

Whoops! Strands of tangled web. I hadn't seen that coming. "Sorry," I said. "It was stupid to say he certainly was gay. He sounded gay. The police implied this was a gay killing."

Paul nodded, and I breathed again.

"I'll do a bit of detecting first thing tomorrow," I said.

Paul came over and sat beside me in the chair. It was too small for both of us, but we managed and fitted our limbs together so that we first got comfortable, then I, and a little later, Paul, got randy so that what started as coziness became an entanglement of sexual gymnastics. Fun all round. I made up for what I'd missed that afternoon.

It had been an easy promise I'd made to Paul the previous evening, though what I could do when it came to the point I wasn't sure. I didn't know where Pete had gone from the cafe the day before. I'd watched him go out, turn left down the road, Marylebone High Street, look back at me through the window, wave and then disappear. I'd told the police the truth. The only thing I knew for sure was that he'd said he had an appointment a quarter of an hour's journey away. Whether it was on foot or by taxi, I didn't know though the way he'd set out so purposefully didn't suggest that he was looking for a taxi.

Suddenly I was saddened by the whole thing. I hadn't known Pete long, scarcely ten minutes in all, but while I had, he'd been alive and vital, and handsome and sexy, and now he was dead. Yesterday it had been a shock, what with the finding of the body and the questions at the police station; now I looked back and felt angry that someone had cut short that life. His last words came back to me: "It'll be fun." Now all fun, as far as he was concerned, had gone for good.

Paul and I travelled into town together on the Underground and, after he got out at his station, I went on to the one nearest the coffee shop. The same guy was behind the counter. He was wiping the counter with a cloth. There weren't many customers in, and I supposed he had to look busy. A badge pinned to his shirt told me his name was Robert—not Bob, which might have been considered cuddly, but the coldly formal Robert.

"Hi," I said. "Do you recognize me? I was in here yesterday."

Robert gave me a look, uninterested, but that was all right because all I wanted was information. "Yeah," he said eventually. "You're the guy that was trying to pick up Pete."

Bull's eye! I felt a bit pissed off by the "trying to" but it wasn't worth quibbling.

"So, you do know him," I said. "What's his other name?"

He looked at me in a rather superior fashion. I probably should have ordered a coffee to start with. "If you didn't get off with him last time, there's no point in trying again."

His angular, rather flat face, twisted into a sort of grimace. I detected in his tone a trace of frustration, perhaps that he'd tried himself and been refused.

Patiently I started again. "It's not like that at all," I said. "The guy's dead. We're trying to trace his movements yesterday. At the moment we don't even know his full name." I purposely tried to make my comments sound official. The "we" I hoped sounded bureaucratic. I also hoped by the sudden bald announcement of Pete's death to shock him into some sort of reaction, but the expression in his face merely changed from supercilious back to deadpan.

"Dead," he said, his voice expressionless. "How did he die? Well, with a job like that, there's always danger."

"What job?" I asked, ignoring his first question.

"Surely you knew. He was on the game."

Now that did surprise me. I've met a few hustlers in my time, purely in the course of my investigations, you understand, but none had behaved like Pete had. With the others it had been money first whereas Pete hadn't even mentioned it. "It'll be fun" he'd said. Surely he hadn't been the sort that would take you back, get you all excited and then come out with the "That'll be fifty quid, guvnor, before we go any further." And then there were his looks. Not that a pretty face isn't an advantage in the trade but he'd looked so open, so honest. Okay maybe I was being naïve, but I sure was surprised to hear that.

"A hustler," I said, hiding my dismay, for I really felt in a way let down. "Okay, now do you know his surname?"

A cunning, mercenary look crept over Robert's face. "What's it worth?"

I was really pissed off with this guy. I took out a notebook I always keep, though really just for appearances. "If you start obstructing the authorities," I said in my best official voice, "You'll find yourself in real trouble, sonny. Now we'll have your name first and then Pete's full name."

He crumpled, like most bullies do. "Okay, okay. No need to act like that. You can't blame a guy for trying. They don't pay millionaire's wages in here. I'm Robert Wilkins. Sure I know Pete's name. It was Palmer."

Palmer? What was going on? The more I heard about Pete, the odder it became. "Do you know a Harold Palmer?" I asked. "Guy about forty?"

Robert gave a nervous glance over his shoulder though there was no one within listening distance. It was so shifty it almost made me laugh. "He's Pete's brother."

"What's he look like?" I asked.

"Nothing like Pete," he said. "He's got a scar on his face." With his thumbnail he drew a line down from just underneath his left eye to the side of his mouth. "He's dangerous. I don't want to talk about him." And that's just what he wouldn't do. In spite of my veiled threats, he refused to answer anything more about Harold Palmer, or indeed about Pete.

"Don't know," he kept on saying. "Don't know nothing about any one. Even though you're the police, I can't say what I don't know."

Before I left I had to disabuse him of this. What if Inspector Skipton or one of his lackeys spoke to Robert later and found out I'd been impersonating a police officer. Then I'd be in real trouble, not that being a murder suspect wasn't enough in itself. "I never said I was with the police," I said.

Robert's eyes, narrowed. "You bastard," he said. "Who are you with then?"

I left without answering.

Was I any further forward? Well, I'd found out that Pete and the elusive Mr. Harold Palmer were brothers. Fratricide isn't all that uncommon, but I couldn't really understand why Harold would have killed his own brother in the flat which presumably they both shared. Hang on a minute! If both lived there, where did they sleep? Of course I'd never got into that last room next door to the bedroom where I'd found Pete's body, but I'd assumed it was a bathroom. Surely Harold's nastiness didn't include incest with his own brother.

And what about Robert? He was an unpleasant enough guy, but did that make him a murderer? If he had fancied Pete and been turned down, or perhaps worse for his ego, told it would cost him big money, was that enough motive to kill him? I doubted it, though I'd have to keep him in mind.

Worse though, I hadn't any other leads to investigate, except, except, I suddenly wondered whether Inspector Skipton might like to have a chat with me. He might appreciate the information I'd gleaned, perhaps even share some he'd found, like the cause of Pete's death.

The sergeant at the desk of the nick was my old friend, Charlie Shepherd. Usually stout and amiable, he regarded me this morning with a less than amiable frown.

"I hear you're in trouble," were his first words to me. Not encouraging.

"It was all a big mistake," I said.

"That's what they all say."

"Do you think I could see Inspector Skipton, Charlie?"

"You're in luck this time. He's just gone out."

"He doesn't really suspect me of being involved in the death of that lad?"

"I doubt it, but I'm only the desk sergeant here. He doesn't tell me anything."

"Why did he give me such a hard time yesterday?"

"I don't think he likes P.I.s."

"Well, that's a change. I thought you were going to say he doesn't like queers."

Charlie smiled. At last a breakthrough. "Don't tell me you're gay!" he said, mock outrage covering his round, amiable face.

He didn't expect an answer so I didn't give one. Instead I changed the subject. "Have they found out how he died?" I asked.

"Well," he said, "I'm not sure I should tell you, but as it's to be released to the press later today, I suppose there's no harm. He was drugged and then suffocated, probably with the pillow."

So that was the reason why there was no trace of violence. Well, if he had to die, I guess, it was as painless as possible. "I had a bit of info for Skipton," I said.

Charlie crossed his arms over his chest looking like a good-humoured Buddha. "'Inspector' Skipton," said Charlie. "You young whippersnappers have no sense of respect for senior rank."

"You call me young!" I said. "Inspector Skipton must be at

least a couple of years younger than me."

Instantly Charlie was serious, and I could see that Skipton's leapfrogging through the ranks had left grievances with the lower echelons. "Shall I pass on a message?" he asked.

"Only that I heard that the murdered guy was the brother of the missing Harold Palmer."

Charlie nodded, not seeming too surprised.

"He knew?" I said. "He knew all the time!"

"Well, it took a little time to leak 'up' to Inspector Skipton, but most of the blokes from constable up know about Harold Palmer. Harold the Hammer, they call him."

"Not a nice guy I hear."

"Certainly not, especially if you're one of the guys who've been under the hammer."

"Literally?"

"Literally."

Suddenly a theory struck me. "So, he'd have quite a few enemies? Enemies who might try to get back at him by bumping off his little brother?"

"Be safer to bump off Harold himself. I guess he'd be rather peeved at whoever done it, and when Harold Palmer gets peeved…" He left the sentence unfinished but I could imagine the rest.

"Got any names for these 'enemies,' Charlie?"

"Sure," said Charlie. "Take your pick: Skip the Wad, Daddy Cool, Canvas Ken, the Padre. They're quite a few others as well."

"And their real names?"

"Sorry, Tim, but you really don't want to know," said Charlie. "They're not the sort of people you want to meet. Best leave it to us, son. I'll tell the guvnor you were here. If you really want to see him, come back tomorrow." He busied himself with some papers, and I knew I'd get nothing more from him that time.

It was, I suppose, good advice, but when I got out into the sunshine I felt I was on a trail. It wasn't so much now that I had to prove I was innocent, but I was taking it personally. Pete, I was sure, had been a good guy, even though his brother might be a villain. Someone had bumped off the good guy, and despite Charlie's warning and no doubt Skipton's disapproval if he should ever find out, I wanted to find out who'd done it.

Now, I've got a friend who knows everything and everybody, on the gay scene that is. His name's Ross. I've never been quite sure whether that's his first name or his surname so you can see we're not exactly close. He's helped me out before though.

"Where've you been, doll?" he said, bubbling down the telephone when I called him from the office. "I nearly crossed you off my guest list. Still with your delicious redhead?"

He knew I was of course. If I hadn't been, by some incredible, almost telepathic means, he'd have been the third person to know about it, after Paul and myself. Though I wondered if he might have found out something like that even before I did.

"Yes," I said. "Ross, I've got myself into a bit of a situation. There's this guy who's been murdered."

"Peter Palmer," he said.

"How did you know?"

"The word gets around." Certainly did as far as Ross was concerned.

"Anyway," I continued, "I just happened to be in the flat when his body was discovered, and I seem to have turned out to be one of the suspects. Not the prime one, of course, but…"

"So, what do you want to know?" Ross asked.

"There were some guys who might have a motive, but all I know are their nicknames. I just wondered if you'd know who they really are."

I'd jotted down the names as soon as I'd got out of the police station so, I could reel them off quite easily. "Skip the Wad,

Daddy Cool, Canvas Ken, the Padre," I said.

There was silence at the other end. "Not heard of them?" I said. Well, it had been a long shot.

"Jeez, sweetie," came a whistling sound from the other end. "When you get yourself involved you really go for it in a big way. These are not the sort of guys you want to play around with."

But I was too exhilarated to concern myself about his warnings. Ross always went way over the top anyway. "Great! You know them. Tell me. All the details, please, and I'll owe you forever."

Ross sighed. "Okay, doll. Skip the Wad, I've never heard of. Daddy Cool and the Padre run the main clubs for Stepney and Marylebone areas respectively. Organize the drugs too I wouldn't be surprised. Certainly any amateur runners get short shrift and soon back out, if they can still walk."

"Canvas Ken?"

"You can give him a miss. He's in prison, not I guess that that could stop him from organizing a killing if he really wanted to, but he's more into the art world scams. I'd forget about him."

"Okay," I said, "so who are 'Daddy Cool' and 'the Padre'?" Notebook out, biro at the ready.

"Real names Ken Roach and David Murdoch. Roach lives in Stepney above one of his clubs, the Commodore, in Commodore Street, not exactly bulging in the imagination department." He paused.

"And Murdoch?" I reminded him.

"Ah…now he's got a big house in the country somewhere. When he's in London though he can usually be found at—er— 12 Henrietta Place. Nice little pied-à-terre," he paused and then added, "I believe."

"You know so much about them, they must both be gay."

"Both gay? Daddy Cool certainly is, likes young chicks, though, treats them reasonably well, as long as they don't get tired of him before he does them. The Padre's probably bi. He's got a wife tucked away somewhere, but he pulls guys like a good'un."

There was something about his tone, the hesitations, that made me wary. "You've been there, haven't you?" I hazarded. "To his house. You've been with him?"

"Okay. I confess. There was an occasion. I was in his club, Gracey's in Connaught Place, and he took a fancy to me. You know me, I'm just a girl who can't say no." I knew exactly. It struck me suddenly that Ross and I weren't so unlike. That worried me a bit.

"What's he like?" I asked.

"Big man, strong, mid-forties. Scary, if you don't do exactly what he says. He's got some interesting little games he likes to play, whips and stuff, but it wasn't bad. I've had worse."

I could imagine. "Thanks, doll," I said. "You've a treasure. We must get together some time."

"Promises, promises! Now you be careful. These aren't your average nelly queens. Remember they're gangsters, and they have guys who'll do anything for them, no questions asked. Even if they don't want to do it themselves, for pleasure."

He rang off.

I made myself a cup of instant brew and then looked up the clubs and addresses Ross had given me in my A to Z. Roach's Commodore Club of course was way out in the East End. If I wanted to go there, I'd have to save it for later on in the evening. Henrietta Street and Connaught Place on the other hand weren't too far away—in fact, in fact it hit me suddenly like a massive brain haemorrhage—walking distance, say ten or fifteen minutes, but more to the point, the same distance from the Coffee Experience, and that was where Pete had been when he'd said he had a business meeting with someone in a quarter of an hour.

Gracey's mid-afternoon looked less than ordinary, at least from the outside. It was in a Regency terrace which could have been at home in any spa town, Bath or Cheltenham, for example.

Originally the houses had been built as elegant town houses with restrained simplicity and imitation Classical Greek pediments, mouldings and pillars. Now most had been divided into separate flats and offices, some not very well. In fact one I noticed had a partition wall built right across the window, dividing it vertically, but Gracey's looked fairly unspoiled. Some steps led up to an elegant portico with a front door painted in a rich dark red on which was a polished brass name plate with just the name. There were window boxes with blue and white flowers flourishing profusely. I tried the door and it opened. I remembered the last time this had happened and wondered what I was letting myself into.

A gorilla of a man stood in the shadowy entrance hall, all muscles under a dark blue suit, which looked as if it could scarcely contain them. He was wearing a white shirt and a tie which just held together the collar around that bull-like neck.

"Good afternoon, sir." The accent was educated, high pitched, almost refined, and I could scarcely believe it came from the same guy, but his lips seemed to be operating in sync with the words. Perhaps the tie was constricting his larynx. "Are you a member of the club, sir?" he asked. "I don't think I recognize the face."

"Er, no," I said, uneasily aware that it wouldn't take much from him to rearrange even a familiar face into something completely unrecognizable. "If it's possible, I'd like to have a few words with Mr. Murdoch."

He fixed me with a look. I wasn't sure if it was hostile or not.

"If he's available," I added.

"You don't have an appointment?"

"No," I said.

"Would you mind telling me what it's in connection with?"

Well, at least the guy could make elementary grammatical gaffes, like ending a sentence with a preposition. "It's about a friend of mine, Peter Palmer."

"Friend" was stretching things a bit, but I felt it was more likely to get a favourable response.

"Ah yes," said the gorilla, "Poor Mr. Palmer, met with an accident, I understand. Such a sympathetic young man." He sounded genuinely concerned and I almost warmed to him. "Your name is?"

"Sinclair," I said. "Tim Sinclair."

"You're not, of course, with the police?"

"No."

"I'll see if Mr. Murdoch is in, Mr. Sinclair."

He moved off into the shadows, walking on the balls of his feet, very lightly for such a big man, and disappeared through a door on the right. I looked around; dark wood panelling. I couldn't see this as a gay club at all, not unless there was some basement downstairs with laser lights and hot smells of sweat and aftershave, and undercover substances available for the right price. Here it looked like the entrance to some very respectable conservative gentlemen's club, but appearances are deceptive: look at gorilla face with his prissy voice and light, elegant movements. Someone, something, cleared its throat. I jumped. I hadn't even heard him return and here he was right beside me.

"Mr. Murdoch will see you, sir."

He walked me to the door, opened it and stood back so that I could go through first, like a lamb to the slaughter. I could see into the room, sumptuously furnished with dark-red flock wallpaper and a figure sitting in an arm chair in front of a fireplace. I walked towards him. Then a ton weight fell on my head, and for a while I knew nothing.

I came to with the mother and father of headaches and slightly blurred vision. I thought I probably had a concussion and hoped it wasn't too severe. Then I wondered if this was the greatest of my worries. Now there were two men staring at me, sitting together side by side though a respectable distance apart. They looked as if they were temporarily united but didn't fancy sitting too close to each other. I didn't know either of them, though I could hazard a guess, and even through the fuzziness, I was surprised. One was thickset, fortyish, grey hair; the other had a scar on his face from just under his left eye down to his chin. Murdoch and Palmer (elder brother), apparently in cahoots and not looking in any way friendly towards me. They hadn't tied me up, but there was scarcely any need. Standing alongside me I could just make out the bulky figure of the gorilla. I wondered who had clobbered me. Presumably whichever of the guys had not been sitting in the chair in front of the fire.

"I don't know him," said Murdoch. "Do you, Harold?"

"Stranger to me," said Palmer.

"What did he say his name was?" asked Murdoch, and I realized he was talking to the gorilla.

"Sinclair," I said. "My name's Tim Sinclair."

For the first time, one of the two men talked actually to me. His tone was neutral, not exactly threatening, but I got the impression that he knew I knew he was very much in charge. "And you claim you were a friend of my brother's? A close friend? I think not, otherwise we would probably have met."

"My brother." Well, that confirmed that this one was Harold Palmer. So the other one was Murdoch.

"I found Peter's body," I said.

"That makes you his friend?"

"Up till then we'd been getting on well."

"What are you doing here?" asked Murdoch suddenly.

"The police found me in the flat. They suspected me of killing Pete. The only way I can get them off my back is to find the real murderer."

"And you think one of us might have done it?"

All of a sudden coming here seemed even less of a sensible thing. "No," I said. "It's just that Pete went to meet someone yesterday, from the cafe. He said he had a business meeting in a quarter of an hour and this place takes about that time to get to.

I thought he might have met someone here."

"He did," said Palmer. "He met me."

His candour was surprising. Even more so was what he said next. "We'd meet every day. He'd pass over the money he'd earned, purely a business arrangement. He had free use of the flat and anything over our arranged amount was his."

So Harold Palmer was his brother's pimp. I wondered whether Pete had tried to back out of the arrangement and whether this could be a motive for murder. What was I doing here? Yet, apart from the crack on the head, these two guys' attitude to me didn't seem, at the moment, threatening. Quite the opposite, in fact, as far as Murdoch was concerned, who seemed to be giving me appraising looks which I could easily interpret as amorous, if that isn't too weak a word for someone whose features reminded me of pre-stressed concrete.

I remembered Ross's comment: "He's got some interesting little games he likes to play, whips and stuff." I certainly wasn't into that!

"Who could have killed Pete?" I asked. I was looking at Murdoch, and he shrugged.

"Can be a dangerous game, the hustling business," he said. "You don't know who you might pick up."

"Pete could look out for himself," said Palmer, giving his partner, or whatever the relationship was, an angry look.

"There was no force," I said. "Pete was drugged and then suffocated with a pillow. He must have trusted whoever it was."

They didn't say anything. "Look," I said. "I'll be honest with you. I'm a private investigator. The rest I've told you is the truth. I met Pete yesterday, and he asked me round to the flat. When I got there, he was dead. Then the police arrived and arrested me."

"They believed your story?" asked Murdoch.

"Well, I'd done some work for them in the past, and anyway I had no motive." I paused. "They're looking for you," I said to Palmer.

"Of course they are. The flat's registered in my name. They wouldn't know I never lived there."

"Is that the only reason you're doing your bit of detective work?" asked Murdoch. "Because you're in the frame for his murder?"

"I didn't know him well," I said, trying to be honest, "but I liked him. Whoever did it shouldn't get away with it."

"You certainly didn't know Peter Palmer well," said Murdoch bluntly. "He was a bastard. Handsome and charming, sexy too, but if you got on the wrong side of him, he'd drop you in it without any hesitation at all. And once in, you'd stay 'dropped'. Not averse to a bit of blackmail either, eh, Harold?"

I saw Palmer give him yet another of those angry looks. I wondered what it was that was holding the two men together. It certainly wasn't personal friendship. Probably business, and that of course almost certainly meant drugs.

"Do you know a guy called Robert Wilkins?" I asked.

Palmer was about to answer when there was the sound of a buzzer. Murdoch switched on a TV monitor and I could see the full length of the hall on the screen. "See who's there, Hubert."

The gorilla (Hubert?) disappeared through the door, and on the monitor I could see his back going towards the front door. He opened it, and there were two men standing outside. Even though the image was slightly grainy, I could recognize the haircut of one of them. It was surely Inspector Skipton, with a uniformed constable in attendance.

"It's the police," I said. "Is there a back way out? I don't really want them to find me here."

"Nor me," said Palmer.

"Pity you have to go," said Murdoch, looking at me. "I might have had plans."

Palmer led the way through another door and down some steps into what was obviously the main club. At this time of the afternoon it was empty and had a sad, stale smell about it, the musty aftermath of too much sweat, body lotion and sex.

"Was Murdoch right about your brother?" I asked.

"He had his little ways," he said and didn't seem to want to elaborate.

"What about the Wilkins guy?" I persisted.

"Now that is a real little shit," said Palmer. "You don't want to get on the wrong side of him. Looks as if a puff of wind would blow him over, but I wouldn't want to turn my back on him in a dark alley."

And this from the guy they called "the Hammer."

I followed him down the centre of the room. On one side was a bar, at the moment in darkness. The only light there was came from some translucent square blocks in the ceiling at the other end. I realized that the room went under the pavement. I could see feet walking overhead though there was no sound. A door just before the blocks led out into the open air, a narrow, rather damp rectangular space and some steps up to ground level.

I looked up at the front door but Skipton and associate had disappeared, presumably inside. I'd like to have been a fly on that wall. We reached the pavement and battled into the passersby. Palmer tapped me on the shoulder.

"I'd leave the investigating to those who know something about it," he said.

"The police?"

"Me," he said. "Oh by the way, you were quite lucky to get out of there." He disappeared into the crowd.

Well, I'd met some of the protagonists who might or might not have been responsible for Pete's death. Had I learned anything? Mainly that I perhaps was wrong about Pete being a good guy, and, in some strange way, I rather warmed to Harold, even though he must have been the one who'd clobbered me. I felt the bruise and winced. Murdoch was creepy. I rather hoped he was the murderer, but he hadn't sounded in any way guilty when he talked so openly about Pete.

So, Wilkins was a dangerous shit, was he? Despite the fact that we hadn't exactly hit it off the last time we'd met, I thought another visit was in order, so I walked back to the office via the Coffee Experience, but Robert Wilkins wasn't behind the counter. Instead a blond late-teen was cheerfully serving coffee, a vast improvement, except that I wanted to talk to Robert Wilkins.

"Hi," I said. "Where's Robert?"

"I can do anything that Robert can," he said.

"And probably more willingly," I said. "Trouble is, I really need to talk to Robert."

"You won't find him here in the afternoons this week," said the lad, whose name, according to his tag, was Alec. "He's on mornings and evenings." He looked at me with a smile. "Are you sure I can't do instead?"

"So he was off yesterday afternoon," I said, ignoring with difficulty the implication of his last question.

Alec nodded.

That meant he could have been to Pete's flat.

"Do you know a guy named Peter Palmer?" I asked.

"Hold on, honey," he said and sashayed down the counter to where a customer was waving a five pound note. I watched Alec's butt with interest, "pert" was the word I'd use; I like "pert." The uniform, white cotton military-style tunic, came just to the top. Then I watched his crotch as he came back, and that was a dream, his tight-fitting white cotton trousers clinging to long, well-muscled legs and embracing his male equipment with a tender grasp, emphasizing its already sizable proportions. He knew I was looking too.

"Now, what were you saying?"

"Peter Palmer," I reminded him.

He pouted. "Questions," he said, "and all about other guys."

"I'm investigating his death," I said.

"You a cop?" he asked, sounding naively excited.

"Private dick."

He smiled. "What's the good of private ones? I only go for those that get shared around."

I tried to concentrate. "You were going to tell me about Peter Palmer," I said. "Did you know him well? What about his friends?"

Someone was waiting to be served. "We can't talk here." He turned towards the back and called, "Sam, take over for ten minutes will you?"

A guy came out, sized up the situation, muttered "Slut" hardly under his breath and started serving. "Ten minutes tops," he said as Alec motioned with his head, and I followed him towards a sign that said, "Gents."

There's a Boy Scout promise that talks about being "clean in thought, word and deed." I'd never have made a good Scout. On the other hand, their motto, "Be Prepared," I was good at.

Not that we made the Gents. Just before, there was an unmarked door which he opened and disappeared inside. I peered in; a cupboard with some mops and buckets. A hand pulled me in. The door was pulled shut and instantly everything went almost completely dark. I stumbled over something and fell face downwards. Someone collapsed on top of me, an outstretched hand landing on the top of my leg, just below my buttock, felt for my groin. For a moment we were struggling together, then I turned over, and he was lying on me, full length, face to face, chest to chest, groin to groin.

"Is this what you intended?" I asked.

"Quiet!" Alec's soft voice from out of the darkness, and as if to emphasize the command, his mouth closed on mine.

Taking that for agreement, one by one I undid the buttons of his uniform tunic and cat-licked my way down the centre of his chest to his umbilicus and after that, unzipped his trousers and pulled down the elastic waistband of his shorts; I tasted the head of his cock which already exuded a transparent drop of excitement.

He pulled me up into another kiss.

The point of his tongue emerged, insistently probing between my lips, past my teeth, into my mouth and meeting mine, tasting the saliva, joining our two tongues. It was as if this inspired a fresh urgency in the groin, each pushing against the other. My hands cupped the cheeks of Alec's buttocks, the middle finger of my right hand now exploring the deepness of the cleft until it found and entered the crinkled hole. Alec sighed.

"I'd like you to fuck me," he said.

I inserted another finger and moved both, enlarging the hole. He opened his legs and raised his knees so that the access could be easier, and my fingers probed deeper.

I said "Be Prepared" was my motto. Cute and willing as this guy was, I wasn't going to risk riding him bareback. I groped in my pocket and found the flat, square packet, broke open the seal and struggled to pull the rubber over my cock. "Hurry up," said Alec. My, this guy was eager. My prick got its protective coating, and I guided it into the waiting hole. He tensed, then relaxed and allowed it to pierce and enter. I felt his flesh surround me, and I pushed, first gently allowing the alien muscle to become part of him. My hand returned to his cock, grasping it, rubbing the outside skin over the rigid central core. His breath panted, sometimes in time with my lunges, at others out of phase, as I varied the stroke.

There we were, assailed from the back, frotted in the front, the familiar feeling building up in my loins, focusing on that centre of my being, my sex, until I could hold back no longer.

Suddenly there were voices outside the door, two at least, possibly more. They seemed to pause, hesitate for a moment as if not certain whether to come in or not. The closeness of people outside added to the excitement. I groaned, and we reached our climaxes, separately yet together, me into him, he into my hand.

The voices receded, faded and finally ceased. There was

a moment's quiet, and then Alec opened the door, letting in a narrow strip of light, just enough to see by. We adjusted clothing. I wiped my hand on a duster. We left the filled condom in the cleaner's bucket.

"Peter Palmer," I said.

"Never heard of him," said Alec, smiling, thinking he'd got away with it.

That made me a bit cross. Not that the episode hadn't been pleasurable, but I objected to being taken for a mug. He was on his way out when I grabbed him from behind between his legs, feeling the soft ballsack through the thin material of his trousers, and squeezed, hard.

"Ow," he said. "Christ. That hurts."

"Peter Palmer." I held on, not relaxing.

"Please," he said, almost a whimper, the cockiness gone. "I'll tell you. What do you want to know?"

"Who might have had it in for him?"

"I don't know. Ouch. I really don't know."

"Was there anyone he saw regularly?"

"I don't know." A squeeze. "Yes, yes. There was. I never saw him, but Pete used to talk about him. Said it had to be a secret, because otherwise the guy might get into trouble. Pete thought it a bit of a joke. Felt as if the guy was, almost, in his power. You know, he could make him do anything he wanted. Please, let go."

I relaxed my grip. The guy must have been in agony. He clutched at himself, tenderly rubbing his abused parts.

"Did you ever see this other guy? Did Pete ever give a hint what he did?"

"No," said Alec. "I swear. Only thing he ever told me was that he used to meet him at Gracey's. That's a gay club at…"

"I know where Gracey's is," I said.

We went back into the cafe, Alec hobbling a little and looking strained.

"Crikey," said Sam, observing from behind the counter. "He must have been good."

It had been a long day, and I thought I'd had enough excitement. I phoned Paul on his mobile to see whether he was home, going home or still at work. And yes, I did feel guilty. I was sore, though probably not as sore as Alec, and I knew that, yet again, I'd done the dirty on my partner, who, I was pretty sure, would never do the same to me. One of these days I'd get found out, and then it would all be over, and I'd be devastated. Paul was everything to me, and yet time and time again I allowed my wretched cock to plough its way into foreign fields.

Paul answered.

"Hi, lover," I said, not without a feeling of hypocrisy, though I meant it fervently.

"How's the sleuthing going?"

"I've been seeing people," I said, "and listening to stuff."

"Got the murderer?"

"Clues," I said vaguely. "I'll tell you when I see you."

"Do you want to go out tonight?" he asked. "Clubbing, film, theatre? It's been a long, boring day, and I could do with some entertainment."

"I'll provide that," I said. It was true, even though I say it myself. This afternoon's little skirmish wouldn't diminish my prowess at all.

"That's something to round the evening off with," said Paul. "Let's paint the town pinkish first."

"Well, we could go to Gracey's. There's a bit of unfinished business there that needs looking into."

"Not too much business. I want some pleasure."

"I promise you that," I said. "See you at home in half an hour."

We ate, showered, dressed ourselves in our trendiest and were off, first to a restaurant which, though not generally considered the acme of smartness, did provide excellent food at a reasonable cost. I drank to my lover's health whilst sitting opposite him and staring into those beautiful eyes, sparkling with fun and amusement, and wondered, for the fifty-millionth time, why I felt the urge to bother with other people when this delicacy was all mine.

I guessed that, to get into Gracey's would cost and was surprised when Hubert on the door greeted me with, "Good evening, Mr. Sinclair." He passed us both in without any fuss at all.

Gracey's was not very different from any other gay club in London, or probably in any city all over the world. It was hot and crowded, dark and noisy, Paul immediately felt at home in it, and I, as usual, a little uncomfortable. It was nine o'clock when we got there and, being Saturday night, approaching its apogee. The dancing area was at its most lively, sweaty bodies leaping and vying with each other to seem the most athletic, the bar at its busiest, the music at its loudest.

A regular flashing beat in time to music. Harsh pounding rhythms with the bass notes on drums and bass guitar, the melody sharper, more intense, weaving in and out of the throbbing pulse. Coloured beams of light which lit up sweat-slicked bodies, maleness and sex, contorted limbs sharpened by the rampant rhythms, dancing to the strident disharmonies of the lights. The persistent, insistent thump gave me, as it always did, an erection.

Some guys were standing in a group over at one side, clustering round a small raised stage. On it, a pair of youths danced, erotically, wearing only the briefest and tightest of shorts, their bodies entwined though not quite touching, their naked bodies shining with perspiration, their faces contorted, mouths open in a mutually soundless cry.

"Beer," I said. "I must have a beer. Do you want the same?"

Paul nodded. I plunged into the throng around the bar.

"Still pretending to be the fuzz," hissed a voice in my ear. It was Robert Wilkins, his usual flat, expressionless face now twisted in what looked like a parody of a sneer.

"I told you I wasn't the police," I protested, waving a ten pound note at one of the barmen, who ignored me completely. I turned back to Robert. "I'm sorry we started off on the wrong wavelength. I just wanted to know about Pete."

"And I told you he was a hustler, and you didn't believe me."

"I was wrong, and you were right," I said. I tried again with the barman. "Excuse me. Could I have two beers." I might have been invisible. I wondered if Robert might still be able to see me. "I found out though that he had a regular boyfriend, call it what you want, and that he often met him here."

"How should I know? He didn't tell me anything." Robert raised a finger and the barman came over.

"How did you do that?" I asked, and then before the barman could disappear. "Two beers, please - no make that three." It seemed the least I could do.

There was no change from the tenner. This wasn't a bar I'd be frequenting regularly, or for long. I pushed the beer towards Robert. "Thanks anyway."

Perhaps he wasn't used to people buying him drinks, but it was as if his attitude suddenly softened. "Don't know his name, but there's a guy he was often with. The one with the spiky hair." He pointed to the end of the bar.

A young man stood there, hair indeed spiked and tinted blond at the ends. He was wearing shades though it must have made everything look very dark in this dim place lit only by the lasers and the lights at the back of the bar. Perhaps the laser beams hurt his eyes. Perhaps it was a fashion statement.

"Thanks Robert," I said and carried the two remaining drinks to Paul. He was still watching the two on the dais. They had now reached a stage of simulated, if not actual, copulation.

"Wow," said Paul, looking at the couple. "It makes me sort

of randy just looking at them." He sipped at his beer. "I don't think I want to stay here long. I guess I'm looking forward to an early night." He gave me a lecherous leer and put his hand on my groin.

"I promise," I said, "but first I must check out a guy."

I steered him towards the end of the bar where spiky-hair was still standing. He was smoking and looking soulfully into a glass, probably dismayed at the price it had cost him. We approached from the rear and thus were able to get close without attracting his attention. As soon as I got within smelling distance I got a whiff of that perfume I hated so much, Homme Epouvantable, and remembered that the last time I had smelled it had been in Pete's flat, just before finding the body. I didn't recognize him, but there was something strangely familiar about him. Had we met before? It worried me that I couldn't remember. I wondered how I could get in touch without arousing his suspicions. Paul and I went back into the crowd.

"That guy with the dark glasses," I said quickly. "I think he's got something to do with Pete's death."

"Do you want to talk to him now?" asked Paul.

"I don't know. There's something familiar about him, though I can't think what. We may have met somewhere."

"I haven't. Do you want me to talk to him?"

I was dubious. "I don't trust him"

"Oh come on," said Paul. "Nothing can happen here. You can keep an eye on me anyway."

"Okay," I said. I gave him another £10 note. "Buy him a drink. Then see if you can get into conversation. Talk to him if you can, try to find out anything about Pete, but be careful."

I watched Paul go to the bar. After a short while I saw the two of them talking. I sat at the bar and sipped my beer. I could see the two reflected in the mirror at the back of the bar.

"Can't you keep away?" said someone next to me.

I turned.

Harold Palmer stood beside me, a smile on his thickset face. It was twisted by the scar, and if anything it made him look more sinister.

"Mr. Palmer," I said.

"At least you remember my name," he said. "You could call me Harold."

He looked round at the crowded bar around them. "I'd like to see you privately, to talk."

"Only to talk?" I asked and hoped it didn't sound arch. "I think I know who killed your brother," I said.

"I thought I told you to leave it to the professionals."

"That's what I am," I said. "Well, if you're not interested."

He grabbed me by the arm. "Don't play with me," he said. The grip hurt. I remembered again Ross's warning. Remember they're not nelly queens.

"Okay," I said. "It was the aftershave. I smelled it in the flat when I got there. Then Alec at the coffee-bar told me Pete was blackmailing some guy he used to meet at the club, and finally Robert pointed him out just now. He's wearing the same aftershave. It's the one at the end of the bar, in the dark glasses with the spiky hair."

"Look again," said Palmer.

I glanced at the mirror. Paul and the guy I suspected were no longer sitting at the end of the counter.

"Where are they?" I said. "They were sitting down there. They couldn't have got out without passing us."

"There's an exit at the back. He went out a coupla minutes ago with the red-haired boy."

"Oh Christ!" I said. I'd let Paul go off with a possible murderer. I forced my way through the crush on the dance floor. At the other end there was a door with "Fire Escape" painted on it and "Push Bar to Open." But the bar to open seemed jammed when I pushed on it. I tried again, frantically but still nothing budged.

Then another body arrived, stocky and obviously considerably stronger than me. With one hand Palmer pushed at the bar. The doors flew open. I felt fresh air on my face.

We were out in what was obviously the back of the house. It was still light enough to see the small courtyard bordered by brick walls with uneven concrete paving blocks through which a few weeds pushed their way. A couple of dustbins stood against the side wall. There was no one in sight.

"Come on," said Palmer and raced away towards the bottom end where a small gate opened onto a back road. The street lights were on and cast an orange sodium glare on two figures, moving rapidly, one stumbling, away to the right.

Palmer shouted, "Stop," and waved his arm in the air. To my horror I saw that he had a gun in his hand. If he fired he would just as easily hit Paul as the other guy. In the gathering gloom I could scarcely make out which was which. "Don't shoot," I shouted, but Palmer took no notice. He levelled the gun. Desperately I knocked his arm, and the gun went off, the bullet presumably going off harmlessly into the air. Palmer swore, turned on me and hit me with the gun. For the second time today I was knocked out. Well, to be strictly accurate, this time I didn't actually lose consciousness. I felt the pain and everything went suddenly awry, the pavement becoming a wall, the wall a sky. I was on my knees and could still see the pair and Palmer taking aim again. Another explosion and one of them dropped.

"Fucking shit," I screamed and staggered to my feet, hobbling down the road after Palmer. I got to where the unhit guy stood, staring down at the body in the road. He turned to me, and it was Paul. "Thank Christ," I said and took him in my arms, squeezing him until he groaned.

"Mind my ribs," he said.

Only then did I look at the other guy. Flat on his back, legs and arms sprawled, no sign of the bullet hole which must have hit him in the back. His glasses had fallen off and lay shattered on the curb. I recognized him. Without the glasses, and even with the spiked hair instead of his usual conventional parting, the identification was obvious. It was Inspector Skipton, in death looking even younger than he had when alive.

"Oh God," I said to Palmer. "You've shot the policeman."

"Get out," he said. "Leave this to me. Get away from here and say nothing. You don't want to get involved. What does accessory to murder sound like?"

He was right. I didn't want to stay around. Woozily, I grabbed hold of Paul, and we went off into the night. Paul drove home.

"Jeez, I'm so sorry I got you involved," I said later when we were home. "And now I've got Skipton killed. There wasn't any real evidence. Just a few bits of gossip and that bloody aftershave."

"He did it," said Paul. "He as good as admitted it when I mentioned Pete, told him how close we'd been and how he shared all his secrets with me. He hustled me out so quickly I hardly knew what was happening. I guess I'd been next, if Palmer hadn't shot him. All I don't really understand is why he did it."

But I did. I saw it all now. Skipton obviously didn't want to come out of the closet. There's no rule that a police officer can't be gay, but it would probably mean a stop on his promotion and even worse was consorting with a male prostitute, brother of a drugs dealer. There have been and no doubt still are gay Chief Constables, but they don't admit to being gay until they've reached the top and almost always not even then.

I explained as much to Paul. "If Pete was blackmailing him, as Robert said he was, then Skipton couldn't afford to let the relationship continue, and if Pete was as much of a bastard as Murdoch said he was, then Pete knew he was onto a good thing and wouldn't let go. So Skipton presumably went back with Pete, drugged his coffee; I remembered seeing the two mugs on the draining board. Then he killed him with the pillow. With Skipton as Inspector in charge of the case, he could make sure that there was no evidence of his being in the flat before I arrived."

"Except the smell of Homme Epouvantable," said Paul.

I might so nearly have lost him. Even now we were not exactly safe. The police wouldn't give up when one of their own had been killed. They wouldn't know that their Inspector Skipton himself was a murderer. Some time, sooner or later, Palmer would surely be arrested, and then what would happen. Would he sacrifice us? But I had to put that out of my mind for the present.

"Promise me you'll never wear that stuff," I said.

"I promise," Paul said, and kissed me.

CHAPTER ELEVEN

Game Boys

"The Amusement Arcade" beckoned. Neon lights spelled out the words in swirls of red and yellow so convoluted as to almost make a nonsense of the name. "Beckoned" was the wrong word; it shouted, commanded, ordered, and like the children to the Pied Piper, they came. In ones and twos, in groups, predominantly male, predominantly young. Even though a small card in an inconspicuous part of the window advised: "Minimum age sixteen. Anyone appearing younger will be asked to leave," many were obviously under sixteen. Some indeed as young as eleven or less, And no one was asked to leave. A tall, thin, possibly, eighteen-year-old, though still with pubescent spots, was ostensibly in charge, but he expelled no one and welcomed all with an expressionless acceptance which was probably more agreeable to the young arrivals than any sort of smile.

Inside there was a burst of flashing lights, screens with figures in athletic contortions as enemies were destroyed with an electronic zap. Boys whose fingers and thumbs worked the keys with practiced dexterity stared at the screens with an almost zombie-like intensity. Some of them wore such a look of innocence, they wouldn't have been out of place in the church choir; others covered their innocence with masks of concentration, and still more of the older ones had expressions of world-weariness.

The arcade didn't beckon me. On the contrary I approached it most reluctantly. As the Bard has it, "a whining schoolboy creeping like a snail unwillingly." It just wasn't my scene. The kids were too young. They talked a different language. I knew I'd feel out of place. Not that there weren't a few older guys sprinkled amongst the youth, older guys with a predatory look on their strained, yearning faces. I fancifully thought I could smell the acquisitiveness in the air. It came from the anxious searching in the older men's eyes and the weary availability in some of the younger ones. It was summed up, I thought, in the dollar sign embroidered neatly on the arse cheek of one young man's jeans.

So what, you might ask, was I doing in this place which I so obviously disliked?

"Good of you to come in, Tim," said Sergeant Shepherd, seated benignly behind the counter of the local police station. He ignored a shrilling phone until it got too much, then he gestured to a constable to answer it for him.

"I had an option, Charlie?" I said when comparative silence fell.

He smiled. Charlie was a mate of mine, or at least as much as a policeman can be a friend of a private investigator who had often been in opposition to the police, and in fact had twice been the suspect in murder cases. He knew I was gay, and it didn't trouble him, and his bland, rather full face always split into a wide grin when he saw me.

"So what's this all about?" I asked. I hadn't really wanted to become embroiled in the doings of this particular area, not after the shooting of the late Inspector Skipton. I knew he had been bent, that he'd in fact been responsible for the death of one Peter Palmer, a hustler, and that he'd been shot by Peter's brother, Harold, but I didn't want to get involved. Reason one being that both my lover and I, Paul Massingham, would have been arrested as accessories as we'd actually been there at the shooting.

But Charlie had phoned me, said that it was important that I come to see the new Inspector and that I could, perhaps, help them out in an investigation. I was intrigued, I must admit, and it would have seemed strange to refuse, almost suspicious, and suspicion was one thing I didn't want to create.

So here I was in the nick with an "invitation" to see Inspector Haskins, the new D.I. The room had its usual green-painted walls; there was no cup of tea, the only welcoming thing was

Charlie's smile.

"What's this Inspector Haskins like?" I asked.

"You'll like him," said Charlie. "Old-fashioned bobby worked his way up through the ranks. Honest but bright. You couldn't slip anything past him, but he'll treat you straight."

"Not like Skipton," I said, and then called myself stupid. I shouldn't have mentioned the subject. I could see conflicting emotions on Charlie's face. I knew he'd disliked the late inspector, but they had both been coppers, and Skipton had been murdered. They don't forget what happens to one of their own, and no one, as far as I knew, knew he'd been bent.

"Okay," I said. "What's he want to see me about? Are you allowed to tell me?"

"He told me to sound you out first. The situation is this. There's an amusement arcade which we think is being used to attract young boys into underage sex. We want someone to infiltrate, find out what's really going on and if we're right, get the guys who are running it."

"Why me?"

Charlie looked embarrassed. "It's got to be someone gay," he said.

I was cross, no, more than that, furious. "I may be gay," I said, "but I'm not a pedophile. Why do you straights think they're the same? Is a so-called normal guy automatically thought of as lusting after little girls?"

"I thought you'd react like that, and you're right. Of course we don't think all gays are after little boys, but you'd know how a gay man behaves. You wouldn't stick out like a police plant. Put a constable in baggy jeans and a leather top, teach him how to mince and lisp and he still looks, walks and smells like a cop."

I nearly laughed. "And you haven't got any gays in the force?" I didn't tell him that I knew of at least two in that very station who were as gay as August Bank Holiday. I didn't, and couldn't, tell him that the late Inspector Skipton had been gay and shafting

Peter Palmer at every available opportunity before the relationship soured up and Skipton killed him to stop being outed.

"We probably have," said Charlie, "but they ain't admitting it. Look, Tim, you don't have to do this, but it's an unpleasant, vile trade if what we suspect is really going on, kids of twelve and thirteen, perhaps even younger, and if we can stop it, arrest whoever's organizing it, surely that's a good thing."

Of course I agreed, which was why I was entering the Arcade, feeling completely out of place and at the moment wishing that I'd said no.

Of course being and looking furtive probably wasn't a bad disguise for a guy who was scouting out the land to pick up underage boys. Certainly no one descended on me, demanding to know what I was doing. In fact the spotty "bouncer," if that was his job, nodded to me, almost as if I were a regular.

I wasn't sure how to proceed so I decided to tell the truth. "This is my first time," I said to him.

He nodded in an unhelpful way. It was obvious that he wasn't going to introduce me to the nearest underage boy and send us off with the key to a nice little fuck-nest.

"'Ere, Sam," said someone from out of the electronic gloom. "This fucker's on the blink."

Sam took this information with as much enthusiasm as he had my comment. If he wasn't going to bounce the kids, then equally apparently he wasn't about to sort out some misbehaving computer game.

"So, Sam," I said, "What do I do?"

Sam shrugged. "You puts your money in and you punches the knobs," he said. "Squeeze the tit or the cock, whichever suits your fancy."

I looked to see if he was giving anything away, but his face was blank. It hadn't meant anything, well, nothing significant I was fairly sure. He turned away, losing interest, wandering off to look at a guy whose flashing fingers and obvious dexterity were achieving spectacular results on the screen.

I cursed the guys who had sent me into this embarrassing mess, but then, someone who was really out to find a chicken for sex wouldn't necessarily be an expert at arcade games. Or would he? Wouldn't the guy bone up on the action so that at least he'd have something in common with the customers. I looked round vaguely.

There was a vacant machine. On the screen a muscle-bound "hero" punched his way round a boxing ring laying out opponents right left and centre. Tentatively I prodded at a button. Nothing happened. I peered closer. There were some instructions on the side. "Insert a £ coin," it said. So much for my listening to Sam's instructions. I put in a quid. The screen cleared and the guy appeared alone in the centre of the ring. I tried a button. He turned around. I tried another. The boxer flashed out his right fist. Another one, and he was a southpaw. This was easy. Another guy, equally beefy, entered the ring. I turned my guy to face him, aimed a blow, missed and I was flat on the floor. The referee counted me out. "GAME OVER."

Someone near to me laughed from out of the gloom. "Ain't much cop in the boxing ring are you, mate?" A face swam into view lit by the alternating lights of a screen, red, green, yellow, blue. A young boy's face, not as young as some here, perhaps sixteen, at least his voice had broken. Dark hair, short, combed into a fringe over his forehead, ears that stuck out a little, and for a moment I was reminded of my lover, Paul, who, when he wore his hair short, also had the same look, but here the resemblance ended. Bright eyes, in the dimness and against the lights I couldn't see the color. Full lips curled into the suggestion of a smile, altogether attractive. Thin body that would fill out into a real athletic build in his twenties and, then, I felt sure, would fatten with lack of exercise into premature middle-age, but now flushed with the health and vitality of the young.

I acknowledged his comment with a wry smile. "I guess not," I said.

"Any good on a motor bike?" He gestured at an amusement down the aisle. Two imitation motor bikes, or at least the seats and handlebars, faced side by side a single screen.

"I used to ride," I said. It was true. I had once had a two-stroke, though gave it up after running into a van which had pulled out of a side road into my path. The only casualty had been the bike, but afterwards I'd decided that a car was safer.

"Give you a race," he said, "if you'll pay. I'm clean out. More fun with two." I looked to see if there was any significance in the remark, but his expression remained bland. His eyes were green, I noticed.

We climbed on to the bikes. I inserted coins for each machine. There was an electronic attempt at a motorbike roar which increased when I wound the accelerator.

I turned to face him. "My name's Tim," I said. He was wearing a dark-blue sweatshirt with two white bands across the chest and the number three, also in white, just above where his umbilicus would be.

"Zack," he said. What sort of name was that? Who in their right mind would name a child these days Zack? Zachariah? Perhaps it was a street name.

I'll give him his due. He kept his speed down while I got to terms with the controls. It was fairly easy. The handlebars did the steering. Right hand accelerated and left braked. The road unfurled on the screen ahead of us, and there were various hazards along the way, zigzags, dangerous corners, other vehicles to overtake or avoid, stupid pedestrians occasionally wandering into our path. In a little while, he accelerated and I twisted the grip to keep up with him.

Zack was lying low over the handlebars, as if to lessen the wind resistance, as if he could actually feel the wind flowing over his back. He flung himself over to the sides as he went round corners. It couldn't have done any good, of course, although, even though my throttle was at the extreme, he was still going faster than I was, and barely slowing down to take the tightest corner. A sign for a humpbacked bridge suddenly appeared. Zack ignored it, but I slowed slightly. Even so, on the screen, my little bike took off, and I realized there was a sharp bend to the left immediately after. I wrenched the handlebars over, braking hard, but my wheels had no traction, not even touching the surface. The bike couldn't clear the fencing at the side of the road. It catapulted upwards, turning over and over before crashing to the ground in a spectacular display of sparks and flame.

Zack turned to me, his face alight, a broad grin splitting his face. "You done good," he said. "Winner stays, loser pays! Try again?"

After a few more goes we ran out of steam, and I figured that this would be the last I'd see of him, but before we parted he asked me if I wanted to get something to eat. "Wanna buy me a burger?" he asked. His blatant materialism, the almost tacit acceptance that I would pay, didn't upset me. His face was frank and open. He asked, and I could accept or not. I didn't think he'd be upset even if I refused.

I nodded, and we made our way towards the exit. Sam, the spotty-faced "bouncer," was deep in conversation with a middle-aged man, their heads close together. As I got nearer I suddenly recognized the other man. It was Dave Murdoch.

Now, Murdoch and I had met before and only recently. He was the owner of several gay clubs, and, I'd been told by a friend who knows about these things, probably a drug dealer. His business partner, Harold Palmer, had been the guy who'd shot Inspector Skipton that time with Paul and me as witnesses. I didn't want anything to do with either of them, but I couldn't understand what Murdoch was doing here. I'd been reliably informed that he wasn't into young guys; Harold Palmer possibly was, but not Murdoch. I'd only met Murdoch once, and perhaps he wouldn't have recognized me again, but I didn't want to take the chance.

"You see that guy there," I said to Zack, turning my back and pointing over my shoulder, "talking to Sam. Do you know who he is?"

Zack peered. "Sure," he said. "That's Big Mac. He owns the

place."

"Big Mac," huh? Last I'd heard he'd called himself "the Padre," but perhaps he used a different name for each of his undertakings. So, he owned the arcade and presumably knew about what was going on there. No one did things behind the Padre's back and expected to get away with it.

I sidled out looking away from Murdoch, and we reached the street without his noticing, Zack giving me a curious look which I ignored. The Burger Bar was a couple of shops down the road on the other side.

I expected him to sit opposite me, but he followed me onto the bench and we sat next to each other, and Zack wolfed down a Double Ham 'n' Cheese with fries and a milk shake. I sipped at a coffee, watching him from time to time. It was still early evening and the place was half empty. There was an innocence about him away from the arcade. It was as if that was his territory, and there he was boss. Outside he was just a kid and seemed to lack confidence.

He finished the food and drank the shake.

"Do you live nearby?" I asked.

Instantly it was as if a defensive shield went up. His eyes looked at me suspiciously. For a moment he looked much younger than the sixteen years I had estimated. A young child stared out. "Why?" he asked.

"No reason," I said. "Just asking. My flat's only a couple of streets away. I assumed you didn't travel any distance to get to the Amusement Arcade. You're obviously a regular there."

He nodded and relaxed; the self-possessed cockiness back. "I ain't seen you there before," he said. I felt a slight pressure as our thighs touched. He'd moved nearer as he drained the shake. "Do you wanta go back to your flat?" he asked. The thigh pressed harder, making the suggestion explicit, but there was nothing sleazy about his invitation. His smile was frank and open, and I knew if I said yes, he'd be just as forthright about the price. Or so I thought.

"Not tonight," I said, nearly adding an automatic "Josephine," but I stopped myself. He might not have recognized the reference and felt it was an insult to his manhood. "I like you, but there are complications. Perhaps we can meet again." I wanted to ask questions but was afraid that, if I pushed it, he'd clam up. "My name's Tim Sinclair."

"Okay," he said, neither upset nor disappointed. His hand reached into my groin and squeezed me. "Yes, I can see you like me." He laughed, and walked out of the Burger Bar. I watched him as he crossed the road and went back to the Arcade. He'd had his meal from me. Now he was off for something else.

Paul was quiet and seemed a little out of sorts when I got home. "You've had a visitor," he said. "Charlie Shepherd called wanting to hear how you'd got on."

"I'd have let them know down at the nick. Couldn't they wait?"

"I think he just wanted a chat," said Paul, giving me a sharp look, which at the time I didn't understand. "He drank three cups of tea."

"Always was one for the tea," I said. "I suppose he told you what they wanted me to do down at the Arcade. What they didn't tell me was that Dave Murdoch owned the place."

"You're getting into deep waters," said Paul, nodding. "The police must have known he owned the Arcade. Why didn't they tell you?" We sat at the table with the remnants of the evening meal between us. Chicken Korma followed by strawberries and yoghurt. Apart from the fruit, it had all come from packets. Two busy working lads didn't have time for real cooking at the end of the day.

"I don't know. Perhaps they thought that a guy going into the arcade wouldn't know anything about the management. All they wanted me to find out was how the links between the kids and the adults were made."

Paul looked worried. "You don't think the police have a suspicion that we are connected in some way with Murdoch and

Palmer and it's all a sort of trap for us, or at least you, to fall into."

"No," I said. "I think that's too devious, even for the new guy, Haskins. Charlie says he's straight. I was quite impressed."

"They don't like one of their own being killed," he said, a dubious frown creasing his forehead. It made him look vulnerable and troubled. I leant over the table and kissed him but he drew back. "So, what did you find out?"

"Well, I made a contact." And I told him about Zack, leaving out the bit about his farewell grope.

"That's all?"

"I'll get back to him tomorrow," I said. "The only way I could get any further was to drag him back to the flat. I guess you wouldn't have approved."

Paul looked at me. "As if you haven't done it before," he said.

"What!"

"Oh, come off it, Tim. Do you think I've been blind all these months?" He got to his feet and the chair he'd been sitting on fell backwards.

"What do you mean?"

Paul counted the names off on his fingers. "Let's see, there was Ted Parry, the policeman, Rod Boyston, Joe, that daft UFO guy, my friend, Martin Kasmir. Charlie told me that you met Pete Palmer in the coffee bar and were going back to his flat for sex when you found him dead, and what about Alec from the Coffee Experience?" He blazed with anger.

The litany of names rocked me back on my heels. They weren't all true. Ted Parry, for instance, had wanted to get me into bed but had failed. Roderick Boyston hadn't got past the groping stage.

"You knew about Joe," I said. "The others were just mistakes. They didn't mean anything." It was a pathetic, blustering attempt at extenuation, and I knew it sounded completely unconvincing. Charlie in his bumbling, chatty way, had completely dropped me in the shit.

But now Paul's anger dissolved into something worse. It was as if something inside him had crumbled. He sagged. "Wasn't I enough for you?" he asked, his face pale and strained.

I had no answer. Paul was my everything, in bed, at home, just being with him. He was the one whose body I held next to mine in lust, pushed aside in anger, comforted, loved, missed when he wasn't there. But there was always something in me I couldn't control. An attractive guy made a pass at me, showed me that he was available, gave me a swift grope and opened the door to his bedroom, and I was there.

And now I'd really blown it.

I could see Paul struggling with his tears. I went round the table and tried to take him in my arms, but he wrenched himself free, turned away and ran from the room. I couldn't believe this was happening. It would all be all right. I'd leave him for ten minutes. He'd have a cry and then I'd go to him. We'd fall into each other's arms. He'd forgive me as he had before. I'd promise it would never happen again, and this time I'd really make sure it never did.

Everything was quiet. I wanted to go to him more than anything, but I forced myself to wait. Outside a car starting broke the silence, the ignition needing to be turned twice before it caught, then the sound of it driving off down the road. Silence returned.

I wasn't sure how long I waited, but it felt an age. I went into the hall. The door to our bedroom was shut. I listened, but there was no sound. I knocked.

"Paul," I said. No answer. I opened the door. I could see straight away that he'd gone. Drawers were open and clothes pulled out. A suitcase from above the wardrobe was missing. He'd taken what he needed and must have gone out of the flat quietly. The car! The car I'd heard starting. I ran to the front door and stared at the empty place where Paul's car had been parked. He'd gone, and I had no idea where.

I didn't sleep much that night. A couple of hours before dawn I dozed off and woke up as the light filtered through the window. I reached out for Paul and found only cold emptiness.

As soon as was civilized, I started phoning, but his mobile was switched off and there was no answer from his work.

I made a cup of coffee, and as I did so, my phone rang. I snatched up the receiver. "Paul, Paul," I said, "please forgive me."

"Is that you, Tim," said a voice I didn't recognize.

"Shit," I said. "Who is that?"

"Zack."

In the state I was in, the name meant nothing to me.

"Who?" I asked.

"Zack," he said. "We met yesterday at the Arcade. Look, I need some help."

"How did you get my number?" I asked.

"You're in the book," he said, "as a private investigator."

So much for my cover. Presumably that meant my job at the Arcade was over, but in fact I felt relieved. Now I could put all my effort into my private problems.

"Okay, Zack," I said. "What do you want?"

"Can we meet? Please, Tim. It's very urgent. At the Burger Bar this morning." He sounded agitated. There was a catch in his voice as if he'd been, or perhaps still was, crying.

I looked at my watch. "Ten o'clock." I said. That would give me two hours to see if I could find Paul.

"Thanks, Tim." He rang off.

I sipped my coffee and tried to think of where Paul might have gone. I doubted whether it would be to his parents. They hadn't taken the news that their son was gay very well. They'd been even less enthusiastic when they learned that he was moving in with me. Not that there had been a screaming, homophobic scene or anything like that, but relations had been frosty. They didn't like me, and I didn't think Paul would have made them his first choice.

There were his friends Martin and John, but now that Paul had learned—how had he done that?—that I'd had a little affair with Martin, again it seemed unlikely that he'd go to them for sanctuary.

The phone rang again. This time I was more circumspect though just as quick at picking up the receiver.

"Hello."

"Tim, it's Charlie Shepherd. I asked Paul to get you to ring me last night. Was there a problem?"

"Yes, Charlie, there was. Thank you for dropping me so deep in the shit that Paul's left me."

There was a pause, and when Charlie spoke again, his voice was low and apologetic. "Christ, I'm sorry, Tim. I thought you and Paul had this sort of open relationship. You know, go with who you like as long as you come home to me. I never realized…" His voice died away.

"Well, it's done now," I said. "I only hope I can smooth things over in time. Anyway, what did you want?"

"D.I. Haskins wants you to report on yesterday and then be back at the arcade this morning."

"My cover's been blown," I said, and told him about Zack and how he'd found out I was a P.I.

"Find out what you can from him," said Charlie. "He may not have said anything to the guys in charge at the Arcade."

"That's another thing," I said. "You never told me Dave Murdoch owned it, and Dave Murdoch knows me."

Charlie gave a whistle of concern. "It's all a bit of a cock-up," he said. "Well, meet Zack this morning as you arranged, see what he has to say and then we'll decide on what to do next. I'll tell Haskins the situation."

So I still wasn't off the hook as regards the Arcade. Now I'd agreed to look into Zack's problem, whatever that was, and there still was my own completely fucked-up private life. I drained my coffee which tasted as bitter as guilt.

I hadn't tracked down Paul, still not able to get him on his mobile, and the word from his workplace was that he'd called in sick. Whether this was true or not, I wasn't sure. He might have given instructions that he was "out" to me. I thought of ringing again under an assumed name, but decided this was taking things too far. What if the receptionist saw through my disguise? I'd feel a complete twat.

I got to the Burger Bar just before ten, and it was packed. Obviously it was coffee time for the offices and shops around. Zack wasn't there, so I got myself a coffee, decided that, although I didn't feel hungry, I ought to eat something, so bought something vaguely meaty and greasy in a bun and sat as close to the door as possible so that I could see Zack when he arrived.

The clock ticked on. Several people looked at me with my drained plastic cup and half-eaten bun. A boy clearing tables caught my eye and gave me a half grin. It was half-past ten. I decided I'd been stood up though I couldn't understand why as it had been Zack who'd been so insistent to meet me. I stood up to go, and a woman who'd been standing behind me and sighing officiously, swept into my seat with a scarcely sub-vocal, "At last."

I could give the whole thing up and devote the rest of the day to looking for Paul, but I'd no idea where to look, so I went to the Amusement Arcade. It was exactly as it had been the day before, the same earnest, intense young faces staring into screens, fingers or arms, sometimes whole bodies, twitching to make the brightly coloured ghosts do their bidding. The same sounds, electronic approximations of real life. Sam, wandering around like an unhealthy zombie. I stopped him in an aisle. "Have you seen Zack?" I asked.

"I expect he's around," he said vaguely. "He usually is."

I couldn't see him. Nor for that matter could I see Murdoch, but that didn't mean anything. The bossman might be anywhere, in another part of his empire, in a back room counting his takings—no, he'd have accountants to do that for him. Perhaps even peering at screens where hidden cameras took pictures of unwanted interlopers into his domain, me, for instance. I looked around guiltily, but no one was staring at me as if I was doing anything suspicious.

I found Sam again. "If you see Zack, could you tell him I was looking for him?" I asked.

"Whatever," he said.

So I went. Standing in the street outside, I called Paul again on my mobile. Still no answer. I tried the nick. D.I. Haskins was out, so was Charlie. I left a message saying I'd call in later. I rang home, hoping against hope that there might be a message on the answer phone from Paul. "You have one message," said the precise, disembodied voice, and my heart leapt. "Your message timed at 10:03 today. First message."

There was a pause.

A voice, harsh, cracked voice, talking with what appeared great difficulty, with gasps between the words. "Tim...yer... gotta...help me...I'm...at..." there was an even longer pause, and I feared that whatever had happened to Zack had been too much when the last words forced themselves out. "Flat 1...7 Hope...Terrace." The message disconnected.

Just after ten Zack had made that despairing phone call and now an hour had passed. I had no idea where Hope Terrace was, nor had any passerby whom I asked, but then they were tourists, office workers, shoppers from out of town, not people born and bred in this part of London.

There was a news-agent just down the road. Surely they would know. They would have to deliver newspapers in the area. A man, thickset and bespectacled, stood behind the counter idly flicking over the pages of an OK! magazine.

"Do you know where Hope Terrace is?" I asked.

Without a glance at me he reached behind and picked up an A to Z. I thought at first he was going to look it up for me, but instead he handed it over and demanded a fiver. Mercenary, but I suppose understandable. After all he was in business. I paid and turned to the index. Hope Terrace, W.C.1. The relevant page showed me that Hope Terrace was a small road actually branching off the one I was in. It was a cul-de-sac.

Hope Terrace was just what it said, a terrace, two lines of joined Victorian houses, their front doors leading straight out onto the pavement. From the general run-down appearance of the buildings, it looked as if hope was all it had left; prosperity had certainly passed it by. On the right hand side were numbers 1, 3, 5 and 7. On the left, 2, 4, 6 and 8. I raced along. Number 7 had bell pushes marked with the flat numbers and/or names. There were three, one per floor, I assumed. I pressed the bell for Flat 1, but nothing happened. Flat 2 had a name in smudged Biro, "R. Johnson." I tried that one, but again there was no answer. Flat 3 had the name neatly printed, "Mrs. Peters."

A thin, quavery voice answered over the speaker. "Who is it?"

"Mrs. Peters," I said. "This is Zack. I've forgotten my outdoor key. Could you let me in?"

"You're back?" asked the voice. "Whom do you want to see?"

"Not back," I said, "Zack. Can you let me in?"

"I can't hear," she said. "I'll let you in, and you can tell me what you want. I'm on the top floor."

The lock buzzed, and the door clicked open. A flight of stairs led upwards; a door with a number 1 on it was on the left. I banged on it. "Zack," I said. "It's me, Tim."

There was a pause, then the door slowly opened.

"Jesus Christ Almighty," I said.

Paul stared into the middle distance. A newspaper article he was supposed to be reviewing lay on the desk in front of him.

He'd already read it twice and still had no idea what it was about. An untouched plastic cup of coffee cooled beside him, a skin forming on top.

He'd spent the night at the flat of a friend he'd gone to college with some six years before. They'd kept in touch, more or less, and the friend had been one of those guys who had kept the easygoing lifestyle of the student even though now he was in a job and going out seriously with a girl. Paul's arriving unannounced and with a request for a bed for the night had been received with curiosity but no great astonishment. The simple explanation that he'd split with his partner—the friend hadn't been aware that Paul was gay—and that the partner was male had been received with casual sympathy.

"Stay as long as you want," he'd said, before disappearing into his own bedroom with his girlfriend and leaving the couch for Paul to toss and turn on for the remainder of the night. The not very subdued sounds of passion from next door hadn't helped of course, but it was the break-up of his own relationship which caused him the most distress.

Paul was one of those people who, when he fell in love, loved absolutely. He'd been in love once before with a guy called Joseph Carter, who had been murdered. It had taken a great deal of time to get over that one, and he'd been tentative about making any sort of commitment with Tim, but he had eventually done so, and even overlooked, as far as was possible, the extramarital affairs that Tim had indulged in. But Charlie's revelation that there had been so many more than he knew about had finally forced a crisis. There was no comprehension in Paul's philosophy that love could be partial or apportioned or put to one side, even for the time being, if someone else attractive and available hove into view.

Now he felt desperately miserable. He ought to feel that his heart was broken, but the discomfort he felt was in the pit of his stomach; perhaps that was the seat of emotions. He'd been hurt but wondered whether his abrupt decision to leave had been sensible or just a spontaneous act of immaturity. He knew, or was pretty sure, that Tim loved him. Wasn't it possible to overlook the other side of Tim's libido? Again? And how many more times?

"Aren't you feeling well?" asked Sheila, his boss, as she passed his desk. As always with her, sympathy was in short supply. She'd had to fight her way to the top and had no intention of showing any sort of compassionate weakness in her own make-up on which others could assault her.

"What? Oh sorry. Yes, I'm okay. Just got a few personal problems," said Paul.

"Don't let them stop you finishing that review," she said shortly. "I want it by midday."

"Bitch," said Paul, under his breath, but her interruption had forced him to stop thinking of himself. He pulled himself together and started the article again. This time it was making a bit of sense. He made a few notes.

Perhaps it was time that he split with Tim, however hard that would be. He would have to see him of course, but later. He needed some things from the flat. He'd go and collect them in his lunch hour when Tim would be at work.

He looked back at the article, and for a second his eyes blurred with tears. Angrily he wiped them aside.

Zack was in the spare room. I'd done what I could for him. I wanted to take him straight to hospital, but he'd refused. Someone had done a really good job at beating him up, but they'd been clever about it. I didn't think anything was actually broken; if it had been I'd have insisted on hospital whatever Zack had said, but it was mainly bruises and cuts that had made him look so terrible when he opened the door to me, his clothes torn, vivid welts over both eyes, blood running down his face.

There was nowhere else I could take him, as he refused to go to hospital and wouldn't tell me where his home was. I got him back to the flat and gently took off his clothes, wincing at the bruises and abrasions all over the tender young skin of his body and legs. Now that I'd gently washed him and put him to bed, he looked better, though felt, he admitted, awful. I fed him some Paracetamol, but understandably he didn't want any food.

"Do you feel up to telling me what happened?" I asked.

He groaned. "Leave it till later," he said.

I nodded and left him there, looking young and vulnerable, his eyes shut, youthful features twisted into a grimace of pain. Hopefully the analgesics would begin to work soon and he'd sleep.

As I reached the kitchen I heard the sound of a key in the lock of the front door. I ran out into the hall. It was Paul, looking pale and strained.

"Oh," he said, as he saw me. "I didn't think you'd be home. I need some things."

"Paul," I said. "Surely we can talk about this. I can't bear it if you leave."

He hesitated, looking at me warily, his hair dishevelled. I wanted to take him in my arms. "It's just that - " he started when there was a sound from the spare room.

"What's that?" asked Paul.

"Tim," Zack called clearly.

"Have you got someone there?" asked Paul.

Oh shit, I thought. I said, "It's that young guy, Zack. I told you about him. He'd nowhere to go and - "

Paul interrupted. "So you did bring him back. No sooner was I out of the way than you're bringing guys back."

"You don't understand," I said desperately. "He was beaten up. He wouldn't let me take him to hospital. Take a look at him. He's in a dreadful state."

"I don't want to see him," said Paul, outraged. "Who do you think you are? Fucking Florence Nightingale." He turned and stormed out of the front door.

"Wait," I said. "Paul, please wait."

But he'd gone, and I heard the car squeal off down the road.

Shit. Why was everything going wrong?

I went in to see Zack. He'd pulled himself into a sitting position, supported against the headrest of the bed. I arranged the pillows so that he was more comfortable. I recalled Paul's jibe about Florence Nightingale.

"Why don't you try to sleep?" I asked, sounding even more nurse-like.

"I can't." There was a pause. "It said in the phone book you were a P.I."

I nodded.

"Are you investigating the business at the Arcade?"

I sat down on the side of the bed, making sure that I didn't touch him. I nodded again.

"For underage sex?"

"That's part of it," I said. "We want the adults who are doing it, not the kids."

"So you weren't trying to pick me up?" There was a trace of a smile on his swollen lips.

"Not exactly."

"But you wouldn't really have minded? You got turned on in the Burger Bar."

"Zack," I said, "I'm married. I live here with a guy. It doesn't stop me lusting a bit but I don't do anything about it." I felt a complete hypocrite but wanted to get the conversation away from dangerous ground. I didn't know what the future was between Paul and me, but I didn't want to fuck it up even further, in case something could be salvaged.

"Not much I could do for you anyway at the moment."

I ignored that. "What happened this morning? Two phone calls, the first you were upset but not like the second one."

"Okay," said Zack. "It was a bad night. The punter had paid

for a full night, but he was gross. When he wanted to do it again in the morning I wouldn't let him. I wanted out. I thought you might be able to help me."

"And then he beat you up?"

"Not him," said Zack. "He left, but must have complained, and a couple of bullies arrived to 'punish' me just as I was about to leave to meet you."

"Who were they?"

"One was a big guy employed at the Arcade for duties, not sure exactly what he does. I've seen him around."

"Was the other one 'Big Mac'?" I asked.

"No," said Zack.

"What about Harold Palmer?" I asked, going on a private hunch.

"Don't know him."

"Guy about forty, has a scar down the left side of his face. Uses a hammer as punisher."

Zack shook his head.

Of course the two goons could have been hired by either Murdoch or Palmer, or in fact by anyone. But the fact that one of them worked at the Arcade owned by Murdoch suggested that he was the boss.

"Tell me how it works," I said.

"Kids are 'recruited' by older ones. Punter pays money in the arcade. I don't know who to. Kids get payment weekly. Just a job, piece work," he said bitterly.

"Who actually gives you the money?"

"The big guy from the arcade."

"Is he running the outfit?"

"Doubt it. He's as thick as two short planks."

So there wasn't much evidence to tie in Murdoch or Palmer. I could tell this to Charlie or Inspector Haskins. No doubt they could arrest the bully, but if he wouldn't talk, if he denied everything, there was nothing to link to the real boss, or bosses. It was obvious that I'd have to get back into the Arcade, be more upfront about wanting to "date" one of the young kids.

"How do I get into the system?" I asked.

Zack gave me a long look from those already blackening eyes. "You want to watch out, Tim," he said. "They don't play games, not if they find you're not what you say."

What was this sixteen-year-old telling me, ten years his senior, to watch out for? But it was nice that he felt enough for me to care. I felt a hand on my thigh. Suddenly I realized that there was a half-naked boy in the bed I was sitting on. Not that I hadn't realized it before, after all I'd put him there, helped him out of his clothes, all except his underwear, and washed the blood off. Before, though, it had been charity, and I'd banished any lubricious thoughts from my mind. Now that hand changed everything. I felt something stir in my trousers.

"Thought you said there wasn't much you could do for me," I said, half jokingly.

"My hand's okay," said Zack and felt for my groin.

A hard choice, but I made it. "Better not," I said, thinking of Paul. I got up, though the erection showed. "I'll be back later. If you need anything, there's food in the kitchen, but sleep if you can."

Zack made a grimace and blew a kiss from twisted lips. "Take care," he said. "Have a word with Sam."

For the second time that day, I went into the Arcade. On the way I'd called Charlie, telling him what I was doing and that, if anyone was the villain, it was probably Murdoch.

"Haskin's out," Charlie had said doubtfully. "Perhaps you ought to wait till he comes back."

"Inspector Haskins," I had said reprovingly. "Haven't you got any respect for authority? I'll let you know what happens."

"Hang on - " but I'd rung off.

It felt almost like coming home. I strode in as if I belonged. There was a young guy, blond, face like a cherub, lips like a cock-sucker, on one of the games. His immature body twisted with the vigour of his actions. His arse, encased in combat trousers, waggled enticingly.

Sam wandered up the aisle looking as indifferent as always. I remembered Zack's parting advice. "That's a nice-looking boy," I said, nodding at the one I'd noticed.

"He's not been in today," Sam said, and when I looked bewildered, added, "Zack. You asked about him this morning."

"I'm not interested in Zack anymore," I said, and casting discretion to the winds, "It's that lad who caught my fancy."

Sam glanced in the boy's direction, but didn't seem to be all that concerned. He just nodded and wandered off into the dimness at the back of the premises. Perhaps he hadn't understood what I was aiming at. He looked stupid enough. I wondered what on earth Murdoch was thinking of when he employed him and for what purpose. He seemed ineffectual enough. In fact I hadn't seen him doing anything.

"Hi," I said to the boy, who gave me a brief, appraising glance and then turned back to his screen. I wasn't sure what the scenario was, but alien looking creatures kept appearing from behind cover and were killed or mutilated by the lad's swift responses. "You're good at that, aren't you? Bet you're good at everything you do." It was an appalling pickup line, and I squirmed as I said it.

The boy gave me another look which expressed his contempt. "Yeah, I'm good," he said, "and worth every penny."

Well, cack-handed I might have been, but it looked as if I'd made contact. "How much?" I asked.

"You better ask at the office," said the boy, gesturing to the back of the premises.

"What's your name, son?" I asked.

"Andy."

I found a door in the gloom and pushed it open. It led into a short corridor with a door on each side and one at the end. I though probably that the end one led out of the arcade. One of the others must be the office. I knocked on one, and, as I did so, I heard the other door open and felt a heavy hand clasp my shoulder, squeezing hard, turning me round. At the same time a delicate, educated voice said, "Good afternoon, Mr. Sinclair."

I recognized the huge figure of Dave Murdoch's gorilla, who I'd last seen at Gracey's Club standing menacingly over me.

"Hubert," I said, weakly.

"Perhaps we should have a talk." It sounded like a suggestion, but I knew it was a command. Keeping his hand on my shoulder he walked me through the door into a small office, where there was a desk and a couple of chairs, and a mirror on the wall. A computer screen was filled by a screen saver in which various brightly coloured fish swam lazily around. There were no windows, and an angled lamp on the desk threw a pool of light, the only illumination. I felt completely cut off, and the outside world seemed a long, long way away. There wasn't even the sound of traffic from the main road outside. Someone could scream in here and not be heard, I thought to myself - and wished that I hadn't.

"Well, fancy seeing you here," I said, trying to make light of the whole situation. "And how's Mr. Murdoch?"

"What are you here for, Mr. Sinclair?" asked Hubert, ignoring my crass pleasantries.

"Oh you know," I said weakly, "I was just looking for a bit of company."

"What sort of company?"

"Young company."

"I didn't realize you was into that sort of thing, Mr. Sinclair. I thought you was a married man, if you takes my meaning." Hubert's educated veneer seemed to have slipped since leaving Gracey's, or perhaps it was just something he put on when he became the West End club doorman. In either case he was just as scary.

"I like a bit of a change," I said. "The seven year itch and all that."

"Have you really been married for seven years?"

"Actually not. That was just a sort of metaphor. We have an open relationship." Very open, I thought, in fact at the moment so open as to be nonexistent.

Hubert grunted, his whole frame expressing disapproval of all things metaphorical. "Why don't you take a seat," he said eventually.

I did so thankfully. I hoped that meant at least that I wasn't going to get beaten up.

Hubert sat himself behind the desk and jabbed the computer into life. From where I sat, I couldn't see the screen, but he looked at it for some time, his lips moving as he presumably read something. Then he typed a couple of words, waited a while perhaps for an answer and eventually looked at me.

"Okay, Mr. Sinclair, that seems satisfactory. I just need a few details. You understand we have to be careful with our clients in this delicate arrangement."

Delicate! And illegal. But I couldn't see Hubert organizing this all on his own. How had Zack described him? Thick as two short planks, and certainly I had never seen him as anyone except a carrier out of orders. Was someone giving him orders now, perhaps over the computer, someone who was looking at us now - through the two-way mirror behind me. I restrained myself from turning round, but I could feel the hairs at the back of my neck curling.

The questions were probing and extensive. I answered as truthfully as possible, and Hubert slowly inputted the answers into the computer. At the end he waited for a moment and then said, "We'll have to check up on this, but if everything is kosher then there should be no problem. We'll need a deposit of £100 to start off. The charges vary on the age of the product and the time you wish to spend with him, also of course what you want to do."

It all seemed cold-bloodied, and I felt sick. "I don't have that sort of money on me," I said.

"Of course not. Now, I understand you're interested in young Andy. As a gesture of goodwill, we're prepared to let the two of you get acquainted this afternoon."

I breathed a sigh of relief. I'd be able to get out after all, then something struck me. How did Hubert know it was Andy I'd been talking to? There may have been CCTV, but surely the arcade was too dark to really make out features. But if Hubert hadn't seen me, the only person who had seen my interest was - Sam. Sam? Dozy, ineffectual Sam? But perhaps a good cover.

Saying nothing Hubert escorted me back into the arcade and to the station where young Andy was enthusiastically still pounding aliens into the dirt. "He's all yours," said Hubert.

"Where do we go?" I asked.

"He knows," said Hubert. "Just tell him you're on a special offer."

I touched the lad on the shoulder. "Care for a burger?" I asked.

"Is that what you call it?" said the streetwise little urchin, flashing a practiced grin. "Come on then."

As we went out I looked back. In the dim recesses I could just make out the hulking figure of Hubert talking, or rather being talked to, by the slimmer one of Sam. From the body language, Sam was very much in charge.

It felt fresher, in spite of the petrol fumes and tired London air, when we stepped onto the pavement. As we did so, though, there was a screech of tyres and a police car pulled up, followed by another, and then a plain van.

"Shit," said Andy. "The filth. I'm outta here." He shot off up the road leaving me standing.

Kids streamed out of the arcade as the police went in. They ignored anyone who looked young but fastened on to any adult. I saw Hubert struggling in the grasp of two policemen, but it needed a third to finally bring him to a standstill.

Charlie clambered out of the second car. "Better make it look legit," he said to me as he put an arm lock on me and hustled me into the van.

"Make sure you get Sam," I said. "Tall, spotty lad, looks young enough to be one of the kids."

But, when we got to the nick and everything was sorted out, it seemed that Sam had been missed and had slipped out with the rest of the kids. Someone wasn't going to be pleased about that.

In fact Inspector Haskins was fairly livid about the whole situation. He had me and Charlie in an interview room and complained loudly that, on the strength of my earlier phone call to Charlie, they'd picked up Dave Murdoch.

"I was probably wrong about that," I admitted.

"You tell that to Murdoch," said Haskins and told a young police constable to bring the angry arcade owner in.

He came in still loudly protesting his innocence, proclaiming that he thought the prostitution of young boys to be repellent. It was certainly not the sort of thing he did. "What's he doing here?" he asked, when he'd run out of steam and was able to notice his surroundings. "He's an interfering little swine. Got it in for me because I made a pass at him once."

"Mr. Sinclair backs you up," said Haskins dryly. "He doesn't think you had anything to do with the vice ring."

"It was just that Hubert was obviously involved, and because he was your doorman at Gracey's, I naturally assumed you were involved. Now I think he was working for Sam."

Murdoch exploded with wrath. "Sam? Sam! That spotty-faced useless wimp. Couldn't organize a piss-up in a brewery."

"That's what he wanted you to think," I said. "All the evidence is on the computer. I assume you've got some experts who can get into it."

Haskins nodded.

"I hope you'll wipe the stuff on me," I said.

"I wish I could get my hands on Sam and Hubert," said Murdoch, still fuming. "I'd teach them to start being entrepreneurs in my business."

"Hubert has been charged and will come to Court," said Haskins. "Unfortunately Sam seems to have slipped away. We'll get him though, never fear."

Murdoch smiled, it wasn't a pleasant sight. "I think I'm more likely to find him, what with the contacts I've got."

I didn't say anything but I thought that Sam would probably prefer to take the consequences of his crimes in a Court of Law rather than that meted out by Murdoch with his own form of justice. I almost could see him lying in an alley with two broken legs.

I got back to the flat, hoping that Paul would have returned, but there was no one there, not even Zack.

And a few of our belongings were missing too. Not many, not really important, a bottle of aftershave, not my favourite. A photograph in a silver frame, of me. A designer shirt belonging to Paul.

So much for being a good Samaritan. I'd know better in future.

CHAPTER TWELVE

Nightfall. A drizzle of rain falling onto the grey expanse of road and pavement. The streetlamps lit up pools of reflection. At first sight it appeared that the road was empty. Indeed, who would want to be out at a time like this, in an area devoid of shops or places of entertainment, even houses? This was the back of King's Cross station, never built to be observed. A few brick buildings which would be occupied by office workers in the daytime but now were deserted. A wide road over which the enormous expanse of bridge provided some sort of shelter. Behind high walls the railway lines stretched out towards the Midlands and Scotland and occasionally the sound of a train as it rumbled in or out of the capital.

But there were a few people around. They didn't make their presence felt, but lingered, taking shelter where they could. Young men, some perhaps little more than boys, dressed not in the sort of clothes suitable for this foul November weather, but rather to show off their bodies; tight jeans mostly, though some wore baggy combat trousers, T-shirts, and for some leather jackets.

A car nosed its way along the street, windscreen wipers working and headlights dipped, but lighting up the road and pavement in front. Instantly there was a flurry of movement amongst the waiting hustlers. They emerged from their shelters and arranged themselves along the curb while the car crawled by, the driver observing, making his pick and eventually drawing up alongside a tall young man, whose blond, cropped hair was lit by the overhead streetlight.

There was a hurried conversation, terms agreed, the lad got into the passenger seat and it drove off. The lad knew where to go, where to find a quieter place where the act could be performed, money exchanged and satisfaction obtained, A short, fairly sordid business but apparently acceptable to both. The remaining men went back to their shelter. It was a bad night, but probably there would be more trade to come.

So there I was, after a year and a half of being in a partnership, living alone. It was my own fault, of course, but that didn't make it any easier. I'd fucked up my relationship with my lover, Paul Massingham, my cock leading me to places where it really had no right to intrude. No wonder, when Paul found out, he had been horribly hurt and distressed, so much so that he'd left me. I felt damn sorry for myself. I missed him. It hurt like hell. Waking every morning I'd reach out for the warm body which ought to have been there beside me, and find nothing. In the evenings, I'd make plans for a meal for two and then realize there was no need for the other half. Later, when we would have sat together and chatted about the day's events, or gone out together to a club, cinema, theatre, or perhaps made love, it had to be a solitary event.

And the ironic thing was that, while I was in the affair, there seemed to be innumerable opportunities for casual sex. Now that I was free, no one seemed to care. Did I now have a sort of aura of gloom and despair about me that put people off? Had I suddenly, overnight as it were, become unattractive, aged like Rip Van Winkle? I couldn't see any difference as I shaved in the bathroom mirror; the same grey eyes, perhaps a little more wary than before, short, cropped dark hair, a smile that, if I put it on, seemed rather forced. Was I thinner than before? If so, perhaps it was to the good. My recent partnership had brought me complacency, a tendency to worry less, eat more of the sugary, fatty types of foods, but I had been happy. And now I was not.

"Golden October had declined into sombre November," as the poet has it. "And the apples were gathered and stored, and the land became brown sharp points of death in a waste of water and mud." To be strictly accurate it was quite a mild November, or at least the start of it, but Eliot's description was spot on for the way I felt. Added to that, I had had no investigations since the affair at the Arcade. My P.I. business had dried up.

So, there I was, staring gloomily out of my office window at the blank wall and fire escape of the next building - the rent of my office was cheaper because it didn't have much of a view - when the telephone rang. Always when that happened, my first thought was that it could be Paul, but I knew deep down that it wasn't.

"Tim Sinclair," I said. "Private Investigator." I'd thought of adding something cute yet intelligent that I could parrot out as an introduction, but my heart wasn't in it.

An educated, quite attractive-sounding, male voice said, "Mr. Sinclair, I have a problem. Would it be possible to arrange an appointment? As early as possible, please. It is rather urgent." There was a strained element in the voice.

I recognized the sound of a person in trouble.

I needed the work, but it didn't do to sound too eager. People might think I was desperate. "I could fit you in this afternoon," I said.

James Marston was a man of perhaps forty, dressed in a sober suit of traditional, rather than designer, fashion. He had dark hair, cut short and greying slightly at the temples, and grey eyes that had a worried expression. He stooped a little, and his manner was a trifle hesitant. He seemed to have some trouble in coming to the point. He remarked on the weather, on the recent terrorist outrage which the papers had been trumpeting that morning, on the difficulty of finding suitable office accommodation. This last I took as something of a criticism. Anything rather than the matter which had brought him to see me. I tried to put him at his ease, but the cup of God-awful instant coffee which was the best I could manage only seemed to make him more uncomfortable. He sipped at it, made a scarcely controlled grimace and put it back down on the edge of my desk.

"Now, Mr. Marston," I said in a businesslike manner, having had enough of this procrastination, "what exactly is the problem?"

He touched his tie, dark blue like his suit, smoothed his hair, scratched his forehead, gave a sort of half smile, and eventually said, "Well, you could say I've been robbed."

"A job for the police," I said.

Marston became even more hesitant and embarrassed. "No, you see, there's something else. I know who did it. A lad I picked up, a young hustler. But I don't know his name or anything. If it was just the money in the wallet, I'd put it down to experience, but it was something important, something valuable."

"And what was more important than the money?"

"Some letters and personal documents. These showed I was married and also that I was a Member of Parliament."

"There are plenty of gay MPs," I said. "Some even proud to come out."

Marston sighed. "But not ones in a high position who have been found to be associating with young hustlers. If this gets out, my career, at least in the upper reaches of Government, is finished, and my wife mustn't find out."

I suppose I saw his point, though I didn't like the man. Cheating on his wife. I guessed he'd only married her to further his career. Many selection boards wouldn't look favourably on aspiring members of Parliament who were unmarried and therefore, by implication, gay. Yet my own treatment of Paul, was my cheating any worse than his?

"So what do you want me to do?" I asked. "Odds are that you'll never hear from him again. He's probably not interested in the letters."

"He phoned me today," he said. "He wants £200."

Blackmail. "Surely you can afford that to get the documents back."

"I wish it were just that. No, he wants £200 a month, no return of the letters. I pay him a wage, in effect, or he goes to the papers and tells all."

"You'd be better to go to the police, they don't like blackmailers.

They can be quite discreet if you haven't committed a crime yourself. I can put you in touch with someone."

He sighed again. "What if the boy was underage? I doubt whether the police would be all that sympathetic in that case."

I was forced to agree. "Tell me about him," I said. "What did he look like?"

"Slim. Nice body, not exactly muscled, but not skin and bones like some adolescents. Dark hair, short and brushed forward. Had a certain brightness, a vitality which was very attractive."

"And he didn't tell you his name?"

"We didn't do much talking," Marston admitted. "He was, you know, all over me. I thought at the time it was lust, usually they just do the business and that's that, but he was quite passionate. Afterwards I realized that all that groping and stuff meant nothing; he was just picking my pocket."

For a moment I felt a bit sorry for him, poor bastard. "And then what?"

"I drove him back to King's Cross, he got out and I went home."

"You didn't feel for your wallet?"

"I'd paid first," he said. "There was no need." It seemed an embarrassing admission, but probably the usual way round. Do the business first, and once the john had got his rocks off, he could easily push the lad out of the car and drive off.

"Whereabouts in King's Cross?"

"There's a known curb-crawling place at the back of the station, York Way. You must know it."

When I confessed I didn't, he seemed to lose a bit of confidence in my abilities. "I thought you're gay yourself."

"I am," I said, "but that doesn't mean I frequent all the pickup places in London, especially rent ones."

He looked suitably abashed, so I said, "Anyway, Mr. Marston, I'll do what I can, though at the moment I can't see what. What if we go back tonight and try to find this guy?"

"Do I have to go? I've got a meeting that's important."

"I'll need you to make the identification," I said. "It's up to you to decide on priorities."

He nodded, and we agreed on a time to meet.

I thought for a while after he'd left and then rang up my friend, Ross. Ross knows everything about the gay scene in London, and for all I know, in the rest of the world. I don't know how he does it because he spends all his time pursuing trade, usually rough trade. Perhaps that's how he does it, quizzing his conquests after or, possibly, during the act. I've never had any personal sexual congress with Ross and, perhaps because of this, had remained friends with him, which, on occasions, has been very useful for me.

"Sorry to hear about you and Paul," he trilled, as soon as he heard my voice. How had he known? I'd told no one, and I rather assumed that Paul hadn't either, but there it was. "Hope you can get back together again. He was good for you. You really must stop behaving like a slut."

This from him! But what he said was true.

"What can I do for you, doll?"

"I'm looking for a hustler," I said, giving him the description Marston had told me. "Hangs out on York Way."

"You are in a bad way," said Ross. "I could put you in touch with someone cheaper and much more reliable."

"It's not for me, it's for a client. And, anyway, what would I want with one of your castoffs?"

"So you're in the pimping trade now are you? I'll have to make a note of that."

I patiently explained the real details, and Ross seemed to believe them. "Well, there are quite a few guys who could answer the description. 'Young,' you said, 'good with his hands.' Not averse to a bit of blackmail? Sounds like Zack."

I started, and, had Ross been able to see me, he would have recognized my surprise. I knew Zack, or at least a young guy who called himself Zack. We'd met during my last case, and he had, as it happened, been the cause, the final straw, as it were, for Paul's leaving me. I'd been innocent in that instance, though not in others. With an effort I struggled back to the conversation. As it was, my failure to answer caused Ross to wonder. "Are you okay, doll?"

"Zack," I said. "Do you know his full name, where he lives?"

"No idea. I've never actually met him, just heard of him through 'friends', if you know what I mean. Where he lives? Well, I doubt whether he's got a permanent place. He bums off acquaintances, probably literally, until he outstays his welcome, and then leaves, usually with a couple of keepsakes."

Yes, I knew that. He'd disappeared from my flat with a couple of those.

"Well, thanks, Ross," I said. "You've been a help."

"No probs," he said. "We should get together some time." He always said that. "Oh, by the way, I hear your delightful Paul is staying with a friend from college. Fielding Road, number 22, down Muswell Hill way, not fashionable at all, but perhaps you might find it useful. Take care, doll."

This guy! He'd be a godsend for MI5 or MI6 or Scotland Yard, or all three, and the FBI as well.

 Muswell Hill, a leafy suburb of North London. I looked at my watch. I could get over there and get back to King's Cross in time to meet Marston, but what could I do even if I saw Paul?

I found Fielding Road, a road of pleasant semi-detached houses, 1930s vintage, I should think, with bow-fronted windows from the ground to the first floor. It gave them a strange look, as if they were large, well-bosomed and stomached dowagers, but the extra window space round the curve made the rooms lighter, I guessed, than a straight window. They were all built on the same model but had little architectural differences; one had its brick frontage, another was pebble-dashed, a third had some dark wooden beams so that it looked almost Tudor-esque, which gave them a look of variety.

I knew that Paul would recognize my car, so much had happened in it, especially in the backseat, before we had set up the flat together, that I didn't want to wait until he returned from work, but I couldn't resist parking for a short while directly opposite number 22 and gazing at it intently. I saw no signs of life. Presumably everyone was out. For a moment I thought of writing a note, but then I wondered whether Paul would see this almost as an action of a stalker. Creepy. So I drove off, stopped for some food at a cheap trattoria I knew of and then set out for King's Cross.

Marston was sitting in his car where we'd arranged to meet. He looked as if he'd been waiting there for some time. He also, I thought, looked apprehensive, perhaps understandably.

We drove off in my car. I argued that his hustler blackmailer might possibly recognize Marston's car, a smart BMW, whereas my almost fit-for-the-wrecker's-yard Volvo would cause little or no reaction in anyone expecting well-off punters.

"In any case," I said, "he'll probably be out with someone if he's as attractive as you say." I didn't tell him that I suspected I might know the guy.

There were some half dozen young men lined up along the pavement as we cruised slowly up York Way from King's Cross Station towards Camden Town. They tended to cluster under street lamps, and Marston peered at them closely, shaking his head as we passed each one. I didn't recognize anyone as Zack either.

"I'll cut through to the Caledonian Road and back so we can do the trip again," I said. I turned left down a narrow road I didn't know but hoped would take us through. As we rounded a corner, I saw flashing blue lights from the tops of police cars. A uniformed policeman stood in the middle of the road waving us down with a torch.

Marston gasped. "Turn round," he said urgently. "Get me out of here."

"Don't be silly," I said. "We're doing nothing wrong. If we turn round and rush off like a startled rabbit, it'll look suspicious."

"But what am I doing in this part of London at this time of night?"

I had forgotten how self-important people in the public eye were. Marston had immediately assumed that everyone would recognize him, and his guilty conscience would imagine tabloid journalists hiding behind every lamppost just waiting to publish all, whether true or not.

"I don't know, visiting friends, going home from a meal."

"In this?" he asked disparagingly, which I felt was unfair to my dear old Volvo.

I drew to a halt beside the policeman. To my surprise I knew him. It was my old friend, Sergeant Charlie Shepherd. He was equally surprised to see me.

"On point duty?" I asked jovially.

He wasn't amused. "Nasty business," he said. "How come you're always in the vicinity when something bad happens?"

"What do you mean?" I asked.

"It's not the first time you turn up just after a murder's been committed."

My amazement must have been obvious. "Who is it?" I asked.

"Young lad, strangled and chucked out of a car, I'd say. Medic hasn't said anything, but that's what it looks like."

A nasty thought struck me. "Who's in charge?" I asked. "Could I have a look?"

I was aware of Marston next to me, digging with his fingers into my ribs. "Er," he said, "I haven't much time." Obviously eager to get away as soon as possible, but I wasn't to be moved.

"D.I. Haskins," said Charlie. "You remember him."

I did indeed.

"Who's your friend?" asked Charlie.

"Jim Marston," I said. "We're on our way home."

Charlie nodded knowingly, tapping the side of his nose with his index finger. Out of the corner of my eye I could see Marston flinch. "Been together all evening," I said.

"Well, I guess you could take a look," said Charlie. "Sometimes you seem to know more than's good for you."

I didn't like the last comment too much but got out of the car, Marston rather unwillingly following me.

Inspector Haskins and another two men were standing over the crumpled figure of a body which lay half on the pavement, half against the wall. Even from a distance I could see the open mouth gaping from its last gasp, the staring eyes. I recognized him immediately. It was Zack. He was wearing a shirt, open to the waist and the zip of his jeans was open, his cock hanging through the gap. It looked pathetic, and I wished someone had at least tucked it back again, made him decent.

I heard Marston gasp behind me.

Haskins turned. "Who's this?" he asked. "My God, Sinclair. What are you doing here?"

"Just passing through," I said, "but I do know the lad there." I pointed to the sad remains of a boy who, in his life, had been the epitome of youth and vivacity, as I had known him, a cheerful rogue, who, while I couldn't always excuse his peccadilloes, I found it easy to forgive him. Now he was dead. A tragic, unnecessary death for someone who had enjoyed life to the full.

"So who is he?"

"He called himself Zack. I don't know what his real name was. I met him in the Amusement Arcade business you put me on. He did upset the guy who was running that, but I wouldn't have thought it was a killing offence. Anyway, he got a beating up for it. Looks like some perverted punter who gets off causing pain, and this time went too far."

"Do you know where he lived?" asked Haskins.

I shook my head. "I don't think he had any sort of permanent address, probably shared with a friend. He was one of the York Way curb boys. Talk to them, probably they'll know, perhaps even saw who he went off with tonight."

He nodded. "I'll be in touch," he said.

Charlie took us back to our car. "So young," he said. "It's a fucking shame. I'm not a capital punishment man, but some guys really need stringing up."

I realized he was referring to my hypothesis that the murderer had been someone who got off on violence, but then suddenly it struck me. There was someone who would be very pleased that Zack was no longer able to continue his activities.

James Marston was no longer being blackmailed.

And how long had James Marston been in the King's Cross area this evening, before I arrived?

I could have quizzed him, but first I wanted to hear what the police could find out. After all, I had some information which I could use as a bargaining point.

I drove Marston back to his car, not sure if I was sitting next to a murderer or not. It wasn't a comfortable feeling, and, more than ever, I wished there were someone at home I could talk to.

The next morning I went down to the nick to see Charlie. He was back in his usual place behind the desk, sitting like a benevolent Buddha dispensing justice and advice (is that what Buddha does?). Anyway, that was impression I got. He was clutching a mug of tea, almost as if it were a permanent appendage to his hand.

"Did you get anything from the York Way boys?" I asked.

"Well, they eventually acknowledged the lad was there, but they couldn't or wouldn't tell us who he'd gone off with. In fact, they were nervous about admitting anything really."

"You don't think they were afraid you were about to arrest them for prostitution?"

"Probably," said Charlie gloomily.

"Should I have a word with them?"

Charlie immediately looked alarmed. "I'd have to get approval from Inspector Haskins. But if I were them, and one of their number had been murdered, I doubt whether I'd be there tonight."

"And if this is their only way of getting money to live off?"

Charlie grunted. "I'll have a word with Haskins," he said.

"Inspector Haskins," I said.

He lumbered off, returned, picked up his tea and disappeared again. A constable came and took his place.

"Is Sergeant Shepherd looking after you, sir?" he said. He was a young lad, fresh complexioned, with steady grey eyes and a neat cap of brown hair. He looked as if he'd just left school. Oh dear, I thought, when the policemen start looking young, I must be getting old.

"Yes, thank you," I said. He sat down and stared into the distance, playing with a pencil. It was awkward without any talk. "Have you had anything to do with the murdered lad?" I asked.

"He was gay," he said. "He was a prostitute."

"True," I said. "Your point being?"

I think he was trying to tell me that Zack had got what he deserved, though he didn't go as far as to say it. I stared at him, and he looked down in embarrassed silence.

Eventually Charlie came back. "Inspector Haskins thinks it's a good idea," he said. "See what you can find out, Tim."

"I thought the modern force disapproves of homophobic attitudes," I said, looking at the constable.

At least he had the grace to blush.

I went along to the local political party headquarters to see if I could get a photo of James Marston. The woman there was only too pleased to provide one and incidentally to sing his praises as much as she could.

"He's such a good MP," she said. "He really does his best for the constituency, and…" her voice dropped to a conspiratorial whisper, "it's rumoured he'll be in the Cabinet at the next reshuffle."

I was almost tempted to tell her that my bet could be that he might well be destined for prison, but I restrained myself. I did though give him a ring to his home from my mobile. A woman, pleasant-voiced, answered saying that James was at the "House." Her emphasis on "House" obviously indicated the Houses of Parliament. I left no message.

I drove to the office, making a detour via Camden Town so that I could see York Way in the daylight. It looked so different, office workers, I assumed, walking down the pavements that later would be populated by the hustlers. It was just an ordinary London street, and I marvelled at the difference the hours of darkness would bring.

I was a few hundred yards from the concourse of the station when I noticed a tall youth with unnaturally blond hair standing on the pavement in a rather posed attitude, right hand on his hip, right leg bent. He seemed unaware of the passersby, who either passed him unnoticed or occasionally gave him an odd look or passed a comment. I recognized him from the night before as one of the young hustlers and luckily was able to stop the car in a vacant spot by the curb. It was a no parking area, but I couldn't see a warden in the vicinity and I trusted to luck.

"Hello," I said to him, and he started out of what obviously a deep reverie.

Automatically, a smile came to his lips. It was a professional smile, without warmth, but it made his face, pretty rather than handsome, attractive. "Sorry, love," he said, "not working at the moment."

"No," I said. "I just wanted to ask you about Zack. I knew him, you see, and now I found he's been killed."

The boy's eyes filled with tears. For the first time he really looked at me, and I recognized true emotion. "What can I tell you?" he asked. "I don't know anything about how he died."

"Look," I said, "I'm parked just up there and will be booked in a minute. Can I give you a lift somewhere, take you to a bar and buy you a drink perhaps?"

He looked at me suspiciously and was perhaps reassured by what he saw, for his frown cleared, and a half smile turned up the corners of his mouth. He looked very young, and I wondered whether he'd actually be allowed into a bar.

"Where do you suggest?" I asked.

"Actually, I think I'd prefer a burger."

Why is it that kids are always hungry? But that was fine with me. On the way, he told me his name was Gavin. I parked more legally, and we went to a Burger Bar on Euston Road, just opposite the British Library. I bought him meat and salad and things in a bun, and a cola.

"I used to know Zack," I said as we sat down. He ate as if he hadn't had a meal for days. Perhaps he hadn't.

"I know," he said, which surprised me, and it must have shown because he went on. "I didn't recognize you at first, then it clicked. He's got a picture of you. Keeps it by his bed." And I remembered the photo that had disappeared when Zack had left. Why he had taken it, and why he had kept it, I had no idea.

"Was he living with you?" I asked.

"It was only temporary," he said, "but we got on well together, and it halved the rent. We often used to discuss tricks and the kinky things some of them wanted."

"Last night," I said, "did you see who Zack went off with?"

Suddenly Gavin looked alarmed. "Are you the police?" he

asked.

"No," I said. "Actually, I'm a private investigator, but this is personal. I liked Zack. I'm afraid the police might just put it down to another gay killing and not really put themselves out. I want to find who did it."

My sincerity must have been obvious for Gavin nodded. "I sort of saw him," he said. "Didn't get a really good look at him though."

"Was it this guy?" I asked and showed him the photo of James Marston.

Gavin looked and started. For a moment the thought went through my mind that we'd got Marston bang to rights, but then Gavin said, "No. That wasn't the guy."

"But you recognized him?" I said.

Gavin nodded. "I've been with him a couple of times," he said. "That wasn't the one Zack went off with. For a start, the car was different. This one's - " he tapped the photograph " - got a BMW, lovely leather upholstery." For a moment his eyes took on a longing look. "I was quite scared of getting stuff on it."

"And the one who picked up Zack?" I reminded him.

"He was driving a small car, Nissan Micra or something like that. Red, I think."

"You didn't see the number plate, I suppose?"

Gavin shook his head. "Wasn't close enough for that," he said.

"What about the guy himself? Was there anything about him you noticed?"

"I think he had a moustache. Couldn't see much at that distance. He had a mop of dark hair. That's about all. Zack used to like blokes with moustaches. He said he liked the feeling on his pubes." Gavin blushed as he said that. He was an odd, even attractive, mixture of innocence and maturity.

A thought struck me. "Is Zack's stuff still at home?"

Gavin nodded.

"The police haven't been?"

"I never told them we were sharing."

"Do you think I could have a look?" I asked. "I think Zack had some letters. Would it surprise you to know he was doing a bit of blackmail?"

Gavin laughed. "I wouldn't be surprised at anything Zack did. He could be a bit of a hard-ass." He got up. "Come on then."

They had two rooms in a three-story house in Camden Town. One of the rooms was a living room with two mismatched easy chairs, the upholstery rather stained and worn, a TV set and an old music centre. In the corner was a kitchen area with a couple of electric rings and a kettle. I suspected they would have eaten out more often than not.

I followed Gavin into the other room. The bedroom had two single beds. What they did if they both brought trade back with them, I didn't ask. Probably had some method of communication that the bedroom was "engaged." I immediately noticed my photo which stood in a frame on a small table next to one of the beds. Gavin went to a chest of drawers and opened the top drawer, taking out a large old-fashioned biscuit tin which he handed to me.

"Those are his things," he said.

I opened the tin. I didn't want to scrabble through his personal possessions, but the letters were lying on top. There was a letter from no less a person than the Prime Minister to "'James,'" and another in a woman's hand, signed "Ann," presumably his wife. I didn't read them there, but it was obvious that these were the incriminating documents which Marston had been so anxious about.

"Can I take these?" I asked. I knew the police would want to see them, but I felt a residual loyalty to Marston, who was still my client, especially as I had suspected him of a dreadful crime.

Gavin came close and looked at them. "Sure," he said, but he didn't move away. I turned to face him, and he wrapped his arms around me, his body touching mine all the way down. He smelled fresh and clean. He kissed me and as we stood, lips to lips, chest to chest, groin to groin, I could feel his erection growing. It felt good and substantial. I decided that perhaps the Rip Van Winkle curse had eventually lifted.

He took his tongue out of my mouth. "Do you want to, you know? I'm not working all the time, and I like you."

I did want to, of course, but I held back. "I really like you, Gavin. You can probably tell - " and indeed my cock was straining at the barriers of material between us, "but I'm in a relationship. Actually it may have just broken up, but I still don't want to have sex with anyone else at the moment."

"Are you sure?" he asked, and his hand snaked down to grasp and hold my cock. He squeezed me gently, and I could scarcely restrain a groan of frustrated desire. It had been some time since I'd had any sex at all. It was all I could do to stop myself hurling him down on the bed and flinging myself on top.

"I'm sorry," I said.

"He must be really something."

"He is," I said and kissed him gently, like a maiden aunt.

"I wish I had someone like that," said Gavin regretfully.

"Shall I take my photo?" I asked.

"Can I keep it?" Gavin asked.

And so I left, taking the letters—wouldn't want to put temptation in Gavin's path. He stood at the door, tall, blond and willowy. He looked sad, but I was sure he was resilient and would bounce back. I didn't mean from my rejection but from Zack's death. I only hoped we could find the murderer and at least remove one danger from the sort of life he had chosen. The thought crossed my mind that perhaps I could influence him into another way of life, but that sounded too philanthropic, and I dismissed the idea.

I phoned Marston. This time he answered personally. I told him that I'd managed to get back his letters, and he sounded mightily relieved. He asked how I'd managed it, but I told him I'd explain when I saw him.

"Come over now," he said. "My wife's out."

From previous experience I knew he wasn't much good at making up lies, which I felt must be somewhat of a disadvantage in a politician, but I said I'd be over shortly. I would have too, but Camden Town isn't all that far from Muswell Hill, just through Archway, Highgate and to the leafy plane trees of Fielding Road. This time I determined to call, but there was no answer to my bell. A next-door neighbour popped out after I'd rung three times.

"They're not in during the day," she said. "Can I take a message?" Her nose twitched inquisitively, and I wondered how she'd react if I asked her to tell Mr. Massingham that I loved him more than anything in the world and I wanted him back into my arms, into our bed.

"No message," I said, "but thanks all the same."

I was just about to start up the car when my mobile rang. As always my heart leaped but it wasn't Paul. In fact, it was Ross.

"Hey, doll," he said. "I guess you haven't done anything positive about Paul."

"Not really," I said shortly.

"In that case, come to a party this evening. It'll take you out of yourself, stop you from moping."

"I really don't feel in a party mood," I said.

"'Course you don't," he said, "which is why you must come. I won't take no for an answer. In fact, I'll call for you and take you along myself. Then, if all you want to do is drink yourself unconscious, I'll be there to get you home."

"But…"

"Eight o'clock sharp in the gladdest of your glad rags. No argument."

He rang off.

The traffic was heavy into London, and it was past three o'clock when I got to Marston's house, two hours later than I'd said I would be. He'd be spitting tacks. The house was smart and expensive, the Regency facade white painted and some black decorative iron railings to keep hoi poloi out. I peered through them, feeling like a Cruikshank waif and stray. A garage that must have put another 20,000 quid onto the asking price. There was a small car on the gravel. No BMW in the garage, so I assumed Marston had had to go out, perhaps urgent summons from the P.M. The gates provided yet more material for the metalworker's art. They were oiled and opened without a squeak.

I passed the little car. Now that was one I'd like, neat, nippy and no doubt reliable. I had a look at the make, Nissan Micra. For some reason that struck a chord, but I couldn't remember what.

The door was answered by a woman with hair that was almost too perfect to be real and a grey suit. She looked composed and excessively efficient and quite capable of dealing with a somewhat untidily dressed P.I. who arrived on her doorstep later than expected. It had been a long, eventful day, and it wasn't over yet.

"Mr. Sinclair," she said. "I'm afraid my husband has had to go out, but he said you'd some documents to leave for him."

Then I remembered. A coincidence surely, but Gavin had said the guy whose car Zack had got into last night was driving a red Nissan Micra.

"Nice little car," I said, pointing to it. "Reliable."

Mrs. Marston seemed a little confused by the change in topic, but she wasn't to be upset. "Not always," she said. "Yesterday it broke down."

"Really?" I said. "What was wrong?"

"Oh I don't know. My husband knows about cars, but it was in for repair last evening. Most aggravating, as my husband was out, too, in his BMW."

"How annoying," I said. "Had to be towed off did it?"

"Well, no. My husband managed to drive it. It was making strange noises, he said. Then he came back and had to use his own car for his engagement later in the evening, but it's all right now. He brought it back this morning completely cured."

She dismissed the subject of the car with a wave of a manicured hand. "Now about these documents."

My mind was whirling. I needed to think. "Er," I said. "I really need to see Mr. Marston personally before I hand them over. Could you tell him, I'll be in touch to arrange another time?"

She looked taken aback. "He was very insistent that I collect them."

"Tell him not to worry. I'll be back."

"Could it be? " I thought. Greased Testicles! It could be.

"Charlie," I said "can I see Haskins? I think I've discovered something."

"Inspector Haskins," said Charlie. "Well, he is in. I'll see if he's free."

"It's very important," I said.

"It always is," said Charlie.

"First," I said, "I've got to apologize for not being entirely open at the start. Marston was, after all my client, and that meant client confidentiality, so I have a sort of excuse."

"What are you talking about?" asked Haskins.

"I didn't tell you about his motive," I said. "You see Zack was blackmailing him. I suspected him from the start, but when Gavin said it wasn't him, that the car Zack had got into wasn't a BMW. That, in fact, the driver wasn't him, didn't look anything like him, had a moustache and lots of black hair, well, I thought I must have been mistaken."

"You're not making any sense at all," said Haskins.

"Okay," I said. "I'll start from the beginning." I told him about Marston coming to see me and how I'd found out that the blackmailer could have been Zack. Then I told him about Gavin who knew Marston but hadn't recognized the driver of the Nissan. Of course, if Marston had used his wife's car, put on a wig and a moustache, then Gavin wouldn't have recognized him, nor, I guess, would Zack until it was too late.

"All of this is supposition," said Haskins.

"But provable," I said. "You can find out if, in fact, Mrs. Marston's car wasn't in a garage overnight. If Zack was actually murdered in that car, there's likely to be some DNA evidence. Was there anything on Zack's body, sperm, etc., that could provide a DNA profile?"

Haskins nodded.

"Test Marston, and if it's positive, it's proof he did it. Get a search warrant for Marston's house. You might even find the wig and moustache. Could have been one of his wife's, but I expect you can prove it if he wore it."

I didn't tell them that I had the letters from the P.M. and his wife. Why? In the back of my mind there was the niggling doubt that I was completely wrong, in which case Marston deserved to get the letters back, and no one would need know.

When it was all over, Haskins said, "I don't know whether to arrest you for withholding evidence or say 'Well done.' We'll follow this up. You'll be called for evidence if anything proves positive, of course. I suppose this Gavin will talk. He wouldn't before."

"Just handle him gently," I said. "He's a nice boy. And don't send your homophobic P.C. to interview him."

Charlie organized a cup of tea, and we cleared up the final points. I was tired. I wanted to go home to bed, and then I thought of the empty expanse of my flat, and I didn't.

The doorbell rang at eight o'clock on the dot. It was Ross. I'd completely forgotten about his invitation to the party. I was still unwashed and unchanged and looked, I suspected, a wreck. He didn't bother to mince his words.

"Great Aunty Nelly!" he exclaimed. "Is this the best you can manage?"

I nearly pointed out to him that I'd once that day already turned down professional (though free) sex with a chicken probably half my age, but I didn't feel up to it. Instead I grunted something to the effect that I'd forgotten he was coming.

"Honey chile," he said. "Quick, off with those smelly togs and into the shower." I protested, but he wouldn't leave me alone. In fact, he so nearly stripped me that eventually I said, "Okay, okay, I'll do it myself."

"Five minutes maximum," he said.

When I got out, wrapped in a towel, he'd organized some clothes for me. Not ones that I'd have chosen myself. In fact, they were some of Paul's that he hadn't collected. I put them on and he hustled me out, into his car, and next thing I knew we were in a restaurant.

"Choose anything you like," he said.

He chattered, as only Ross could, all the way through the meal about people we knew, people I had only heard of, people everyone knew and what they were all doing and with whom. The tabloid press lost a treasure by never signing on Ross, but then they'd probably have been bankrupted with lawsuits as I'm sure half of what he said was made up.

I felt better afterwards, quite cheerful, but I still didn't feel in party mood, so when he said, "Right, the entertainment begins," I complained that it was too late. "You're sinking into the Ovaltine Age," he retorted and dragged me back into the car.

The party was in Hampstead. I had no idea who was giving it. Not sure even that Ross had either, but he seemed to know everyone and everyone knew him. Even I recognized a few faces from the past, and we kissed and asked what had happened to each other and why we never kept in touch and we certainly must in the future. The usual things.

At last I found myself sitting with a guy I remembered vaguely meeting some years earlier. We didn't have much in common, and it was pretty obvious that he was as interested in me as I was in him, so he wandered off and left me with a glass of supermarket red for company.

I let the sound of the party wash over me. I thought I could probably drop off to sleep if I wasn't careful, and I felt miserable again. Through the animated conversational pairs and groups and dancing couples, I could see someone on the other side of the room. From the posture of his body, he looked as miserable as I felt, shoulders hunched, head forward, hair…hair! A bright golden red color that caught the light from a standard lamp next to him and reflected it in glowing brilliance. No one had hair like that except…Paul!

I got up and crossed the room. As I got near to him, he looked up and briefly an expression of such resplendent joy crossed his face that I knew, I knew that he wanted me as much as I wanted him.

"Paul," I said and sat down on the floor beside his chair. My head was level with his knees. I laid my head in his lap. "I've missed you so much," I said. I felt his hand on the back of my head, his fingers stroking my hair. I didn't want to say anything more. I didn't want to move, ever. But then I got cramp in my left leg and I had to struggle up, groaning and kneading the muscle until the pain lessened.

"Let's dance," Paul said.

We moulded into each other's bodies. It was a mixture of the familiar and the new. The body I knew so well, every single part of it and yet, after our separation, the return made it somehow new and exciting. I wanted to explore every crevice, every opening and rediscover how I fitted into him. With the palms of my hands I investigated his face, the flat planes under his cheekbones, the angular cut of his jawline. My lips caressed the tender place under his earlobe, and my tongue tentatively probed into the curled interstices of his ear. I felt rather than heard a deep and profound sigh, and his body shuddered and forced itself against mine so that it seemed as if I was experiencing every bone, every sinew, every muscle, especially that hard probing one which lay beside mine, upright and demanding. I stroked his hair, feeling the soft coarseness, the springy curl and I looked at the rich color, the vivid highlights, gazed into his brown eyes.

Paul's lips, soft and inviting, pressed like a contract against mine. I opened them to allow his agile tongue to enter my mouth, to find and embrace my tongue, to play up my hormones and arouse my prick even more so that our erections pressed hard against each other. I felt my emotions surge. Here was my love, my life, my all. I had never felt like this about anyone else before, and was sure I never would again. The kiss seemed to go on forever. The world turned, the music played, the people carried on with their trivial party conversations, but for us everything stayed still.

Until Ross found us and pried us apart.

"Come on," he said, "I'm taking you both home."

We sat in the back of the car, cuddled together, touching as much of each other as we could. I knew I'd have problems with other guys, but the grief I'd felt from Paul's absence this time meant I'd try, really try to be faithful in the future.

Idly I asked, "Ross, did you know that Paul would be at the party."

"Of course," said Ross. "I invited him."

I owe you, I thought, before locking on to Paul's lips again.

Some time the following day, woozy with sex and love, wearing Paul's aroma like a second skin, I was awakened by the insistent ringing of the telephone. I groaned and roused myself from the debris of the bedclothes like a beached porpoise.

"Leave it," said Paul, pulling me down on top of him again. "Let the answering machine take it." He pulled me onto him, and I was filled with his scent.

But I'd switched off the answer phone the previous evening because I had intended to stay in, and if Paul had rung I would have answered straight away. Then Ross had arrived, and I'd forgotten to switch it on again.

We tried to hide the sound from under the bedclothes but it wouldn't stop.

In the end I staggered up and, naked, answered the phone. Not graciously. "Yes," I said.

"Sinclair," said the voice which I recognized through my own sexual miasma as belonging to James Marston. "Thank God I got you at last. I want those letters."

I struggled to think clearly. "What's the hurry?" I asked. "I'm busy at the moment."

"Come back to bed," said a voice, low and seductive. My lover lay on the bed, the covers thrown back. He was naked and obviously willing.

"Gotta go," I muttered thickly down the phone.

But something had snapped with Marston. He was shouting. "You give me those letters. I'll come over and get them."

"No. No," I managed, but it made no difference.

"Ten minutes," and the line went dead.

"Shit," I said, not too worried about Marston, I could handle him, but more concerned how the interruption would affect my love life. "Sorry, darling, something's come up."

Paul grinned lewdly.

"There's a guy coming over, a client. He wants some letters I have. I'll have to see him."

"Like that?"

I saw myself reflected in the full length mirror of the wardrobe, a piece of self-indulgent furniture Paul had insisted on when he'd moved in. He was a bit of a narcissist on the quiet. I saw myself, naked, looking tousled and covered in the evidence of last night's indulgences, the remains of a hard-on caused by

Paul's invitation still obvious.

"Shit," I said and made for the shower where I removed some of the more obvious signs. I'd scarcely towelled the surface moisture off when the front doorbell rang. Christ! What had Marston used to come over, a space shuttle? I pulled on a pair of jeans and a pullover and thrust my sockless feet into a pair of trainers.

"I'll get rid of him," I promised and raced downstairs.

Marston wasn't on the doorstep, but his BMW was parked at the curb, engine running, the passenger door open. He was sitting at the wheel peering at me. He beckoned me over. The wind was chill and I shivered. I was scarcely dressed for November weather.

I stood at the open door of the car.

"Where are they?" Marston demanded.

In my rush of course I hadn't remembered to pick the letters up. "Shit," I said for the third time that morning and turned to go back in, but something had obviously caught Marston's attention in the driving mirror. He turned round, and I saw a police car nosing round the corner and turning towards us.

"Get in," said Marston, and, when I hesitated, he grabbed me by the pullover and hauled me into the car. At the same time he crashed the car into gear and raced off. The passenger door was still open, wildly swinging, and it caught the side of another parked car which forced it shut. I managed to get settled in the seat.

"What are you doing?" I said.

"They're after me," he said. "The police have been to my house taking DNA samples, sequestering my wife's car, searching my house, taking the clothes I wore last night. They're trying to pin the murder of that boy on me."

He drove the car at forty down the centre of the road and swung it, tyres screaming, to the left at the next turning. I flinched as we passed within a hairsbreadth of another car approaching.

I tried to put on the seatbelt, but groping behind me I couldn't find it.

"Racing off like this will only make them more suspicious," I said. "Slow down. Don't be a fool."

"The letters are the only things that can link me with him," said Marston, not slowing his speed and swinging the car recklessly round another corner.

There's me, I thought. Even if you had the letters, I'd still be able to tell them. In fact, of course, I already had, though he wasn't to know that. I said nothing, just clinging as hard as I could to the seat and bracing my feet against the floor.

The police car behind started its siren, the wailing sound echoing down the suburban street. People would be coming out of their houses, staring out of their windows at the pursuit.

I tried to grab hold of the wheel, a bad move; the car veered and scraped along the side of a parked van. Marston half turned and hit out with his fist, catching me a glancing blow on the side of the face. It wasn't hard enough to do damage, but it stopped me trying to interfere anymore.

He took the road that led towards the motor-way. Once on it, his powerful car might be able to get away from the pursuing police car, but what was the point? They'd have taken his number and would know who he was, even if they hadn't been following him all the time. I wondered why they hadn't arrested him but assumed that the real proof lay in the interpretation of the DNA, and until then they didn't have too much to go on. At least they could have taken him in for questioning. I'd have a word to say to Haskins when I next saw him, and then it struck me. It wasn't "when," but "if." Marston had no intention of allowing me to go free. What plans there were going on in his fucked-up mind certainly didn't include me, or not as a living, breathing witness for the prosecution at any rate. This was Tim's last case, as far as James Marston M.P. was concerned.

We squealed round the roundabout and roared up the slip road onto the motor-way, pulling out in front of another car.

The driver punched his horn, but Marston paid no attention. He jammed his foot on the accelerator and I saw the speedometer needle jerk up, sixty, seventy, eighty, Christ, ninety miles an hour. And me without a seatbelt. The peripheral thought shot through my head, for, even with one on, at this speed, if we hit anything, survival would be at best unlikely.

Way back in the distance, I could see the police car, but it certainly wasn't gaining. Marston was getting away.

Then it happened.

Marston was driving in the fast lane and another car was hogging the road in front of him. He sounded his horn, but the driver of the car in front wasn't about to give way. Marston swerved inwards to the left, but at the same time a van in the inside lane, the slow one, drew out to overtake a slow lorry. Marston saw his available space diminishing and jammed on the brakes. They locked, and he started skidding across the road, first to the lorry on the left and then, as Marston swung the wheel round, to the right and into the back of the van.

There was an enormous bang, metal crunched and scraped with a screaming whine. The door on my side swung open, perhaps it had been weakened by the initial knock when Marston first pulled away from my flat. Anyway it swung wide, and I was flung out. Luckily, if anything can be said to be lucky in the pile-up, the BMW struck the van at an angle so the speed was gradually rather than abruptly lessened. I hit the road hard and skidded, leaving shredded clothing and skin on the tarmac, but I wasn't knocked out, and no speeding car behind finished the job by running over me. Marston's car, though, squealed on, seemingly welded to the back and side of the van, and eventually both slowed and stopped in a tangled wreck.

The police car drove up and two officers got out, one coming up to me. Covered as I was with blood, I think he expected me to be dead, when I groaned and tried to sit up.

"Lie still, for a moment," he said. "There's an ambulance coming."

And so my last case didn't end with my death, though it very nearly did. Marston, though, was killed. His side of the car was completely crushed, and the van driver was unhurt.

With the prime suspect dead, the police might well have suspended and closed the case, but the forensic department was already in the process of analysis. Anyway Haskins wanted to make sure they'd got the right man. The evidence was there. As there was no Marston DNA on Zack, it seemed that Marston hadn't had sex with him before killing him, but Zack's DNA was discovered in the passenger seat of Mrs. Marston's car and also on the clothes Marston had worn. I was right as well about the wig. He had been wearing a black wig belonging to his wife. There was no record of the Micra being in any of the local garages.

My injuries were largely superficial, though very painful, and I made the most of them to Paul who was suitably caring and sympathetic. Again and again I swore undying monogamy. Paul smiled. He knew me of old, but I really meant it. Really. Really!

Some time later while walking through the West End, I saw Gavin, He was still as slim and willowy and camp as a row of tents, but he looked happy. He was accompanied by a dark man in his mid thirties. I wasn't sure whether to acknowledge him, but he stopped and smiled seraphically.

"Tim," he said. "This is my partner."

The man smiled and looked possessive and almost proud.

"I'm happy for you," I said.

"What about you?" asked Gavin.

"Yes," I said, "Paul and I are back together again."

Gavin smiled and his friend smiled and I smiled. It was a good day. I hoped it was the start of many more.

THE END

MICHAEL GOUDA was born and raised in London, England. He served as a National Serviceman in the RAF where, he claims, he lost his virginity. Then he went back to the commercial life. After a change of direction in his thirties, he left the world of commerce and entered that of education becoming a teacher at a Comprehensive School in Worcestershire, England. Since retiring he lives in a limestone cottage in the Cotswolds with a neurotic Border Collie. He also writes under the name of Michael Duggan.

CPSIA information can be obtained at www.ICGtesting.com
Printed in the USA
BVOW051001120911

271055BV00001B/3/P